THE ART OF DEATH

The third man stepped back, examining his handiwork. After a moment's thought he reached into the bag again, this time removing a broad calligrapher's brush.

Dipping the soft bristles into the paint pot of blood formed by the hole where Hawksworth's left eye had been, he loaded the brush and drew three quick characters across the blanched surface of the general's forehead. The characters, in Mandarin, spelled out two words:

Black Dragon

"Dark ... Graphic ... Inspires awe"
Publishers Weekly

Other Avon Books by
Christopher Hyde

HARD TARGET

BLACK DRAGON

CHRISTOPHER HYDE

AVON BOOKS ◈ NEW YORK

AVON BOOKS
A division of
The Hearst Corporation
1350 Avenue of the Americas
New York, New York 10019

Copyright © 1992 by Christopher Hyde
Published by arrangement with the author
Library of Congress Catalog Card Number: 91-48229
ISBN: 0-380-71878-2

Published in hardcover by William Morrow and Company, Inc.; for information address Permissions Department, William Morrow and Company, Inc., 1350 Avenue of the Americas, New York, New York 10019.

First Avon Books Printing: September 1993

AVON TRADEMARK REG. U.S. PAT. OFF. AND IN OTHER COUNTRIES, MARCA REGISTRADA, HECHO EN U.S.A.

Printed in the U.S.A.

RA 10 9 8 7 6 5 4 3 2 1

This one is for Barrie Jones,
my old true friend, the only one who knew me
when I didn't have a beard.

CHAPTER 1

THE MAN WAS naked, spread-eagled on the bed in the forward cabin of the yacht, wrists and ankles tied down with soft, braided ropes of silk designed specifically for bondage.

He was in his seventies, the vitality of his middle years fading now into the softness of old age. His hair was thin and white except for the thatch over his groin that was still dark. With age he'd run to fat, his torso pear-shaped with an apron of pale flesh that drooped over his thick, limp sex organ, but his face was lean and square-jawed, the handsomeness of his youth like a shadow beneath the lines and crow's-feet of a lifetime's experience.

His eyes were closed, and his lips were parted, a thin line of saliva coursing from the corner of his mouth down across his chin. He was breathing noisily in a half-stupor, a faint rattling repeated regularly in the back of his throat and nasal sinus.

His name was General William Sloane Hawksworth, most recently the Supreme Allied Commander, Europe, or SACEUR for the NATO forces there, now in Washington for his appointment as the new director of the Defense Intelligence Agency and senior military advisor to the president's "drug czar."

His uniform was neatly set out on an upholstered chair in the corner of the cabin, the right breast of the jacket heavy with ribbons and medals recounting an air-force career spanning half a century, beginning with the Doolittle Raid on Tokyo.

The woman with him in the cabin of the borrowed yacht was young, less than a third the general's age. Except for a short yellow silk kimono jacket, she too was naked as she went about her business at the small desk beside the bed.

By any standards she was exceptionally beautiful, slightly shorter than average in height, her hair jet black and long, reaching halfway down her back. Her breasts were small and perfectly formed, her belly flat and smooth, her legs slim. Her skin was flawless, colored a deep honey shade, her eyes faintly almond-shaped, the pupils as dark as her hair. Skin and eyes reflected her polyglot heritage, a mixture of black, Polynesian, and Chinese, springing from her Hawaiian origins. Her name was Amanda Chung Kilau, and she was a whore.

Amanda worked studiously at the desk, her ears casually noting the breathing patterns of her client. In front of her on a small wooden tray were a variety of implements. There was a small clay pot, an alcohol lamp, several, long pearl-knobbed needles, and a stained ten-inch-long bamboo tube, one end fitted with a chased silver bowl.

Taking up one of the needles, she dipped it into the pot, then removed it, a small lump of brown paste adhering to the needle's tip. She held the needle over the burning wick of the lamp, watching as the paste began to sizzle and expand, swelling into an almost transparent bubble. Delicately squeezing the globule between thumb and forefinger, pressing it flat, she then dipped the needle into the pot again and repeated the process. She did this half a dozen times until she had a crisp, nut-sized ball on the end of the needle. When it was done to her satisfaction, she picked up the pipe, heated the tiny opium egg once more over the lamp, then plunged it, smoking, into the silver bowl. She put the other end of the pipe to her lips and drew in a breath, making sure the dose was well lit, then took the fuming pipe to the bed, where she sat down, crouching on her knees between the dozing general's legs.

"General," she whispered, her voice soft. There was no reply. She spoke again, and this time Hawksworth stirred, his eyes fluttering open. The pupils were wide, the pale blue-gray irises watery.

"What?" he muttered, lifting his head slightly from the pillows, his wrists fluttering against their bonds.

"Smoke," Amanda said. She leaned forward and pressed the end of the pipe to the older man's lips. He shook his head.

"No more. 'Nuff."

"Smoke," Amanda insisted. "And I will give you more love." She pushed the pipe against the general's mouth again, and this time he succumbed, taking in a long, deep breath, filling his lungs. He shuddered, and the woman took the pipe away from his lips. She watched as the smoke began to trickle from his mouth and nose, then took the pipe back to the desk. She laid it on the tray, blew out the lamp, then returned to the bed, removing her kimono jacket before kneeling between the old man's legs again.

She gripped his organ, squeezing lightly, her nails biting into the soft flesh. She felt him stir in her fingers, and he made a soft moaning sound. Smiling to herself, she dipped her head, taking him into her mouth, her long hair fanning out over his almost hairless thighs.

Old perhaps, but still strong, she thought, feeling him grow within her mouth, the heavy, plum-shaped head of him slipping out from under its darker-skinned sheath. She'd had younger, bigger men with less to offer.

The woman lifted her head for a moment, continuing to work the wet, glistening tube with one small hand. She looked at the man's face. He had fully succumbed to the smoke now, the skin and flesh of his cheeks slack. She smiled again, almost sadly, knowing what was to come. With that knowledge came whatever compassion her own unhappy past could muster; she would give him a last drink at the well of paradise before he drowned in the waters of hell.

She reached between her legs and inserted two fingers of her left hand, stroking herself slowly, feeling the thick juices left behind from his previous exertions. After a few moments she withdrew the fingers, then slid them under the sagging bag of his scrotum, simultaneously lowering her mouth over him again. Taking him between her lips, she pushed her fingers back between the cheeks of his buttocks until she found the puckered hole of his anus.

She worked the lubricated fingers into his rectum while her mouth slid up and down more quickly, bringing him to his fullest size against her throat, tongue, and palate. She searched for, then found, the hard kernel of his prostate, and began to knead it slowly with the sensitive pads of her fingertips.

He grew even larger in her mouth, the head swelling, deep in her throat. Sensing the first salt tang of fluid, she quickly withdrew both fingers and mouth and in a single, sinuous motion lifted herself above him, gripping his organ with her hand, pushing it between the already swollen lips of her vulva.

Easing herself downward, she took him deeply inside her and was rewarded with a single, drawn-out moan from the head of the bed. She was impaled, but it was he who was the prisoner, and with him captured, she began to move, humming softly to herself, a calm, whispering melody from her infancy, a lullaby for children.

Moments later, almost lost in the song, she felt a motion not her own as the yacht rocked gently at anchor. She turned her head in time to see the three men enter the room, all dressed in black, heads covered in woolen ski masks, clothes streaming with water.

Nodding in acknowledgment of their presence, she lifted a silencing finger to her lips and kept up her own rhythmic movements, sensing that the old man beneath her had almost reached the brink. The three men ignored her ministrations, and one stepped forward, pulling a heavy, single-edged knife from the sheath at his belt. Before she could react, he had leaned across the bed and lashed out with his knife hand, the blade slicing across her throat and cutting so deeply that it grated against the bones of her spine, almost decapitating her.

The severed head fell back, a spout of still-pumping blood gushing out of her neck and falling in a viscous deep red torrent over the general's thighs and belly.

The first man stepped away, and the second of the silent trio took his place, gripping the woman's hair and pulling her roughly from her perch on the old man's genitals. Hawksworth stirred at his pleasure's interruption, his eyes opening, seeing the horror but still not understanding it.

The third man moved to the head of the bed, using one hand to sweep the opium tray from the surface of the desk, replacing it with the small black bag he had been carrying. He opened the bag and took out a small device—two large, barbed hooks, joined by a short leather thong.

Hawksworth, his dulled mind finally realizing that something terrible was happening, began to struggle at his bonds, his mouth opening in a scream. The man with the hooked device reached out with his free hand and gripped the old man's jaw, pulling it down, while his other hand slid into Hawksworth's gaping mouth, practiced fingers inserting the hook into the tongue, fixing it firmly in place. Gripping the thong, the man pulled hard, dragging the general's already bleeding tongue out of the old man's mouth as far as possible, cutting off the welling screams of pain. The man pulled harder still, then embedded the second hook deeply in the soft flesh of Hawksworth's chest, making sure that it was snagged securely, the barb well down in muscle tissue. Hawksworth's thick tongue was now fully extended, acting as its own gag.

With the general silenced, the three men began to work, oblivious to the old man's mad struggles against the silk ropes that held him down, his body arching off the bed as the pain began to consume him.

The first two men pulled the lolling corpse of Amanda Kilau off the bed while the third man reached into his bag again and took out three short-handled knives, their blades as fine as scalpels. He handed a knife to each of the men, retaining one for himself, and then all three men began to cut, working with quick, sure strokes, slicing deeply into Hawksworth's flesh, carefully avoiding any major organs. Within five minutes the old man was bleeding from more than forty wounds, and the cabin was choked with the dark, tangy reek of heated copper. Through it all the old man struggled, his gurgling screams becoming bubbling, high-pitched squeals of animal pain as he twisted and pulled against his bonds, bladder and bowels emptying with his terror.

Their work almost complete, the first two men stood back, the acid stink of their sweat adding to the abattoir stench in the cabin. Reaching into his bag, the third man took out a small, spoon-shaped implement and bent over the writhing figure. He held the old man's head firmly with his free hand, then slid the implement into first the left, and then the right, eye socket, blinding the general with the casual grace of a chef coring apples for a Waldorf salad.

With the same deftness, the man took up his knife again and sliced off the general's ears, leaving them where they fell on the pillows. The figure on the bed was only twitching now, what was left of the old man's consciousness having retreated deeply into shock.

The third man stepped back, examining his handiwork. Satisfied, he nodded to himself, replacing both spoon and knife in the bag. After a moment's thought he reached into the bag again, this time removing a broad calligrapher's brush.

Dipping the soft bristles into the pain pot of blood formed by the hole where Hawksworth's left eye had been, he loaded the brush and drew three quick characters across the blanched surface of the general's forehead. The characters, in Mandarin, spelled out two words:

BLACK DRAGON

The man who had wielded the blade that killed Amanda Kilau grunted his approval and spoke. The language was Vietnamese, the words muffled by his ski mask.

"Cai do tot." Finish it now. The third man nodded. He put the brush back into the bag and then pulled out a simple pair of kitchen shears.

Opening the scissor blades, he slipped one beneath Hawksworth's yawning tongue, the other above, as close to the root as possible. He snipped once, firmly, and the severed slab of meat jerked forward onto the old man's chest, pulled by the taut leather thong.

Dark blood began to well up from the stump, filling the mouth. The three men left the cabin as quietly as they had entered it, leaving General William Sloane Hawksworth to drown alone.

CHAPTER 2

JAMES CHANG STOOD at the floor-to-ceiling corner window of his office and stared out over the city. During the day gray clouds had been building steadily, and now a light, drizzling rain was staining London's stonework from a low lead-colored sky.

Black Turtle Tea, and its parent company, Limehouse Trading Corporation, were headquartered on the fifty-third floor of the National Westminster Bank tower on Old Broad Street. The tower, built in the early seventies, was still the tallest building in England, and LTC had occupied the top floor from the day the tower opened.

From his vantage point almost six hundred feet in the air, Chang was often able to see across all of London and several counties beyond. Today, with the weather closed in and his view obscured, he had to content himself with looking down on the canyonlike courtyards of the Bank of England, then beyond to St. Paul's sooty dome and the muddy-brown and sluggish serpent line of the Thames. Even in the rain it was a view Chang treasured. It was a vision his grandfather, the first Chang Chin-Kang, had been able to see only in his mind, and that he, the third so-named in his lineage, had been able to make manifest. Looking out over the city, Chang felt connected to his past and let that feeling give him strength and feed the endless subtle anger that was his most valuable inheritance.

He turned away from the window and crossed the

large, softly lit room to his desk, a massive creation of solid oak that had graced the captain's cabin of a China clipper more than 150 years ago. The hardwood floors were partially covered by a scattering of exquisite Chinese carpets, and scores of niches built into the grasscloth-covered walls displayed a collection of jades worthy of a museum.

Chang picked up the phone on his desk and tapped the intercom button. Doris, the personal secretary guarding his office door, answered instantly.

"Yes, sir."

"Five minutes. Tell Li Wen to have the car ready."

"Yes, sir. Will you be available?"

"No," Chang answered. "I'm going home for the day." A lie, but necessary.

"Yes, sir," Doris replied. The line went dead as she hung up. Chang allowed himself a brief smile. Doris was no fount of intelligence, but she did exactly what she was told. An earthquake could swallow up their warehouses in Rotherhithe, and he would remain undisturbed at home.

He slipped out from behind the desk and went through a narrow door leading to his private bathroom. Hanging the jacket of his Savile Row suit on the door hook, Chang rolled up his shirtsleeves, washed his hands, and splashed water on his face, ignoring his reflection in the mirror over the sink. At sixty-six he was still a handsome man, flecks of white only now appearing in his jet-black hair, but he avoided looking at himself almost out of habit—unwilling to stare into the evidence of his own flint-blue eyes, eyes that had no place in the face of a true Chinese. Unbidden, without the taunt of the reflection, a name and lineage came into his mind, as it had come a thousand times before: Sergeant Albert Doakin of his Majesty's Royal Hong Kong Constabulary, born April 3, 1816, in London, England, died with his throat slit from ear to ear in Li Po Street, Hong Kong, August 6, 1858. The man who

raped his great-grandmother, Chang Wei-Ming. A forgotten moment half a world away and a century and a
half in the past. The source of his hated nickname:
Blue-Eyed Chang.

"D'iu ne le mo," Chang breathed, scrubbing his face
with a towel. The curse was as potent now as it had
been in the past. Still avoiding the mirror, Chang rolled
down his sleeves, buttoned them, then shrugged on his
jacket once again.

He left the bathroom, bypassed his desk, and went to
the wide burled-walnut double doors leading out of his
office. He paused there and let his neatly manicured
fingers reach out and stroke the large jade sculpture on
its own pedestal by the entrance.

The sculpture, carved from *"haieh,"* or lacquer black
jade from Yarkand, Chinese Turkistan, was almost
seven hundred years old and depicted a dragon-headed
turtle rising from a whirlpool. In a stylized form the
dragon turtle appeared on every box of Black Turtle tea
and was the logo for the Limehouse Trading Corporation. It was also something more.

Chiao yu, the turtle, was also *chan shih,* the warrior,
symbol of endurance and guardian of the northern
sphere. Chang let his hand trace the powerful neck and
dragon head, down to the humped enclosing shell.
Much more than a company symbol.

Chang slipped a pair of lightly tinted sunglasses from
the breast pocket of his jacket, put them on, and opened
the door to the outer office. He gave Doris a few brief
instructions, then followed the narrow carpeted corridor
down to his private elevator.

CHAPTER 3

THE DARK BLUE Rolls-Royce Silver Spur whispered through the midafternoon traffic of the City, turning right onto Threadneedle Street, easing past the rain-teared facades of the Royal Exchange and the Bank of England. Hidden behind the smoked-glass privacy screen, Li Wen the chauffeur guided the Rolls onto Cheapside, and as they glided past St. Paul's, heading west, Chang opened the small sports bag on the seat beside him and pulled out a well-worn industrial-green coverall.

He changed quickly, glancing out through the tinted windows as he pulled on the coverall and zipped it up around his neck. Just before Holborn Circus Li Wen turned sharply onto St. Andrew Street, then ducked into the shadowed entrance of the parking garage at the intersection of Shoe Lane. By the time the Rolls came to a stop on the third level, Chang had completed his change. He tapped a button on the console in front of him, and the privacy partition lowered. Chang glanced at his watch, then gave Li Wen his instructions, speaking the rapid, slightly grating Cantonese dialect of the Hong Kong streets.

"It's four-thirty. I'll be back at eight. Tell Mrs. Li that I would like dinner for our guests served at nine. Yes?"

"Of course, sir," Li Wen nodded, his aging face expressionless. Li Wen and his wife had worked for Chang's father and were overdue for retirement, but

11

neither of them had any family except for Chang and absolutely no inclination to return to their native village in the New Territories.

In lieu of a pension Chang had deeded the couple a small restaurant just off Regent Street, which Mrs. Li operated with an iron hand. As well as serving excellent food, the restaurant was also useful as a discreet meeting place for gatherings such as the one scheduled for that evening.

"Eight then," Chang repeated, then let himself out of the Rolls, bringing the sports bag with him. He closed the door and watched the automobile move off. He knew that Li would wait on the main level for ten minutes and then use the St. Andrew Street entrance again.

Footsteps echoing, Chang crossed to a low retaining wall. Parked tight against the wall was an unassuming Honda Civic. Using the keys in the pocket of his coveralls, Chang opened the door, entered the vehicle, and turned on the ignition. He headed down the ramps, following the signs that led to the New Street Square exit from the parking garage.

He left the garage, threading up the narrow road to New Fetter Lane. He paused there, checking his mirrors, then swung left without signaling, watching for any sudden movement in the traffic behind. There was none. Relaxing slightly and beginning to enjoy his total anonymity, Chang headed down to Fleet Street and the Inns of Court, turning west again, gliding easily in and out of the traffic moving toward the Strand.

Chang reached Charing Cross a few minutes later, puttered quietly around Trafalgar Square, and slipped onto Cockspur Street. Taking the roundabout at the rear of Canada House, he circled back on Pall Mall East, obeying the One Way signs, then turned due north on Whitcomb Street with the imposing bulk of the National Gallery on his right. He swept past the Royal Trafalgar Hotel, checked his mirrors once again, then turned onto Panton Street, finally reaching Leicester

Square. Logic told him that the complex system of ensuring his privacy was probably unnecessary, but prudence told him that avoidable errors should be avoided. For those like Chang, who followed in the footsteps of the *Chiu Chao,* sudden death was often the price of hindsight.

Chang piloted the Honda around the northern perimeter of the square, then turned into a narrow alley. The lane had once led to the side entrance of the now-vanished Chapel School that once faced the square, but now it was used mostly as a way of getting from the Leicester Square tube stop to the shops and restaurants on Little Newport Street.

Steering the small car into the alley, Chang drove into the shadows and parked. He left the car and locked up. Looking once over his shoulder, he moved off down the dogleg lane, carrying the sports bag in one hand.

He reached the end of the unnamed passage and paused, taking a deep breath. Nothing else in London smelled like it—an orchestra of odors, a hundred culinary instruments played in mad sequence combining to become a single voice telling him that this was his own. *"Tong Yan Kai"*—China Street, a twelve-block sector of what had once been the poorest part of Soho, now the cultural mecca for fifty thousand Chinese living in London and an equal number scattered around the rest of the country.

Chang swung to the right onto Little Newport Street, cutting through the browsing crowds of his countrymen who were sampling the wares of the surrounding herb shops and food stores, ignoring the drizzling rain.

Most of the hundred thousand Chinese living in England were involved in the food business, but it was only here, in Soho's Chinatown, that they were able to purchase the necessary ingredients for their own cooking, and not the laughable concoctions prepared for their *"gwei-lo"* round-eyed clientele. Here there were the makings of baked crab with ginger, shark's fin soup, white vegetables and sweet beans.

Chang went into a tiny variety store and nodded to the shrunken, wizened man behind his makeshift counter. The shop, selling soft drinks, racked packets of crisps, and cigarettes, rarely made enough money to pay the rent, but the man behind the counter was collecting squeeze from half a dozen sources, acting as lookout for several of the nearby basement gambling dens as well as spotting for Chang himself.

"Loto Pai," Chang said politely, asking for a package of American Camel cigarettes. The old man nodded, reached up, and took down a package, placing it on the counter. Chang paid for the cigarettes and scooped them up, dropping them into the pocket of his coverall. He nodded, then turned and left the shop. Had the little man given him *Luji Pai,* or Lucky Strikes, Chang would have known that his rendezvous had been prejudiced. As it was, he now knew that the coast was clear.

Between the herb store at number 34 Little Newport and the acupuncturist's at number 36, there was a short flight of steps leading to an unmarked solid-wood door painted a sooty red color that was an almost perfect match for the surrounding brickwork. Reaching into the deep side pocket of his coverall, Chang brought out a ring of keys, chose one, and stepped up to the door. He unlocked it, slipped into the narrow vestibule beyond, and pulled the door closed behind him, locking the dead bolt with the same key. Directly in front of him a long, steeply angled flight of stairs led upward, lit by a single yellow-bulbed fixture in the pressed-tin ceiling.

Climbing the stairs, Chang reached the second-floor landing and paused. On his right was another door. Choosing another key from the ring, he unlocked the door, opened it, and stepped inside.

The suite of offices had once been a tiny flat made up of a front bed-sitting room overlooking the street, a small living room, and an even smaller kitchen with toilet facilities leading off from it. The door from the hallway outside opened into the living room. The walls were papered with a faded rose pattern, the floor was covered with gray, brown-speckled linoleum and the only furniture was a narrow sleeping mat and a wooden kitchen chair painted a shocking electric blue.

Chang sat down in the chair and shrugged off the coverall. Removing the cigarettes he'd purchased from the coverall, he stood, brushed down his suit, and smoothed his hair. He opened the package of cigarettes, lit one with a dull, gunmetal Cartier lighter, and walked into the front room.

A slope-shouldered, middle-aged man in shirtsleeves was waiting for him, standing behind a plain office desk, his back to the trio of small windows looking out over Little Newport Street. A small portable computer was set out on the desk, a sheaf of papers and a ledger off to one side.

The name on the man's British passport was Abbot Fong and described him as being a resident of London, England, and a businessman. He had been born Fong Ching-Kuo in the New Territories village of Man Kam To, and he was *Pak Sze Sin,* or White Paper Fan, in the organization of which James Chang was leader. The passport and the attendant paperwork that gave Abbot Fong legitimate status in England and around the world had been purchased in Hong Kong at a cost of U.S. $175,000.

"Shan Chu," said Fong, using the appropriate "Dragon Head" honorific. "Punctual as usual."

"Abbot." Chang nodded. He dropped down into a comfortable armchair across from Fong. "Presumably there are no snakes among the dragons?" Both men spoke in low-toned Cantonese.

"The rooms were swept an hour ago," Fong answered. "We are free to talk."

"Excellent," Chang replied. A dozen police agencies

would have gladly expended their entire annual surveillance budgets to gain access to the weekly meetings between the 489 and 411 of the Black Dragon Triad.
Then, of course, there was the competition.

"Shall I make my report then?" Fong asked. Chang
nodded, smoked his cigarette, and half listened as his
second in command droned out a seemingly endless list
of figures and facts relating to their international holdings. Chang sighed inwardly, part of him wishing that
he were living in the world faced by his grandfather so
long ago. A simpler time of adventurous beginnings.

Black Dragon had begun with the first Chang Chin-
Kang and the six pounds of Patna opium he'd managed
to smuggle off the *Torrington,* a Jardine-Matheson
schooner in the trade. "Brilliant" Chang spirited the
drug into the warrens of Limehouse and Ratcliffe Highway, founding a criminal empire that had lasted for
more than a century and spanned the globe.

The opium had purchased a small holding in the Oriental ghetto made up of rat-infested alleys with names
like Ming Street and Canton Lane. Originally a tea-
house and opium den for Chinese and Malaysian seamen pausing briefly in the city, the Black Turtle
expanded to include a brothel, which in turn led the
first Chang to expand further, establishing "cribs"
throughout the East End and eventually in more refined
parts of London. His trade in opium and women opened
up other opportunities, and utilizing a string of coffee-
houses throughout the city, he soon had a broad-based
and tremendously effective criminal-intelligence network. He knew of raids before they happened, knew
which of the tea clippers were also carrying illicit
opium, and knew who had what stolen goods to sell.
Within a few years "Brilliant" Billy Chang was to
crime in London what Lloyd's was to insurance. And
that was only the beginning.

James Chang blinked, pulling himself back into the
present. Abbot had almost reached the end of his report

on the ebb and flow of their operations for the week. Chang stared at the pudgy administrator thoughtfully. The Fong lineage with the Black Dragon Triad was almost as long as his own. Fong's great-uncle, Lo Yu Sheng—Big-Eared Sheng—had been White Paper Fan to Chang's grandfather, and an assortment of Shengs and Fongs were scattered throughout the Black Dragon organization around the world, as well as holding a variety of positions within Limehouse Trading, Black Turtle Tea, and their complex of associated companies in a score of countries. Recently it had been occurring to Chang that perhaps there were in fact too many Shengs and Fongs working for him. It wouldn't be the first time that a man's worst enemy turned out to be his closest ally.

"I think that just about does it," said Fong, tapping a key on the computer and squinting at the screen. "I haven't included some of our operations in Taiwan— the book and computer counterfeiting, for instance. I'm still waiting for the quarterlies on them."

"Good enough," Chang said. "What about the shipment into Vancouver? Any problems?"

"None that I know of," Fong answered with a tired shrug. "The *Orient Star* docks today. Our Vietnamese colleagues assure me that the system is foolproof."

"I hope so," Chang grunted. He leaned forward and stubbed out his cigarette into a small ashtray on the desk. He settled back into the chair. "We've risked seventy kilos of product to test it."

"The container port has been in use for too long. Too many people not our own have become involved—the motorcycle gangs, for instance. They virtually control the terminal."

"And are they to be trusted any less than the *'chu ju'?*" asked Chang, using a common derogatory term for the Vietnamese.

"The 'pygmies' are somewhat less than human," offered Fong, "but at least they share the same family tree as we do. They are not *'gwei-lo.'* As you know, I have had reservations about using them from the beginning, but you agreed that we had very little choice in the matter. They also provide an effective smoke screen between ourselves and the authorities."

"When will we know if they have succeeded?" Chang asked.

"Tonight," Fong answered promptly. He glanced at the computer again, struck another key, then folded down the top. "Which brings us again to the meeting you have requested."

"Plans are proceeding then?" Chang asked calmly. He knew that Abbot Fong had been against the conference from the beginning, and wondered if his White Paper Fan was about to try and deter him once again.

"Plans are proceeding as you requested, *Shan Chu,* although as you know I have advised against such an assembly." Fong cleared his throat. Chang lit another cigarette, blowing smoke up to the low yellowed plaster ceiling. "There have been some problems," Fong continued.

"Such as?" Chang asked.

"Our Sicilian friends are nervous about the venue. They're balking."

"The last time they organized a policy meeting such as this one was at Apalachin, New York, in 1957," Chang replied. "The FBI appeared, and they fled like rabbits. Having our meeting aboard *Orient Star* gives us absolute control over who shall be in attendance. The ship is owned by Coronet Seaways, and the tickets have all been booked through the Halpro Agency."

"Both of which are owned by LTC." Fong nodded. "I am aware of that, *Shan Chu.* Nevertheless . . ."

"Calm their fears, Abbot," instructed Chang. "The Sicilians are as aware as any of us that this meeting must take place, and must take place soon. All of us are threatened by the Colombians and their lunatic methods. They are businessmen, as we are. So are the yakuza. The Colombians are less than animals. Together we can stop them." Chang smiled at his chief adviser, softening the moment. "Perhaps when all is said and done, the American Drug Enforcement people will give us a medal. Do you think so, my loyal *Pak Sze Sin?*"

"Anything is possible," Fong muttered. "If I can organize and coordinate a meeting between the American Mafia, the Chinese triads, and the Japanese yakuza, anything is possible."

"We live in interesting times," Chang grinned, paraphrasing the ancient proverb.

"As I recall," Fong answered dryly, "Confucius meant that to be a curse."

"Then let me live a cursed life by all means." Chang laughed. "At any rate, the date has been set?"

"Yes." Fong nodded. "The *Orient Star* leaves for Alaska from Vancouver in three days. She arrives back two weeks after that. We board for the Hawaiian cruise two days later, on the twenty-seventh."

"Excellent!" breathed Chang. He clapped his hands together. Fong stood, gathering up his papers and the portable computer. The handclap signaled the end of the meeting. Fong let out a slow breath, staring at his master with an odd look of both fear and envy.

"The girl is waiting in the kitchen," he said quietly. He came around the desk. "She is from Sheung Shui village in the New Territories."

"A Hakka?" Chang asked.

"Yes." Fong nodded. "Of course." Chang pursed his lips thoughtfully.

"I wish to know about the Vancouver shipment," he said softly. "You should have word in time for the dinner tonight." It was not a question. Once again, Abbot Fong nodded.

"Of course," he answered. Chang stood up, bowing his head and shoulders briefly. It was a gesture of dismissal.

"Thank you, Abbot."

"Good-bye, *Shan Chu.*" Fong left the room, and a few seconds later Chang heard the soft sound of the door closing and the lock being thrown. He waited briefly, staring out through the rainswept windows, then turned and went back to the small bedroom next to the kitchen. The room was almost totally dark, lit only by a weak spill of light from the hall.

"*Pi nu!*" he called, using an old word for servant girl. Within a few seconds a small figure filled the doorway. Slim, long-haired, dressed in a plain cotton dress that gave no hint of her figure.

"Yes, lord?" The accent was rough and uneducated. He felt a faint ripple of memory and anger. His grandmother would have had much the same kind of accent.

"Closer," instructed Chang, still speaking Cantonese. The girl stepped forward with only a small hesitation. The light from the hall caught her cheek. She was pretty, no more than sixteen. Chang studied her for a few moments. "Remove your dress," he said finally.

"Yes, lord." There was no hesitation now. She was following instructions that had been drilled into her for weeks now. She took a single step back and drew the dress up over her head. She folded it carefully and draped it over the chair with Chang's coverall. Beneath the dress she was wearing a plain white bra and panties. The breasts were small but well formed, and the hips were slight. Best of all was her skin, creamy smooth and unblemished. She had been a good choice.

"You are from Sheung Shui?" Chang asked, switching to Hakka. The girl looked surprised, then frightened.

"Yes, lord." The eyes would not meet his. He put his index finger under her chin and raised it. Her eyes were shining black, with a spark of intelligence, even anger. A very good choice.

"What is your name?"

"Huh'ng Fah," she answered. Chang smiled. "Fragrant Flower." Every village mother had at least one child with that kind of name. "Almond Blossom," "Little Clever One," "Bright Moon." Names from bad love songs. Romantic names for hopeless lives.

"Do you have many brothers and sisters?" Chang asked.

"One brother, three sisters," she answered.

"And you were the youngest?" Chang suggested. Surprisingly, the child-woman shook her head, the hair waving around her bare shoulders like a dark shadow.

"Second-youngest," she said. "But my little sister has a . . ." The girl frowned and lifted one foot, gripping the heel.

"Clubfooted?" Chang suggested. The girl nodded happily, as though his comment had formed some kind of bond between them.

"So you were the prettiest then," Chang said. The girl shrugged.

"Our family is very poor." Poor enough to sell her into servitude for a fixed fee.

"How long is your contract?" asked Chang.

"Three years," she answered. Three years' training in a *chi kuan* crib here in London, or perhaps in Manchester. If she did well and listened to her mistress, she might be one of the lucky ones. Whatever happened, he knew, the three years was only the beginning. She would never see her village again, or her family. He sighed. And perhaps that was just as well.

"Are you a virgin?" Chang asked coldly. He knew that she was, but the question reinforced his authority. The girl flushed.

"Yes, lord."

"And do you know who I am?" he asked.

"Yes, lord," said the girl, eyes lowered. "You are *Shan Chu* of the Black Dragon. You are responsible for giving my father great wealth and face."

Responsible for turning her father's daughter into a whore. But for Chinese daughters that had always been the manner of it, Chang knew, one way or the other. Time had changed nothing but place, and the old laws remained.

"Do you know what the place of the *Shan Chu* is?" asked Chang.

"Yes, lord," the girl replied, the words learned recently by rote. "The *Shan Chu* is leader of the *Hui*, the Dragon Head. He defends the lineage and the honor of all those in his care. His word is law."

"Do you know what your place is?" asked Chang. The girl nodded, and he could see the faint quivering of her shoulders.

"Yes, lord," she whispered.

"Then show me," said Chang.

CHAPTER 4

ABBOT FONG SAT in a corner seat in the almost empty subway car, swaying easily with the hypnotic motion of the tube as it carried him toward his meeting with Chang and the other senior officers of Black Dragon at Madame Li's restaurant.

His cheap light gray suit was rumpled, his tie loose, the top button of his shirt undone. Between his legs was a battered medium brown briefcase of the old-fashioned sort normally given to junior government clerks.

In the briefcase was a welter of files, papers, and documents, all of them in Chinese and none of them relating to the affairs of the Triad. The briefcase and his somewhat dumpy appearance gave him the look of a slightly befuddled, unassuming, and totally benign small businessman, which was exactly the impression he wanted to give to anyone showing interest in his affairs.

Fong kept a perfectly legitimate office in the eastern suburbs of London, doing business as a letter writer, immigration consultant, and tax adviser to the Chinese community there. Any investigation of that office, official or otherwise, would have revealed nothing that didn't jibe with that minor-key role with the exception of his laptop computer, which was kept in a small fireproof safe built into the wall.

The computer, which he used for Triad business, was programmed to wipe out all the information it contained if anyone without the proper authorization tried to access the data, and Fong backed up the information each day, transferring it to a disk that was then placed in a location known only to Fong and the *Shan Chu*. Even Chang was unaware that Fong kept a second disk copy for himself as insurance.

The middle-aged man allowed himself a moment's weakness, leaning his head back against the cool glass of the window behind his seat. Under the present circumstances his second-disk insurance might well prove to be useful.

He had spent months organizing the new channel for the Triad's Pacific shipments of Black Dragon powder, and the plan had seemed to be foolproof. Now it lay in ruins. Seventy kilos of uncut Heroin had vanished, and the security of the Triad and its members had been compromised.

Worse, on the eve of Chang's long-awaited summit with the Japanese and the Sicilians, Black Dragon had lost an unbelievable amount of face. Beyond the obvious financial loss, the disappearance of the goods would seriously prejudice its position at the meeting. Black Dragon, suffering from what Fong believed was a weakness of leadership and direction, had problems enough without this. The *Shan Chu* was going to be furious, and rightly or wrongly, that fury would fall upon Fong's shoulders. To be White Paper Fan for an honorable society such as Black Dragon was a position most Chinese of his generation would envy, but it had its drawbacks. He shivered, his mind, unbidden, conjuring up the dark, pockmarked features of Kom Tong-Ho, the organization's Red Pole. To Fong, Black Dragon's tall, cadaverous enforcer was the personification of Chiang Shih, the legendary ghost vampire, devourer of men and violator of women. Kom did nothing to dispel the image, dressing in black and keeping his graying hair long and loose about his shoulders. Even Chang feared the Red Pole's barely suppressed ferocity, knowing that his only true loyalty was to Death itself. As a bill collector Kom was without peer.

Fong pushed the image of the Red Pole from his mind and tried to concentrate, assembling the information from his contact in Vancouver, adding it to what he already knew concerning the plan he'd put into effect. He went over every detail, trying to put the puzzle pieces into place, assembling a vision of his defeat. It would have begun at Vancouver's Canada Place cruiseship terminal with the docking of the *Orient Star.*

CHAPTER 5

THE "CANADA PLACE" complex in Vancouver, British Columbia, lies at the foot of Burrard Street in the downtown core of the city, jutting out into the harbor like some enormous landlocked China clipper, the twelve soaring "sails" of the roof above the building arching upward in a sculptured bright white homage to the port city's earliest days.

Built as the Canadian pavilion for Vancouver's Expo 86 trade fair, the complex is made up of the sail-roofed exhibition hall, an adjoining trade and convention center, and the towers of the Pan Pacific Hotel. In addition, the massive base structure is also used as a cruise-ship terminal capable of berthing and seeing to the needs of any-sized passenger vessel, including the *QE2*.

The terminal regularly plays host to vessels from virtually every major cruise line, including P&O, Cunard, Royal Viking, Sitmar, and Princess Cruises. During the peak summer and fall seasons it is quite common to see both main berths on either side of the terminal filled, and ships like the *Rotterdam, Island Princess,* and the *Fairsky* are often seen entering and leaving the harbor beneath the sweep of the Lions Gate Bridge at the head of the harbor two-and-a-half miles to the west.

Snugly moored to the starboard side of the cruise-ship terminal, the Orient America passenger liner *Orient Star* was neither the longest nor largest ship to dock there, but she was certainly one of the most impressive. At 820 feet in overall length and 45,000 tons gross tonnage, she was heavier and larger than the *Rotterdam,* but smaller than the *QE2* or the *Norway.* She had twelve decks and accommodation for thirteen hundred passengers, and could travel at a top speed of over twenty knots. Painted an unpleasant beige by her original owners, she was now the same brilliant white as the sails of the building beside her.

Commissioned by the Hong Kong–based Dominion Far East Line in 1958, and christened *Prince Marco* at her launching in 1960, the ship was purchased in 1985 by Orient America Cruise Line, a subsidiary of Pacific Marine Transport Corporation, itself a wholly owned subsidiary of PATCO, or Pacific American Transport Corporation, with its head office in San Francisco. Both companies were in fact owned by Limehouse Trading.

After a complete refitting and upgrading, the ship was reborn in 1987 as *Orient Star,* covering several different cruising routes, depending on the season. During the spring and summer she went from Hong Kong to Hawaii, and then from Hawaii to either San Francisco or Vancouver. Half a dozen times during this season she also did San Francisco, Vancouver, and Alaska. During the fall and winter the *Orient Star* went back and forth on the Honolulu–Los Angeles–Puerto Vallarta triangle.

From the sundeck, eighty feet above the oily surface of the harbor, down to E-deck, *Orient Star* was fitted out luxuriously with rich carpeting in her corridors, fine wood paneling in her four separate dining rooms, her lavish staterooms serviced by a swarm of stewards dressed in crisp white uniforms. On the upper decks the thunder of the massive turbines deep below was reduced to a gentle whisper of vibration barely felt, and to the passengers, food, drink, clean linen, and freshly laundered clothing simply appeared as if by magic.

From E-deck down to the double bottom below H-deck, it was a different world. Carpeting and paneling vanished, replaced by utilitarian, heavily painted steel. Crew and staff, totaling more than seven hundred men and women, were crammed into scores of cabins squeezed in between below-deck facilities like the laundry, quartermasters' stores, the print shop, baggage rooms, and food-handling areas. Corridors were narrower, ceilings lower, and the overall noise level was much higher, even with the ship resting at her berth. With new stores being taken on for the voyage north to Alaska, half a dozen different languages could be heard: Goanese from the stewards, Filipino from the cooking staff and seamen, Cantonese from the laundry staff, and even English when a junior officer appeared from the purser's staff.

Of all the ethnic groups represented on board the *Orient Star,* the Chinese laundry staff were the least involved with the social structure of below-decks life. Like virtually all cruise-ship lines, Orient America hired its laundry workers from one of several large companies in Hong Kong, in its case using Sun Bright Laundry Services, yet another company owned by Limehouse Trading through a complicated screen of subsidiaries.

For *Orient Star* Sun Bright provided a staff of nineteen Hakka workers broken down into three 6-man shifts with one overall supervisor. The men worked around the clock handling thirty-five tons of laundry a week in their steam-filled dungeon deep down on G-deck. The laundry flowed in from all sectors of the huge ship—galley, officers, crew, and passengers, with linen constantly being changed in the dining rooms, as well as towels and sheeting being replaced daily in each of the 720 cabins.

The laundry staff, with separate accommodation and cooking facilities from the rest of the crew, lived entirely apart, and except for occasional meetings between the laundry supervisor and the hotel-services manager aboard ship, there was no contact between the Chinese and anyone else on board. The laundry staff all worked on short-term contracts, never more than a year, after which they were rotated back to Hong Kong for a one-month vacation before they were reassigned to another ship. It was a system that had worked flawlessly for a number of years, and since the purchase of *Orient Star* there had not been a single laundry-related complaint.

Chen Han Lu, laundry supervisor on *Orient Star* and also a 49 or foot-soldier member of the Black Dragon Society, pushed the fully loaded linen trolly down the main service corridor on G-deck, head lowered and paying no attention to the throngs of stewards and cooking staff milling around him. They had reached Vancouver early that morning, and the first of the new stores were now being brought aboard through the crew-and-provisions entrance in the aft section of the cruise ship.

Chen was in his late forties, his short, stocky body heavily muscled from years of manual labor. A native of Hong Kong's mud-flat slums at Aberdeen, Chen had worked for Sun Bright for eleven years and had been a member of Black Dragon since early adolescence. He had little or no ambition to rise within the ranks of the organization, content to follow orders, knowing that the Society would always be there to take care of his needs and those of his family. He remitted half of his wages from Sun Bright to his aging parents, now living in a Choi Hung Housing Authority flat, and Black Dragon matched the amount each month. Upon his parents' death the money would be banked for Chen by the Society as a pension for his own retirement.

Reaching the linen store, Chen unloaded his trolley, placing the freshly laundered sheets and pillowcases in their appropriate niches. He then exchanged his emptied trolley for a bulging canvas-and-aluminum cart filled with soiled linens from the upper decks and returned to the service corridor.

Yan Fu, one of the laundrymen, was waiting for him at the midships freight elevator, a large orange plastic

refuse bag resting on the floor beside him. Wordlessly
the younger man took the canvas cart from Chen and
wheeled it into the elevator. Chen then picked up the
garbage bag and took the companionway stairs one
deck down, the garbage bag slung easily over his shoulder. Through the thin plastic it was easy to see that the
bag was loaded with empty aluminum cans, most of
them bearing the distinctive Coca-Cola logo. If anyone
had noticed Chen or the bag, he would have assumed
that the cans came from the large refrigerated dispenser
at the entrance to the laundry, put there for the exclu-
sive use of Sun Bright employees. Only a very observ-
ant witness would have noticed that Chen's biceps were
straining with the burden of a bag that should have
weighed no more than five or six pounds.

Fifty feet down a wide, low-ceilinged corridor on
G-deck, Chen reached the full-width hold that had once
been used to ship automobiles owned by the passengers. One section of the gloomy area was still used for
this purpose, but for the most part the hold was a convenient place to stow the scores of containerized refuse
bins used on each voyage.

In the early days of cruising, garbage hadn't been a
problem, with the ocean used as a convenient and forgiving dump. In the eighties and early nineties in-
creased environmental awareness had necessitated a
more prudent method of waste disposal, if for no other
reason than good public relations. Although organic
food waste was still discreetly tipped over the side during the night, everything else was placed in one of the
minidumpsters, glass, plastic, and aluminum being divided for recycling.

Threading his way between the rows of dark blue
containers, Chen found the one with the stenciled
number he had been given in Hong Kong. Peering into
the bin, Chen checked to make sure that it was indeed
for aluminum. Satisfied, he swung the orange bag up-

ward, muscles bulging, and emptied the contents into the Dumpster.

Yan Fu had completed the exercise once before, and now, with the second load, the job was done. Seventy kilograms of China White Heroin, eight troy ounces to a bag, each bag inserted into a specially made Coca-Cola tin and hermetically sealed, were now ready for the next stage on their way to the addicts of North America.

Feeling pleased with his work and the five-hundred-dollar bonus it would give him, Chen lit a cigarette and headed back to the laundry, wondering how much of a share in the five hundred he would give to Yan Fu. The bonus, paid in cash, would be given to him that evening at a restaurant in Vancouver's Chinatown by a member of the local Black Dragon cell.

To those who trade in illicit substances, there is nothing particularly exciting or exotic about the business. Opium, Heroin, cocaine, marijuana, and hashish are nothing more than commodities provided for a specific market, and the prices of those commodities are established using the same criteria as pork bellies or orange juice—supply and demand.

In the case of Heroin for the North American market, demand was generally constant and had been so since the mid-seventies, with an average addict population of about 750,000. The upsurge in cocaine use during the eighties had no impact on the number of users except to marginally increase supply due to the focus of police and customs interdiction swinging to the "new" drug. The biggest change in the Heroin industry was a steady increase in the percentage of the drug coming from Southeast Asian sources and a decline in the amount coming from Pakistani, Turkish, and Afghani sources, mostly for political reasons. Even now, several years after the Soviet withdrawal, the opium crop in Afghanistan was only 30 percent of what it had been in the late sixties, and the Turkish, Iranian, and Pakistani crops were almost nonexistent.

The most serious problems facing the modern Heroin druglords were the same as they had always been: transportation and time. A major exporter of Heroin could invest millions of dollars in a shipment, which would then take weeks and sometimes even months to get to its market, tying up the often borrowed money at heavy interest. Relatively small amounts—three or four kilos—could be transported by air, but airport security and surveillance made that a risky business.

With pure Heroin worth 400 percent more by weight than cocaine, major dealers were also not about to engage in the outrageous cowboy antics of the Colombian cartels, preferring discretion and patience to expensive grandstanding. Still, time was money.

Abbot Fong had originated the Coca-Cola can scheme almost a year before, realizing that their normal routes using Heroin smuggled inside various ship containers was tying up too much money for too long a period. The method also put the product out of their immediate control for extended periods, and they were forced to enlist the aid of those who handled the containers once they reached their destinations.

The Coca-Cola idea had a number of strong points. A small factory owned and operated by the Black Dragon Society was already making novelty radios using fake soft-drink cans, giving then access to the containers, silkscreens for the designs, and the equipment used to seal them. Unlike the real containers, the radio cans were made of sheet metal, not aluminum.

The cans, filled with Heroin and sealed, were then brought aboard the *Orient Star,* interspersed among real cans destined for the Coke machine in the laundry. Arriving in port, the Heroin containers would then be mixed with real aluminum empties and pitched into the appropriate Dumpster.

The next stage of the process was equally straightforward. A small waste-disposal company, in Vancouver's case a Vietnamese firm called Mau Len Transport, would pick up the aluminum-can consignment and take the cans to its recycling depot. At the depot a large magnet would be used to "fish" the sheet-metal cans out of the aluminum empties. On a standard Hong Kong–Hawaii–Vancouver cruise the product would be in transit for only twenty-one days, and at no time would it be out of Black Dragon control.

On the last two cruises Abbot Fong had done full dry runs using cans filled with sand, and the system had worked flawlessly. Fong had even instructed that a Hong Kong Preventive Service drug-sniffing dog be kidnapped, and the creature had completely overlooked several sealed tins of Heroin mixed in with a real case of drinks.

Chang's second in command knew that in terms of drug surveillance and customs Vancouver was somewhat more efficient than the overburdened ports of San Francisco and Honolulu, and if the system worked in Canada, it could be applied to any port *Orient Star* found herself in.

At 11:35 A.M. a dark green flat-cabbed, front-loading Mack waste-disposal truck turned off Powell Street in Vancouver's waterfront district, following Centennial Street through the bedraggled maze of warehouses and piers that stood below Chinatown. The truck was driven by Nguyen Thu, with his assistant, Tran Dinh Diem. Both men were refugee Vietnamese, and both had served together in the same unit of the Army of the Republic of Vietnam. Although both men were the same age and had held the same rank in the army, Nguyen was senior of the two because he had managed to successfully smuggle out his black-market booty before the fall of Saigon while Tran had not been so fortunate. Nguyen had also managed to keep up his contacts with other black-marketeers who had escaped during the final days, and had an ongoing relationship with the or-

ganized substrata of Southeast Asian criminals who had
established themselves in southern California's Orange
County. The relationship had been a profitable one and
had provided the additional financing he'd needed to
establish Mau Len Transport as a reasonable front for
his other activities. Normally neither Nguyen nor Tran
would actually have driven one of the Mau Len trucks,
but today, as both men knew, was special.

Nguyen piloted the heavy truck along the debris-
lined pierside road, eventually coming out into the open
area of crisscrossing railway lines that had once served
the old Canadian Pacific station at the foot of Granville
Street. On their left a forty-foot-high artificial embank-
ment kept the industrial area hidden from the downtown core, while ahead and to the right they could see
the trademark sails of B.C. Place. Today the portside
berth was empty, while the starboard pier was taken up
by the romantic, streamlined form of *Orient Star.*

Crunching down through the unfamiliar gears,
Nguyen slowed the truck and steered to the left, following a single curving arrow painted on the roadway and
passing a sign announcing that the road was for service
vehicles only. A security guard in a booth at the cavernous entrance to the lowest level of the cruise-ship terminal gave them a bored wave and they lurched into
the dimly lit garage area.

"Ben trai," Tran instructed, pointing. Nguyen nodded
irritably, dragging the heavy wheel around to the left.

"I know, I know," he answered, peering ahead. Most
of the parking slots were empty, but Nguyen resisted
the temptation to cut directly across to the pierside exit.
A moment later they had reached the pier itself and began to drive hesitantly down the canyon created by the
concrete parking garage and the sleek white flank of the
Orient Star. Nguyen and Tran weren't alone. There
were half a dozen other trucks on the oil-stained roadway, all of them clustered around the forward provi-
sioning entrance and the broad conveyor belt that led

into the ship's interior. There was also a Canadian Customs car parked at an angle by the conveyor, two uniformed officers watching as cases of bonded provisions were loaded aboard. One of the customs men was smoking a cigarette, and the other was picking at something in his right nostril. Both men looked utterly bored.

Masking the welling panic he felt, Nguyen pretended he was just as bored as the customs men and guided the truck beyond them to the forward cargo hatch. Here there was a broad ramp rather than a conveyor belt, and a score of dark blue BFI minidumpsters had already been arranged along the pier. Nguyen eased his foot down on the brake and brought the truck to a hissing stop. Tran, carrying a clipboard, climbed down from the passenger side and began the process of identifying the bins containing aluminum waste.

Within half an hour all the bins had been emptied into the belly of the truck, and Nguyen and Tran were on their way out of the terminal. As they moved off the pier, Chen Han Lu, who had been watching the entire procedure from an E-deck porthole, exited the ship across the A-deck passenger gangplank and flashed his seaman's pass to the woman at the Immigration desk on the landward end. She waved him through, and he gave her a quick bow before heading for the elevators that led up to the main floor of the terminal and the waiting bank of pay telephones. As far as he could see, everything had gone exactly according to the plan laid out so carefully by Abbot Fong.

Twenty minutes later the careful plan ended in total disaster.

The Vietnamese district in Vancouver mimics world geography, the small neighborhood appended to the much larger and well-established Chinatown section. East of Main Street and from Hastings Street down to the bleak, windowless warehouses along the water was

home to the nearly destitute and utterly friendless sprinkling of Vietnamese who came to Vancouver during the
midseventies.

Over time the few had managed to carve out a reasonable place in the city, emulating the Chinese by going into the food business and establishing restaurants
as well as greengroceries, and even a few truck farms
in the rich soil of the delta region close to the United
States border. But even after more than fifteen years the
strip of East Hastings from Main to Campbell Street
was still called Saigon Alley, and the produce warehouses, noodle factories, and rice brokers' offices were
still located in the gloomy industrial wasteland that ran
close to the waterfront from Gore Street to Hawks.
There are no trees, grass grows long and strawlike out
of broken glass and cinders, and there is no sign of
children anywhere.

The Mau Len Transport company's "recycling depot"
was located at the foot of Hawk Street, occupying a
small, windowless bunker that squatted between the
Gold Dragon Auto Body Shop and an empty, sag-
roofed wooden warehouse that looked like an arsonist's
dream. There was a small door at the front of the depot
that opened into a tiny office, and an alley between the
depot building and the auto-body shop that led to a hidden courtyard and a rear loading dock. A chute, made
of salvaged sheet plywood, had been built onto the
loading dock, allowing the trucks to dump their contents directly into the building. The chute led to a high-
sided conveyor belt that carried the aluminum cans to a
small hydraulic crusher set up in the center of the depot
floor.

The crusher created forty-pound "ingots," which
were then placed on dollies, loaded onto a stake truck,
strapped down, and carried to a large reclamation plant
in the suburbs of Richmond where they were sold. The
whole operation was simple, straight-forward, and reasonably profitable. From time to time the depot was

also used as a way station for hijacked cigarettes and gray-market electronic equipment. Several times a year the depot was used as an assembly point for illegal refugees entering the United States.

Nguyen and Tran reached the Hawk Street building within fifteen minutes of leaving the Canada Place terminal, and Nguyen nosed the truck into the alley, fully expecting Li Doc, Tran's cousin, to meet them at the loading bay. The four other employees, none of whom knew about the special consignment from the *Orient Star,* had been given the day off.

The loading dock was empty as Nguyen eased the Mack into the courtyard, and Tran shook his head angrily. It wouldn't be the first time his cousin had brought him shame. As Nguyen jockeyed the truck into position, Tran jumped down from the cab and went up the steps to the loading-bay door. Li he knew, was probably comfortably settled in on the toilet, with a cigarette in one hand and a copy of *Hustler* in the other.

Muttering curses under his breath, Tran ducked into the shadows beyond the gaping freight doors, stepping around the conveyor belt. He reached one arm over the side of the belt housing and rummaged around with his hand, listening to the sound of clattering aluminum cans. He cursed again. Li had been told to empty the belt and the crusher before they returned. And why was the depot dark?

"Li!" he called out. "Where are you hiding?" No answer. Stumbling, Tran skirted the cables leading to the crusher and stamped across the concrete floor to the breaker panel beside the closed door to the toilet. To his right he was vaguely aware of Nguyen backing the truck up to the chute.

Tran reached the breaker box and discovered that the main switch was in the Off position. He palmed it on angrily, but nothing happened. Furious now at his cousin's stupid game, he hammered on the toilet door. There was no response. He grabbed the knob and swung it open.

As he'd expected, his cousin was indeed seated on the toilet, trousers around his ankles, and there was a copy of *Hustler* on the urine-splashed floor at his feet. Instead of a cigarette in his mouth, however, Li's limp, uncircumcised penis dangled from between his lips like some hideous alien tongue. Between his legs there was a deep red stain, slowly turning to brown. A squadron of silent flies was gathered there, feeding happily.

Retching, Tran backed out of the cubicle, head bent and turned to one side, his eyes squeezed shut against the horrible vision of his dead cousin. He briefly felt a cold sensation behind his right ear, and then he died as a single bullet, its sound muffled by the flesh of his neck, exploded into his brain, then exited above his upper lip, the chips and shards of his front teeth clattering against the doorframe of the toilet like tiny hailstones.

Outside, the gusty roar of the Mack's engine had blocked out the small sound of the weapon as Nguyen backed the truck into position. When he had the rear gate of the truck aligned with the chute, he grunted to himself happily and switched off the engine.

He sighed deeply, glad to have the hard part of the job done, then opened his door and climbed down to the ground. Hearing a small sound, he turned, and died as quickly as Tran had a few seconds before, never fully recognizing the barrel of the shotgun six inches from his head.

Two thirds of his face dissolved away as the weapon fired, sheeting back onto the half-open door of the truck, and then the dead man slumped to the ground.

A slight, dark-haired figure appeared on the raised loading bay. The man was in his early twenties, Vietnamese, wearing tight jeans, black lace-up shoes, and white socks. Even though the weather was hot, he was also wearing a black nylon jacket. The second man, still standing over the slumped body of Nguyen, was dressed identically.

"Ong toi dau," said the man beside the truck. "His head hurts!" The man on the loading bay laughed. The sound was high-pitched and nervous.

"Mine is done as well. He spit out his teeth."

"Cai." The man on the ground nodded, pleased with their work. He gestured with the shotgun, pointing at the wooden flank of the chute. "Make the words as we were told."

The man on the loading bay grinned, then reached into the pocket of his windbreaker. He brought out a tin of Canadian Tire Candy Apple Red spraypaint and set to work, marking the side of the chute with the ragged characters he'd practiced the night before.

"Co dur'oc khong?" he asked. The man on the ground nodded again, scanning his companion's handiwork with the spraypaint.

"Dung." Perfect.

The characters, inscribed in old Mandarin, dripped blood red down the stained secondhand sheets of plywood, spelling out the same message as the one painted in blood on the forehead of General William Hawksworth:

BLACK DRAGON

CHAPTER 6

THE TUBE BOOMED noisily into the brightly lit Regent Street Station, and Fong stepped out onto the platform, the heavy briefcase weighing down his right arm. Wearily he made his way down to the exit and began the long escalator ride up to the street. From there, Madame Li's restaurant was a short walk away.

According to his contact in Vancouver, the local Asian Crime Squad had been notified of the killings by way of an anonymous telephone call. As far as the contact knew, the Vancouver ACS had not made any connection between the murders in Little Saigon and the *Orient Star.*

If the Vietnamese garbage workers had done as they were told, there would be no written records of their pickup at Canada Place, but any dealings with the *"chu ju"* were potentially troublesome. Thankfully he'd warned Chang about that earlier in the day—it was one of the few points in his favor. Not that it made much difference, since the use of Vietnamese go-betweens had been Fong's idea in the first place.

Even more unsettling was the message left behind by the killers. His organization wasn't the only importer of Black Dragon powder, but it had invented the name and was the largest exporter of the product from Chiang Mai and Bangkok. Initially the Vancouver police would almost certainly put the deaths of the men at Mau Len Transport down as a localized, gang-related problem, but any serious investigation might well result in the revelation of Black Dragon's involvement. Even without a police investigation it was obvious from the message that somebody was making a direct challenge to the Triad's hegemony over the West Coast drug trade.

Fong reached the top of the escalator, walked out of the station, and ducked out into the cool evening air. The rain had stopped long ago, leaving behind the familiar, slightly acid scent of damp stone and concrete. Ignoring the wash of bright lights all around him, Fong headed up the street for his meeting.

The pudgy man gripped his briefcase more tightly and grimaced. He'd been looking forward to his meal at Madame Li's. Instead of his regulation chips and eggs at the local takeaway, he'd be offered fine black eggs, cold, steamed chicken strips, shrimp and vegetables, and small green beans. There would be mushrooms in dark sauce, followed by prawns in their shells, with sweets to follow—probably lotus seeds in syrup.

With the clients' palates cleansed, the old woman would proudly bring out the main courses of baked fish and pork, set off with savory meatballs or perhaps even her legendary frogs' legs. There would be rice, of course, and through it all an endless supply of steaming hot *pai ka'rh*, the potent, 60 percent alcohol wine that had originated in Chekiang Province and that was almost impossible to get in England or anywhere else outside the New Territories.

Fong sighed. A wonderful feast, one to make the mouth water. But his mouth was dry; he had no appetite for what might be the last meal of the condemned. Frowning, he turned off Regent Street onto Maddox and trudged slowly toward his fate.

CHAPTER 7

Phillip Dane sat behind his desk at the front of his store on M Street and watched the rain trickle down over the window, tear tracks fanning across the black-and-gold letters of his sign:

BLIND JUSTICE
Used and Antiquarian Books
Specialists in Law, Jurisprudence
and True Crime

He lit a cigarette and leaned back in his squeaky, old-fashioned wooden office chair. The chair, like the sign and the store itself, had once belonged to his grandfather, Judge Conrad Dane, a retired Supreme Court justice who'd run the bookshop as a hobby after losing his sight to glaucoma. The judge had been dead for seven years now, and Blind Justice belonged to Dane.

Dane turned away from the window and returned to his work, snipping away at the pile of newspapers in front of him, putting the clippings in their appropriate folders. After his grandfather died, Dane had left his job at the Defense Investigative Service, but the old habits died hard, and he still maintained clipping files on anyone he considered interesting within the Defense establishment. The files were more than just a hobby; he'd been called in as an independent assessor a score of times since leaving DIS, and he was still considered a top-ranked analyst and trouble-shooter in the arcane world of "sensitive personnel investigations."

Dane clipped another Hawksworth obit and added it to the growing folder beside him. Not such an arcane world as all that, when you considered the implications. Thousands of Defense contracts were put out every year, and scores of them involved research or manufacture deemed "secret" or at the very least "secure."

Dozens, hundreds, sometimes even thousands, were employed to fulfill the contracts, and invariably key people had to be granted security clearance. Most of the work was mundane, but from time to time there were interesting situations. He glanced at the pile of Hawksworth death notices. A good example.

At seventy years old the general had been offered a key post, but from the looks of things no one had taken a close look at his medical records. There might not have been any way to avert the heart attack that had killed him, but if the DIA or the president had known about a possible major heart condition, they could have saved themselves some embarrassment by offering the job to someone with a cleaner bill of health.

Now they'd have to spend all sorts of time and energy trying to find someone else to head up what *Time* magazine was calling the "Cocaine Commandos." Dane dragged on his cigarette and snorted. Maybe this time they'd be a little more careful, but it was doubtful.

Coming out of a long career in Military Intelligence, he'd taken the job at DIS expecting some reasonable level of competence and integrity. He'd been wrong. DIS turned out to be a paper mill, grinding out approvals and reports to suit the needs of the contractors and the people lobbying for them within the maze of corridors in the Pentagon. A congressional committee discovered that DIS had an approval rating of 94 percent of applicants for clearance, which was higher than the approval rating for District of Columbia sanitation workers.

His grandfather's death and the inheritance of Blind Justice had been the perfect opportunity to bail out with a little of his dignity still intact. Another couple of years rubber-stamping files and he would probably have stepped into a minefield like the Walker spy scandal.

Dane butted his cigarette out in the already overflowing ashtray beside him on the desk. He wondered what had happened to the DIS officer who'd approved *that* personnel file. On the other hand, working for Defense did give him the occasional opportunity to actually talk to someone.

He sighed and looked around the store. Four thousand square feet on two floors, the main floor crammed with fifty thousand titles cataloguing every vice and perversion known to man, the second floor taken up by his apartment. Three quarters of the store's business was mail order, finding books and abstracts for the clientele his grandfather had built up over the years, and on a day like this the chance of anyone setting foot in the store was almost zero.

Dane lit another cigarette and stared at the telephone, half-buried beneath the stacks of file folders and piled newspapers. Early afternoon in the nation's capital and he couldn't think of a soul he wanted to call.

"I'm living in library hell," he muttered, glancing at the shadowed aisles of floor-to-ceiling bookcases around him. The life of a divorced, childless, forty-two-year-old antiquarian book dealer. The sweet-sour smell of old volumes and their bindings, horse glue and leather, printing ink and yellowing paper. Days and nights alone. Memories of more exciting times. Dead friends and a forgotten war. Creaking floorboards.

The telephone rang.

"Blind Justice."

"Colonel Dane?" An alarm bell went off. Who would call him "Colonel" these days? The voice was male, evenly modulated with an underlying note of tension.

"Yes."

"We were given this number."

"We?" Dane asked.

"Yes, sir. By General Cutter." Cutter had been Dane's direct superior at DIS.

"That doesn't tell me who 'we' is," Dane answered. But he knew. Spooks gave off their own particular scent, even over a telephone line.

"DIA sir," said the voice. "My name is Lawson. Major Dennis Lawson."

"What can I do for you, Major?" Dane asked.

"We need a curator, sir. Immediately."

CHAPTER 8

WITHIN THE HIERARCHY of the Defense Investigative Service there were three main jobs: investigator, analyst, and curator. An investigator gathered information, an analyst analyzed the information gathered, and if necessary, a curator manipulated the information gathered and analyzed.

At DIS Phillip Dane had performed all three functions, but it was the curatorial work that had interested him most. In bald terms a curator's job description called for a combination novelist, historian, archivist, private eye, and unrepentant pathological liar.

From time to time security clearance was required for a potential employee with a suspect, or sensitive, past—a Soviet defector perhaps, or in days gone by, a Nazi scientist needed for the space program. It was the curator's job to create a "legend" for the employee, building up the necessary documentation, deleting information from old files, and providing new identities.

When required, the curator was also responsible for "decreating" people if there was a problem, erasing any evidence of their connection with sensitive areas within the Defense establishment. In the manuals this was called "protective deniability."

After two tours in Vietnam and a few years as a Defense information officer at the Pentagon during the Nixon era, Dane was cynical enough to see the direct relation between a curator's occupation and Winston Smith's job rewriting history in Orwell's *1984*, but for most of his tenure at DIS he could rationalize the work both because of "national security" and, even more, because he thrived on the creativity of it.

Oliver North and Irangate had cured him of that; there was no rationale for greed in the name of patriotism, and enjoying yourself was no excuse for protecting people from their well-deserved and just deserts. Better to live a benign and uncompromised life in library hell than to wake up at the end of your life and look back at a career built with the bricks and mortar of deceit.

So why, given such a holier-than-thou philosophy, had he agreed to the meeting at DIA headquarters in suburban Maryland? The question had nagged him throughout the rain-soaked drive, irritated him in the parking lot behind the big industrial complex just off the parkway, and confounded him while he went through the rituals of half a dozen security checks that took him up to the third-floor conference room. The only answer he came up with was curiosity, but deep in his soul he knew that answer wasn't good enough.

The conference room was small and bare with a set of windows that looked out into the parking lot below. The furniture consisted of a long, leather-covered table and four chairs. A coffee machine stewed in one corner, and a fluorescent fixture buzzed in the ceiling, making the gray overcast outside seem even more oppressive.

Major Lawson revealed himself to be a balding thirty-year-old flack in a crisply starched air-force uniform with a lot of flashy patches and service bars that marked him as ex-NATO.

His boss was a man named Cordasco, an army general with the blowsy face of a drinker and stars and bars enough to take him back to Vietnam in the early sixties. As soon as he made the introductions, Lawson vanished, leaving Dane and Cordasco alone in the conference room.

There were two things on the table in front of the general: a blue-striped "dead" file with Dane's name on

it, and an unmarked eleven-by-fourteen manila envelope.

"You did some good stuff while you were working
for Cutter," said Cordasco, making a little show of leaf-
ing through Dane's file. "He said you were the best.
Sad to see you go."

"Personal considerations," Dane answered, trying to
be noncommittal. Cordasco nodded, a polite smile
washing briefly across his face.

"Your grandfather. Yes, I know." He nodded. There
was a long pause. Dane watched as the general's hand
gently touched the manila envelope. There was a West
Point ring on Cordasco's third finger. Old Guard. He'd
play it by the book. Dane reached into the pocket of his
slightly damp Harris tweed jacket and took out his cigarettes. He lit one, then looked around for an ashtray.
There was a stack of tinfoil saucers beside the coffee
machine.

"Mind if I get some coffee?" Dane asked.

"By all means," Cordasco answered. Dane stood up,
poured himself a Styrofoam cupful, and added artificial
creamer. He picked up a foil ashtray and came back to
the table. Cordasco had opened up the manila envelope
and removed its contents—a stack of eight-by-ten photographs. He kept both palms over the pictures as Dane
seated himself again.

"Lawson said you need curatorial help," said Dane.
He sipped his coffee. It tasted foul.

"Yes." Cordasco nodded. He sighed heavily. "I'm
just wondering if you're the man for the job."

"And I'm wondering if it's the job for the man,"
Dane answered. "I won't know that until you tell me
what you want." He sat back in his chair and waited for
Cordasco to remind him that he was still bound by the
National Security Act and the Compartmentalization of
Information rulings. He was pleasantly surprised when
the red-cheeked man got right to the point.

"What do you know about William Sloane Hawksworth?" Cordasco asked.

"Three-star general," Dane answered promptly, glancing at the two stars on Cordasco's shoulder boards. "Supreme Allied Commander Europe for NATO up until a few weeks ago. Resigned to take over as head of this place with a special mandate to take over all narcotics intelligence functions for the president. He died yesterday. Heart attack."

"No," Cordasco answered.

"No?" asked Dane, wondering what part of it he'd got wrong.

"Not a heart attack." The general picked up the stack of photographs and fanned them in front of Dane.

"Jesus," he whispered. The pictures were Kodacolor and left absolutely nothing to the imagination. Long shots, close shots, every detail. They looked like production stills from a horror movie. Dane reached for his coffee and took a long swallow, ignoring the taste.

"The woman is a prostitute named Amanda Chung Kilau," said Cordasco. "The room is a cabin on board a yacht called the *Terpsichore* owned by a senator named Lang."

"Democrat from Ohio," murmured Dane.

"A war buddy. They served together in the Pacific. Lang let Hawksworth borrow *Terpsichore* while he was in Washington."

"Does Lang know about ... this?" Dane pushed a finger at the array of photographs on the table. Cordasco nodded.

"Yes. He's terrified that he's going to be involved. Prostitution, drugs, and ritual murder. This a hard-line law-and-order type. He'd be ruined."

"So, in other words, you're telling me he'll cooperate."

"Yes," the general answered tersely. "He's put himself in our hands."

"What about local involvement?" Dane asked.

"There is none," said Cordasco. "Lang found Hawksworth and the woman and got in touch with us right away. We cleaned it up."

"So there's been no investigation?"

"Not yet. With Hawksworth's appointment to DIA the whole thing is incredibly sensitive."

"No idea who might have done it, or why?" Dane asked. The general shook his head.

"None. Except for the message."

"The Chinese characters on his forehead?"

"Yes. According to our linguists, they spell out the words 'Black Dragon.' "

"What's the reference?"

"Black Dragon is a Heroin brand name. Like UniGlove or Red Star. Thai. Mostly out of Bangkok."

"Presumably no one here had any idea that Hawksworth was tied in to Heroin," said Dane.

"We still don't know that," Cordasco responded stiffly. "You're talking about a man who won the Congressional Medal of Honor, Colonel Dane."

"Mr. Dane," he corrected. "I've been out of uniform for a long time now."

"You're still on the list," Cordasco answered. A veiled threat. Dane ignored it.

"So what exactly do you want me to do?" he asked finally. He stubbed out his cigarette and lit another one, his eyes still drawn to the glossy obscenities in front of him. It was the kind of thing tailor-made for an upcoming Woodward or Bernstein.

"We can't put any of our own people on this," Cordasco said, after a moment's thought. "It's bound to come out eventually, but a civilian investigator can do more for us until we're ready to answer questions."

"What kind of legitimacy would I have?" Dane asked. "I'd need a legend of my own to get anywhere." He was making it sound as though he were still making up his mind about taking the assignment, but both men knew better. If Dane refused the job as a civilian,

Cordasco would pull the appropriate strings to have him put back in military harness. His employment was a fait accompli.

"It's standard practice to assign a biographer to an outgoing director," said Cordasco. "And we use civilians all the time, you know that." The general paused, frowning. "He hadn't taken over officially, but I don't think anyone will question someone making the rounds. If somebody balks, you can refer them to me."

"I'll need the book on Hawksworth," said Dane. "Everything you've got. Nothing kept back."

"Lawson's putting it together right now."

"Budget number?"

"Already assigned," said Cordasco.

"You don't miss a trick," Dane answered. The general made a snorting sound. He looked as though he needed a drink. Dane didn't blame him. They were both staring into deep, dark, and dangerous waters.

"We missed a trick all right," Cordasco said finally. "We chose the son of a bitch to be director."

"I gather he didn't get your vote," said Dane.

"No," Cordasco responded shortly. "He did not." There was a long pause. The two men stared at each other across the table, the photographs lying between them like an awful stain.

"A question," said Dane finally. The obvious one.

"Yes?"

"I want to know if this is a backstop operation. I want to know if I'm a character in someone else's scenario." He didn't want to be any more specific than that. God only knew what kind of bugging equipment was hidden in the walls. The general's features twisted into an ugly sneer.

"This isn't our kind of thing, Mr. Dane," he said, sweeping a hand over the photographs. "We're as much in the dark about this as you are. Fair enough?"

"It'll have to do," Dane answered. "I just don't like the idea of being somebody's pawn."

"We're all pawns in this game, Mr. Dane," the general answered. "I'd have thought you'd learned that lesson by now."

"I'm a slow learner, I guess," Dane answered. He put out his cigarette. "I presume that time is of the essence?"

"You presume correctly." Cordasco nodded. He stood up, shuffled the photographs back into a pile, and slid them into the envelope again. "Lawson will give you a secure number to use. Keep in touch. Let us know how you're doing." Dane stood up, and the two men shook hands across the table. "If you wait here for a few minutes, Lawson will give you everything you need."

With that, the general left the room. Dane sat down again and resisted the urge to light yet another cigarette. He stared at the clear expanse of leather where the pictures had been laid out. Outside, the rain was still slanting down from a gray sky.

"Shit," he whispered, leaning back in his chair. He looked out at the rain and waited for Lawson to bring him Hawksworth's past and his own uncertain future.

CHAPTER 9

WITH BULKY KOSS headphones clamped over his ears, David Copperfield Mo sat in the tiny, darkened apartment and stared blearily at the television screen a few feet in front of him, occasionally glancing at the motionless needle of the VU meter on the radio receiver that was balanced precariously on top of the TV.

To his right, mounted on a tripod at the curtained window, a British-made PPI surveillance video camera was tilted steeply downward, offering a bird's-eye view of New York Chinatown's Pell Street, eight stories below.

Using the small switcher unit in his lap, the young man could pull back to get a long view of the narrow, neon-choked street, or zoom in on the doorway of his target, the offices of Red Lotus Travel, less than fifty feet in from the corner of Bowery. It was 8:45 P.M. in New York, and Pell Street was jammed with cars and taxis, the sidewalks overflowing with people coming in and out of restaurants like the Palm, Ting Fu, and the Temple Garden.

The young man's head bobbed up and down as he watched the scene on the television, his headphones connected through the switcher to the radio receiver and also to a Sony Walkman beside him on the overstuffed couch.

At the moment he was listening to Ziggy Marley's version of his father's reggae song "Natty Dread." David Copperfield Mo, although ethnically Chinese on both sides, had been born and raised in Kingston, Jamaica, and had been accused by some people of speaking Cantonese with a Rasta accent.

The Marley tape ended, and Mo peeled off the headphones, his eyes still on the screen in front of him. He yawned, stretched luxuriously, and picked up a package of Marlboros from the table beside the couch. He lit one, yawned again, and used his free hand to rub at his right eye. The cramped, low-ceilinged apartment stank, staring at the monitor was making his eyes ache, and he felt as though he hadn't exercised in a week.

He'd been at his post since seven-thirty that morning, and above all he was monumentally bored. Young lawyers fresh out of the University of Miami weren't supposed to spend their days cooped up in matchbox apartments that smelled faintly of barbecued pork and egg noodles. On the other hand, the money was twice what he could make articling with a big firm, and a U.S. Department of Justice secondment to the "Jock" Squad was a quick way up the legal ladder.

"Jock" was the International Joint Organized Crime Task Force, a loosely organized multinational group developed out of proposals made at an international conference on organized crime held in Vancouver, Canada, in 1989.

By that late date in a so-called "war" that had gone on for the better part of a century, it had become abundantly clear that groups like the FBI, the American Drug Enforcement Administration, Canada's RCMP, and the myriad other agencies in the UK, France, Germany, Italy, and the rest of Europe were doing virtually nothing to stem the enormously successful growth of worldwide organized crime.

The Vancouver symposium isolated several main problems in dealing with organized crime. Logistical, bureaucratic, and jurisdictional mayhem was at the top of the list.

In the United States alone there were a score of major agencies dealing with organized crime, including the DEA, FBI, CIA, DIA, IMNS, NYDETF (New York Drug Enforcement Task Force), OCDETF (Organized Crime Drug Enforcement Task Force), the U.S. Coast Guard, the U.S. Marshal's Service, the Bureau of Alcohol, Tobacco and Firearms, IRS Criminal Investigations, the U.S. Postal Inspection Service, the Federal Air Marshals, and the U.S. Customs, Special Investigative Division, not to mention more than seventy major metropolitan police forces, all with organized-crime units.

In theory these agencies were supposed to share information through the U.S. Central Bureau of the International Police Organization (Interpol), the National Crime Information Center (NCIC), and NADDIS, the Narcotics and Dangerous Drugs Information System.

In practice all of the agencies jealously hoarded their information, intent on making their own cases, and almost never disseminated information. The same was true in the United Kingdom and Europe.

This in turn pointed out another serious problem—intelligence, or rather the lack of it. Some investigative agencies in the United States and the United Kingdom had been working on organized crime for decades, but there were rarely any meaningful prosecutions. In 1991 one of the DEA's most "successful" deep-cover agents retired, saying that his more than twenty years in the business had been a waste of time, and that on more than one occasion bad information had led to the death of both friends and colleagues. Beyond that, he was exhausted by a life where the bad guys drove Rolls-Royces, while the good guys had to beg on bended knees for an expense account meal at McDonald's.

Which led to the third main problem addressed at the Vancouver convention: money. Most of the world agencies dealing with organized crime were underfunded, and their employees, by definition, were underpaid. Bribery and corruption were rampant, both in the field and at higher administrative levels. In some cases the corruption had actually been given an official stamp of approval.

In Vancouver itself the Asian Crime Unit regularly had its investigators transferred to other duties as a matter of police-department policy—making it virtually impossible to open any long-term investigations because of staff turnover and thus preventing any in-depth work to be done regarding the upsurge of Hong Kong triad activity in that West Coast city.

Tar-pit bureaucracy and internecine rivalry, poor communication and intelligence, lack of funding and rampant corruption. Everyone agreed that a single, unconnected organization with adequate funding was needed to put together a new and untarnished "book" on international organized crime. The "Jock" Squad was the result.

A steering committee was created, manned by a single, high-ranking official from the Department of Justice in each of the member countries, answerable only to the head of that department—the attorney general in the case of the United States. The Justice official then organized funding through a nonpolice division of the department.

At the DOJ in Washington the funding came from the Foreign Claims Settlement Commission through the Office of Intelligence Policy and Review—about as far from the FBI and the DEA as it was possible to get. The budget was authorized directly by the U.S. attorney general and was "black," which meant it appeared on no documentation available for congressional perusal.

Staffing was the next consideration. Because of the potential for corruption, only a small number of seasoned policemen with field experience were recruited, and in the United States none were brought in from major centers like New York, Miami, or Los Angeles, where there might be a possibility of already existing collusion. Instead, most of the Jocks were plucked fresh out of law school, or were recent university graduates with degrees in criminology or related or useful disciplines, including Asian studies, computer science, and international banking.

The ethnic background of potential Jocks was of critical importance, and early in its development the IJOCTF realized that there would have to be several subsquads within the group, each with its own mandate. For instance, there was no point using a Jock agent who spoke only Cantonese to gather intelligence concerning the Taiwanese United Bamboos, who spoke only Mandarin.

The U.S. division of the task force had been split into seven distinct "desks." Hong Kong, of which David Copperfield Mo was a member, dealing with Cantonese-speaking triad operations; Taiwan for Green Gang, United Bamboo, and other Mandarin-speaking operations in the United States; Hispanic for Mexican and Colombian work; Sicily/Italy for the Old Guard Mafia/Cosa Nostra; Japan for the yakuza, which had begun to make inroads on the West Coast; Vietnam for the rise in street-gang and gambling activity; and finally, the Harleys—jokingly named but deadly serious considering the intrusions made by several large motorcycle gangs into Teamster and dockyard activities on both coasts.

The initial task of all seven "desks," expected to take from three to five years, was to assemble as much information as possible relating to the members of various organized-crime groups, their activities, and their holdings.

Although having no powers of seizure or arrest, Jock agents had access to virtually any crime-related data base within the organization through their own online information net, almost limitless operational funding for surveillance and travel, and carte blanche when it came to wiretapping and "plumbing" jobs. All in all it was a

heady and exciting environment for a young man like
David Copperfield Mo.

Out of the corner of his eye the Jock agent saw the
VU meter on the radio twitch. He pulled on the headphones again and switched over from the Walkman
channel. He listened, keeping his eyes on the screen in
front of him, the Marlboro hanging from the corner of
his mouth.

The slightly hollow voice using the bugged telephone
in the Red Lotus Travel office belonged to Nelson
Fong. On paper Fong was the owner of Red Lotus
Travel, but both Mo and his superiors thought it unlikely that a twenty-eight-year-old man who'd emi-
grated from Hong Kong less than a year and a half
before and who had no apparent business skills could
have been so successful so quickly.

The Jock Hong Kong desk monitored all Chinese immigration into the United States by quietly tapping into
the Immigration and Naturalization computers, and a
backcheck with the task-force office in Kowloon spit
out a report on Fong that was absolutely spotless with
the exception of a note that he was distantly related to
a man named Abbot Fong, a naturalized UK citizen living in London.

Abbot Fong was suspected of being associated with
the near-mythical Black Dragon Triad. The association
was vague, but it was enough for the U.S. Jocks to put
the newly arrived Chinatown resident under surveillance.

Flipping open the steno pad on the arm of the couch,
David Mo jotted down the time of the telephone call
and continued to listen. Fong was speaking rapidfire
Cantonese with the tense Hong Kong intonation Mo
had come to recognize. Fong was ordering a limousine
from Gold Star Livery, a limo service with its lot under
the Manhattan Bridge approaches at Division Street and
Forsyth, only a couple of blocks away. It wouldn't take
long to arrive. Fong gave his destination address, and

David Mo smiled. Apparently the owner of Red Lotus Travel was intending some high-priced R&R.

Mo waited until the call was complete and then made one of his own, using the telephone on the floor at his feet, checking the code list at the back of the steno pad before he dialed. It was answered on the second ring.

"It's Rastaman," he said. "The subject is taking a limousine to Arizona."

"Repeat the destination, please, Rastaman."

"Arizona."

"Thank you, Rastaman."

"You're welcome, and if anybody's looking for me, I'm going out for a burger and fries."

"Roger that, Rastaman."

CHAPTER 10

THE IMPOSING FOUR-STORY building on the corner of Fifth Avenue and Fifty-third Street had been designed by the renowned architectural firm of McKim, Mead, and White in 1894 and was constructed of a light pink Milford granite that had darkened to a deep gunmetal after almost a hundred years of exposure to the Manhattan atmosphere.

Originally designed as the new home of New York's Academy Club—a private pied-à-terre for East Coast Ivy League alumni—the building actually had seven floors hidden behind the four-level facade, comprised of lounges, dining rooms, and a total of seventy-six bedroom suites. In effect it was a small, discreet, and very luxurious hotel.

After the demise of the Academy Club itself in the late twenties, the building had gone through a number of transformations until its purchase by a Bermuda corporation in the mid-1980s. After a complete renovation the building was reopened in 1988 as the Pacific Club, catering almost exclusively to Asian businessmen staying in New York. The initial seventy-six suites had been cut back to sixty-three, all of which were booked at least six months in advance.

Beyond its value as a much-needed oasis of sophisticated Oriental culture in the Foreign Devils' wasteland, the Pacific Club was also immensely profitable. The dining rooms and lounges on the first and second floors brought in a solid income, as did the gaming tables on the third and fourth floors. The real money, however, was produced within the sixty-three bedrooms.

Freed from the rumor-ridden confines of Hong Kong and Tokyo, and released from the prudish constraints of family pressure, Pacific Club members enjoyed the finest New York had to offer at an average rate of $2,200 per night, tasting the various delights offered by some of the most accomplished male and female professional sex partners in the Eastern Seaboard. Even with an overhead of close to 50 percent the rooms generated a net profit of almost $75,000 per night, or $2.2 million per month, all cash, all tax-free.

Using several different names and corporate fronts, Limehouse Trading operated seven similar clubs in Boston, Toronto, Miami, Nassau, Dallas–Forth Worth, Los Angeles, and San Francisco, which netted in excess of $200 million per year.

Han Chao Shun, nominally a 438 or Incense Master of the Black Dragon Triad and known to the IJOCTF as Danny Han, sat behind his desk in the Pacific Club's basement money room, feeding stacks of currency into an industrial-sized Burroughs counting machine and casting an occasional glance at the bank of Sony Trinitrons built into the far wall.

Over the past five years Han had watched an incredible assortment of sexual practices being performed on the screens in the money room, and he'd long ago become completely inured to the never-ending parade of contortions, erections, and ejaculations. For Han the whispering chitter of the counting machine provided far more erotic satisfaction than watching yet another turgid Oriental organ vanish into yet another *gwei-lo* orifice.

On the other hand, whatever pleasure he found in the money room was offset by a negative sense of frustration. Although supposedly the overseer of all Black Dragon activities from Toronto to Miami, manager of

the East Coast Pacific Club operations and leader of
more than seven hundred foot-soldier 49s, Danny Han
knew full well that in the hierarchy of Black Dragon he
was nothing more than a clerk. The real decision-
making was undertaken by others employed by the
Shan Chu and trusted by him. Han knew that if it
weren't for his marriage to Lily, Chang's beloved firstborn, he'd be hunched on a Kowloon street corner using an abacus to count begged pennies. And Chang
never let him forget it.

"Bastard," Han muttered. He lit a cigarette and
watched the fluttering bills pile up in the counter's receiving tray. The preprogrammed machine pinged softly
as it counted off another twenty thousand, then paused.

Han scooped up the bundle, slipped it into a vacuum
bag, and used the heat sealer to the right of the counter.
Job done, he dropped the airtight "brick" of money into
one of the two-cubic-foot moving boxes on the floor.
Taking another handful of loose money from the desk,
he loaded it into the Burroughs machine, tapped the Re-
set button, and began the whole process yet again. The
task was a boring one, but anything was better than being at home, watching his wife drifting in and out of
the alcoholic haze that seemed to have been her normal
state for the past seventeen years. And anyway, Nelson
Fong was due at any moment with the day's take from
Chinatown; best to appear industrious.

Han took a deep drag on his cigarette and raked one
hand through his thinning black hair. At fifty-four he
was running to fat, belly spilling over his belt, thick
folds of flesh squeezing over the tight collar of his
shirt. Too much liquor, too many cigarettes, and no exercise at all—an unhealthy, aging yin to Nelson Fong's
dapper youthful yang.

The corpulent man frowned and drew in a short
breath, trying to take some comfort in the faint scent
of his expensive after-shave. Fong, he knew, was
dangerous—young, aggressive, and nephew to Abbot

Fong, the Triad's White Paper Fan. Everything was pointing to Nelson being groomed for larger things within the organization. At the very least, the young man's increasing power base meant that Han was losing face within Black Dragon. At worst it meant sudden death with a loop of piano wire around his throat.

Han poked a thick finger between his neck and the starched collar of his shirt. His position as Chang's son-in-law afforded him some protection, but the escalating attacks against Black Dragon interests and the upcoming summit meeting in Hawaii were almost certainly making the *Shan Chu* nervous. Why else would he be making this sudden, unscheduled trip to America? The time was rapidly approaching when sides would have to be taken, old scores settled, and new alliances made. Han had to make sure that his choices were the correct ones.

The door buzzer went off, and Han jerked upright, startled. He butted his cigarette and poked at the electric switch under the desk. The metal-clad door of the money room opened, and Nelson Fong entered, one hand gripping the handle of a dark blue Samsonite suitcase. He was dressed in a well-cut charcoal suit, his thick hair neatly groomed. He looked like a stockbroker.

"Nelson." Han nodded, trying to keep his tone casual.

"Uncle," Fong answered formally. He swung the suitcase up onto the desk, fiddled with the combination locks, and opened it. He began lifting out blocks of money, each three-inch stack bound with a thick rubber band. Emptying the suitcase onto the desk, he reached into the inside breast pocket of his suit jacket and gave Han a neatly folded strip of paper tape.

"A good day?" Han asked casually, keeping his eyes off the tape. With Chang arriving within the next few hours, a strong profit picture would be better insurance than being married to his daughter.

"Not bad," Fong answered, eyes on the television screens. In one of the rooms the chief financial officer of a large Japanese entertainment conglomerate was being swallowed whole by a statuesque blonde with a marked resemblance to Madonna.

Han unfolded the tape: $622,000—a day of drugs, gambling, and extortion within a twenty-two block area of New York. Deliveries later that night would see an equal amount come in from Black Dragon operations in New Jersey. An enormous amount of money, but not enough. They were down for the month by almost 15 percent. Han could feel the sting of sweat in the corner of his eyes.

"What about the murder of the general?" Han asked, trying not to think about declining profits. "Is there any word on the street?"

Nelson Fong turned away from the television screens, reached into the pocket of his jacket, and brought out a package of Marlboros. He lit one with a slim Dunhill lighter and blew out a plume of smoke.

"Nothing," he said, his voice cool. Han knew he was walking a fine political line. His job was money, not enforcement. But he *was* the *Shan Chu*'s son-in-law. "Definitely not the Ghost Shadows or the Flying Tigers. From the looks of things they were probably Vietnamese, hired from outside."

"The contract for the Vancouver shipment was with the Vietnamese as well, was it not?" Han asked.

"That is not my concern, Uncle," Fong answered. The implication was clear in his voice—the subject was no concern of Han's either.

"And the *Shan Chu?*" asked the fat man.

"He arrives at JFK in two hours," Fong replied. He grinned. "I've been asked to meet him there."

"Yes?" Han said, as casually as he could.

"Yes." Fong nodded. "I have been asked to extend his regrets to you, Uncle. His schedule does not permit a visit to his daughter. I have been asked to take him to the airport at Newark. He will be going on to San Francisco tonight."

"Ah," Han said, putting the appropriate note of disappointment into his voice. He cursed silently. Another loss of face. Fong was being utilized as a chauffeur, but that was better than being ignored. Han's position within Black Dragon had slipped down another subtle notch. He swallowed hard, trying not to show his anger or his concern. It was time to make up his mind, before the decision was made for him.

"Well, then," said Fong, "I'd better be on my way." He grinned. "Too bad I can't stay for the show." He nodded toward the television screens. "Must keep you from getting bored, though, eh, Uncle?"

"I pay no attention," Han answered coldly. "I have more important things to concern myself with, Youngest Nephew." The term was a mild insult, but Fong chose to ignore the slight.

"Never tempted to try out their wares?" The younger man smiled.

"Never," snapped Han, lying.

"Very wise of you, Uncle," Fong said. He smiled, but there was no humor in it. He nodded politely, turned away, and left the room, closing the door behind him.

Fuming, Han lit another cigarette and stared at the television screens. He thought for a moment, drawing one hand along the smooth skin of his cheek. He'd memorized the telephone number weeks ago, and now it was time to use it, but not from here. The walls in the Pacific Club had ears as well as eyes.

CHAPTER 11

JAMES CHANG, SHAN Chu of the Black Dragon Triad and Tai Pan of the Limehouse Trading Corporation, sat in the almost-empty first-class section of the British Airways 747, eyes closed, head back against the seat, letting his mind fill with the steady throbbing of the massive engines.

He sat alone. Abbot Fong, his most trusted adviser, was traveling to San Francisco on an Air Canada great-circle flight that would take him to Vancouver first. Even without the problem in Canada Fong would never have traveled on the same flight as Chang for security reasons.

Chang's eyes fluttered open, and he glanced around the first-class cabin. An elderly couple sat in the first row of seats close to the rounded bulkhead at the nose. Directly in front of Chang a well-dressed, middle-aged woman snored softly. Chang had already declined the ministrations of the flight attendant on two separate occasions, and he hadn't been bothered since. So far the flight had been completely uneventful—four hours of limbo over the Atlantic.

He was grateful for the peaceful interlude. The murder of General Hawksworth and the hijacking of the Vancouver shipment were deadly omens that didn't bode well for the immediate future. The organization he had worked so long and so hard to develop was at a turning point, its criminal and corporate hegemony threatened now both from without and within. He had created an empire only dreamed of by his father and never even considered by his namesake, the first Blue-Eyed Chang, and now that empire was in danger of being utterly destroyed in a single instant.

Chang sat up in his seat, sighing quietly, and lit a cigarette. His grandfather, the tiny, wizened man he knew only from photographs shown to him by his father, would have predicted this situation, of course. Chang knew that in a basic sense such vulnerability was almost inevitable. The original Limehouse Company and its dark corollary, Black Dragon, had been born out of desperation, poverty, lust, and greed. His father, the second of the Blue-Eyed Changs, had built upon that expanding web, playing weak against strong and deceit upon treachery in an effort to destroy his competition.

Through the twenties and thirties Limehouse and Black Dragon had infiltrated virtually every ethnic Chinese community in the world, forging alliances through fear that seemed invulnerable. By 1939 Limehouse had become a major force in legitimate commerce, and Black Dragon had an army of ghostly warriors that spanned the globe.

To James Chang, wearing the conservative uniform of a British-run private school in Rangoon, the future seemed secure. By 1945 that future lay in ashes, as did the remains of Limehouse and Black Dragon. The war destroyed it all, killing his father and leaving James Chang with a bitter inheritance of nothing more than memory.

Incredibly Chang had managed to resurrect both organizations within ten years, but none of it would have been possible without General William Sloane Hawksworth. Now it seemed that the source of the Limehouse/Black Dragon resurrection was potentially going to bring about its downfall.

It was the fundamental flaw that had haunted his father, and his father before him. Treachery begets only treachery and never honor; lies beget only lies and never truth. Unless he acted quickly and with deadly force, those conspiracies would almost certainly be uncovered and all the lies revealed. Hawksworth. It seemed so long ago.

In 1942, fleeing the Japanese invasion of Burma, James Chang, sixteen years old, orphaned and with the last remains of his father's fortune out of reach in England, had found his way to the railhead at Myitkyina in northern Burma, doing odd jobs for the beleaguered British forces there as he tried to find some way out of the country. By early April it was clear that the Japanese intended to sweep northward to cut off the Burma Road supply route from China.

Even with a valid British passport and documentation, Chang's Oriental heritage put him low on the list for evacuation, and after several fruitless attempts to beg any sort of transport west into India he headed north across the border into China, arriving at K'unming on April 20, two days after the Doolittle Raid on Tokyo.

The ancient city was in chaos, with Nationalist and Communist forces vying for power as the greater conflicts of the war raged around them. Chang's fluency in both Chinese and English was a useful commodity, and in an effort to avoid the dangers of life in K'un-ming itself, Chang drifted out to the air base on the outskirts of the city, headquarters of Claire Chennault's infamous Flying Tiger Squadron.

By April 30 James Chang's concerns about staying in Burma had been borne out as Myitkyina fell to the Japanese, blocking the Burma Road, effectively cutting off any supplies from the British to Chiang Kai-shek's forces in K'un-ming. At the same time, the first survivors of the Doolittle Raid began arriving at Chennault's headquarters as news of the attack on Tokyo began to spread.

In the British Airways jumbo, James Chang stared

into the blackness of night, forty thousand feet over the
Atlantic. He smiled faintly at his dim reflection in the
oval glass of the window, surprised at the vividness of
his memories. He let the smile broaden. He'd only been
a boy, virgin still except for a single embarrassment
with a Rangoon whore the year before, but even so,
when the moment came in K'un-ming he'd known it
for what it was, and had seized the opportunity.

It had been raining heavily for two days, and the ter-
rain around the carefully tended airstrip was a quag-
mire. Searching for someplace dry to spend the night,
Chang had discovered the apparently empty C-87 cargo
plane parked beneath a stand of blighted trees on the
near side of the field. The closest center of activity was
a rough hardstand and maintenance area a hundred
yards away, with a flight of three battered P-40 fighters
arranged in a semicircle around a tool hut. Chang could
see a rain-caped sentry squatting under the wing of one
of the shark-mouthed P-40s, but the C-87 was un-
guarded.

Keeping one eye on the sentry in the maintenance
area, Chang ducked under the nose of the transport,
then boosted himself up through the open hatch into the
wheelbay. Squirming, he edged himself through the narrow observation door below the navigator's position
and then back into the main cargo section.

The long aluminum-ribbed cavity was dark, with
only faint light coming through the rows of windows on
either side of the fuselage. The cargo bay had been fitted with three high, scaffoldlike stretcher holders. The
interior of the aircraft smelled of blood and death, but
at least it was dry.

It had been weeks since he'd had a proper bath, and
the tattered remains of his school uniform hadn't been
washed for even longer. Even to his own nostrils Chang
reeked. In the faint hope of finding soap left behind in
the curtained lavatory at the rear of the aircraft, Chang

picked his way along the center aisle, heading for the tail section.

And discovered the bodies. Four of them—three arranged one above the other on a single tier, the fourth set off by itself. All four were covered by thick blankets. Chang examined the bodies in turn. There were three Chinese, all wearing Nationalist uniforms. The fourth was an American. Covering the faces of the Chinese once more, Chang stripped the blanket off the American and wrapped it around his shoulders. Callousness born out of desperation and cold; in other times he would have never considered doing such a thing.

He stared at the pale face as the thin rain drummed lightly on the fuselage of the transport. Young, perhaps twenty-five or so, wearing the soiled uniform of the United States Army Air Force, the single gold bar of a second lieutenant on the collar of his leather jacket. There was a large patch on the left breast of the jacket—the stylized black-and-red Thunderbird insignia of the 34th Bombardment Wing.

The teenager sat back on his heels, wrapping the blanket more tightly around himself. He'd seen the patch before, worn by one of the men who'd come in the day before—Hawksworth, the one they were calling a hero. He let out a long breath, the chill air turning it to vapor.

He let his eyes rove over the body. No obvious wounds, no torn flesh or gangrenous stumps like those he'd seen in the littered streets of K'un-ming. So what had killed him, leaving him to lie here in the darkness, deaf to the soft sound of the rain while his colleagues lived, basking in the glow of their superiors' commendations?

It didn't matter. All the boy really knew was that the dead man no longer had a need for his jacket, while he did. Chang paused for a moment, listening to the rain, tense for any sudden sounds, then moved quickly.

Throwing off the blanket, he shuffled forward, gripped the corpse by the shoulders, and rolled it over, pulling the sleeves of the jacket back as he did so, grunting with the effort. He'd strip off the felt patch and the rank insignia, and no one would be the wiser. Springtime came late to K'un-ming, and the nights were bone-chillingly cold.

Bending down to haul the jacket from the dead man's back, he finally saw what had killed him. The collar of the jacket had hidden a large, star-shaped wound at the base of the man's neck. The shot had been from very close range; the skin around the swollen, petallike rent in the man's flesh was spattered with the tattooed marks of hot gases and unexploded grains of powder. The second lieutenant lying on the stretcher had been executed.

Grimacing, Chang rolled the body back into its original position and replaced the blanket, covering the man's face. He slipped on the man's jacket and stood up. Something was weighing down the inside pocket. He felt around and withdrew a palm-sized notebook, bound in dark green buckram. The corners were worn, and the book appeared to have been well used. Moving to the other side of the aircraft, he held the book up to the weak light from one of the windows and opened it.

"HOLY GHOST"
Personal Journal of Lieut.
Vernon Wendell Cates
USAAF
—if found plse. return to Eglin Field Fla.—

The boy turned and glanced at the shrouded body of the man behind him. For a moment he thought about slipping the journal into Vernon Cates's trouser pocket, then decided against it. He tucked the small black book into the jacket and zipped the garment up to his chin. He already felt warmer.

There was no way that he was going to spend the

night with the bodies of four dead men, so Chang made his way back to the nose of the transport and let himself out the way he'd come in. The sentry guarding the trio of P-40s was asleep now, back against one wheel nacelle. Chang slipped into the night, using the stand of trees as cover while he made his way toward the main gate of the airfield. He moved into the shadows behind the sandbagged mess hall and under the protective overhang of the corrugated-metal roof. Dropping down behind a row of trash bins, he pulled his hands deep into the accommodating sleeves of the leather jacket and was asleep almost instantly.

He awoke to the sound of shouting voices and the stuttered wail of a hand-cranked siren. The rain had stopped, and dim light was bleeding up over the distant hills. Dawn was breaking; he'd been asleep for several hours. The boy in the leather jacket watched from the shadows beneath the roof overhang as half-dressed men ran toward a billowing pillar of smoke and flame in the middle distance. It was the C-87, now a funeral pyre for its uncaring occupants, three Chinese and an American named Vernon Wendell Cates.

An ancient truck, fitted out with a water tank and mechanical pump, careened across the hard-packed stones of the runway, horn bleating as it made for the flaming transport. It was far too late to salvage anything; beneath the roiling pall of smoke the ribs of the fuselage were visible now, the interior of the cargo hold a white-hot furnace.

The young man had been on the aircraft only a few hours before, had considered sleeping there, in fact. The ground outside had been soaked by forty-eight hours of almost constant rain, and there was nothing aboard the C-87 that could have initiated such an inferno. No smell of aviation fuel, no volatile cargo. Only four dead men.

Watching the crowd forming around the flaming wreckage, Chang gently touched the Thunderbird breast patch of his new jacket, feeling the hard rectangle of

Vernon Cates's journal beneath. Somehow, even then, he knew its importance and understood its inherent danger, but to capitalize on his new asset, he first had to survive.

He did survive, and so did the journal, even though the jacket had been traded for food long before he left K'un-ming more than three months after the fire. Now, half a century later, the journal still existed, sealed in an airtight archival container, safely locked away in Chang's personal safe at Naloa, the sprawling family estate on Oahu.

Caught in the tangled skein of his memories, James Chang barely noticed the lights below the aircraft, marking their arrival in New York. He looked up as the uniformed male flight attendant suggested in a whisper that he do up his seat belt, and for a moment the attendant's face was that of Vernon Cates, his secret, silent partner for so many years.

CHAPTER 12

PHILLIP DANE DROVE his aging Fiat Spyder across town with the top down, daring the gray slabs of cloud looming over the nation's capital to vent their wrath on his worn leather upholstery. The dirty-shirt sky and the moist rush of air moaning around the dull black sports car suited his mood exactly. A filthy spring day in the Secret City, and here he was, bleaching the government's dirty laundry for it once again.

Booming around the Columbus Monument in front of Union Station, he turned right into the busy mid-morning traffic on Delaware Avenue, cut in front of a sluggishly moving bus, and then keyholed his way across Constitution Avenue and onto the grounds of Capitol Plaza.

As usual there were workmen toiling on the decaying East Front of the Capitol itself, but he managed to find a parking slot among the plumbers' vans and painters' trucks in the half-circle lot directly in front of the main steps. He keyed off the engine, listening to it rattle and die with its familiar grunting swan song, then picked up his briefcase from the seat beside him and clambered out of the car.

He paused long enough to light a cigarette, then crossed the roadway and began to climb the broad flight of granite steps leading up to the entrance. Tacking slightly to avoid a nattering swarm of Japanese tourists, he nodded to one of the uniformed National

74

Parks security guards and stepped into the building FDR had once referred to as "Freedom's Fortress."

Stubbing his cigarette out in the virgin sand of a free-standing ashtray, Dane consulted the scrap of paper with his directions and turned right in the foyer immediately in front of the entrance to the Rotunda. He climbed a half-flight of stairs and stepped into the high vaulted corridor that ran past the old Senate Chamber.

It was familiar territory to an old Washington hand like Dane, but he still found his eyes drawn upward to the complex brightly painted designs on the fluted columns and vaults of the marble-floored passage. Birds, boats, and swords being turned into ploughshares, all done in reds, blues, and golds, representing the lifework of a nineteenth-century Italian pacifist named Constantino Brumidi.

Pleasant enough if you liked that sort of enthusiastic opulence, but to Dane it was faintly reminiscent of a Venetian whorehouse or something that should have been painted on velvet and sold at a "starving artists' " auction. He snorted softly. Maybe it was just his mood.

Conrad Lang's Senate office was the last on his right. The very fact that he had an office in the Capitol itself, and not in the blockhouse buildings on Constitution Avenue, was proof of his long-standing seniority and power. Power that could vanish instantly if he was ever connected to the slaughter aboard *Terpsichore*. Dane wasn't looking forward to his interview with Lang at all.

He tapped lightly on the recessed door and entered the outer office. Ornate Oriental carpet, dark paneling, and leather couches, the doorway to the inner office guarded by a heavy wooden desk and its occupant, a steel-eyed, iron-haired woman who looked as old as the Capitol dome itself. A brass nameplate for the benefit of anyone courageous enough to approach announced that her name was Mrs. Ethel Ignatz.

"Yes?" Voice as hard as ball bearings. Dane felt sorry

for any casual constituent from Ohio who dropped in for a chat unannounced.

"I have an appointment with the senator."

"You are?" said Mrs. Ignatz.

"Dane. Phillip Dane."

Mrs. Ignatz ran one gnarled finger down a list on her desk blotter. She looked up at Dane and frowned.

"You're early."

"I'm afraid so, yes," Dane answered, offering a small smile. It was refused. He could guess the reason for her frown.

Dane was no one she knew, there would be no title beside his name on the list, and Lang had almost certainly not told her anything about the appointment. Mrs. Ignatz was a woman who frowned on ciphers in her life. Dane was an anomaly, and therefore not to be trusted.

"Please be seated," she said, pointing her very square chin at one of the leather couches. "The senator will see you as soon as he is finished."

Finished what? Dane thought, but didn't ask. He sat down on the couch farthest from Mrs. Ignatz's position and snapped open his briefcase. He had a little time to go over the file he'd put together.

The Lang family was rich and had been almost from the day the Langs realized that the future of America lay in powered flight. The senator's grandfather had been a Dayton, Ohio, hardware-store owner and one of the earliest investors in the fledgling Wright Aeronautical Corporation.

Like his contemporary Henry Ford, Jurgen Lang recognized early on that the real money was in parts, and by the 1930s his Lang Aviation Company was supplying bits and pieces to everyone from Piper to Northrop. Lend-Lease made the company even richer, and the aftermath of Pearl Harbor turned Lang Aviation into an industrial giant, still firmly rooted in Dayton, Ohio, but with interests around the world.

During the early years Jurgen Lang had purchased shares in many of the companies he sold parts to, and his son, Otto, had continued the practice.

By 1941 Lang Aviation had become Lang Aviation & Manufacturing, and Jurgen's grandson Conrad had joined the United States Army Air Force with a major's commission, forming a direct but discreet link between LA&M and its biggest customer, the federal government.

In October of 1945 the relationship was cemented even more completely as Conrad, complete with a colonel's eagle on his shoulder and the green, blue, and gold of a War Department General Staff I.D. on his sleeve, took over as chief liaison officer for the newly formed Air Transport Group, headquarters in Hawaii.

The ATG was responsible for the transportation of all military personnel and equipment to and from occupied Japan as well as to all military bases located around the Pacific Rim, including the Philippines, Southeast Asia, and Australia. Since the army air force didn't have anything like enough aircraft to do the job, it was authorized to employ civilian aircraft companies on lucrative long- and short-term contracts.

After a year traveling all over the Pacific, establishing ATG operations in a score of far-flung locations, Conrad Lang resigned his commission and within days established Pacific Air Transport Corporation of America, or PATCOA, complete with the Flying Gryphon logo he'd borrowed from the 50th Bombardment Wing, operating a fleet of aircraft that were mainly surplus DC-3s, ordered by the air force in the military C-47 version but never handed over. The pilots were all experienced ex-military men, used to flying the identical aircraft in conditions that ranged from terrible to worse.

PATCOA was the first and largest of the early civil airlines operating in the Pacific, and it wasn't surprising that Lang's company won most of the transport bids put out by the Air Transport Group and its successor, Air

Transport Command. Lang Aviation and Manufacturing had a new winner on its hands, and Conrad Lang rode it all the way into the Senate, winning the 1952 campaign in a landslide. He'd been there ever since, supposedly at arm's length from his business interests but clearly in complete command. From his voting record and committee chairmanships it was obvious that Conrad Lang had a very simple philosophy—if it was good for him, it was probably good for Ohio.

There was a buzzing sound, and Dane looked up from the open file folder in his lap. Given his personal horror of pagers and cell phones, Dane knew the noise hadn't come from him, so it had to be Lang. He looked toward Mrs. Ignatz expectantly, but she seemed completely involved in a document in front of her on the desk. No sign that she'd even heard the sound. A few seconds later the buzzer went off again. This time Mrs. Ignatz favored Dane with a brief, cold look.

"The senator will see you now," she said. He stood up, and she followed suit, beating him to the inner door by a yard. She put her hand on the knob, looked at Dane once again, then opened the door. Dane entered Lang's private office, and Mrs. Ignatz closed the door firmly behind him.

CHAPTER 13

THE INNER OFFICE was a large rectangle with a pair of windows that looked out over the East Lawn to the heavy stand of trees obscuring a view of the Supreme Court. The wall-to-wall carpeting was gray, the walls plain white and hung with scores of photographs. Lang's desk, flanked by a United States flag and an Ohio state pennant, was parked between the two windows, and Lang himself was parked behind the desk. He stood up as Dane approached.

Old age generally makes men either fat or skinny. Lang had gone the thin route. He was a pipe cleaner in a dark blue pinstripe and wing tips, his nicotine-colored hair buzzed in an old-fashioned crew cut. From his pale coloring and almost invisible eyebrows it was obvious that Conrad Lang had been a redhead once upon a time. He wore a heavy gold ring on his right index finger and what looked like a Skull and Bones charm on the watch chain drooping across his vest. Which fit. Dane's file mentioned Yale and a degree in engineering.

"You're Colonel Dane," Lang said, offering his hand as he came around the desk. Dane shook it. Warm and dry, no obvious nerves. Out of the corner of his eye he noticed a door leading out of the room on the far wall. The source of the buzz? Some kind of early warning system for Mrs. Ignatz? A discreet exit for a visitor who didn't want to be seen by the nosy curator from the DIA?

"Mr. Dane will do just fine, Senator. I haven't used the rank or worn the uniform in quite some time."

"Prudent in this case, I suppose," Lang murmured. He waved Dane to a leather armchair to one side of the desk. Dane seated himself, letting his fingers run along the arms, wondering who'd sat there only a few moments before. The senator seated himself behind the desk again, hands clasped over the green felt blotter.

Dane pulled his briefcase onto his lap, popped the latches again, and took out a steno pad. Closing the briefcase, he put it aside and reached into the breast pocket of his jacket, taking out a felt pen. At the same time he pressed the Record button on the microcassette machine in the pocket. The Radio Shack recorder was wired to a small microphone behind the U.S. flag pin on his lapel. The machine was voice-actuated and had a range of about fifty feet. The note-taking was a blind; Dane was a firm believer in word-for-word transcriptions.

"I understand you had known General Hawksworth for quite some time," he began. The senator nodded.

"We served together in the Pacific."

"He was second in command of the Air Transport Group?"

"That's right," Lang agreed. "I was War Department liaison. I assessed the need, and General Hawksworth found the solutions." Lang blinked. "He was a colonel then, as I was."

"And you became friends?" Dane asked, scribbling a few notes.

"Over time," Lang answered. "We worked together very closely, both in Taipei and later in Hawaii."

"After you left the service."

"That is correct."

"Hawksworth was assigned to Hickam?"

"Yes." Lang nodded. "He was made deputy chief of the Special Activities Group—7612 Air Intelligence."

Dane tried not to show his surprise. The official biography he'd been given by Cordasco never mentioned SAG. According to the DIA, Hawksworth had been an administrator for Pacific Command. SAG's "Special Activities" included a lot of transport operations with OSS, and was effectively an early version of the Central Intelligence Agency's infamous Air America.

"At that time you were setting up PATCOA, is that right?" asked Dane.

"Yes."

"Did you have any direct connection with Hawksworth?" Dane said.

"Only socially," answered the senator. "That was shortly after his marriage to Cynthia."

Dane knew about that part of it. Cynthia Torrance was the daughter of one of his uncle's colleagues on the bench. A Washington blueblood, smitten by the hero who'd won the Congressional Medal of Honor. She'd died in an automobile accident several years after the marriage. No children.

"You knew Mrs. Hawksworth?"

"She was my cousin," the senator responded. The closed circle of the Washington elite, Dane thought. It wasn't surprising.

"So there was no working relationship between yourself and the general?" he asked.

"No," the senator replied testily. "I told you that."

"Yes, you did," Dane answered. He paused, wondering how muddy the water was going to get, and how much he dared stir it up.

"You spent almost four years in Hawaii."

"Yes."

"And the general?"

"He remained at Hickam until the Korean War. Then he was assigned to Yongsan and later to Yokota in Japan."

"By that time you were back in Dayton and here in Washington?"

"Correct."

"You maintained your friendship with General Hawksworth?"

"At a distance," the senator replied. "We met occasionally when he returned to Washington. He had an office at Fort Belvoir."

SAG again. Fort Belvoir was headquarters for the Air Force Special Activities Center. It looked as though Hawksworth had been something of a spook, and the senator obviously knew about it. His connection to DIA was beginning to make sense. Dane cursed Cordasco silently. Not only were the waters muddy, they were deep, and probably full of sharks.

"After Korea General Hawksworth was assigned to Saigon?"

"I believe so, yes," the senator agreed. "And then he was made director of European Air Intelligence."

"That was 1977. Lindsay AFB, Germany," said Dane.

"Yes," said Lang. "Followed by his appointment as CINCU-SAFE in 1980."

"Commander in Chief, U.S. Air Force, Europe."

"Yes," said Lang. All very cut-and-dried, right out of the official bio.

"Then SACEUR, Supreme Allied Commander, Europe, a NATO position."

"Yes."

"And the DIA appointment."

"Yes," said Lang.

"You were one of his strongest supporters for the job."

"Yes."

"Why?" Dane asked.

"Because I thought he'd do a good job," the senator answered blankly.

"Not because of your previous association?"

"My personal knowledge of General Hawksworth formed part of my impression."

"You had no knowledge of his involvement with drugs?"

"I still have no knowledge of that," snapped Lang. "As far as I'm concerned, it could easily have been a setup."

"Setup?" Dane asked.

"Of course," the senator answered coldly. "This is Washington, Mr. Dane. We all have our enemies. General Hawksworth played hardball; he stepped on a lot of toes."

"Why don't you explain that," said Dane.

"He was instrumental in convincing the Thais to crack down on Heroin production, even as far back as the Vietnam War. He saw the Communist Chinese drug involvement in the North as an act of war. He did something about it. He made enemies."

"And they killed him?"

"Yes."

"With the added bonus of possibly destroying your career in the process."

"That has occurred to me, yes," Lang said, teeth clenched. Dane took a deep breath, contemplating a move onto very shaky ground.

"What about the prostitute, Amanda Kilau?" he asked.

"What about her?"

"Did you know her?" Dane asked. The implication was obvious. Lang's face darkened.

"Certainly not." It was a lie, and they both knew it. Lang had gone sharesies with his old friend. Dane tried not to think about the cigarette he wanted and concentrated on putting it all together. Maybe his curatorial job was to protect Lang, not Hawksworth's reputation.

"So there's no chance that anyone would have seen you with her at any time?" he asked. Lang pursed his lips and thought about it for a second.

"No. I did not know the woman."

"And had no idea she was on *Terpsichore* with the general?"

"No."

"You never visited Hawksworth aboard the boat?"

"I showed him around the first day he was in Washington."

"And the woman wasn't there?"

"No." Another lie.

"No sign of drugs?"

"No, of course not. General Hawksworth loathed anything to do with narcotics. My God, man! He was being made head of the president's task force!"

Sure, thought Dane, and the civic politicians didn't smoke crack either. The autopsy on what was left of Hawksworth showed that he'd ingested an enormous amount of opium. The resin under his fingernails alone was enough to stone a dozen junkies. The coroner's best guess was that he'd been on a bender for two or three days at least. There'd also been enough type-and-match semen residue in Amanda Chung Kilau's various bodily orifices to impregnate the entire Woman's Air Corps.

"Is there anything else you can add?" Dane asked quietly.

"No. Not really," said the senator. His hands unfurled on the desk blotter; he held them palms flat, staring intently at Dane. "From what I've been given to understand, your job is to . . . smooth out the jagged edges."

"Something like that."

"You sound more like an investigator. As though you're looking for . . . something."

"I'm looking for anything that might cause a problem, now or in the future, Senator. You can't cover up something unless you know what it is you're supposed to be covering."

"You're very blunt."

"I have to be," Dane answered. "I'm not here to win friends and influence people." He paused. "That's for the politicians," he added, unable to resist the shot. Lang ignored it.

"You have a reputation on the Hill," the senator said after a few moments. "I've checked. You're known for your discretion."

"I've been in the information business for a long time, Senator Lang. If I weren't discreet, I'd be a gossip columnist." The man was reaching for something. Dane waited, not wanting to push.

"There is something," the old man said finally. "A woman."

"Not Amanda Kilau?"

"No," the senator answered, shaking his head. "It was a long time ago."

"And this involves the general, not yourself?"

"Yes."

"Go on."

"General Hawksworth was a very . . . vital man."

"So I gathered," Dane said quietly. For vital, read "stud."

"His marriage to Cynthia was never a very solid one. It was . . . perhaps political is the right word."

"The Hero and the Debutante?" Dane suggested.

"Something like that, yes," agreed the senator. "At any rate, Cynthia didn't take well to life at Hickam, or Hawaii in general. She was used to a somewhat higher level of sophistication. They separated within a year. She came back to Washington."

"And General Hawksworth took a mistress," said Dane, the pieces falling into place.

"Yes."

"Did his wife know about it?"

"Yes," said the senator. "She was in the process of filing for divorce when she had her terrible accident."

"She was hit by a car?"

"Yes. Hit-and-run. They never found the person responsible."

"Was she divorcing the general because of his relationship with the other woman?" Dane asked. The senator shrugged.

"It may have been the catalyst. I don't think it was the direct cause." Lang paused again, rejoining his hands, staring at the big ring on his finger. "Cynthia was too sophisticated to be terribly upset by a dalliance."

"Was it just a dalliance?" Dane asked.

"In the end, no. It was more than that," the senator answered.

"How much more?"

"He supported her for many years. The relationship was ongoing."

"This was in Hawaii."

"It began in Taiwan, before he married Cynthia. It continued in Hawaii. Eventually he moved her to San Francisco. I believe she's still there."

"Do you know her name?" Dane asked. The senator nodded.

"Leung. Kim Chee Leung."

Dane sat back in the chair. The Medal of Honor winner with a Chinese mistress and a blueblood wife. In someone like Bob Woodward's hands it would be a blockbuster. At worst it would be wall-to-wall headlines in the tabs.

"Did you know her at all?" he asked finally.

"Yes. I employed her, both in Hawaii and in San Francisco. She was a secretary."

"Made it convenient."

"William Hawksworth was my friend," said the senator.

"And Cynthia Hawksworth was your cousin."

"We were never close." A twitch there. The senator was lying again. Dane's desire for a cigarette was becoming overwhelming. There was something very nasty back there in the past. Something Lang didn't even want to think about. They didn't need a curator for this job; they needed a bulldozer for the cover-up.

"Who knew about this woman?" asked Dane.

"Almost nobody. Cynthia only knew that there *was* a woman, a Chinese. She never knew who it was. Maybe a few people at the PATCOA office in Honolulu suspected that something was going on, I'm not sure."

"What about your wife? Ever confide in her?"

"No."

"Does the Leung woman have any close friends that you know about? Someone she might have told?"

"Not to my knowledge."

"All right," said Dane. "I suppose I'd better go to San Francisco and talk to her." He looked at the senator. "I don't suppose you have a current address for her?"

"Yes." The old man nodded. He opened a drawer in the desk and took out a single sheet of paper and a Montblanc fountain pen. He scribbled down an address from memory, folded the sheet, and handed it across the desk to Dane. He dropped it into the open briefcase on the floor beside him.

"Do you have her name and address written down anywhere?" Dane asked.

"Perhaps in an old address book," the senator answered.

"Destroy it. Make sure there's no connection between yourself and her."

"Yes," said the senator. Dane looked down at the steno pad thoughtfully. He doodled an elaborate border around the name "Kim Chee Leung." Something was wrong.

"Lots of men take mistresses. Even Medal of Honor winners and generals about to be confirmed to high-ranking posts. You think this is different. Important enough to mention. Why?"

"There are certain . . . sensitive connections."

"Such as?" Dane prodded. The senator was actually perspiring now, hands knitting together and coming apart again and again.

"William's . . . relationship . . . with Kim Chee began in Taiwan, where he had met her previously."

"Where?"

"Chungking."

"This was after the Doolittle Raid?"

"Yes, immediately after. He was being treated as a hero, wined and dined before being sent on to K'unming and a flight out to India."

"And he ran into this Kim Chee Leung woman."

"More a child," said the senator. "I think at the time she was twelve, perhaps thirteen."

Dane closed his eyes briefly and shook his head. Along with all the other skeletons in Hawksworth's closet, he'd just added statutory rape.

"How exactly did he meet her?" Dane asked.

"She was a maidservant for a high-ranking woman who had chronic medical problems. A nurse's aide, in effect. General Hawksworth was a houseguest there while he was in Chung-king."

"Who was the high-ranking woman?" Dane asked, fairly sure that he already knew the answer.

"Is that necessary?" asked Lang.

"I think so, yes."

"The woman was Mei-Ling Soong, better known as Madame Chiang Kai-shek, the Generalissimo's wife."

CHAPTER 14

THE MARRIAGE OF James Chang, third of the Blue-Eyed Chin-Kangs in his lineage, to Kwang Shen-Li had resulted in the birth of three children within a four-year period between 1949 and 1953.

Lily Chang was first of the three, and weakest, now married herself to Han Chao Shun and living in New York. The second child was Victoria, married to Samson Kee, White Paper Fan of the western division of the Black Dragon *Hui*. The third child, and the one whose birth had resulted in the death of Kwang Shen-Li, was James Chang's heir and was named for him as fourth of the Chang Chin-Kang's, usually referred to as Jimmy, or Younger Brother, to differentiate between him and his father. Jimmy Chang was *Cho Hai*, or Straw Sandal, of the *Hui*, and oversaw Black Dragon activities in Hawaii and Hong Kong from the family estate on Naloa, their private island compound eight miles offshore from Oahu. Jimmy, just three years younger than his older sister Lily, had married her husband's sister, Han Mu-Chen.

Between them, the three children of James Chang had given him ten grandchildren, and through Jimmy Chang's young son, Robert, had guaranteed the continuation of the Chang name, thus ensuring the survival of the *Hui* into the twenty-first century.

With the exception of White Paper Fan and Red Pole, the most important positions within Black Dragon were held by direct family members, or those related to their spouses. This included the family names of Han, Kee, Pau, Lum, Lee, Lau, Chin, and Shu and provided a network of people representing every ethnic Chinese community in the world, each member of that network firmly connected to the Dragon Head, James Chang.

Western sociologists and cultural anthropologists have often applauded the Oriental's strong sense of family, assuming that it has something to do with perpetuating personal principle and morality. The truth is much simpler—keeping it in the family simply makes good business sense, and above all the Chinese are good businessmen. It is much more difficult to lie, cheat, steal from, or betray your family, and if it occurs, you are much more likely to be found out by other family members than you would be by an anonymous employer.

Except for sex, with all its variations and permutations, Victoria Chang Kee's ruling passion in life was the study of her lineage. She knew in the depths of her being that it was only by an accident of biology that she was denied her position as rightful heir within the *Hui*, and no day passed without some thought of that irony. Kingdoms had been lost for want of a nail; she would lose hers for want of a dangling piece of flesh between her legs. Lily was a slobbering drunk, and Jimmy was a boasting fool. Had she been born a male, the position would have been hers by right.

But knowing the lineage with all the subtle strengths and weaknesses of its members could, and did, give her power, even though that power was rarely appreciated and never acknowledged. Her father knew, though; she'd seen it sometimes in those cold blue eyes, impossible even for him to disguise. At the compound on Naloa with her brother Jimmy boasting of how much he was doing for the *Hui* while her husband, Samson Kee, listened politely but could not quite hide his anger— yes, her father had seen it then: the same hunger in her that had taken him to greatness. And something more:

the recognition that she was far better suited to become leader of Black Dragon than her brother.

But that, of course, would never happen.

Victoria Chang Kee stood up and walked to the floor-to-ceiling window of the penthouse apartment she rented. The building was on the summit of San Francisco's Nob Hill, overlooking Huntington Park. Far below and well to the east she could look down onto Grant Avenue and Chinatown Gate. A hundred years ago it would have been worth her life to set foot outside the boundary that it marked, and now she soared above it like an eagle. Times changed, yes, but not quickly enough. She was like some benighted vampire in reverse—the penthouse was the fairy tale she lived in during the hours of daylight; at nightfall she returned to play the dutiful wife in the house of her husband.

Humiliating, but a game she had to play for the sake of appearance, and a daylight fantasy was better than no fantasy at all. She stared down on the sunlit city. There were fifty thousand women hidden there, Chinese like herself, or Korean, or Vietnamese, employed by five hundred sweatships, half of them owned by her husband and her father, stitching clothes with designer labels for the *gwei-lo* and being paid peasant wages. Any one of those women would have done anything to switch places with her. It was something to remember.

Gathering the soft folds of her dark blue silk robe around her, Victoria turned away from the window and returned to the low, ornately carved table. She sat down, knees together, gazing at the huge, unrolled scroll of the lineage. It had taken her more than a year to create, each entry on the engineer's graph paper neatly inked, line linking line, name linking name, fine-handed notes made concerning role, status, and function.

It was far more than a family tree; it was an indictment, and her husband would almost certainly slit her throat if he knew of its existence. Beyond its value as

a genealogical chart of her family, it was also in effect
an organizational chart of Black Dragon, explicit, clear,
and detailed: In Bangkok on the infamous Sampeng
Lane, Mark Kee, her husband's cousin, controlled
opium transportation, prostitution, and the smuggling of
gold. In Honolulu, another cousin, one of her own,
Steven Pau, was in charge of gambling and illegal immigration. In Amsterdam, Bernard Fong, in Hong
Kong, Wilson Han—the list went on and on.

Victoria slid a mentholated cigarette from the package on the table and lit it with a platinum Dunhill, enjoying the heavy clicking sound as she snapped away
the flame. With one long coral-pink fingernail she
touched her husband's name on the yardlong chart
spread out in front of her. Strong, powerful, important,
but not a Chang, only married to one.

A good man, handsome, virile, and intelligent to be
sure, but he knew that his role, even as *Pak Sze Sin* for
the Pacific, would always be subordinate to Jimmy's
when he assumed the position of *Shan Chu* following
the death of their father or his retirement.

Her eyes still on the chart, she let one hand slip
under her robe, splayed fingers gently touched the
smooth skin above her breasts. The fingers roamed,
covering the firm flesh, lightly pinching the already
erect nipples. She felt the first warming nudges of ex-
citement, and after carefully placing her cigarette in the
ashtray on the table, she stood again.

She walked across the living room, entered the pale
green bedchamber, and went to the large walk-in closest
beside the en-suite bathroom. The left side of the closet
was filled with a wide variety of clothes on hangers,
while the right was made up of a score of built-in drawers for accessories and racks filled with shoes. The rear
wall of the closet was a floor-to-ceiling mirror, lit by a
panel in the ceiling.

Standing in front of the mirror, Victoria reached up
to the nape of her neck with both hands and unpinned

her long black hair, letting it fall across her shoulders. She shrugged gently, and the robe fell away from her body, slithering to the soft gray carpeting at her feet. Examining herself critically, she smiled, pleased with what she saw.

At forty-two she looked at least a decade younger. Her lightly tinted amber skin was unblemished, small breasts rising above the flat stomach, firm and perfectly formed. Her pubic hair was neatly trimmed to an exact triangle between her legs, its apex offering the barest hint of the pale pink flesh below. Her legs were strong and well shaped, feet pleasingly small.

Turning, she offered up her profile to the glass. She had the narrower, high-checkboned features of the South and not the pie-faced cliché of the Manchurians, and she was grateful that her father had married into the purer bloodlines of the Shanghainese aristocracy, rather than the mongrel gene pool of the North.

Looking over her shoulder, her eyes followed the smooth line of her spine down to the cleft of her small-checked, almost boyish, buttocks. She smiled again, wondering if her husband's almost obsessive interest in that part of her body said something about his hidden desires.

Not that it mattered; she was more than happy to accommodate his pleasures and his male stalk. It was no hardship to let him be the master of her body, when she knew that she was the secret master of his soul. At any rate, the buttocks, like the breasts, showed no sign of aging, free of wrinkles, cellulite, or any other blemish.

Satisfied and still naked, she turned away from the mirror and padded back to the living room. Kneeling down at the table, she finished her cigarette, scanning the chart in front of her, waiting. Less than five minutes later she heard the sounds of a key being turned in the lock of the penthouse door, and she turned toward the sound, knowing perfectly well what kind of picture she was presenting.

A woman appeared, dressed in a modestly cut cream-colored suit and carrying a tooled-leather attaché case in her right hand. Like Victoria, the woman was in her early forties. She wore her hair barely shoulder length, and here and there, even from a distance, Victoria could see that it was shot with silver the woman made no effort to hide. The face was handsome rather than beautiful, the slim body beneath the suit lithe and strong. Victoria felt a sudden surge of heat in the pit of her stomach, and a rash of color began to spread unbidden across her chest.

"You are looking very businesslike and efficient, Yu-Mei," said Victoria, standing and turning in a single fluid movement.

"I've spent most of the day with your husband's bookkeepers," answered Norma Chung, whose Chinese name was Chung Yu-Mei. She was madam of the five brothels operated by Black Dragon on the West Coast and actively controlled the largest of them, located in San Francisco. In addition she was an acquisition scout for new girls, spending a great deal of time in Bangkok, Manila, and Hong Kong. She was the only woman within the *Hui* with an official position of real power, which was part of the reason Victoria Chang Kee had cultivated her friendship long ago. The other reason was simple lust; as a sexual partner Yu-Mei had no peer.

"Would you like something to drink?" asked Victoria. Yu-Mei shook her head. She crossed the room and stood within a foot of her naked friend. Smiling, she put down her attaché case and slipped out of her suit jacket. Stepping forward, Victoria helped with the buttons of her blouse, her lips seeking out the hollows of the other woman's neck as her fingers worked.

"You're very eager," Yu-Mei whispered, using her hands to push her skirt down over her hips. Beneath it she was wearing nothing, and Victoria was suddenly overwhelmed by the woman's musky scent.

"I've been thinking about this all day," she answered. She found Yu-Mei's lips with her own and pressed her hands against Yu-Mei's larger, softer breasts. "Feel," she whispered, taking one of Yu-Mei's hands in her own. "Feel how wet I am for you." Victoria guided the other woman's fingers between her legs, and for a few moments Yu-Mei caressed the soft, swollen inner folds, feeling the shivering of her companion's thighs. Yu-Mei withdrew her two fingers then and brought them up to Victoria's lips, wetting them with the slick gloss of her own secretions.

"Let me taste you," she said, and they kissed again, both fully naked now. They parted briefly, Victoria's head nestled in the other woman's shoulder while Yu-Mei's hands fluttered like butterflies across her back.

"Where?" asked Victoria.

"Here," Yu-Mei answered. She stepped back, using her hands on Victoria's shoulders to push her gently down toward the scattering of pillows around the table. Victoria did as she was told, knowing what was to come, her legs parting slightly as Yu-Mei knelt and pushed the catches of her attaché case. Inside, nestled in felt-covered niches, were a variety of appliances used by women of her profession for centuries in the Middle Kingdom. There were silver clasps and implements, "Jade-Step Polishers," "Cockscombs" and several types of "Lively Limb," some very old and made of polished wood, others fabricated from more prosaic materials.

Yu-Mei studied the contents of the attaché case briefly, then withdrew a large, double-ended dildo, the thick twin stalks made of a deep pink natural rubber, the bulbous heads covered in a softer, more forgiving latex. Each shaft of the V-shaped device was a full eight inches long, and at its apex, held by two small silver rings were long ropes of softly braided silk.

"Oh, yes," Victoria whispered, looking up and seeing Yu-Mei's choice. Her companion smiled and, with the *Yang-Wu* in her hands, knelt between her friend's legs.

She bent forward, pressing a soft kiss onto Victoria's belly, then brought her mouth up to the woman's nipples, licking each in turn. Victoria moaned softly at the touch, and her thighs fell open even wider. As they did so, Yu-Mei pressed forward, the large head of the *Yang-Wu* parting Victoria's sex easily, then swallowing its entire length.

Yu-Mei reached down and found one of the silk ribbons, bringing its free end up and placing it in Victoria's right hand. She took the other ribbon in her own hand, swung her legs outside of Victoria's, then eased back, impaling herself on the other stalk of the *Yang-Wu*. The two women, joined by the device, began to move slowly, first one, then the other, pulling alternately on the silk ribbons in their hands in a steadily quickening rhythm.

"So wonderful, so wonderful!" Victoria hissed, feeling the huge stalk and head moving within her. She began to pant, hips twisting and bucking as Yu-Mei moved above her. "Tell me everything!" she whispered into Yu-Mei's ear. "Tell me all the things you have heard today!"

CHAPTER 15

SAN FRANCISCO'S CHINATOWN, once given the generic name *Tangrenbu*, "Place Where the Chinese People Came," is a twenty-four-block enclave in the northeast of the city that is bounded by Broadway to the north, Sutter to the south, Mason Street to the west, and Kearney Street and the Financial District to the east. Except for New York's Chinatown it is the most crowded urban area in the United States, with a population density of 228 people per acre.

Twenty thousand Chinese actually live in the community, and all eighty thousand Chinese residents in San Francisco do business there. Built on the smoldering ruins of the first *Tangrenbu* after the 1906 earthquake, it is still a ghetto of tiny garish storefronts, narrow alleys, and warrenlike corridors and tunnels invisibly linking one basement to another. Once ruled by the infamous "Six Companies," it is still a city unto itself, as secretive as it was a hundred years before.

For the *gwei-lo* public officials of the city Chinatown is a colorful tourist attraction, famed for its exotic restaurants and Saturday markets. For the area's power brokers, Samson Kee among them, it was the capital city for ethnic Chinese around the Pacific Rim, with three quarters of its residents foreign-born and with an average income of ten thousand dollars—less than half the median income of the city as a whole. Initially made up of overseas Chinese migrants from the Nomhai, Punji, and Shunteh districts of Guangdong

Province in the 1850s, it had been overlaid with a complex pattern of Koreans, Vietnamese, Cambodians, and Thai, who provided a continuing source of cheap labor for the area's sweatshops.

Using an umbrella operation called Pacific Sewing Company, Samson Kee, husband of Victoria Chang and son-in-law to James Chang, *Shan Chu* of Black Dragon, controlled sixty subcontracting sewing companies, all of them nonunion and all of them paying far less than minimum wage. Like the other major piecework corporations involved in the $3.5 billion garment trade in San Francisco, Pacific Sewing subcontractors assembled pre-cut fabric for Byers, Esprit, Fritzi, Foxy Lady, Gunne Sax, North Face, and Twin Peaks.

Following the strategy laid down by the *Shan Chu* years before, Pacific Sewing had no direct connection to any of the San Francisco subcontractors. Instead PSC financed the smaller companies with between $30,000 and $70,000 capital, allowing them to employ anywhere from five to fifteen workers. The money was just enough to rent space, rent or buy a few second-hand sewing machines, and pay for electricity. The subcontractor would then advertise for people needed to operate sewing machines—and work would begin. There was never any lack of non-English-speaking legal and illegal immigrants to fill every position advertised, and the piecework itself was brokered through another division of PSC. It was a closed circle, made even more secure by the Pacific Sewing system of splitting jobs between several different locations so that no one subcontractor ever completed a single contract. PSC made money charging incredible interest rates for the money it "loaned" to the subcontractors, made money again on commissions for obtaining the contracts from the large garment wholesalers, and made money a third time charging a minuscule "adjustment fee" on each finished item.

Since virtually all of the subcontractors operated on

a shoestring, the majority of them also practiced an unemployment-insurance fraud scheme. Part-time workers were registered as full time and thus were eligible for unemployment benefits, premiums paid for by the subcontractor. Once on benefits the worker would then be paid part-time wages under the table. Once again PSC charged a fee for setting up the fraudulent books, deducting yet another tiny amount from the workers' paychecks.

Of the 25,000 Asian garment workers employed in the Bay area, 7,300 were controlled by PSC with an average total fee-per-worker of $7 a day, or slightly less than $1.5 million per month. This did not include commissions or financing fees, which nearly doubled the amount.

The headquarters of Pacific Sewing Company was located in a nondescript four-story building on Lum Square that had once housed the Chinese Congregational School and Mission. From his office window Samson Kee could look out over the artificial tiers of the "park" covering the Portsmouth Square parking garage, and between the Holiday Inn and another tower farther down the hill on Montgomery he could see the glittering spike of the Transamerica Pyramid.

During the day Samson would often see old men at the checker tables, or doing t'ai chi exercises, and he sometimes wondered if his view from the window was actually a vision of his future. He could think of worse fates than a quiet old age spent in the dappled sun with old friends and older memories. He could also think of better.

At forty-six Samson Kee was in his prime, both physically and mentally. He worked out each day in the Holiday Inn Health Club, ate carefully, and with the exception of ten rigorously monitored cigarettes each day, enjoyed no vices. He was even reasonably faithful to his wife, which, for a man in his position was almost unheard of.

At five feet ten inches he was relatively tall for a Chinese, something that he was secretly proud of but that also embarrassed him.

He knew that among his people physical size was thought to indicate slowness of thought, so he went out of his way to downplay his height, wearing plain dark suits without shoulder padding and crepe-soled flat shoes without heels. At the gym, on the racquetball court, or in bed with Victoria, it was a different story, though, and he reveled in his strength and power. A weakness perhaps, but a hidden one; unlike Danny Han's women and drugs or Jimmy Chang's arrogance and his fiery temper.

Samson Kee swung his chair away from the view out his window and glanced around the office. Small, utilitarian, efficient. Filing cabinets, a desk, a small, plain rug. Pale green walls, unadorned except for a red-and-gold calendar from the Golden Dragon Restaurant on Washington Street, a block away to the west. Braised noodles with barbecued pork and cabbage.

Kee smiled to himself. That was another fate awaiting him, of course, less benign that t'ai chi in the park below. His brains blown into the lo-mein noodles, mixing with the beef and tomatoes courtesy of some holligan youth from the Hop Sings or the Wah Chings. It had happened before. In 1977 a group of Joe Boys had come into the Gold Dragon armed with shotguns and assault rifles. Five had died, and eleven were seriously injured.

The beeper in the breast pocket of his white short-sleeved shirt went off, and Samson Kee reached for the package of Winstons on the desk in front of him. He lit one with a disposable lighter and leaned back in his wooden office chair, drawing in a luxurious cloud of smoke. He exhaled cautiously. His fifth of the day.

Tonight was dinner with the *Shan Chu,* a lavish family event at the Harbor Village in the Embarcadero Center, well away from Chinatown and any potential trouble. Just to make sure, Samson had rented the entire restaurant for the evening, and metal detectors would be used at both the staff and guest entrances.

Kee had taken every security precaution for the dinner tonight, but he knew most of it was for show. As in any conflict between opposing groups or nations, the leaders or the generals were very rarely personally involved in the fighting, and any attempt on the life of the *Shan Chu* would be deemed an outrageous act of bad faith.

Drawing lightly on his cigarette, Kee flipped open the expensive, leather-bound binder on the desk. He turned the pages as he smoked, going over the rows of neatly inscribed Chinese characters one more time. Tonight, after dinner, he would present this to the *Shan Chu* for his edification—a complete quarterly report on the West Coast activities of Black Dragon from Vancouver, British Columbia, in the north to San Diego in the south.

Cloaked in a variety of euphemistic codes, the document listed every major criminal enterprise of Black Dragon's, including prostitution, loan-sharking, robbery, extortion, illegal immigration, pornography, gambling, and drug distribution. Profits for the past three months were in excess of $1.2 billion, most of it laundered through several Hong Kong and San Francisco banks for eventual distribution among Limehouse Trading's various legitimate operations around the world. The figure was up almost 15 percent over the previous year, and was well above the East Coast totals of Danny Han.

Hopefully the report would be enough to soothe any anger the *Shan Chu* might have regarding the unfortunate loss in Vancouver. Kee took a last drag on his cigarette and stubbed it out into the cheap aluminum ashtray he used. He wasn't directly responsible for the incident—happily that role belonged to the local Canadian 432, Marvin Lok, but one way or the other he would be asked to make good the loss. The least he could do was find out who the hijackers were, and so far he'd had no luck beyond some vague rumors about a new gang operating in the area called the Holy Ghosts. Not much to go on, and not much to give the *Shan Ghu*.

Kee glanced at the plain-faced Seiko on his wrist and sighed. There was still a lot of business to take care of before the dinner. Pushing the report into the attaché case beside his desk, he shrugged into his suit jacket and left the office. Taking the pedestrian bridge across to the Holiday Inn, he found his way down into the bowels of the underground parking garage and climbed into a dark green Pontiac Tempest, one of the three cars he used in random order. Thirty-five minutes later, after fighting the traffic streaming toward the airport, he pulled into the vehicle-strewn yard of the warehouse in Burlingame, a few blocks in from the Bay.

The blocklong wood-frame-and-sheet-metal building was owned by a Black Dragon holding company and had been divided into half a dozen shops rented to a variety of businesses, including a wrought-iron works, a fiberglass boat builder, and a manufacturer of vacuum-formed key-chain bottle openers. Across the street, in another ramshackle building, there was a venetian-blind company and several yacht brokers. The whole area, bounded by a branch-line railroad track and the highway overpass, was a maze of oil-stained service roads and buildings like the one managed by Samson Kee.

The tall Chinese parked his car in front of the shop at the far end of the building, then picked his way through the litter of cars, boats, and anonymous lumps of machinery until he reached the metal door of the shop. A small, faded sign identified it as T.K. MANUFAC-TURING LTD. Using a key from the ring in his pocket, he unlocked the door and stepped inside the windowless building.

Metal-strapped crates were piled to the ceiling of the

rudely partitioned foyer, each one stenciled with the three letters TKM and a Hong Kong address. From behind another door he could hear the grating sound of a band saw, and the air was thick with the odor of burned bone, overlaid with a pungent chemical smell. Opening the inner door, he stepped into the main shop area and paused for a moment.

The shop was a hundred feet long and thirty wide, the corrugated-metal ceiling twenty-five feet overhead. A platform of four-by-fours and plywood had been built over the rear third of the shop for added storage space. The floors were raw concrete, and the walls were covered in unfinished plasterboard, marred with spray-painted graffiti in both English and Chinese.

There were eleven men at work in the big room, all stripped to the waist in the claustrophobic heat, the older ones wearing bandannas over their faces, the younger men preferring the more efficient surgical masks to keep the cloying dust and reeking chemicals out of their lungs.

There were four band saws at work, the cutters being handed racks of raw horn by their teenage apprentices, who moved back and forth from the storage bins under the elevated platform to the saws out front. The horn racks, tens of thousands of them, were hacked from the carcasses of a seemingly never-ending supply of deer and elk provided by professional hunters from Colorado to Alaska. The racks, cut down to manageable pieces three or four inches long, produced seven or eight pounds of horn worth about $350 on the wholesale market. TKM crated more than twenty tons of horn a month, almost all of it destined for Hong Kong, Bangkok, and Manila. The deer and elk populations of China, Thailand, and the Philippines had been decimated decades before; and among the herbalists and practitioners of holistic medicine in those countries, the horn was almost as valuable as gold.

Samson Kee made his way toward the rear of the

shop, his shoes crunching on the powdered fragments of horn that lay everywhere. To the right of the saws and ranged along the side wall of the shop, there was a long line of tables forming a makeshift assembly line, beginning with an antiquated white enamel freezer.

Fifty-pound bags of rock-hard entrails and organs, perfused with chemicals, were removed from the freezer and passed along the line. Wearing boots and long rubber aprons, workers stripped off the plastic bags and "cracked" the frozen lumps of flesh with heavy wooden mallets, sweeping most of the contents into plastic garbage containers below each table. What remained, purplish fist-sized organs, was passed along to the next worker, who used a butcher's cold-cut slicer to produce thin, still-frozen sections. The sections were then weighed carefully and bagged at the end of the line, where a runner took them to the freeze-drier on the far side of the shop. One in every ten organs was quartered and poked into a plastic container, then topped off with a liquid preservative. These were bear gall bladders, historically the rarest aphrodisiac and potency-inducing substance known to Chinese medicine. The gall bladders were gathered by the same hunters who provided the antler racks, the mutilated corpses of the murdered creatures left to rot where they lay.

Kee held his breath as he walked quickly past the tables but still managed a smile. He knew that the entrails in the garbage containers would be thrown away rather than put to some other use—something that would never have been allowed in Hong Kong when he was a boy. There everything had a value, even garbage.

He climbed the narrow flight of wooden steps that led to the platform above the rear storage area and nodded at Charlie Ong, his foreman. Charlie, vaguely related to Benny Ong, the infamous former "mayor" of New York's Chinatown, was one of the "new" Chinese who'd entered the United States illegally through Vancouver less than a year before.

Now twenty-five, Charlie had been a Hong Kong gang member from the age of eight, graduating from the festering slums of the Walled City with a long knife scar that ran the length of his narrow, handsome face. Charlie's mother had been a part-time prostitute who also worked in a "Fragrant Flesh" butcher store making cocktail sausages from dog meat. His father had been a Guangdong petty criminal who'd disappeared before he was born.

With no past and a predictably tragic future, Charlie had been a perfect recruit for Black Dragon. Utterly ruthless and totally amoral, Charlie Ong knew that his life in America was paradise compared to the unimaginable horrors of the Tung Tau Tsuen Road, and that paradise had been provided by Black Dragon. His loyalty to the *Hui* was absolute.

"Charlie," said Samson Kee, reaching the top of the stairs. Ong bowed stiffly, the formal gesture at odds with the Metallica T-shirt and sweatpants he was wearing.

"Mr. Kee," he said politely. "Very good to see you."

"Shipments going out on time?" asked Kee. He sat down gingerly on a stool beside the makeshift desk crammed into one corner of the loft "office."

"Yes, sir." Charlie nodded. "Would you like to see the order sheets?"

"No, that won't be necessary." Kee smiled. The boy knew that any shortfalls in the orders would result in punishment, perhaps even a forced return to Kowloon.

"I have finished the crates you asked for," said Charlie. "The ones with the false documentation."

"Good," Kee said. "I want that order to go out just as we discussed."

"Of course," answered Charlie Ong.

The harvesting of antler horn and bear gall bladders was highly illegal in both Canada and the United States, and over the years some effort had been made to halt the incredible slaughter, but there was no law against importing either horn or gall from abroad.

From time to time there were raids made on stores selling gall and horn in Vancouver, Toronto, San Francisco, and New York, but if the store owner could show that the material had come from Hong Kong, there was nothing the authorities could do. Several years previously Samson Kee had devised a system of packaging the bear gall with labels from a fictitious company in the New Territories, then putting those packages in crates complete with Hong Kong markings and forged customs clearances. The crates were then taken to the San Francisco docks and surreptitiously included with legitimate offshore shipments. Shipments of horn were too cumbersome for the system, but at two hundred dollars an ounce for the gall, it was eminently cost-effective.

"Any problems with the workers?" asked Kee, glancing over the two-by-four railing of the platform. Charlie Ong shook his head.

"No, sir." Kee knew it was a rhetorical question. The cutters and packers below were even more indentured to Black Dragon than the women who worked for Pacific Sewing, and they were all illegals, most from the ethnic Chinese communities of Cambodia and Laos. For them, return to their native countries was a death warrant.

"Good," said Kee. He knew that his trip to Burlingame had largely been for show, but it was necessary to reinforce his authority occasionally. He stared at Ong blandly. The young man had worked out well; a few more months and he could be moved on to other, more important business. "Keep up the good work," he said, standing.

"Yes, sir." Ong nodded. "Of course."

Samson Kee smiled at his employee, then headed down the stairs again. Ong watched him go, listening to the sound of his own heart as it slowed. Below him one of the saws hit a dense section of horn and screeched loudly. Kee left the shop, and Charlie pulled a crumpled package of cigarettes out of his back pocket. He lit one, puffing furiously, and looked at the cheap plastic watch on his thin, hairless wrist. Another minute and the call would have come through while the bastard was still here. Shit!

The old-fashioned black dial phone on the desk rang, and Ong felt his heart jump. He let it ring a second time, then picked up the receiver. The tinny voice on the other end of the line spoke in the clipped, high-speed dialect of his childhood. Ong had a brief, terrible vision of the rat-pattering alleys and dripping walls of his birthplace.

"Everything is ready for tonight." It wasn't a question.

"Yes," Ong answered. He could feel sweat explode in his armpits, the sour smell of his own fear mixing with the reek of the chemicals in the shop.

"We'll see you there," the voice continued. "We expect no problems of any kind. Is that clear, Mr. Ong?"

"Yes." Charlie nodded. "Yes, it's clear."

CHAPTER 16

THE ADDRESS GIVEN to him by Senator Lang led Phillip Dane to a neatly kept Victorian cottage on Liberty Street in San Francisco's Noe Valley district. Once upon a time the hilly area in the southern part of the city had been home to a blue-collar population of factory workers, but the migration to the suburbs shortly after World War II saw a decline in the community that went on until it was seen as an attractive alternative to downtown life by the city's burgeoning gay residents during the 1970s. The Noe Valley's demographics changed again during the eighties as more committed-to-the-city young professional families moved into the neighborhood.

Dane squeezed his rental car into a spot across the street from Kim Chee Leung's small house, set the hand brake to keep from rolling down the steep hill, and stepped out into the cooling late-afternoon sunlight. He yawned, trying to shake off the aftereffects of the previous night's red-eye flight from D.C., and took a long breath of the hyacinth-scented air.

From where he stood, he could look down over San Francisco's interior landscape, a sea of pale houses, dark rooftops, and swatches of greenery, undulating down to the skyscrapered city core and beyond to the sun-coppered mirror of the Bay. Pretty and serene, a perfect place for someone like Hawksworth to cache a secret mistress.

Dane checked the voice-activated recorder in his

pocket, crossed the street, then climbed the long flight
of wooden steps up to the front porch of the house. The
cottage was clean and neat but showed none of the renovated touches of its neighbors on either side. The window frames were original, the glass covered with
old-fashioned lace curtains, and the flower beds and
bushes in the small front yard were thick and lush.
From what Dane could tell, Kim Chee Leung's house
had remained unchanged for decades. According to
Lang's information, she'd lived there for more than
forty years.

Pausing to catch his breath at the top of the steps,
Dane shook his head. Almost half a century in the same
house; no one lived that way anymore—it was a world
and a lifestyle that simply no longer existed.

He'd lived in his grandfather's place for seven years,
and for Dane that was a record. He'd lived on a dozen
different military bases before he was fourteen, and after the death of both parents in quick order, a year later
there had been a succession of private schools, followed
by military-academy dorms and a blur of Bachelor Officers' Quarters marking the various stages of his career
in Military Intelligence.

Dane crossed into the shadows of the porch and
tapped the button of the front doorbell. The Georgetown bookstore was the closest thing he'd ever had to
a real home, and even there he still felt like a guest, his
presence always overshadowed by the aura of his
grandfather. In some ways it was comforting, but in the
end he knew that it probably wasn't healthy.

He snorted softly. This was the wrong time for personal introspection; if he didn't concentrate on the job
at hand, he'd never get back to Georgetown for the opportunity to find out if it was healthy or not.

The front door opened, and Dane found himself staring through the outer screen door at a small Chinese
woman wearing a plain dark smock. If she was twelve
or thirteen in 1942, that put her in her early sixties now,

but she looked a lot younger. Her hair was jet black with no trace of gray, piled up at the back of her neck in a thick, braided knot. The skin of her oval face was smooth and unwrinkled, and her posture was erect.

"Yes? Can I help you?" she asked. Her voice was soft, with only a faint accent.

"Are you Kim Chee Leung?" Dane asked.

"Yes. That is my name," she answered. "What can I do for you?"

"I'm sorry to intrude," Dane said, trying to put on a polite smile. "My name is Phillip Dane. I wonder if I could ask you a few questions about General William Hawksworth." He reached into the pocket of his jacket and took out the little leather wallet Cordasco had provided. The badge and identity card described him as being an officer in the Records and Archives Division of the United States Air Force. He opened the wallet and pressed it up against the screen. The woman glanced at it briefly, then nodded.

"Of course," she said quietly. "Please come in." She unhooked the screen door, pushed it open, and stood aside. Dane entered a wide, wallpapered hallway. Kim Chee Leung hadn't shown any curiosity at all, as though she regularly had air-force officers asking her questions about dead generals. Either she was inscrutable as hell, or she'd been expecting someone like him to come along.

The woman closed the two doors carefully, then brushed past him, leading the way along the hall to a bright summer kitchen at the rear of the house. There were counters, cupboards, and appliances along two walls and windows everywhere else, allowing splashes of light to gild the white porcelain gas stove, the blue-and-green speckled linoleum countertops and the fifties-style refrigerator. The floor was honey-colored wood plank, the cupboards lemon yellow. A kitchen from a nostalgic movie.

In the center of the room there was a large maple table with four plain varnished wood chairs, one on each side. A whistling kettle was singing on the stove.

"I was about to make tea, would you like some?" asked Kim Chee. She gestured toward one of the kitchen chairs, and Dane seated himself, surprised at how comfortable he felt in the room. The woman possessed a grace that put him instantly at ease, and he felt an unaccustomed guilt for pushing himself into her life.

"That would be very nice," he said. She nodded, took two cups without handles down from the cupboard beside the stove, then poured hot water from the kettle into a fat brown pot. She brought the cups to the table, then went back to the stove and picked up the teapot. She placed it on a woven rattan square in the center of the table, then sat down across from Dane. She looked at him expectantly, but without any trace of nervousness or fear. Once again Dane had the feeling that he'd been expected. "This is a wonderful room," he offered, not wanting to begin his questions.

"It has always been my favorite," she replied, smiling gently. "Since I came to live here."

"That was a long time ago, I suppose," said Dane, easing into it. She smiled at his caution.

"I have lived in this house since 1949," she answered. "The year my . . ." She let it dangle.

"Yes?" said Dane quietly.

"Nothing," she answered. "A passing thought." She drew the pot to the cups and poured. Green tea, the aroma suddenly filling the room. She placed a cup in front of Dane two-handed. He let it sit, enjoying the fragrant wisps of steam that drifted up to his nostrils.

"How long had you known General Hawksworth?" he asked.

"Since 1942," she answered promptly.

"You must have been very young." He smiled.

"Thirteen." She nodded. "But not so young for a Chinese girl in those times. In Chunking. Not so young."

"You were a nurse's assistant for Madame Chiang Kai-shek, is that correct?"

"For Mei-Ling Soong. But I was no more than a scullery girl, really. Nothing so glamorous as you suggest."

"She was ill?"

"She had a bad back. An accident several years before." Kim Chee smiled briefly. "And she had terrible trouble with her teeth."

"So you attended to her needs."

"Yes."

"You met the general shortly after the Doolittle Raid."

"Yes. He stayed with us for only a few days."

Dane took a moment to lift the small cup to his lips, wondering how to proceed. He sipped the hot liquid, then placed the cup back on the table.

"Presumably your . . . relationship with the general didn't begin at that time."

"No. But I was aware of his interest." She paused and took a small mouthful from her own cup, then smiled. "A woman knows, even at thirteen."

"So you met again?"

"Yes. Eight months later."

"Where?" Dane asked.

"Washington," she answered. Dane stared.

"D.C.?"

"Yes, at the White House."

"Good Lord."

"You seem surprised." Kim Chee smiled. "A scullery girl from China in the presidential mansion." The smile widened. "Actually I found Mr. Roosevelt and Mr. Churchill quite entertaining. Especially Mr. Churchill, with his cigar and his very poor attempts at speaking Chinese. His accent was quite atrocious."

"We're speaking of President Roosevelt and Prime Minister Winston Churchill?" Dane asked, totally bemused by the small woman's story.

"Of course," she answered. She took another sip of tea and looked up at Dane, eyes twinkling with her amusement. "You must remember, Mr. Dane, that I was traveling in the company of Mei-Ling Soong and her entourage. She was Madame Chiang, of course, the Generalissimo's wife, but she was a Soong and very powerful in her own right. Her family controlled hundreds of millions of dollars in this country. Billions, if you believe the stories."

"She visited here?" Dane said.

"She was educated here, Mr. Dane, a fact which many people forget. And yes, she visited. At that time it was for her health. She had her back attended to in New York, as well as her wisdom teeth extracted." Kim Chee allowed herself a small laugh. "Not that it did anything to quell her temper."

"You met with Hawksworth."

"Yes, as I said. It was shortly after he received his Congressional Medal of Honor. There was a reception."

"And your liaison began."

"After a fashion," she answered. "To put it bluntly, your General Hawksworth was extremely drunk and raped me in one of the upstairs bedrooms."

"Raped? In the White House."

"It is the only word which describes the occurrence, Mr. Dane. It was not a pleasurable experience. He apologized profusely the following day, sent me flowers, called on the telephone, but it did not change the fact of it."

"It hardly seems the way to begin a long-term relationship," said Dane weakly. He took another sip of tea.

"Nevertheless, that is what happened."

"Did anyone else know about it?"

"Certainly." Kim Chee nodded. "Madame Chiang, for one. She accused me of trying to seduce him."

"At thirteen?"

"It was nothing Mei-Ling Soong would have balked

at. I think it impressed her ... my supposed deviousness."

"What was the result of all this?" asked Dane.

"The general ... colonel then, formally asked for my forgiveness in the presence of my mistress. I accepted, of course. After the apology he asked Madame Chiang if it was necessary for me to return to China. She knew what he meant immediately, and they negotiated."

"Negotiated?" asked Dane.

"To her I was nothing more than a chattel," Kim Chee explained. "I had no family, no power, no position. Nothing but my femaleness."

"What did she stand to gain?"

"A great deal, actually," Kim Chee answered. "A large part of the Soong family business revolved around foreign-aid payments made to the Generalissimo. At that time black-market American dollars were trading at almost three thousand to one. The formal exchange rate was twenty to one. William Hawksworth was a bona fide hero and potentially useful to her cause. It was a small thing ... for her."

"What happened?"

"General Hawksworth was formally based in San Francisco. When Madame Chiang returned to Chungking, I remained there. I was given a job as a maid in the house of a man named Jih Iung Woo. He was chairman of the Bank of Canton in San Francisco. The owner of the bank was Tse-An Soong, Madame Chiang's younger brother."

"Very neat," Dane commented.

"It was the way in which the Soong family operated."

"You stayed here then?" asked Dane.

"Until the end of the war, yes."

"And continued your relationship with the general?"

"Yes, from time to time, when he was in the city. Later I was moved to Okinawa and then again to Honolulu."

"By this time Hawksworth was married."

"Yes. It never seemed to conflict, though, and the marriage was a brief one."

"The situation never bothered you?" Dane said. Kim Chee sighed, small hands playing with the rim of the cup in front of her.

"You must understand, Mr. Dane, that I was very young. I had no family. I barely spoke any English, and I was without documentation. I had no wish to return to China, I can assure you. To be a concubine to a man such as your general was no hardship under the circumstances, and over time I learned to . . . appreciate him."

"I see." Dane nodded. Kim Chee smiled.

"No, Mr. Dane, I very much doubt that you do see, but that doesn't matter. Not now."

"So you came back to San Francisco in 1949."

"Yes."

"Did you go back to work for Mr. Woo?"

"No." She shook her head. "In Hawaii I had worked as a clerk for Pacific Air Transport Corporation of America. PATCOA. I continued that work here. My English had improved by that time, and the company did a lot of business with what you call Taiwan. I was useful as a translator and interpreter."

Dane nodded. This was the connection to Lang. Hawksworth had needed a "beard" to hide his relationship with the Chinese woman, and a job with Lang's company had provided it.

"So you worked for PATCOA here."

"Yes." Kim Chee nodded again. "Until they were bought out in the early 1950s."

"Did Hawksworth buy this house for you?" asked Dane.

"Not directly. It was owned by the company. It was deeded over to me in lieu of a pension."

"You still saw the general?"

"Rarely." The woman smiled. "By then the bloom had gone off the flower, you might say. He had other interests by then. A number of them, from what I understand."

Dane was silent for a moment as he tried to put the pieces together. Hawksworth had shunted aside his shopworn dalliance as his career developed. A Chinese mistress had no place in the long-term plans of a rising star. Believable enough, but if that was true, why had he gone to such lengths to ensure her security? Blackmail? He glanced at the woman on the other side of the table. It didn't seem likely.

"When did you last see General Hawksworth?" he asked finally.

"In 1968," Kim Chee responded promptly. "July." Almost twenty-five years ago.

"Was there any particular reason for the meeting?" Dane asked. In 1968 Hawksworth had been head of the 7612 Air Intelligence Group out of Yokota Air Base in Japan and Tan Son Nhut in Saigon.

"No," she answered, looking down at her cup. "Just a friendly visit. He was on his way to Washington." She was lying. But why? Dane pushed back from the table.

"I think that just about covers it," he said, standing. Kim Chee Leung followed suit. "You've been very cooperative."

"What are all these questions for?" she asked bluntly.

"Just background, Mrs. Leung," Dane responded lightly. He knew she didn't believe him. "We're preparing General Hawksworth's official obituary for the files. We like to have as much information as possible."

"And will I be part of that official document?" she asked.

"I very much doubt that," he answered truthfully. Kim Chee Leung was an object lesson in the need for curators. Dane knew that every evidence of her part in the murdered man's life would be carefully sponged out of the records by Cordasco and his people.

Beyond that he knew that the woman would be put on a "watch list" by DIA for the rest of her own life, and perhaps for years afterward. Her existence, especially considering the connection to the Soongs and Chiang Kai-shek, was a potential string of firecrackers that could be dropped down a presidential gum boot at any time. Even if he logged her as a "no threat" to Cordasco, Senator Lang would be onto the DIA man like a dirty shirt.

Dane followed the woman as she led him back down the hallway to the front door. There was a row of simply framed photographs over the telephone table, and he paused briefly to examine them. One in particular caught his eye.

The picture had obviously been taken in front of the house he was standing in, at the foot of the steps outside. The foliage to the left was thinner, the giant hyacinth bush considerably smaller than it was now. In the photograph Kim Chee Leung, dressed in slacks and a light-colored blouse, was standing with her hand protectively placed on a young boy's shoulder. He was dressed in high-top running shoes, short pants with suspenders, and a white short-sleeved shirt. One his head he was wearing a Davy Crockett coonskin cap, complete with raccoon tail dangling over his neck, and a pair of child's sunglasses. He appeared to be eight or nine years old. The Disney series starring Fess Parker had been popular during the mid-fifties, which put a rough time frame on the picture.

"My nephew, David," said Kim Chee, turning back to stand with Dane.

"I had a hat just like that," he said. "And the lunch box that went along with it."

"He wore it everywhere," Kim Chee said. "He liked it because his name was David too. He insisted that everyone call him Davy."

"A long time ago," Dane said.

"Yes, a very long time," Kim Chee answered. She took Dane to the door and let him out. He stood on the porch for a moment, looking at her through the screen again.

"Thank you again, Mrs. Leung."

"You're welcome, Mr. Dane." And then the door closed.

He went back down the steps, pausing at the place where the picture had been taken. He reached into the pocket of his jacket and switched off the recorder. He crossed the street and climbed into the rental car. Dane was reasonably sure he'd heard her correctly, but he'd check the tape later, just to make sure:

"I was very young. I had no family. I barely spoke any English, and I was without documentation."

A nephew needed an aunt or an uncle, and that meant a brother or a sister for Kim Chee Leung, who'd said that she had neither. So who was the boy in the coonskin cap?

He started the car and drove down the hill, back to the city, humming under his breath:

"Davy, Davy Crockett, king of the Wild Frontier."

CHAPTER 17

THE HARBOR VILLAGE Restaurant is located on the upper galleria floor of No. 4 Embarcadero Center in San Francisco's financial district. The restaurant's interior, including teak and rosewood paneling, crystal chandeliers, etched-glass panels, and thick carpeting, was shipped from Hong Kong in three gigantic containers. There is a rumor among the Embarcadero Center management staff that the stunningly beautiful hostesses in their slinky cocktail dresses had been shipped in the containers as well. The Harbor Village is the perfect expression of upscale Hong Kong money, and there is not a red dragon wall plaque or a fish tank full of carp to be seen.

The restaurant offers two views, one of the prettily lit Ferry Building and the Bay beyond, the other of the striking glass-and-steel architecture of the Hyatt Regency Hotel at No. 5 Embarcadero on the other side of Sacramento Street. The two addresses are connected by an underground plaza of stores, fast-food outlets, and boutiques.

Samson Kee had planned the dinner well, situating his father-in-law's table in the center of the large room, his back protected by a high, angled wood-and-glass divider topped by a mass of artificial plants. The table offered a pleasant view of the Ferry Building, but was well away from the floor-to-ceiling slabs of glass that formed the Bayside wall of the restaurant.

The main table was reserved for actual members of

119

the Chang lineage and their immediate families, seating
for the other guests, almost seventy of them, ranged in
a broad fan shape that gave James Chang a full view of
everyone.

The *Shan Chu* of Black Dragon was tired from his
long trip and would have much preferred the peace and
quiet of Samson Kee's Seacliff mansion overlooking
the Presidio, but he knew the dinner was an absolute
necessity. After the murder of Hawksworth and the hijacking of the Vancouver shipment, it was clear that
Black Dragon was under attack, and to show weakness
at this point would be fatal.

Ignoring the pleasant chatter of his daughter and his
grandchildren all around him, he looked out over the
low-lit room to Son Wei Kuo's table. Big-Eared Son
was in his eighties, a gnarled walnut of a man, his
large, bald head splattered with liverish age spots,
rheumy eyes set impossibly deep in dark-rimmed sockets. Beside him was Benny Kong, his Red Pole, moon-
faced and dressed like a bookkeeper. Benny's working
name was *Chuan-Tsao,* the Screwdriver, his tool of
choice.

Big-Eared Son was the unofficial mayor of San
Francisco's Chinatown and *Shan Chu* of the Suey Sing,
one of the largest and most powerful tongs in California, with branches all over the United States. The Suey
Sings and Black Dragon had coexisted for years without any trouble, but the relationship was a fragile one,
based mostly on the fact that their interests rarely coin-
cided. Big Ear distributed drugs for Black Dragon on a
wholesale basis in the western United States but had
never shown any interest in actively engaging in its im-
portation. The old man had ruled the tong for more than
half a century and had long since defined his territory.
As long as Chang and Son stayed at arm's length, there
would be no problem.

Julian Yao, five tables to the right, was cut from different cloth. Yao, in his mid-fifties, was dressed in a

tailor-made silk suit, wore monogrammed shirts, and had voracious sexual appetites that were legendary on both sides of the Pacific. He had a weakness for young white women, usually blondes like the one seated next to him.

James Chang could feel the muscles in his jaw tense and let out a quiet breath to ease his anger. Yao's slut was the only *gwei-lo* in the room, and her presence was an affront. It was also a message. Julian Yao was aware that Black Dragon was undeniably the most powerful of the international triads, but by bringing the woman, he was demonstrating his lack of respect for Chang's position.

Yao was Hong Kong Chinese and had inherited his own position as *Shan Chu* of the Hip Sing Triad when his father had died peacefully two years before.

The Hip Sings had been a major influence in San Francisco and Los Angeles since the early 1900s, but under Yao's leadership the organization had been expanding internationally. They were also gaining a reputation for extreme violence using their association with the Wah Ching gang and the outlaw Vietnamese groups in South Orange County. Until he was given better information by Abbot Fong, Yao and the Hip Sings were Chang's most likely suspects for the Vancouver hijacking.

There were several other people at Yao's table in addition to the white woman, but the only one Chang recognized was Tu Sheng, the Hip Sing counterpart of Screwdriver Kong. Unlike Kong, Tu Sheng fit the part of Red Pole perfectly. Taller than Samson Kee, Tu Sheng was a hulking figure, his bullet head balanced on a thick sinewy neck, the muscles of his shoulders and chest obscenely large, pushing the fabric of his cheap suit out of shape. A throwback to the days of meat-cleaver tong wars at New York's Five Corners. Chang smiled, thin-lipped. The brutal-looking creature reminded him of Odd-job in the James Bond movie; the only thing missing was a bowler hat. Chang shook his head; Yao's choice of Red Pole was an indication of the Hip Sing leader's melodramatics and lack of taste.

"Father?" It was Victoria, seated on his left. Chang blinked, pulled from his reverie back to the noisy reality of the table.

"I'm sorry," he said quietly. "An old man's mind tends to wander."

"You're not old, Father." Victoria smiled. She was dressed in a dark green dress that set off the pale, perfect texture of her skin. Of his two daughters Victoria was most like her mother, Shen-Li, dead now so many years. The memory laid truth over her gentle lie. He was old—much closer to the withered figure of Big-Eared Son than the sleek middle age of Julian Yao. His time was passing.

"Your flattery is a kindness, daughter, if a misplaced one," Chang said. "I'm afraid that mirrors are without compassion."

"So are wristwatches," Victoria answered, lifting her hand to show him her slim Patek Philippe. "You asked me to remind you when it was nine-thirty."

"Yes." He nodded. "I have a small business matter that must be attended to, then I shall return."

"And find us gone, I'm afraid," said Victoria. She placed her hand on the drooping head of the child seated to her right—Andrea, youngest of her three children. "I have to get the little ones home to bed."

"All right." Chang nodded. "I'll see you there later."

"I think Samson wants to talk to you," said Victoria, nodding across the table at her husband.

"Toby has some questions about the bank," explained Samson Kee, poking with his chopsticks at something on his plate. "We'll wait for you to return, *Shan Chu.*"

Chang nodded again and rose to his feet. Tobias Woo was director of the San Francisco branch of Limehouse Trading's bank, First Pacific Orient. The bank was a key element in laundering illicit funds from the *Hui*'s offshore enterprises.

As Chang stood up, Samson Kee made a small gesture, and two young men from a nearby table stood as well. The two men were brothers, Terry and Norman Kwok, Black Dragon 49s normally employed as runners for the *Hui*'s gambling interests in the *Tangrenbu* district. The Kwok brothers were cousins to Samson Kee, born and raised in San Francisco. They were both armed with Belgian machine pistols carried on slings under their jackets, two of the half-dozen weapons Kee had allowed into the restaurant.

The Kwoks made small, deferential bows to their *Shan Chu*, joining him as he headed out of the Harbor Village, one in front and one behind. Most of the stores in the complex were closed and shuttered, and the five-minute walk to the lower level of the Hyatt Regency was uneventful.

Still accompanied by his bodyguards, Chang rode up to the seventeenth floor, then announced himself as "Mr. Sung" at the concierge's desk. The seventeenth floor, and the levels directly above and below, made up the fifty-four rooms of the hotel's elite Regency Club, a private enclave for wealthy guests. The trio of floors was a hotel within a hotel, complete with its own kitchens, bar, lounge, and game room.

"I would like to see Mr. Lee," Chang said quietly. "I believe he's in room 1740."

"One of our corner suites." The uniformed attendant nodded. "Just a moment." The man tapped at a discreet phone unit on the desk and spoke briefly into the receiver. A few seconds later he hung up the telephone and smiled at Chang again, extending one hand to the left. "Just at the end of the hall," he directed.

"My colleagues will remain here," Chang answered, gesturing to the Kwok brothers. The concierge looked at the two men, slightly surprised, but recovered swiftly.

"Certainly, Mr. Sung. I'll just get the gentlemen some chairs."

"That won't be necessary," Chang instructed. "They will stand."

"As you wish," said the concierge.

"Yes," said Chang. He turned away and went down the broad, well-lit corridor, leaving the Kwoks and the concierge behind. Reaching the slightly recessed door of 1740, he knocked once. The door opened instantly.

"Abbot," said Chang, bowing.

"*Shan Chu,*" Abbot Fong replied, returning the gesture, then standing aside. Fong was down to his shirtsleeves and had no tie. His reading glasses were halfway down his nose. Fong never stopped working, but it was never completely clear if he was working for himself or others. Chang smiled as he walked down the short entrance hall to the suite's living room.

Abbot Fong was perfectly capable of working for himself and the *Hui* simultaneously, to the mutual benefit of each, all of which could be explained by the man with any number of spreadsheets. Always spreadsheets. If Abbot sold his soul to the devil, he'd get it back with a spreadsheet.

The living room was expensively, if blandly, decorated in varying shades of gray. A floor-to-ceiling window looked out over the Ferry Building, its outline picked out with hundreds of tiny lights. A few cars whisked back and forth on the Embarcadero Freeway, standing between the Ferry Building and the hotel.

He'd first seen the terminal at the Port of San Francisco half a century ago. No boutiques or lobster restaurants had lined the port's hundred wharfs then. The Bay was thick with moored freighters waiting to unload, the fishing fleet bustled back and forth, and here and there you could see the tall masts of sailing ships still working the cargo trade up and down the coast.

Chang pulled the curtains closed over the scene below and sat down on a deeply upholstered chair. In front of him the coffee table was a litter of papers, with

Fong's beloved portable computer as a centerpiece. A tray held the remains of Fong's dinner—steak and a baked potato.

"Hardly fit for a celestial gentleman such as yourself, Abbot," Chang commented, gesturing at the tray. "I should have brought something for you from the dinner."

"Chinese food must be cooked by someone who knows what he is doing," Fong replied, dropping down onto the couch opposite Chang. "When I am away from home, I rarely eat it because I do not trust it."

"A prudent philosophy." Chang smiled.

"Quite so, *Shan Chu.*" Fong cleared his throat and glanced down at the papers in front of him.

"I suppose you want to get down to business," said Chang.

"There is much to talk about." Fong shrugged. Chang took out his cigarettes and lit one.

"The Vancouver incident?" he prompted.

"Yes." Fong nodded. "I spoke with Marvin Lok yesterday." Lok was the Black Dragon Straw Sandal in Vancouver, supposedly a local restaurant owner but actually in charge of the *Hui*'s West Coast Canadian affairs. As it was with most of the *Hui*'s "officer class," Lok was part of the Chang lineage, related through marriage to Danny Han in New York.

"How is Marvin?" Chang asked.

"Frightened," answered Fong.

"He has no reason to be frightened if he acted in good faith." Chang shrugged.

"There is no question of his loyalty," said Fong. "But he was responsible for setting up the Canadian part of the procedure, and that is the part which failed. It is a matter of poor judgment on his part—or so he thinks."

"Is that the case?"

"Perhaps," said Fong. "He put the Vietnamese in place. I wondered about that at the time . . . as you know."

"And I approved it," said Chang. "The responsibility is mine, not yours or Marvin Lok's."

"Still . . ." Fong let it dangle.

"You can tell Marvin that I hold him blameless," Chang said. "It was my decision."

"There is more to it than that, *Shan Chu,*" Fong said quietly. "Another element."

"Yes?"

"Sheng Ling," said Abbot Fong. "Does that mean anything to you?" Chang frowned. Even in Cantonese the term was obscure.

"Spirit of Holiness?" For an accurate translation he would have to see the actual characters written out.

"Holy Ghost," said Fong. "More specifically the Protestant missionary version rather than the Roman Catholic."

"What is the connection?"

"A rumor," Fong replied. "A secret, very small organization, never drawing attention to itself. One of Lok's contacts in the Vancouver Police Department mentioned it."

"Do they run anything in the city?" Chang asked. It seemed unlikely. The senior triads in Vancouver were 14K and Green Bamboo. Black Dragon had worked with both for years without any major problems. The city was far too important for *all* the triads for any one to prejudice for short-term gains.

"No," said Fong, shaking his head. "I spoke with Tam of the Fourteen K and Wah Heung at Green Bamboo . . . only rumors."

"Exactly what sort of rumors?"

"The story is that Holy Ghost is financed by *Ching Fang.* The Black House." The euphemistic name for Communist China's Secret Service. Chang extinguished his cigarette and sat back in his chair.

"This changes things," he said.

"If the rumors are true," Fong agreed.

Chang's goal was to create an association of various

organized-crime syndicates stretching from Europe to Southeast Asia and across the Pacific to North America. The shipboard meeting in Hawaii was the first step in the creation of that association. On the surface it was simply a question of economics; if the separate groups could be brought together, everyone would profit by coordinating their efforts. On another level, though, it was a distinctly political act. Fong's spreadsheet analysis was absolute—such an association would create an entity with a financial base of $500–$700 billion per year, more than the combined profits of all the Fortune 500 companies. "The Coca-Cola Corporation of Crime," as Fong had once jovially described it. Such an entity was clearly a threat to the government of any country not enjoying the benefits of participating in its activities. Virtually the only major country fitting that description was Communist China.

"It makes sense," murmured Chang. "The murder of Hawksworth was far too sophisticated for anyone here."

"It had no other purpose than being a signal," Fong agreed. "And the use of the *Hui*'s name in both Washington and Vancouver links the two events. It was meant to."

"But why us?" Chang asked. "Fourteen K is more powerful in Hong Kong and in Europe, and Green Bamboo has direct connections with Taiwan and what's left of Chiang's people. We've never had any direct political connections."

"Except for Hawksworth," said Fong.

"Few knew about that," said Chang, shaking his head. "And he served his real purpose long ago."

"If you don't mind me saying so, *Shan Chu*, I think you're underestimating his importance," said Fong. "Hawksworth was a decorated hero and about to be made head of Defense Intelligence. He was directly linked to the President's Office on Drug Abuse with a mandate to increase military participation in the prosecution of narcotics offenses. Noriega and the Panama incursion was the opening move in that game, as you are aware."

"No," said Chang firmly. He lit another cigarette. "We're missing something, Abbot. If the Black House is involved in this, then why didn't they wait until Hawksworth had been confirmed as head of DIA? His murder and his association with us would have had far more impact that way. In fact, why not just leave him alive and leak the information? In terms of propaganda, Hawksworth squirming on a televised Senate debate would have been much more useful."

"And potentially disastrous for us," said Fong. "You're right." He ran a hand across his brow. "What is it that we're not seeing?"

"Is Hawksworth still being investigated?" Chang asked after a moment. Fong nodded.

"Yes," he said. "Lang has been interviewed, and what they call a 'curator' is now in place. A man named Phillip Dane."

"Where is he?" Chang asked.

"Here by now. In San Francisco."

"Will he find out anything?"

"It's possible." Fong shrugged. "He knows about Kim Chee Leung. We have our people watching."

"What do we know about this 'curator'?"

"Military background. He worked for MACV in Saigon. Intelligence. Joined Defense Intelligence after that. A lobbyist in Washington for a time. He operates an antiquarian bookstore in Georgetown now."

"Why him?" asked Chang.

"He has a reputation for discretion," said Fong. "And he's been away from Defense long enough not to be tied to any particular faction."

"I need to know more," said Chang.

"About Dane?" asked Fong. Chang nodded.

"Yes," he said. "And about *Sheng Ling* . . . this Holy Ghost."

CHAPTER 18

JIMMY CHANG HATED Bangkok. He hated its over-crowded streets, he hated its filthy pall of smog, he hated the pervasive odor of rot that seemed to seep even into your clothes, and he hated the garbage-choked open sewers of its *khlongs,* the canals that threaded through the city like liquid alleyways. Most of all he hated the fact that he had to do business there.

At three o'clock in the morning, standing in a ground-floor warehouse on a backstreet off Boriphat Road, he could in no way convince himself that he was anything other than yet another "chink" preying on the frailties of his neighbors. The fact that he represented one of the most powerful criminal organizations in the world was irrelevant. No matter how you cut it, he was a drug dealer, not a businessman. That worked on Naloa, or in his Honolulu office, but not here, with the stink of Bangkok in his nostrils.

Jimmy Chang, at thirty-six, was James Chang's youngest child and only male heir. In many ways he was a younger version of his father—lean, physically fit, and narrow-faced, and carrying the same shameful blue-eyed hallmark of the Chang Chin-Kangs. On occasions such as this, when he was away from home, Jimmy Chang had adopted the practice of wearing dark-tinted contacts to hide his "deformity." He also used a host of aliases, each with its own documentation. Tonight he was Howard Ting, the same name as the one he was using at the Hotel Mandarin on Rama IV Road and that appeared on his Hong Kong passport.

Jimmy Chang looked around the dimly lit chamber, checking his preparations once again. The warehouse was empty, but the air was filled with tiny particles of the milled-rice flour it normally contained. The floor was concrete, raised on metal-clad stilts to keep out rats and river rot, while the walls and ceiling were made of corrugated sheet metal.

There were three other people in the thirty-by-forty warehouse, young members of the Red Fan gang from Sampeng Road. They were uniformly dressed in jeans and T-shirts, and each wore a twisted blood-red bandanna around his forehead. They were armed with war-surplus Sterling submachine guns and had spent the last two hours exchanging fierce glances and smoking cigarettes. Chang wasn't really worried about violence, but the trio of guards was a necessary window dressing.

He sneezed, then pulled a linen handkerchief out of his suit-jacket pocket. The rice dust was everywhere. Skirting the old Volkswagen van and the skid holding the big flatbed scales he'd brought to the warehouse, Chang walked to the open loading doors and looked out over the narrow conduit of Khlong Bang Lam. He could smell putrid flesh, rotting vegetation, and fish, but there was no sound of an approaching outboard.

Tonight's delivery was coming from the waterside and would arrive aboard one of the bargelike sampans that plied the *khlong* network of the city day and night. Black Dragon's representatives in Bangkok regularly paid off the appropriate people in the Narcotics Suppression Office, but once in a while you ran into incorruptibles like the infamous Colonel Juttimita, so it didn't hurt to be discreet.

Jimmy Chang lit a cigarette and stared over the water. On the far side of the *khlong* he could make out the lights of the Pahurat Cloth Market and beyond to the Grand Palace. He let a trail of smoke dribble out onto the heavy, humid air. Like Hong Kong, Bangkok was a city of black and white. The poverty and squalor of the *khlongs* within sight of the Temple of the Emerald Buddha. A city built to house a thousand temples and populated with an army of five hundred thousand prostitutes, some available for as little as four American dollars.

The man cleared his throat and spit into the water. What did he care? Bangkok was a different world, a hell in fact, which he visited as rarely as possible. A recurring nightmare perhaps, but no more than that: a dream.

Chang heard the small puttering sound of an approaching outboard and peered into the darkness. Two hundred yards upriver a spindly wooden footbridge spanned the *khlong,* and from underneath it he could just make out the approaching darker shadow of a barge. He turned briefly and snapped his fingers. The three Red Fans doused their own cigarettes and straightened, weapons at the ready. One padded across to the streetside wooden door and waited, while the other two came to stand by the van and the weigh scale.

Jimmy Chang stepped back and flipped the switch on the scale's pedestal-mounted control console. A dozen zeroes lined up in glowing red on the digital display. Before bringing the removable chip insert to the warehouse, he'd calibrated it to account for the packaging weight. He took the rectangular insert plug from his jacket pocket and plugged it into the console, making sure that the pins were aligned correctly. He grinned to himself; the scale was really a marvel of modern technology. He went back to his position at the *khlong* side doorway and watched the barge approach.

Originally designed for the U.S. Atomic Regulatory Agency by an independent weights-and-measures lab in Houston, Texas, the scale was intended to give accurate readings of the weights of fissionable products created by American nuclear-weapons manufacturers, conform-

ing to the regulatory commission's requirements of ac-
countability. Using microchip technology, the scales
could assess weights down to an infinitesimal fraction
of an ounce.

A bright young entrepreneur connected to the drug
trade in Florida, who happened to have a degree in
electronic engineering from CalTech, saw another ap-
plication for the device and knocked off a version of his
own that was now standard in the industry. Each unit
like the one in the Bangkok warehouse cost almost half
a million dollars and was capable of calculating the exact weight of currency based on the tiny differences between denominations. Once set to "see" money rather
than plutonium pellets, it worked as a wonderfully accurate bulk-counting machine.

The barge slid out from under the bridge and cut its
small engine, coasting forward through the dark water.
When it was fifty feet away, Chang called out the pass-
word for the night and was given the proper response.
He turned to the Red Fan beside the van and gestured.

"Hsing Tung," he instructed. The teenager nodded
and slung the Sterling across his shoulder. He crossed
to the door and went down the steep flight of wooden
steps leading to the minuscule loading wharf. A half-
naked figure on the barge threw the boy a rope, and the
barge was made fast. Chang could see at least half a
dozen loinclothed men on the barge, surrounding the
tarpaulin-shrouded shape of its cargo. Several of the
men began stripping away the tarp as another man appeared, this one dressed in the uniform of a major in
the Thai Provincial Police. The major stepped off the
barge carefully and climbed the flight of steps. Behind
him, the men in loincloths began unloading neatly taped
two-cubic-foot cardboard boxes, each bearing the distinctive logo of a well-known American moving-and-
storage company. The company had no connection with
the drug trade, but the boxes were useful because of
their uniform size and weight. Each one was capable of

holding exactly $84 million in U.S. twenty-dollar bills, or $2.62 million in ten-dollar bills. As previously arranged, that night's shipment was all twenties. There were ninety-two boxes on the barge: $368 million.

The major, dapper in his uniform complete with ascot in royal blue silk, reached the top of the stairs and *"wai*ed" Chang, hands pressed together, bowing slightly. Chang returned the gesture.

"Sawadee khrap, Major Chakri," said Chang politely.

"Kawpkun," replied the major. *"Sabai dai ru?"*

"Well enough," answered Chang, speaking English, their language in common.

"Good," said Chakri. "Enjoying your stay in Bangkok?"

"As always," Chang said dryly. Both men stood aside as the workers began bringing up the boxes and loading them onto the meter-square bed of the scale.

"This becomes more cumbersome with the passing of each season," commented Chakri, pointing his rounded chin at the scale.

"Success has its burdens." Chang shrugged. The money being loaded on the scale was the result of transactions between Chakri's associates in the northern border states and other major Heroin dealers operating in Southeast Asia, not Black Dragon. Since Chakri was involved, the money was probably from Green Bamboo, or one of the local Thai organizations still foolish enough to operate directly into Europe via the old, long-established Mediterranean channels—the so-called French Connection.

Chang took a small notebook out of his pocket and began logging in the numbers as they skittered upward on the digital readout. So far everything was as it should be. The process went on in silence, broken only by the heavy breathing of the workers and the creaking of the stairs leading down to the water. Within fifteen minutes the transaction was complete. The workers returned to the barge, and Chang's Red Fans began loading the boxes into the Volkswagen van.

"Dee maak?" asked Chakri. Chang nodded and put away the notebook.

"Dee maak, Major." He nodded. "Just as we agreed."

"Good." Chakri offered another *wai,* which Chang ignored. He went to the passenger compartment of the van and spun the dials on the combination locks of his briefcase. He took out an envelope and returned to where Chakri was standing by the river doors. The Thai opened the envelope and examined the sheaf of small rice-paper notes. Each slip of paper bore the handprinted figure of a dragon in black ink. Except for the pictogram the paper was blank.

Chakri counted them carefully. There were ninety-two, each one worth $4 million.

"Sabai dai kawpkun, Mr. Ting."

"Kawpkun, Major. Until next time."

Chakri tucked the notes back into the envelope, placed the envelope carefully into his uniform blouse, and made yet another *wai.* Chang nodded, and Chakri went down the steps and into the waiting barge. One of his men cast off the line, hopped into the stern of the sampan, then started the outboard engine. Within less than a minute the boat had vanished into the darkness.

Only then did Jimmy Chang fully relax. For all his politeness Major Chakri was a Shan from the North, and thus utterly unpredictable. For a man such as Chakri, loyalty was assessed in dollars, and betrayal was a way of life.

Chang rolled the river door closed and threw the bolt that locked it. He snapped his fingers again, and the man standing guard at the street door pulled it open. The two other Red Fans climbed into the VW, started the engine, and drove slowly out of the warehouse, picking up the third Red Fan on the way out. Chang followed them, stepped outside, and pulled the metal door closed, then sealed it with an impressive brass padlock that was as much for show as Chang's Red Fan boys. No one in his right mind would break into a building with the bright red triangular symbol above its door.

The young Chinese man lit another cigarette and tried not to breathe too deeply. It was very late, but his body was still on Honolulu time, and the meeting with Chakri, uneventful or not, had left him feeling pumped with adrenaline. He thought briefly about going to one of the lush, ultramodern massage parlors on the Patpong, but dropped the idea quickly. Bangkok was fast becoming the AIDS capital of the world, and the last time in Bangkok he'd wound up with a *gatoei* transvestite and didn't realize his mistake until it was far too late.

Trying to suppress that particular memory, Chang crossed the narrow packed-earth street and unlocked the driver's side door of his rental Renault 5. He rolled down his window, wishing he'd asked Hertz for a car with air-conditioning, took a last drag, then flipped his cigarette butt out onto the street. He started the engine and did a U-turn, heading south toward the Chao Phraya River.

He'd do it just the way his old man would—methodically. Back at the hotel he'd hook up the Porta-Fax to the telephone in his hotel room and send a confirmation message off to the office in Honolulu. When that was done, he'd ring the man waiting for his call at the local Kwikchek office and tell him the cash was on its way. Only then would he make himself a drink. Or two.

Chang spit out the window, then jammed a hand into his jacket, looking for his cigarettes. Just like his old man, he thought coldly. Fucking business before pleasure—always. Scowling, still thinking about his father, Jimmy Chang reached the river, then turned east along the Songwat, heading for his hotel. None of it mattered, in less than twenty-four hours he'd be back at home again.

In San Francisco the *Shan Chu* of Black Dragon rose with the dawn, his sleep disturbed by dark dreams and premonitions of the future. The very fact that he'd even dreamed was the most disturbing; James Chang prided himself on his careful logic and had always avoided falling into the easy, superstitious habits of most elderly Chinese.

Even that avoidance was based on logic; to understand your enemy, you had to know how he thought— that was elemental, so Chang had always cultivated Western *gwei-lo* ways. Not for him the *feng shui* adviser or the herbalist; if he wanted to build a house, he called an architect; if he felt ill, he went to a doctor.

James Chang swung his legs out of bed and fitted his feet into the waiting pair of slippers set out for him by his daughter. Standing, he slipped on the dressing gown laid out across the foot of the bed, belting it around himself. Shivering slightly in the cool morning air, he gathered his cigarettes and lighter from the bedside table and left the guest room.

His daughter's Seacliff house, like many of its neighbors, was enormous, with far more rooms than the family could ever use. Spread out over three levels above China Beach, virtually every window on the ocean side offered a view of Golden Gate or the rocky cliffs of Lands End. Samson Kee had justified the building's out-of-scale proportions by insisting that it was as much a house belonging to the entire Chang family as it was his and Victoria's, but the *Shan Chu* knew that its size had more to do with Samson Kee's roots in the cramped housing of Hong Kong than it did with his sense of family.

Chang padded quietly down a series of seemingly endless broadloomed halls until he reached the curving, overly dramatic stairway leading down to the main level. Reaching the entrance foyer to the house, he went down another hall until he found the kitchen. He smiled softly as the rich smell of Kona coffee reached his nose. Victoria knew his habits and had set the automatic coffee maker to brew an early pot.

The kitchen was as out-of-scale as the rest of the house. In Kowloon it would have provided room for half a dozen people and their possessions. There were appliances everywhere, and the counters were covered in slabs of burnished slate and polished granite rather than Formica.

Chang poured himself a large mug of coffee and left it black. Few of his friends drank coffee at all, but he'd acquired the taste years ago, when he'd first lived in Hawaii, and he still enjoyed one strong cup in the morning and perhaps another during the day.

Picking up a dishtowel on his way out of the room, Chang opened the sliding glass doors leading out onto the deck and went outside. He wiped off the seat of a chair set before a round patio table and sat down, sighing with simple pleasure. He took a sip of coffee, lit a cigarette, and sat back to survey the broad expanse of ocean beyond the beach. The days ahead would be extremely busy, and there would be few opportunities for moments like this one.

Bad dreams. Snakes and dragons breathing fire, visions of his father on the dock at Hong Kong, putting him aboard the steamer bound for Rangoon and school. It was the last time he'd seen his father alive. His father had known that war was coming, of course—the school in Rangoon was simply an excuse to put him out of harm's way.

Images of his mother too, fainter than his father, impressions more than memories, like the faint scent of a flower dried between the pages of a book. The smell of death. The taste of metal. Empty sockets in the eyes of a temple god, slowly filling with blood. Chang took another sip of coffee and shook his head. Dreams like that would throw a Kowloon fortune-teller into fits of joy. He put them aside.

The dinner had gone well, even though his meeting with Abbot had posed more questions than it answered. Holy Ghost was a cipher to be investigated and dealt with before the meeting in Hawaii aboard the *Orient Star,* but for now it was nothing but a rumor.

His discussions with Toby Woo and Samson Kee later in the evening had far more relevance. By then, most of the guests had gone, including Julian Yao and Big-Eared Son. With the family table to themselves Woo had given his *Shan Chu* a detailed explanation of the Pacific Orient Bank's progress over the past four months.

The bank was really little more than a suite of offices in a building owned by Limehouse Trading on Bush Street in the Financial District and offered no ordinary banking services. There were no tellers or loan officers, only Tobias Woo and a platoon of computer traders and commodity analysts. What Pacific Orient really did was electronically move money from one place to another, filtering the transactions through more than a hundred corporations around the world. Other than the computer hardware and complex telephone and telex system, the bank's only real asset was its ownership of a company conceived of by Samson Kee—Kwikchek International Corporation.

For almost a hundred years the financial transactions of Chinese tongs and triads had been handled through a complicated banking system usually fronted by gold shops and manufacturing jewelers. Illicit funds would be exchanged for gold vouchers much like the notes Jimmy Chang had given to Major Chakri of the Thai police. These vouchers could be cashed in for bullion at any of a thousand shops in Hong Kong, Macao, Singapore, and throughout Southeast Asia. Eventually the gold would be sold again for cash in a legitimate transaction that would stand up to official scrutiny.

Following the war in Vietnam and the resulting enormous increase in the number of Heroin addicts in the United States, the volume of real cash involved in the drug trade grew dramatically, and the old system became unwieldy and inefficient. A host of money-laundering schemes evolved over the years, but the one devised by Samson Kee was remarkable for its simplicity, its efficiency, and the added bonus that the system itself made a profit on each transaction rather than moving the money at a discount.

To Samson Kee the idea of Kwikchek seemed obvious. Based on a number of different check-cashing businesses in the United States, Kwikchek, with 350 outlets in the United States and another 400 strategically placed around the world cashed people's checks for a small percentage of the face value. The checks, usually state or federal welfare, old-age pension, or unemployment insurance, were paid in cash by Kwikchek in "dirty" money, which was then put back into circulation by its completely innocent clientele. The checks were deposited to Kwikchek accounts, and that was that—the money had been cleaned and could then be used for perfectly legitimate purposes, moved around electronically by various branches of Pacific Orient Bank.

The system had worked flawlessly for the last five years without the slightest indication that any police or other official organization had any suspicions.

No one, it seemed, had noticed that almost every Kwikchek franchise was operated by ethnic Chinese. The few franchises not run directly by Black Dragon were not part of the money-laundering loop and operated without any knowledge of the *Hui*'s other activities.

There was only one problem with the Kwikchek operation—the idea had come from Samson Kee and not Jimmy. Within the organization both men were 438s—*Fu Chan Chu* within their operational spheres, supposedly with equal power. In reality every member of the *Hui,* from Abbot Fong down to the lowest *Sze Kau* footsoldier, knew that Jimmy Chang was heir to the position of Dragon Head by right of ancestry.

James Chang liked Samson Kee and trusted him, both as leader of the San Francisco *Hui* and as a son-in-law. The development of Kwikchek had also proved the man's worth on an international scale. But he was a member of the Chang lineage through marriage alone, and so far Victoria had given birth only to daughters.

Jimmy, his youthful arrogance and stubbornness aside, was married to Han Mu-Chen, binding the *Hui* even more strongly through her brother in New York, and had already borne him two grandsons in Hawaii. It was through Jimmy and his children that the Chang lineage would endure; it was a truth that could change only with the spilling of blood.

At first he had seen the competition between son and son-in-law as constructive as the two men vied to prove their worth to him, but over time and abetted by Victoria's own feelings about her brother, the relationship had soured. More and more James Chang found himself listening to his son's less-than-subtle comments about Kee, and Samson's feelings, though never openly expressed, were equally negative.

James Chang sighed and took another swallow of his cooling coffee, the sweet-tart taste reminding him of the family's estate on Naloa. The privately owned island, once a thriving ranch established by one of Hawaii's "five kings" was the only place in the world he really thought of as home as well as being a monument to his father and his father before him. It was also the seat of Limehouse Trading and Black Dragon operations throughout the Pacific, and Jimmy treated it like his personal preserve.

The morning fog was starting to burn away, and Chang could see the towers of the Golden Gate Bridge beginning to appear. In a few minutes the children would start to wake up, and his moment of peace would be over. He would spend the day with Victoria and his granddaughters, playing at being the doting *lao yeh* grandfather, buying them sweets and gifts while Victoria scolded him for spoiling them.

Chang felt his eyes sting with welling tears and cursed softly under his breath. He lit another cigarette and blinked, staring hard out over China Beach. Like everything else these days, the beach reminded him of the past. Once upon a time it had been home to impoverished Chinese fishermen, trying to eke out a living on the rocky shore.

The waves smashing in so thunderously at the western tip of the cove were breaking over rectangular paving stones dumped there after the 1906 earthquake, their shifting weight creating a dull, rumbling death-rattle clatter as they rolled down the sloping beach with the movement of the waves. Omens and portents, like his dreams. Muttered complaints, like the troubled members of his family.

Family. The Chinese salvation and its curse. In the West the family supported its individual members. In the East it was the reverse—yin-yang, the individual members responsible for the survival of the family. It was a concept that went back more than twenty-five centuries to the time of Confucius, and was totally misunderstood by the *gwei-lo* mind. The individual subjugated to the family's needs and will, protecting at all costs the pivot between past and future that an American sociologist had once dubbed the "Continuum of Descent."

For James Chang it was simply a way of life, the only one he had ever known. The family was a braided rope of infinite length, stretched from the distant past to the unseen future, its thicker strands the family groups, individual fibers being male members carrying the name. As long as one fiber remained, the rope existed. James Chang, Chang Chin-Kang, was that single fiber, and carried in his soul the personification of all his forbears and descendants yet unborn. He existed only because of his ancestors, and his descendants existed only through him.

James Chang wiped at his eyes angrily. This was a time for strength, not weakness. The Present, the Now, was a gleaming razor poised over him, capable of slicing through the frail rope at any moment. If that happened, the ends would fall away from the center, and the lineage would be no more. It would be as though it had never existed at all.

From behind him, inside the house, he could hear the bubbling laughter of his grandchildren and the rapidfire sound of his daughter as the day began. He gathered himself together with a long, shuddering breath and concentrated on the blue sky and the dark sea beyond the beach.

"Fool," he whispered to himself, and wiped his eyes again.

CHAPTER 19

Phillip Dane sat in an office of the sixteenth floor of the San Francisco Federal Building and waited. The office was long and narrow and looked out onto Golden Gate Avenue and the rear of the old State Building. It was lunchtime, and the street below was filled with the noon-hour crowd from the assorted buildings that surrounded Civic Center Plaza.

The office belonged to an assistant U.S. attorney named Benson Chin who headed up the Asian Crime Task Force in San Francisco, a shoebox-sized department within the Department of Justice. The room was crammed with filing cabinets, odds and ends of ancient government-issue furniture, wire baskets overflowing with documents, and a lone fan on the windowsill that moved the still air in the room and fluttered the loose corners of the maps pinned up on the wall.

Chin's office was the end of a bureaucratic quest Dane had begun several hours before at the Immigration and Naturalization Office ten floors down. All he had to go on was the name David, and a hunch. It had led him here.

Using his cover story about a Defense Investigative Services records search, he'd asked to see the file on Kim Chee Leung. A bored clerk had offered him a two-inch-thick dossier crammed into an old-fashioned expanding file. The dossier contained a variety of forms and memoranda stretching back to Kim Chee's arrival in the United States in 1942 and included her naturalization papers, dated 1954. It also contained a birth certificate issued by the administration office of Honolulu's St. Mary's Hospital registering the birth of a male child born to one Leung Kim Chee, O.O.W.—Out of Wedlock. Attached to the birth certificate with a rusting paper clip was the faded carbon of a receipt. The bill for medical services provided to Kim Chee had been paid in cash. The birth certificate listed no name for the child and no name for the putative father.

Following up on this information and assuming the obvious, Dane had made the rounds of the State Building on the other side of Golden Gate Avenue, searching for any information about a child named David Leung who might have arrived in California in 1949, the year of his birth, and the year Kim Chee had moved into her house in the Castro district. After an hour and a half he came up with a Social Security number and a driver's license number issued in 1965.

The Social Security number rang bells when Dane asked it to be run through the central computer, and a notation showed two "tags" on David Leung's record. One indicated an interest by the Selective Service Administration and a local draft board in San Francisco, while the other showed that a juvenile criminal file was in existence, although sealed.

After a little more digging, Dane discovered that David Leung had been arrested for drunk driving several times in 1965 and 1966, and that he'd been drafted into the United States Army on August 22, 1968. According to Selective Service, the nineteen-year-old Leung had never showed up for his induction. A federal warrant had been issued for his arrest on September 17, 1968, but had never been exercised. There was no record of a later request for amnesty. The only other notation was a file number from the U.S. Attorney's Office, which had taken him to Benson Chin's office and the listless fan on the windowsill.

Chin reappeared in the doorway to his office, carrying a slim file folder under his arm and packing down a bent briar pipe. Chin was in his thirties, partially bald, round-faced, pot-bellied, and wearing a wrinkled pinstripe suit. The tails of his white shirt hung out over his trousers, and his overwide tie was askew. Benson Chin was a cheerful-looking slob.

Jamming the pipe into his mouth, he crossed the office, went behind his desk, and dropped down into a metal-and-vinyl swivel chair. He plopped his feet up on the desk and lit his pipe with a Zippo lighter, keeping the file folder in his lap.

"You really expect me to buy this shit about a DIS employment-application search?" he asked, grinning broadly. His pipe made gurgling, sucking noises as he drew on it. Clouds of smoke appeared and were wafted in Dane's direction by the fan. Dane smiled back.

"Believe what you want," he answered. "I'm just doing my job. Same as you."

"Right. Toilers in the federal fields together," snorted Chin.

"Buddies," Dane agreed.

"Bull," said Chin pleasantly. He flipped his lighter onto the paper-strewn desk and snapped open the file in his lap. "As far as the record goes, David Leung was a draft-dodger who dropped off the face of the earth in 1968. You're trying to tell me he's applying for a Defense job twenty-five years later?"

"I'm not trying to tell you anything, Mr. Chin. I'm just asking a few questions."

"I'll bet you're wondering why we've got any paper on him at all," said Chin. He blinked in Dane's direction. Chin might be a slob, but he wasn't a fool.

"The thought had occurred to me." Dane shrugged. "But basically I'm following any lead at all."

"More bullshit." Chin smiled agreeably. "But who am I to argue? I couldn't care less, actually."

"Just curious," Dane said.

"Something like that."

"About David Leung," Dane prompted. Trading quips with Chin was fun, but it was going to wear thin any minute.

"Think again," the lawyer answered. "When is a Leung not a Leung?"

"Explain."

"David Leung was a draft-dodger in 1968, living in San Francisco with a federal warrant out on him. Those were the days of Haight-Ashbury. A few bits and pieces take him along the Underground Railroad to Blaine, Washington, and then into the bush around Abbotsford, British Columbia. Poof! He's gone."

"He went to Canada?"

"Either that or Sweden, which I doubt," said Chin. "But that's not the end of the story."

"Not quite. He pops up again about a year and a half later, back in San Francisco, back in the Haight. Except this time he's not running from Vietnam, he's dealing dope. Or buying it, really. Chemicals mostly. Acid, mescaline, DMT, MDA, the whole alphabet."

"So why wasn't he arrested on the draft charge?" Dane asked.

"We didn't make the connection. Two different people. David Leung had turned into Dave Long, complete with Canadian I.D. The Canucks were doing good work back then. The dodgers and the deserters were given some very high quality documents. All history now, of course."

"I'm surprised he got away with it," Dane said after a moment. "If the FBI had him under surveillance, you'd think the penny would drop eventually. They had photo files as long as your arm back then. There couldn't have been that many Oriental draft-dodgers, or hippie dope dealers, for that matter."

"Ah so," smirked Chin. "You round-eyes think we all look alike. Big mistake." He dropped his feet off the desk, sat forward, and handed the file across to Dane. There were two pictures clipped to the top page. One was a photocopy of a California driver's license, the other was a grainy reproduction showing a young, long haired man coming down the front steps of a house. Neither one of the pictures showed a Chinese.

The face in the photographs was that of a clean-shaven youth with high cheekbones and a large, distinctive nose. The eyes were definitely Western. It dawned on Dane that the picture he'd seen in Kim Chee Leung's house had shown her "nephew" wearing sunglasses. He'd simply assumed the boy was fully Chinese.

"I'll be damned," he said quietly, staring down at the photographs. A long way from the child in the Davy Crockett cap.

"Looks like there was a bit of white bread in the woodpile, so to speak." Chin laughed. Dane nodded as the pieces fit together. David Leung, also known as Dave Long, Kim Chee Leung's child, born in Hawaii and raised in San Francisco, was General William Sloane Hawksworth's son.

"Presumably it didn't end back there in the sixties," Dane said, turning the pages slowly. "Or this file would have been buried in the archives long ago."

"You're right." Chin nodded. "Read through it. . . . As David Long he's been in and out of San Francisco and L.A. for years, always on the fringes of things. He'd show up as a name on someone else's record, and his file would get updated. I came across him by accident. There's a guy named Dennis Long who works as a 49 for the Hip Sings. A couple of years ago I was putting together a report and asked for his jacket. Someone down in records gave me that file in your hands instead."

"Any current information on him?" Dane asked. The last entry in the dossier was three years old and merely noted that David Long had passed through Oakland Airport on his way to Hawaii. Normal enough procedure by customs when it came to a man with a known drug background.

"Not a thing." Chin shrugged. "He's either retired or running on a very fast track."

"And you don't think he's retired," Dane commented.

"Guys like him retire with a small-caliber hole in their foreheads." The lawyer grimaced. "They're not big on pensions."

"You think his home base is still in Canada?"

"Probably," Chin answered. "Vancouver's nice and pretty much wide open. He's probably staked out a patch for himself and runs it with connections down here. Dope, money laundering, who the hell knows."

"So he comes and goes as he pleases?"

"Pretty much," said Chin. "We can't arrest him on the draft charge—the laws have changed, and there's nothing else but suspicion. Shit, we'd have to spend six months, just trying to prove that Dave Long is actually David Leung. There's no point; the son of a bitch has managed to slip through the bureaucratic cracks in the justice system. Go figure. The IRS nails Willie Nelson, and this guy gets a pass."

"You seem pretty blasé about it," Dane commented. He handed the file across the desk to Chin. The lawyer raised one hand and made a seesaw gesture.

"You have to take it all with a grain of salt, Mr. Dane," he said. "I'm one guy in an office in San Francisco. We've got maybe thirty or forty more like me spread out across the country. Match that with over a million Chinese living in the United States, half a million living in Canada, and another fifteen million living in other countries outside of Hong Kong and Taiwan. We figure there's around fifty to seventy million dollars a *day* coming into San Francisco alone. When you get right down to it, I'm nothing but an observer, Mr. Dane." Chin smiled. "The really interesting question to ask is just what *you* are. More than an observer, I'll bet."

"I'm not a spook," Dane answered. He stood up and held out a hand to Chin. "If that's what you're getting at." Chin stood up himself and shook the offered hand. "You've been a big help," Dane added.

"Not too big a help, I hope." The lawyer grinned. He came around the desk and walked Dane to the door of his office. "Heaven forbid that I be too cooperative. It might ruin the department's image."

"Have no fear," Dane answered. "The secret of your efficiency is safe with me."

"*Au revoir,* Mr. Dane, good hunting," said Chin.

Dane smiled, waved a farewell hand, and left the office. Four hours later, back in his hotel room, Dane was making notes for his preliminary report to Cordasco back in Washington. The television was on, tuned to KPIX, the CBS channel.

He watched, transfixed and horrified, as the newscaster calmly read a story about an early-morning fire in the Castro district. The home of an elderly Chinese woman named Kim Chee Leung had burned to the ground shortly after 5:00 A.M. The cause was thought to be a gas explosion in the kitchen of the house. Mrs. Leung, a longtime resident of the neighborhood, had been alone in the house at the time. There was videotape of the smoldering ruins and an interview with Kim Chee Leung's next-door neighbor. According to the woman interviewed, there had been a single, thunderous explosion that threw her out of bed. By the time she managed to get outside, fully expecting another earthquake like the one in 1989, the entire house was in flames. At that point the woman bent down and picked up a two-inch-square piece of glass from the sidewalk opposite the ruined shell of Kim Chee Leung's house. She held up the glittering shard, demonstrating the force of the explosion, which had blown out the windows of Kim Chee's house and sent out a hail of shrapnellike fragments for a hundred feet. When asked to describe what her neighbor was like, the woman being interviewed could only say that she was "quiet" and "nice."

Thirty seconds after the interview had ended, Phillip Dane was on the telephone to Washington, trying to reach General Cordasco.

CHAPTER 20

GENERAL ALEXANDER CORDASCO, out of uniform, wearing a dark blue suit, sat in the small office on the third floor of Humphrey's Hall at Fort Belvoir, Virginia, and contemplated the stack of file folders on the wooden desk in front of him. On the other side of the desk, and also dressed in civilian clothes, a younger, dark-haired man with a neatly trimmed full beard waited patiently.

Fort Belvoir, located on the old Fairfax estate a dozen miles from Washington, D.C., was primarily the home of the engineers' school, as well as several other military/academic annexes, including the Defense Systems Management College. Once a week Cordasco taught a course in intelligence logistics at the DSMC. As well as being a welcome relief from his usual chores at Defense Intelligence, the teaching job also provided discreet cover for his work with the Justice Department.

The man seated with him in the small, bare room was a United States attorney named Francis Klawitter. Klawitter was Cordasco's unofficial contact with the Joint Organized Crime Task Force and assumed that the general was working as liaison with Defense Intelligence. He was completely unaware that the information he provided Cordasco with each week was never seen by anyone at DIA.

"Why don't you give all this to me in a nutshell," Cordasco said, waving a hand over the file folders. "I'm already swimming in paper." The older man settled back into his chair. Outside the window at his back the hot midafternoon sun was baking the grass on the lawns to a yellow brown.

"We've been getting little feeders from all over the place," began Klawitter. "Nothing very specific from any one source, but when you put it all together, it's obvious that something big is coming together."

"Go on," said Cordasco.

"We're seeing movement in all the Hong Kong groups," Klawitter explained. "The big ones anyway— the Wo Syndicate, Sun Yee On, Ah Kong, Green Gang. Mostly among the upper echelons—*Shan Chu*s and 438s. They're dropping out of sight."

"The Mafia used to call it 'hitting the mattresses,' " murmured Cordasco. "You think they're getting ready for a war?"

"We don't get any sense of that," Klawitter answered. He plucked at his beard thoughtfully. "It's too widespread. The same kind of thing is going on in Taiwan with United Bamboo."

"What about here?"

"The same. We had a guy named Fong spotted by one of our people in New York. Turned out he was chauffeuring for a big timer from England."

"This Blue-Eyed Chang character you've been telling me about?"

"That's the one." Klawitter nodded. "Chang wound up going to San Francisco for a meet with the Hip Sings, the On Leongs, and the Suey Sings."

"And you think Chang is important?"

"It's fuzzy." Klawitter shrugged. "He's the CEO of a trading company that's been around since the 1900s—Limehouse. Right up there with Jardine-Matheson. It almost went belly-up during the Second World War, but Chang apparently put the pieces back together again."

"But Limehouse is legitimate?"

"On the surface." Klawitter nodded. "Tea importers,

mostly. But there's always been a smell to it, going back to the fifties. Chang got too big too fast. Limehouse is into everything now—travel agencies, banking, airline interests, the lot."

"Anything you can make a case with?" asked Cordasco.

"Not a thing." The U.S. attorney sighed. "There's about a hundred filter companies between Limehouse and anything nasty. The word is that Chang is *Shan Chu* of the Black Dragons, though."

"Black Dragon is a Heroin brand name, isn't it?" asked Cordasco blandly, shielding his interest. In his mind's eye he could see the photographs of William Hawksworth.

"It's also a legend," said Klawitter. "Its chop is a dragon-headed black turtle. They press it right into the opium bricks and stamp it on labels. The design is the only tangible thing we have tying Black Dragon and Limehouse together. Limehouse markets its tea under the name Black Turtle."

"Pretty thin," said Cordasco.

"It's the best we can do." Klawitter cleared his throat and picked at his beard again. "We have Chang meeting with some pretty hard people."

"No crime in that," Cordasco grunted, lifting his shoulders. "What else?"

"Odd thing," said Klawitter. "Maybe just a coincidence." The lawyer smiled bleakly. "But you don't believe in those, do you?"

"No," said Cordasco. "I don't."

"We're getting the same kind of signals from the yakuza in Japan and our Sicilian friends."

"Battening down the hatches."

"Maybe. A lot of high-end types suddenly going out of circulation anyway. The top man in the Yamaguchi-gumi heads off to Waikiki for a vacation at the same time as his opposite number in the Sumiyoshi-rengo lands in Vancouver. Capos from New York, Chicago, and Detroit drifting down to Miami and Nassau all in the same week. That's a lot of chess pieces in play at the same time."

"You obviously have a theory," said Cordasco.

"It's not just me," said Klawitter. "The computers have never seen anything like it."

"So?"

"A summit conference," offered Klawitter.

"Apalachin for the nineties?" scoffed Cordasco. "A bit farfetched, don't you think?"

"No," Klawitter answered firmly. "I don't think it's farfetched at all. It's already happened several times on a smaller level. The triads here have a general working relationship. East and West with Denver as the dividing line. The yakuza in Japan have the same kind of arrangement—Yamaguchi in Kobe and Osaka, Sumiyoshi and Matsuba split Tokyo, Inagawa runs Yokohama and the docks ... and you know the Mafia's had their arrangement in place for almost fifty years."

"So now you're saying everyone's getting together on a worldwide scale?" said Cordasco.

"Something like that."

"What about the Colombians?" asked the general. "You'd think they'd fit into this somewhere."

"We think they're the reason for all of this," said Klawitter.

"How so?"

"They've been stepping on everyone's toes for the past eight or ten years," the lawyer answered. "Statistically the Heroin trade has been a steady growth industry ever since the end of the Vietnam War. Nice and controlled without a whole lot of violence, at least Stateside. Then the Colombians come along and throw everything into the dumper. Too high profile and a very erratic market. Too much price fluctuation. Bad PR with crack in the schoolyards. Not to mention the fact that they're starting to intrude on other people's territory. It's not business, it's Frontier Time."

"So the Chinese, the Japanese, and the Sicilians gang up on South America . . . come on." Cordasco laughed.

"It makes sense," Klawitter insisted. "It's the only thing that *does* make sense. Three against one. Heroin has been the basic commodity of organized crime since it was invented by the people at Bayer. Cocaine is the new kid on the block. It's a hostile takeover."

"With this Chang person playing Vito Genovese?" Cordasco smiled.

"Read the files," said Klawitter, a growing note of irritation in his voice. "He fits the profile."

"You have someone on him?" Cordasco asked.

"At a distance," Klawitter answered, standing up. "We can't do much more than monitor things . . . gather information like this. As you know, the JOCTF doesn't have any arrest powers. We're just flunkies." It was obvious that the U.S. attorney didn't like the role.

"Maybe that will change," Cordasco responded, soothing the younger man with a lie. The general and the people he reported to had no intention of giving the task force any powers at all. Even now there were too many cooks spoiling the broth. He thought about Dane and the woman in San Francisco and cursed Lang silently. *That* had been too close for comfort.

"I'll keep you advised," said Klawitter stiffly.

"Do that." Cordasco nodded absently. He put on a brief smile. "And I *will* read the files. I promise."

Klawitter grimaced, turned on his heel, and left the office. Cordasco spun his chair around and looked out the window. The air around the red brick building was still, and shimmers of heat were coming up off the winding paved pathway that meandered across the grounds.

"I'm getting too old for this shit," he muttered, watching a group of uniformed students walking across the wide lawns.

"I beg your pardon?"

Cordasco turned his chair around and looked at the figure who had just stepped into his office. The man closed the door and sat down in the chair recently vacated by Klawitter. He was Chinese, in his late fifties, with close-cropped graying hair, an oval face, and small, slightly protruding lips. He wore thick-framed black plastic eyeglasses and was dressed in a plain light gray suit. His name was Yu Zhensan, and until his defection to the United States in November of 1985 he had been a high-ranking official in the *Guojia Anquanbu*—a senior division of the Chinese Secret Service.

"Our young friend was most forceful," said Yu, lighting a cigarette. The bug in Cordasco's desk had relayed every word of Klawitter's report to Yu in the office next door. The Chinese man's English was a slightly accented Hong Kong British.

"He's getting good information," Cordasco agreed. "It confirms everything we've been thinking."

"Including what I told you about the esteemed Mr. Chang," said Yu.

"Especially the information about Chang." The general nodded. "The whole damn thing's coming unglued. Hawksworth, PATCOA, Holy Ghost—all of it."

"These things all have their time." Yu shrugged. He puffed on his cigarette, held two-fingered in his right hand. The ring on his third finger was gold and set with a large jade stone. A slim platinum Rolex was just visible under the cuff of his white shirt.

"We'll have to get things under way now," said Cordasco. "I'm afraid we no longer have a choice in the matter."

"We never did," said Yu. He blinked at the general. "So I may tell my people that we will be proceeding?"

"Yes," said Cordasco. The Chinese man gave a little nod and stood up.

"Allay your fears, General," said Yu calmly. "In this case the end will most certainly justify the means."

"I hope so," Cordasco answered. "If it doesn't, then we're all going to be left swinging in the wind. This is the kind of thing that brings down governments."

"Things must change," Yu said with a smile. "Even governments." He stepped forward and placed his free hand on the file folders Klawitter had left behind. "I suggest that these be destroyed." He smiled again. "And that Mr. Klawitter be given some other task. Curiosity has a way of killing more than just cats."

"That had already occurred to me," agreed the general.

"I'm sure," said Yu politely. "I'll see you later on today?"

"Yes."

"Excellent." Yu blinked, smiled, and left the office, closing the door softly as he went.

"Asshole," said Cordasco, frowning. He'd loathed the son of a bitch from the moment he laid eyes on him two years before when all of this had started. To be a traitor for a cause was one thing, but Yu had turned betrayal into a way of life.

The DIA man laughed at that; over the past few years he'd learned that in China and among Chinese betrayal *was* a way of life. Considering their complex hierarchy of family ties, it was a necessity; to keep the family safe sometimes meant switching political or economic horses in midstream, often more than once. Yu was a case in point.

The dossier on him that Cordasco had read was like something out of an episode of *Knots Landing* or *Dallas*. Yu Zhensan was the grandson of Yu Mingzhen, who was in turn the father of Yu Dawei, Taiwanese minister of defense from 1954 to 1965, brother-in-law to Chiang Ching-Kuo, president of Taiwan in direct line of succession from his father, Chiang Kai-shek. That was on the Nationalist side. On the Communist side his grandmother was Jiang Qing, second wife of Mao Tsetung himself. To top it off, his great-aunt had been

Mao's mistress, and after the death of his father, Yu
Qiwei, Zhensan had been adopted by Kang Sheng, head
of the Communist Secret Service.

Central Intelligence analysts had never been quite
sure who Yu was working for between 1950 and 1965,
but in 1975 he'd been in charge of the *Waishiju,* the division of State Security responsible for the surveillance
of foreign nationals and had "turned" several of them,
including a French journalist named Boursicot. When
his boss, Kang Sheng, died in that same year, Yu's future looked uncertain, but with the help of other family
connections he managed to survive and in fact climb
even higher within the Secret Service. There were
enough hints and rumors during much of his career to
suggest that he was also working as a "mole" for
Chiang's Nationalists on Taiwan, but nothing could
ever be substantiated. What could be proven was his information about a man named Jin Wudai, alias Larry
Wu Tai Chin.

Chin had been recruited by Defense Intelligence in
Japan in 1952. A year later he was turned over to the
fledgling CIA, which put him to work on the island of
Okinawa at the CIA's listening post. At the same time
Chin was working for the Taiwanese under the aegis
of Liao Chengzhi. Chin was eventually made an officer with the CIA's Radio Diffusion Department in
Langley, where he worked for the next thirty years.
Throughout that time and even beyond his retirement,
complete with CIA pension, Larry Wu Tai Chin was
also working for the Communists. His cover was finally blown with Yu's defection. Chin was arrested,
tried, convicted, and jailed. He committed suicide in
his cell.

Cordasco shook his head wearily and gathered up the
files on his desk. The list of names, ranks, organizations, and political affiliations was enough to give him
a headache. As far as he was concerned, it all added up

to one thing—Yu Zhensan, and those he was connected to, were not to be trusted. Then again, he thought, smiling wanly as he headed for the door, he wasn't to be trusted either.

CHAPTER 21

Phillip Dane reached the Oakland Amtrak Terminal at Sixteenth and Wood Streets in the late evening and climbed aboard the Coast Starlight with twenty minutes to spare. The train was a hodgepodge mixture of old Heritage cars, double-decker Superliners, and regular Amfleet coaches. According to the ticket agent in San Francisco, it would take almost twenty-four hours for the train to reach Seattle. From there he'd rent a car and drive across the border into Canada.

Flying would have been much more efficient, of course, but he'd decided to take the train to give him some time to think. He'd known that he was getting into deep water as soon as he saw the photographs of Hawksworth's mutilated corpse, but the death of Kim Chee Leung was beyond the role of a curator. Someone was running a black-bag operation, and he was in it up to his neck. Cordasco was either in on it or was being blindsided himself; there was no way to tell, not yet anyway—he'd never been able to reach the DIA man in Washington and had finally given up.

He asked the sleeping-car attendant to set up a folding table for him in the bedroom he'd reserved, and by the time he'd put away his bags and spread his files out, the train was in motion. He slumped down onto the seat, lit a cigarette, and watched as they clicked slowly through the outskirts of Oakland and into the suburban community of Richmond. He had a last, dramatic view of San Francisco and the bay, and then they began to speed up, rocking noisily into the night.

Dane pulled down the blind, promising himself an hour's work before a quick drink in the bar car and then sleep. Using a felt pen and a yellow pad, he began to doodle, listening to the squeaks and rattles all around him, trying to put his thoughts in order.

HAWKSWORTH. Hotshot flier with Doolittle's boys, gets the Congressional Medal of Honor and never looks back. Marries a blueblood but has an Oriental mistress who pops a child in Hawaii with his name on it. Marriage fails, mistress is quietly bought off with a house in San Francisco and some money, while the flyboy goes on to bigger and better things. Obviously some connection to private industry through Lang, but Hawksworth makes his career in the air force, particularly intelligence. Korea, Vietnam, NATO, and then he gets tapped for the DIA top spot. Gets whacked before he can take the job, along with a hooker from Hawaii. Clearly a drug connection. All sorts of opium paraphernalia on the boat, the name of a Heroin brand written on his forehead, and an autopsy showing he'd been ingesting large amounts of the old *Papaver somniferum.* All the signs of a Chinese mob hit.

KIM CHEE LEUNG. An odd one. Direct line to Madame Chiang Kai-shek. Meets Hawksworth in China, then again in Washington. Hooks up with him in Hawaii on a permanent basis and has a job with Lang's airline to keep her busy when the flyboy's not around. The kid she has with Hawksworth turns sour and becomes a draft-dodger and a doper. Very poor PR for the general if that ever came to light. The woman appears to be living a genteel, lower-middle-class life and then gets blown to hell in a "gas" explosion within a day of being interviewed by a DIA investigator. Possibly a coincidence, but highly un-likely.

SENATOR LANG. What was the real connection there? It had to be something more than old war bud-dies helping each other out. Lang does liaison with Hawksworth after the war, handing out cargo con-tracts. Lang gives Hawksworth's mistress a job in Hawaii with his airline. He continues the "beard" in San Francisco. The senator is the driving force be-hind the lobby that gets Hawksworth voted to the top slot at DIA, and it's Lang's boat, the *Terpsichore,* where Hawksworth meets his gory end. A relation-ship that lasts almost fifty years and based on . . . what? Nothing that was obvious on the surface.

Dane leaned back in his chair, closed his eyes, and fought off a yawn. Everything and nothing. Obvious and obscure. You could spin a hundred scenarios on the basis of the facts on hand and justify all of them, but that wasn't what a curator was supposed to do. He'd been press-ganged into his present occupation to sponge out those scenarios, not create them. His job was to obfuscate and cover, not clarify and reveal.

Or was it?

He put down a new heading and underlined it twice.

PHILLIP DANE. Born into the military, lots of expe-rience in Military Intelligence. Vietnam, the Defense Investigative Services, then a solid career as a curator with DIA. Knows Pentagon politics, knows the Hill, and has some connections. Severed now for all in-tents and purposes.

He was out of the loop, as they said. Unmarried, no close friends. Hired by Cordasco because of his quali-fications for the job? A nice bit of ego stroking, but there had to be a score of curators at DIA who were just as capable and much more easily controlled.

Much more easily controlled if Cordasco was running the project within DIA. If he was running it outside, it would make perfect sense to bring in someone who was completely isolated from the agency. Someone like Phillip Dane.

"Shitfire!" he whispered under his breath. He stubbed his cigarette out into the built-in ashtray and lit another one. Not a curator, methodically opening up all the closets and removing the skeletons. A bird dog. A point man. A Judas goat to bring out victims like Kim Chee Leung.

It made sense. Ego stroking or not, he was very good at his job. He could find things out that the Woodwards and the Bernsteins of the world never dreamed about. This was no ordinary curatorial task—a matter of neatly altered records or missing files. Hawksworth and whatever secrets lay buried in his past were important enough to be destroyed altogether. What Dane discovered, Cordasco and his people would remove—violently if necessary.

Dane stared down at the scrawled doodles and notes on his pad, arrows and lines wriggling from one name or phrase to another.

What if it had all started with Hawksworth? What if Hawksworth's murder, dressed up to look like some bizarre sex and drug ritual, was actually the first step in the operation? Dane blinked, his eyes stinging with fatigue. What was the McGuffin? What was the reason for all this?

He tore the top sheet off the pad and started a new list, flipping back and forth through the files in front of him as he worked.

LANG:	Ohio, Okinawa, Hawaii, Washington
HAWKSWORTH:	China, Okinawa, Hawaii, Washington
KIM CHEE:	China, Hawaii, S.F.

All three had Hawaii in common. Lang's airline, PATCOA, had been headquartered there, with flights ranging all over the Pacific and Southeast Asia, right up until the 1950s. Kim Chee had worked for PATCOA in Honolulu, and Hawksworth had been stationed at Hickam Field.

It didn't quite fit together. After the war there had been a number of serious scandals involving cooked bids and wholesale fraud concerning surplus aircraft, and to his knowledge, no one on a variety of investigating committees had ever pointed the finger at Lang, PATCOA, or Hawksworth. Whatever the general had been doing with his private life, it hadn't impacted publicly, and Lang must have been running a relatively clean operation or he and his airline would have been implicated.

Still . . . the connection was too clear. Dane made a note on the pad to dig into the background of Senator Lang's company. There had to be something there, and it had to relate to Hawksworth and Kim Chee. Something the powers that be deemed worth killing for.

Dane threw down his pen and rubbed his eyes wearily. He glanced at his watch. He'd been at it for an hour and a half. He reached up to the narrow control console on the wall and toggled off the overhead light, throwing the cell-like compartment into sudden darkness. He pushed up the blind across his window and looked out.

The train had slowed to a crawl. They were rumbling across the drawbridge spanning Suisun Bay. To the left, lit by a ghastly network of light poles that had turned the world a jaundiced yellow, thousands of gleaming Japanese imports waited in the huge storage areas by the docks. Closer in and covered in ghostly mothballing paint, hundreds of World War II merchant-marine vessels waited for sea orders that would never come.

Dane stood up and allowed himself a single, luxurious stretch. It was time for that last drink before bed.

Leaving the bedroom dark, he stumbled out into the corridor and closed the door behind him.

The bar car was almost empty. A young couple opposite the long, plastic-topped bar with at least a dozen empty Budweiser cans on the table in front of them. Dane was surprised that they could have sucked back so much in so short a time, and then he remembered that the Coast Starlight originated in Los Angeles and not San Francisco—they'd probably been drinking for hours. They were dressed identically in jeans and Grateful Dead T-shirts. The girl was nineteen or twenty, blond, and large-breasted. The boy looked a little younger and had long, crinkly hair. Both were asleep, heads lolling back, mouths open. Deadheads by name and deadheads by nature, Dane thought, grinning.

"Got on in Oakland," said the black bartender, noticing Dane's interest. The steward swabbed away at the already spotless counter and shook his head. "Wanted their first beer even before I done the cash up from L.A. Drunk all that since. Said they were going to a Dead concert in Eugene, Oregon." The bartender pronounced it "E-You Gene," slowly and carefully. He continued to shake his head. "Now who in their right mind would want to go to a place like Eugene, Oregon, for a concert, much less a dead one?" He gave his head one last shake. "Get you anything, sir?"

"Vodka rocks," said Dane, stepping up to the counter. The bartender nodded and started to work. Dane smiled to himself. There was a lot more intelligence behind the man's eyes than the Stepinfetchit act indicated. The little name tag pinned to the breast pocket of his white jacket said ARTHUR.

"Here you go." He put down a plastic glass half filled with ice cubes in front of Dane with an airline-size bottle of Smirnoff beside it. Dane laid a five-dollar bill on the counter and waved away the change.

"Much business tonight, Arthur?"

"Just them, the lady in back, and now you," the bartender answered. Dane glanced down the car. At the last table on the right at the end of the car a dark-haired Chinese woman was reading a book, ignoring what looked like a Bloody Mary in front of her. For a split-second he thought he was seeing a young version of Kim Chee Leung, and then he brushed the thought aside, realizing with a start that he was feeling guilty about the old woman's death. He snapped open the little bottle and began to pour vodka over the ice cubes in his glass.

"She get on in Oakland too?" asked Dane. The woman was pretty, in her late twenties or early thirties.

"Uh-huh," said Arthur. "Squandered her life savings on that tomato juice she's nursing." Obviously not a big tipper.

The train lurched as it entered a curve, and Dane slopped liquor down the side of his drink. Arthur picked up the glass with two fingers and swabbed the counter off, slipping a paper coaster down in a single smooth motion. The bartender knew his business.

"Maybe I'll check it out," Dane said. Arthur gave him a quick once-over and shrugged his narrow shoulders. He offered up a philosophical smile.

"You could do that," he said slowly. The voice of experience wasn't giving very good odds.

"Worth a try," said Dane. He picked up his drink, coaster now glued to the bottom of the glass, and carried it along the car, swaying with the motion of the train. He dropped down into a seat across the aisle from the woman and put down the drink. He lit a cigarette and looked out into the night. The train was bucketing along at a good clip now, rolling steadily past the fields and truck farms beyond Davis, with the steady glow of Sacramento in the dark distance.

He turned his eyes away from the window, took a sip of his drink, and glanced across the aisle. The woman was reading Mary Benjamin's *Autographs,* the classic, definitive work on the buying, selling, and forging of people's signatures. His grandfather had done a steady business in autographs and other holographic materials, and Dane had a copy of Benjamin's book in the original 1946 edition. It seemed like an odd choice of book to bring along on a train trip.

"Interesting book?" he asked, raising his voice slightly over the rhythmic rattle and hum. The woman lowered the book slightly and looked at Dane guardedly.

"It has its moments," she said. There was a rasp in her voice: a Chinese Lauren Bacall.

"Fascinating subject," said Dane. "Especially since so many famous people used different names at one time or another. You might get a Sebastian Melmoth and not know it was actually Oscar Wilde. Beaconsfield was actually Disraeli, and A. M. Barnard is Louisa May Alcott."

"You sound as though you know something about it," the woman responded. This time she put the book down on the table in front of her.

"A little bit." Dane shrugged. He motioned with his drink. "Mind if I join you?"

"No, come ahead," she answered. He stood up, crossed the aisle, and slipped down onto the seat across from her.

"I'm a rarebook dealer," he said. "Phillip Dane." "Rarebook dealer" sounded better than "used-book seller." He held his hand out across the table, and she took it. The grip was surprisingly strong.

"Erin Falcone," she said.

"You're kidding." He smiled. "You don't look like an Erin or a Falcone."

"My mother loved green, and I married an Italian stockbroker. What can I say?" She took a sip of her tomato juice, then put it down on the table again. She stirred it slowly with a plastic swizzle. "My maiden name was Lam, which I'll be going back to any day now."

"Divorced?" asked Dane.

"Almost," she said. "Like I said, any day now."

"Most people go to Reno; you're headed in the other direction."

"I'm going to Vancouver to see relatives."

"Vancouver, Washington, or Canada?" Dane asked.

"Canada," she answered.

"Me too."

"The train used to run right across the border. I'm not looking forward to the bus ride." She made a face, and Dane laughed again.

"I'm renting a car in Seattle," he said. "I'd be glad to give you a lift." Suddenly the guarded look was back on her face again.

"I don't know about that," she said after a moment. "After all, I hardly know you."

"We can get acquainted tomorrow," Dane offered. He took a last swallow of his drink, more ice water than vodka now. He slid away from the table and stood up. "What coach are you in?"

"Two back," she said. "Roomette nine."

"I'm three cars back," he said. "Bedroom A."

"Okay." She smiled. "Where shall we rendezvous? Your place or mine?"

"Neither," said Dane. "I have to prove to you that I'm not a Ted Bundy, remember? How about the dining car for breakfast?"

"Sounds great," said Erin Falcone.

"Eight?"

"Seven-thirty—let's beat the rush."

"Great." Dane gave her a little wave, then headed back through the cars to his bedroom. While he'd been in the bar car, the steward had tidied up his files, removed the table, and pulled the bed down out of its niche in the wall. His briefcase was on the bed, the files sitting in a neat pile beside it.

Dane shrugged off his jacket, hung it on the hook to his left, and bundled the files into his briefcase. He slid the briefcase under the bed and turned on the tiny rubber-vaned fan located high in one corner of the little room. He lit a cigarette, flipped off the overhead light, and pushed open the window blind again. Seated on the edge of the bed, he looked out onto the brightly lit late-night sprawl of Sacramento. From here they'd turn north toward Marysville and Chico. By morning they'd be in Oregon.

He tapped his ash into the wall ashtray and thought about Erin Falcone, the fair colleen with the almond eyes and the Mongol cheekbones. As a teenager he'd bummed across Europe and the States, often traveling by train, and he'd often had the fantasy of meeting a girl and making love to her in a darkened bedroom just like this one, the mutual sounds of passion drowned out in the mournful wail of the diesel's horn, the rhythm of their lust echoed in the thunder of iron wheels on big steel rails. X-rated Woody Guthrie with some Sean Connery thrown in à la *From Russia with Love*. Great stuff; the trouble was, it never happened, not to him or anyone else he'd ever met.

So why now? And why him?

It was all too neat, especially the bit with the book. It was the kind of conversational hook no one could turn down. The only thing better would have been for him to be a writer and walk in on her reading one of his books. It was a perfect fantasy come to life. He wondered what would have happened if he hadn't gone into the bar car. The same trick but in the dining car at breakfast? Maybe. Probably. One way or the other she would have staked him out and made sure the connection was made.

So who the hell was she, and why had she tagged him? He groaned, then butted his cigarette. He was too tired to think about it. He pulled down the blind and dropped back against the pillow, still fully clothed. Within seconds he was asleep.

CHAPTER 22

DUTCH KAPONO CHEWED the lip of his Styrofoam coffee cup, his eyes darting back and forth, trying to watch all twenty surveillance monitors in the cluttered Security Control Office of the Honolulu International Airport. It was 6:05 in the morning, an hour when anybody in his right mind would be still sleeping, but the grim-faced senior customs patrol officer had already been up for hours.

Kapono was a weatherbeaten fifty-eight, his once-blond hair gone the color of nicotine, his deeply lined face a blurred combination of his Hawaiian father and Scandinavian mother. He was a Honolulu native, and except for a ten-month stint in Korea with the marines, he'd never lived anywhere else.

Kapono had been with U.S. Customs for thirty-five years, and he'd loved every minute of it. As far as Dutch was concerned, it was his sacred duty to keep the Islands safe from the "A-holes," an all-encompassing term he used to describe anyone who wasn't Island-born, regardless of race, sex, or creed. It was also his name for the pudgy insurance salesman who'd had the effrontery to marry his ex-wife, Liana, and who was playing daddy to Kapono's two boys, Victor and Eric.

Dutch's regular shift at the airport didn't officially begin until nine, but the majority of Asian flights touching down on the Reef runway began landing at six, keeping up a steady flow until after ten. The ones he was most concerned with these days came in from

170

Hong Kong, Taipei, Manila, Osaka, and Toyko—dozens of 747s every morning, disgorging hundreds of bleary-eyed, camera-toting passengers into the arms of Paradise. And sometimes into the arms of Dutch Kapono.

On paper, Kapono and his four 10-man teams of CPOs were supposed to be on the lookout for Americans returning home and trying to slip in illicit booze, cigarettes, and the odd black-market Rolex from Kowloon. On a more elevated level they were also supposed to be on the lookout for professional smugglers trafficking in gems, bullion, and other high-end goods.

They caught enough of those to keep the bosses back in Washington happy, but Kapono's real concern was the mountain of drugs being imported and exported from the Islands and the various and sundry "A-holes" who went along with the trade. With the drugs—cocaine, Heroin, marijuana, ice, and all the rest, came the peripherals—gambling, prostitution, extortion, and money laundering.

None of which were supposed to be his concern. The big stuff was supposed to be left to the "professionals" like the DEA spooks and FBI pickle-up-the-ass types who occasionally roamed the corridors and concourses of Honolulu International. The local cops, Honolulu County, Five-O, and all the rest knew better. DEA and FBI meant paperwork, bureaucracy, time wasted, and bullshit. Dutch Kapono meant business. He'd spent his entire adult life accumulating information about every sleazy operation, every dope dealer, and every private patch of Kona Gold around. Of the five hundred hookers working Waikiki at any given moment, Kapono knew at least half by sight. He could give you the price list at any massage parlor or "poruno" shop on Kalakaua Avenue and quote you the odds being given on the Knicks at the Tobaku joints in Little Saigon. Best of all, he could spot a yakuza *"oyabun"* at twenty yards—or on a video monitor in a darkened room.

"There," he said quietly, spitting out a fragment of Styrofoam. "Monitor six. Coming through the gate."

"Which one?" asked the shirtsleeved man at the control console in front of Kapono.

"Three of them. Two skinny ones with the punch-perms and the lumpy one in the suit. *Oyabun* and a couple of *kobun* to keep him company."

"Recognize any of them?" asked the man at the console.

"The *oyabun* is a guy named Masao Kimura. Ichiwa-kai in Osaka. Not a real big-timer, but he's getting up there."

"So what do you want to do?"

"Get Mike to shadow him. I want to know where he's staying."

"Right." The man in shirtsleeves spoke into the gooseneck microphone on the console. On the number-six monitor Kapono watched as a telephone rang and one of the two uniformed men at the customs gate answered. The security man with Kapono gave his instructions, and the uniformed officer hung up the phone. He nodded briefly to his partner, who chalked the flight bags carried by the three Japanese and let them pass through and out of sight.

"What flight were they on?" asked Kapono. The shirtsleeved man checked the schedule monitor flickering on his right.

"Six-oh-two from Tokyo. JAL."

"A-hole's a tourist then." The more intelligent criminals coming into Hawaii knew that customs and the other authorities kept their most careful watch on direct, international flights. Anyone serious about trying to bring anything into Hawaii would use a less vigilant "gateway" like Seattle, then fly into Honolulu on a domestic flight.

"Still want Mike to watch him?"

"Yeah," said Dutch. He took a swig of cold, sweet

coffee and made a face. "We've been getting too many of these guys lately, from all over."

"Like that Italian guy you got so hot about yesterday?" asked the shirtsleeved man.

"Yeah, like him," said Kapono. The "Italian" from the day before had come in on a United flight from L.A. and points east—either Chicago or New York. The face had set off a vague alarm bell, so he'd checked the passenger list. The man turned out to be Carmine Randazzo, and a quick check of his "book" back in the office described him as being the *consigliere* of the ruling Mafia family in Rockford, Illinois. Randazzo's ticket was a first-class open return and he'd booked in at the old Royal Hawaiian in Waikiki.

Kapono clapped the shirtsleeved man on the shoulder, then tossed his chewed-up coffee cup into a wastepaper basket.

"I'll be in the office if anybody's looking for me."

"Okay, Dutch."

"And if I'm not there, I'm on the beeper." Kapono did a quick check to make sure that the little Colt Mustang on his belt was hidden by the drape of his garish, pink-pineapple-motif shirt, then left the room.

He made his way slowly through the maze of corridors, ignored the chattering throng of new arrivals in the main concourse, and climbed the long flight of spiral stairs to the upper level. Passing through a pair of swinging doors marked OFFICIAL USE ONLY, he followed another series of corridors to his office.

It was a large, windowless room, walls lined with filing cabinets and containing a metal desk, government-issue swivel chair, computer terminal, telephone, and fax machine. The only decoration in the room was a large scale map of Honolulu mounted on cork tiles. There were hundreds of colored pins poked into the street map, each one identifying the location of a suspect business or individual. There were so many pins in the map that it looked as though it had been sprinkled with confetti. Some of the pins went back almost twenty years; for Kapono the map represented a visual history of crime in Honolulu.

The current myth going around Hawaiian Customs was that when Dutch Kapono died, all the pins in the map would fall out suddenly, and every "A-hole" in the Islands would give up his life of crime, ushering in a new era of sinlessness. Dutch had heard the story and enjoyed it, but the concept of a sinless Hawaii was laughable—the missionaries had seen to that 150 years ago. As far as Kapono was concerned, they were the first smugglers, bringing in fire, brimstone, smallpox, and the clap.

Ignoring the computer, Dutch went to the bank of filing cabinets against the far wall and started rooting through them. Before the Reagan era the filing cabinets had been referred to in memoranda and reports as the Yakuza Documentation Center, or YDC. Over the years Kapono had assembled thousands of dossiers on Japanese organized-crime incursions into Hawaii, but during the trickle-down reign of Ronnie I the yakuza, the triads, and even the Mafia had taken a backseat to the Colombians. There was no more money for the YDC, and even less to keep tabs on the growing Asian crime presence on the Islands.

It started in the mid-seventies with Yonekura, the Olympic boxer turned gun-runner, followed by a wave of sex- and drug-related operations that seemed to be directly linked to the rise in Japanese tourism. By the mid-eighties the Tokyo press was calling Hawaii the forty-eighth prefecture, just the way the Americans referred to Canada as the fifty-first state. In 1985 almost a million Japanese vacationed in Hawaii and spent a billion dollars. That much again was generated illegally through prostitution, gambling, and the exporting of amphetamines from Oahu to Japan.

Tourism was the key, of course, providing cash and victims both. And the yakuza was right that there would be all kinds of cheap labor willing to work legitimate jobs and make some extra on the side. It was a tidal wave that an army of Dutch Kaponos wouldn't have been able to stop.

They even took a run at the City Bank of Honolulu in a much-publicized scandal, and Dutch knew that was just the tip of the iceberg. Hawaii had always been a pivot point in the Pacific, and now it was becoming a way station for Japanese, Hong Kong Chinese, and Taiwanese gangsters on their way to the Mainland.

It took Dutch the better part of fifteen minutes to cull the files he needed from the three 5-drawer cabinets. He took them over to the desk and sat down heavily. He wished he still smoked, but instead he reached for one of the empty Styrofoam cups he kept stacked beside the computer and began to shred it with his long, meaty fingers.

He was almost sixty, and according to his doctor, a yuppie little prick who'd gone to the Punahou School, Dutch was forty pounds overweight, drank too much beer, and ate too much red meat. He had high blood pressure, swollen ankles, varicose veins, and he was damn lucky not to have prostate cancer, lung cancer, and hemmies.

So he quit smoking his forty Luckies a day, just to be on the safe side, and took to shredding Styrofoam cups. It drove everybody in the airport crazy, but at least you could always find him by following the trail of little white chips.

Humming under his breath, Dutch switched on the computer and called up the chart he'd been putting together over the past few weeks. He checked through the files on his desk again, making sure that his CPOs were filing their updates, then added the new A-hole, Kimura, to the list on the computer. He leaned back in his chair and examined the result.

"It's a fucking convention," he grunted, tearing at the cup in his hands. It was mostly small time so far,

yakuza *kobun,* triad 49s and wiseguy *caporegimes*—
nothing higher. But it was a trend. This was like the advance men for a political campaign, sniffing out the territory before the big cheese arrives.

He hit a key, and the chart vanished and reappeared,
this time showing him where his quarry was staying.
Half in Waikiki, a few on the North Shore, and a couple
on Maui. No pattern, no linkages. Happy gangsters on
holiday. Dutch snorted loudly; he sure as shit didn't believe that for a minute.

Groping in the back pocket of his jeans, he dug out
his address book and flipped through it. He found the
number he wanted, reached forward, and tapped out a
long string of numbers. He kept on humming while the
connection was being made. It took less than thirty seconds for him to reach Washington, D.C. Daybreak here,
early afternoon there.

"S.I.D? Yeah, my name's Kapono ... no, ma'am,
that's with a *K,* not a *C.* Right. I'm chief CPO at Honolulu International.... Sure, you go right ahead
ma'am, I don't mind at all.... Sure. Kapono, that's it
ma'am, just like I said.... Well, what I'd like is a
number for a guy I met last year who came through
here with the task force. He was a U.S. attorney, name
of Klawitter, Francis Klawitter...."

CHAPTER 23

CONRAD LANG, SENIOR senator from Ohio, sat in one of the Lang *Polestar's* leather club chairs and sipped his bourbon and branch water, watching the Virginia countryside drift by, twenty-eight thousand feet below. The cabin interior of the company jet was divided into three, a passenger compartment designed to carry eighteen people, a small stateroom/office, and a rear baggage hold. The passenger compartment was decorated in the standard Lang Industries blue-and-gold, the bulkheads were burled-walnut veneer, and the monogrammed crystal came from Venice. The *Polestar* was an American-made clone of the French Falcon 900, traveled close to the speed of sound, and had a range of almost four thousand miles. It wasn't *Air Force One,* but it was the next best thing.

Traveling with Lang was a short, broad-shouldered man in his late sixties with the crow's-foot squint of someone used to looking out over long distances. He was almost completely bald, his skull patched with age spots, and he looked uncomfortable in his dark, chalk-stripe business suit. Once upon a time he'd worn the leather jacket and flight-boot uniform of Claire Chennault's Flying Tigers, and he still balked at wearing cuff-link shirts and neckties. His name was Tucker Barnes, and he'd been involved with Lang family interests all his life.

"I dunno, Connie," he said slowly. "It's a bad business, especially for old men like you and me." He shook his head wearily, his gnarled fingers picking at the label on the beer bottle in his hands. "Jesus wept, Connie, shriveled-up farts like us should be thinking about retirement."

"The world is ending, Tucker. Our world, at any rate. No one is going to remember any of the good we did; they just want to dig up the bad." The senator sipped his drink. "I won't go out on a rail, Tucker. I won't do that."

"How much does this Dane character really know?" asked Barnes.

"Not much. Not yet," said Lang. "But that's not the point. The very fact that he's being employed at all is a signal. I'm being thrown to the wolves."

"I always thought we *were* the wolves." Barnes grinned. "Do these people know who they're tangling with?" The grizzled little man made a snorting sound and took a long swallow of beer.

"I thought they did." Lang shrugged. "If they throw me to the wolves, they have to know I won't go alone."

"So there's nothing to worry about, Connie. Tempest in a teapot."

"Perhaps," said Lang. He glanced out the window again. In two hours they'd be in Dayton, and then he could rest. He turned and looked at his old friend. "Whatever Cordasco is doing goes very deep. There's a dozen senators and twice that many people in the House I could bury if I told all that I knew. He's risking a lot."

"I still think you're worrying too much, Connie. The Country Club's never been a problem in the past. They need you." "The Country Club" was a derisive term for DIA that had been in use for years. Intelligence yes-men telling the Pentagon what it wanted to hear.

"It's all connected to Bill," Lang mused. "It all seems to turn on him and his whore."

"Poor bastard," Barnes grunted. "No one deserves to go out like that."

"And now the woman is dead as well. They're cleaning house."

"Starting from the back and moving to the front," said Barnes. "Billy goes back a long way. Almost as far as me, and that's saying something."

Lang nodded absently, thinking about the past. Tucker Barnes had been a bomber pilot with the Flying Tigers out of Chungking and had met William Hawksworth there at a testimonial dinner given by the Generalissimo in honor of Doolittle's Raid. The two men had a lot in common and had quickly become friends.

At the end of the war, with Chennault forced to resign his commission, Barnes had followed his old boss to Taiwan and a job with Civil Air Transport, the civilian airline established to help the Nationalists after they were thrown off the Mainland by Mao Tse-tung. It was Barnes who'd introduced Lang to Hawksworth and smoothed the way for the first contracts between PATCOA and Air Transport Command. Lang had repaid the favor by hiring Barnes away from ATC at twice the salary and a position as manager of PATCOA's operations in Southeast Asia.

"We're going to have to do some housecleaning on our own," said Lang after a moment.

"Like what?" Barnes asked, a note of enthusiasm in his voice. His present job as chairman of Lang Industries Aviation Research Division was a sinecure; he hadn't worked actively for years.

"There's a paper trail going back to 1946," said the senator. "Decades' worth of documents, a lot of them with Billy's name on the bottom."

"That why we're going to Dayton?" asked Tucker Barnes. The PATCOA archives were buried deep in the bowels of the Lang Industries headquarters.

"One of the reasons. I want you to set up a meeting with Gollinger too."

"Shit, Connie, you're not going to drag all that up again, are you? The Canton Island stuff?"

"No choice, Tucker," the senator murmured. "He's the last one alive who was part of it—except for you and me, that is."

"That's right. Casey was the only other one who knew, and he's gone."

"And Woodward never got a sniff, not even in that book of his with the old bastard dying of a brain tumor."

"Gollinger still on Howard's Cay?"

"As far as I know." Tucker Barnes nodded unhappily.

"I want to see him as quickly as possible," Lang instructed. "And rent us something you're rated on that's a little less conspicuous than this." He waved one hand, gesturing at the interior of the *Polestar*.

"Okay." Barnes sighed. "I'll get on it as soon as we land." The old bomber pilot shook his head sadly. "Fucking Japs . . . I thought all that was over and done with."

"It's never over and done," the senator answered, looking out the window. "Never."

Thomas John Gollinger walked along the wide beach on the western side of Howard's Cay, enjoying the feel of the onshore breeze riffling the shaggy thatch of snow-white hair that protected his large head from the Caribbean sun. He was wearing Birkenstock sandals and lime-green shorts, while a baggy yellow shirt covered his thick, muscular torso. Under his arm he carried a hardcover copy of Hillel Schwartz's *Century's End,* one of his favorite books.

Schwartz's theory was a simple one: According to him, social history—patterns of human behavior—were predictable in their cyclic nature. Victorian conservatism was reflected in fifties stodginess, and the rebellious sixties were simply a repeat of the Roaring Twenties excesses.

That was on a short-term level. On a larger canvas the historian maintained that at the end of every century societies tried to purge themselves of sins that had accumulated over the past hundred years. At the end of millennia whole civilizations went through an orgy of angst, their fears probably based on a pantheon of cross-cultural mythologies that only counted to one thousand. Hitler's Third Reich being a modern-day example. In his simpleminded madness the Führer had said that his Germany would last a thousand years, assuming that no other vision of the Fatherland would follow it since the world would have ended.

Gollinger chuckled to himself as he walked, the green-blue shallows of the reef on his left, the surreal, oven-hot length of his landing strip two hundred feet to his right. He particularly liked Schwartz's description of what was going on as the twentieth century reeled toward its conclusion—the finale monitored by what he referred to as "New Age Woo-Woos."

At seventy T. J. Gollinger was as far from being a Woo-Woo as any man could get. In 1940 he'd been a twenty-year-old recent graduate of a Jesuit college in upstate New York, intent on getting a postgraduate degree in law. Instead, recommended to Wild Bill Donovan by a family friend, Francis Cardinal Spellman, he'd become an early recruit into the newly formed Coordinator of Information Office, COI. In 1942 COI became the Office of Special Services—OSS—and Gollinger was made deputy head of its Far East Research and Analysis Department.

Gollinger spent most of the war hopscotching around the Pacific, following up on OSS operations in China, Burma, and Thailand, soaking up information, learning half a dozen languages in the process. He'd spent some of his time in Hawaii, but for the most part he was based at a remote air-staging base on Canton Island, a mid-Pacific atoll two thousand miles southwest of Honolulu. Now, almost fifty years later, he occupied another island in the sun—one that he owned.

Howard's Cay was situated in the shallow waters thirty-five miles southeast of Nassau, and from the air the four-mile-long island looked like a rusted, upside-down fishhook. There were half a dozen old cottages on the northern hoop of the hook, while the southeastern tip—the point of the hook—was bare except for scrub brush and sea grape. The hoop and the point created a serene and safe harbor where a score of yachts could easily moor, while the long shank of the fishhook provided the prefect site for a landing strip. The Cay's amenities were rudimentary; water came from cisterns, and electricity came from diesel generators. There was a battered, ten-bedroom hotel above the harbor, a store, an empty dive shop, and a hundred-foot-long L-shaped dock with a trio of decaying fuel pumps.

Before the arrival of T. J. Gollinger, Howard's Cay had been a favorite stopping-off place for wandering yachtsmen and small groups of adventurous diving fanatics. It was an easy one-day cruise from Nassau and a twenty-minute flight aboard a Chalk's charter. There was nothing particularly exciting, but the dive shop and the hotel did enough business to stay open in the high season.

That had all changed abruptly when Gollinger appeared at a real estate office in Nassau and purchased three small properties on the island, paying cash. He opened a total of eleven accounts at various Nassau banks, all under different corporate names, depositing a total of $3.5 million, once again in cash.

The local authorities, including officials at the banks, assumed that the money came from illegal drug deals and turned a blind eye. Gollinger purchased a comfortable but unpretentious Chris-Craft and spent the next few years commuting back and forth between Howard's Cay and Nassau to do his banking—always in cash. He also began buying up Howard's Cay, beginning with the airstrip and the dock. He informed the longtime owners of the hotel and dive shop that the airstrip would no longer accept charter flights, and the dock would no longer provide fuel to either the dive shop or incoming yachtsmen. With access choked off, the dive-shop and hotel owners sold out to Gollinger within three months. The Cay's other half-dozen permanent residents quickly followed. Complaints by the onetime hotel owner precipitated a brief investigation, once again centered around the possibility of drug involvement, but no evidence was found one way or the other.

Gollinger began developing his new home quickly. He brought in a dozen Nassau natives, all male, all black, and all single, to maintain the dock, his boat, and the airstrip. He imported a dozen Dobermans to patrol the island freely, purchased a state-of-the-art satellite television setup from Atlantic Satellite in the Royal Palm Mall as well as an equally sophisticated radio-communications station and a combination solar/wind electrical generating system and battery backup. As a final step, the television, radio, and electrical grid was then run through an extremely powerful computer array designed to Gollinger's specifications by Nassau Data Systems. Less than a year after his first appearance in the Bahamas T. J. Gollinger was fully established on Howard's Cay, and no one knew what the hell he was up to.

The only facts anyone had to go on were the regular filing of flight plans to the island by a company called Southern Air Transport out of Miami and deposits of enormous amounts of cash into Gollinger's Nassau accounts. The only checks that surfaced came out of a Delaware corporation called Air and Sea Supply Limited, payable to TJG Consultants, Inc., with its corporate headquarters on the other side of Cuba in the Turks and Caicos Islands.

Prudently, no one in authority was interested in digging too deeply into the affairs of T. J. Gollinger or the people he dealt with, and local publications and cruising guides began advising people to "avoid Howard's Cay" when preparing their itineraries. Over the better part of the next decade neither Gollinger nor the cay received any publicity except for a brief moment of interest when Walter Cronkite, an avid yachtsman, arrived in the harbor one day and was summarily informed that he would not be allowed to dock.

Gollinger came to the end of his walk and turned away from the beach at the northern end of the cay. He followed the path through the seagrass to the top of a low hill overlooking the harbor. To his left was the squat shape of his house, the radio tower, and the satellite dish, while to the right he could look down the shank of the cay to the windblown Quonset hut and assembly of wooden shacks that marked his private "airport." Directly below him he could see the old wooden hotel, the dive shop, and the dock. One of his employees was washing down the cruiser, and two more were climbing into a Jeep in front of the dive shop, preparing for yet another circuit of the narrow crushed-stone road that ringed the cay. Gollinger nodded to himself; nothing out of the ordinary, just the way he liked it.

Skirting the base of the radio tower, he entered his house through the back door and crossed the hall to his office. The house was thick-walled and cool, broad-slat jalousies in the windows feeding a comfortable cross-current of air. The office, however, was windowless and air-conditioned; the communications and computer equipment it contained was far too sensitive for the salt-sea atmosphere of the cay.

One wall of the room was racked with a variety of shortwave radios and large Revox log-tape recorders. A second wall held his television-monitoring equipment, capable of recording broadcasts from more than two hundred stations around the world, while a third wall was lined with bookcases containing hundreds of identical three-ring binders, each neatly labeled. The fourth wall was home to his computer workstation.

He sat down at the already booted terminal, keystroked in his security code, and typed in a single word: HAWKSWORTH. The screen cleared, then offered up a selection of files under the subdirectory. He keyed in the file name ROYAL BANK OF THAILAND, and a slow, sour smile spread across his features as the screen began to fill with information.

In late 1945 T. J. Gollinger and a small Research and Analysis team from OSS entered Tokyo with the first Occupation forces. Gollinger, fluent in Thai, already knew that virtually the entire gold-bullion deposit at the Bank of Thailand had been spirited out of Bangkok by the Japanese during the early days of the war, vanishing into a number of Tokyo bank vaults and other private caches in Japan. By the spring of 1946 Gollinger had located and retrieved eighty-seven-and-a-half tons of gold. At thirty-five dollars an ounce, the hoard was worth an estimated $98 million.

Given the chaotic state of postwar Thailand, it wasn't difficult for Donovan and his OSS colleague Nelson Rockefeller to convince the Bank of Thailand that the bullion would be better off in New York rather than Bangkok for the interim. Gollinger was authorized to arrange shipment of the gold from Tokyo, and following regular channels, he approached William Hawksworth and Air Transport Command.

At that point Gollinger's job was officially at an end, but after six months in occupied Japan he'd discovered just how corrupt large military and civilian bureaucracies could be in a postwar environment, and just how vulnerable. Utilizing the wide-ranging facilities of the OSS, he kept his eye on Hawksworth and the bullion.

Initially things appeared to be in order. Hawksworth, inundated with demands for military transport and suffering from a shortage of aircraft, put out the bullion contract for private bids. There were three main contenders: Civil Air Transport, the newly formed airline, headed by Claire Chennault of Flying Tiger fame, Transocean, an equally young operation based in Oakland, and Pacific Air Transport Corporation of America—PATCOA, operated as a subsidiary of Lang Aviation. Gollinger knew that Conrad Lang was working with Hawksworth as a liaison officer, so he wasn't surprised when the contract went to PATCOA. Pork-barrel politics perhaps, but not illegal in the strictest sense of the world. And PATCOA did have a spanking-new fleet of war surplus DC-4s at its back and call.

The contract called for nine aircraft to make the delivery, each DC-4 carrying approximately ten tons of gold, close to the vehicle's maximum payload. The gold was to be loaded into small aluminum-clad crates, each crate weighing 110 pounds and containing ten 5-kilogram bars, 180 crates to each aircraft. The bullion was to be ferried from Tokyo to Oakland, then transferred by rail to New York.

Once again, nothing seemed out of the ordinary to Gollinger. What did arouse his curiosity was the route proposed by PATCOA. At full payload the DC-4 had a range of slightly less than 2,500 miles. The most efficient way across the Pacific would have been Tokyo-Wake-Honolulu-Oakland. Instead, Tucker Barnes, head of the team flying the bullion, decided on a route that would take them much farther south: Tokyo—Guam—Truk—Ponape—Canton—Honolulu and finally Oakland. The rationale offered up by Barnes was that with the aircraft so heavily loaded, a route involving a larger number of short distances would be safer.

Gollinger was suspicious, but at that point there was very little he could do, and a few days before the transfer was to take place, he was called back to New York for a number of meetings. As a precaution the young R&A man copied as many of the key documents as possible that related to the shipment.

It was a good thing that he did; when he returned to

Tokyo three weeks later, the bullion shipment had been sent out, and his office had been moved. In the move all his material on the shipment had been lost.

His suspicions now thoroughly aroused, Gollinger began to do some discreet checking, tracing the shipment to its final destination. At first glance everything seemed to have gone smoothly, the bullion flown its circuitous route to Oakland, put onto the New York train, and delivered without incident.

A closer look, using the documents he'd copied for comparison, told a different story. Nine DC-4s had made up the convoy, making the forty-hour flight over a five-day period, but according to the delivery manifest handed over in Oakland, each aircraft had carried 108 of the bullion crates, not 180. Somewhere between Tokyo and Oakland, 648 crates had vanished, containing gold bars worth more than $39 million.

And the only person who knew about it was T. J. Gollinger. At that point the ex-Jesuit knew he was being faced with a critical life decision. Hawksworth was a Medal of Honor winner, Lang's family were major industrialists with immense political power, the bank the gold had been delivered to was owned by a high-ranking OSS official, and the Royal Bank of Thailand—eventually managed by God only knew which of the factions now fighting for control—would be happy to get *anything* back from the Japanese.

For Gollinger's eminently practical mind it was a question of logic over ethics. Ethics said he should inform someone about the theft of the gold. Logic told him that there was no one he could tell who would either believe him or care. Ethics cried out for justice, logic whispered caution. It would be hard to call back the dogs once they were unleashed, and the most probable result of speaking out would be a quick and violent end in some back alley in the Ginza. Logic also said that if justice wasn't to be served, then why not the interests of T. J. Gollinger?

Logic won out. Gathering up his evidence, Gollinger took a Civil Air Transport flight from Tokyo to Wake and dropped in unannounced on Lang and Hawksworth at ATC headquarters. That meeting began an association that lasted almost fifty years, and it wasn't over yet.

Gollinger scrolled through the file slowly, pursing his thin lips as he read. It was ironic; he'd built an information empire on that one incident, yet it was that single event that was coming back to haunt them all. He reached out and tapped the cover of the Schwartz book. History repeating itself.

He keyed his way back to the main menu on the computer and sat back in his chair. The hum of the air conditioner blocked out the sounds of the rushing sea outside.

With Hawksworth's death it was obvious that some kind of process was about to begin, and Gollinger knew that inevitably he would become involved. After half a century of keeping secrets and telling lies, he understood that the acorn of the missing gold had grown into a giant oak, involving people who didn't even know the source of their involvement. But Lang knew, and he'd be the first to move.

"You're on your way, aren't you?" Gollinger said, whispering to the computer. "You're on your way to see your old friend Gollinger."

The white-haired man smiled, knowing that he was right, as usual.

CHAPTER 24

"It was just like I thought it would be," said Erin Falcone, lying close beside him on the narrow bed. The bedroom was dark, lit only by tiny shreds of light from around the edges of the blind covering the window.

"Gee, thanks." Dane laughed. "I was really that predictable?"

"Don't be an idiot," she answered. "I mean the whole idea of it . . . making love to a total stranger on a train." She let her fingers trail along the line of hair that ran from his chest down to his belly.

"Well, we're not strangers anymore," he said, turning on his side. He fitted his palm into the curve of her small hip and slid even closer. He felt himself harden against the warm, honey-colored flesh of her thigh. He kissed her, tasting her cold tongue, and she lifted one leg, hooking it over the small of her back, drawing him inside her with an almost imperceptible movement of her groin. He felt her draw in a sharp breath as he entered her fully.

"Not bad for a round-eye," she whispered, fingers digging into the muscles below his shoulder blades.

"You're pretty inscrutable yourself, Ms. Falcone," he answered. He pushed deeper and swung above her, feeling her smooth, muscular legs lock around him. He began to move in a slow, easy rhythm, matching the swinging movement of the train. It was the third time they'd made love in the last four hours, and he felt as though he could go on forever. She bit his lower lip gently.

"Racial stereotyping," she said, matching each movement of his hips with small lunges of her own. "All us Chinee girls think you white guys have big shlongs."

"You're mixing us up with the blacks."

"And you never saw Mr. Falcone with a hard-on," she answered. "The original Italian Stallion."

"Oh, shut up." He grinned, easing himself up even harder against her.

Twenty minutes later Dane was sitting on the edge of the bunk, pulling on his pants. The train had slowed and was clattering methodically over a steady procession of switch points.

"Where are we?" murmured Erin Falcone from behind him. Dane checked the glowing dial of his watch.

"I'm not sure. Albany maybe, or Salem." He stood up and put on his shirt. "Not too far from Portland anyway." He buttoned his shirt. They'd be in Seattle by early evening, four or five hours away. The fun and games were over; it was time to act. "You want some coffee?" he asked, turning to look down at the figure of the young woman on the bed.

She had the twisted sheet drawn up around her small breasts, and the dark fan of her hair was spread wildly across the pillow. Dane pushed his feet into his shoes and combed his hair into some kind of order with his hands.

"Sure." Erin nodded, stretching luxuriously. Dane watched appreciatively. She was small but surprisingly strong, her hands especially.

"How do you like it?" he asked.

"Black, two sugars." She yawned. "I'll just take a little nap while you go fetch."

"Yes, ma'am." He grinned. He checked himself in the mirror on the back of the door, then let himself out into the corridor, blinking in the sudden burst of light. He bent down and looked out. Endless fields of strawberries, sugar beets, and nut trees. A light rain was falling, but the sun was shining brightly.

Turning away from the windows, he made his way up through the train to the bar car. All the tables were taken, and the air was thick with cigarette smoke. Voices were raised, laughing, heavy with alcohol, and Arthur was doing a roaring trade in beer. The two deadheads were awake now, arguing hotly in low voices. They both looked hung over.

"Missed their stop at Eugene." Arthur smiled as Dane stepped up to the bar. "Blaming each other." He shook his head. "Hafta get off at Salem now."

"Too bad," said Dane.

"For me," said Arthur. "Means I hafta put up with them for another half hour." The bartender sighed. "Get you something?"

"Two coffees. One black, two sugars, one regular, light on the cream."

"Two?" Arthur smiled briefly. "Looks like you did okay after all."

"You could say that," Dane answered.

"Rail romance," Arthur grunted, pouring the coffee expertly into two large Styrofoam cups. He began adding cream and sugar. "I could write a book."

"Why don't you?" Dane said.

"Nobody'd believe half the shit I seen go down." The bartender capped the cups, and Dane handed him three $1 bills.

"How long to Portland?" Dane asked, waving away the change again.

"Twenty-five to Salem unless there's a freight. Hour and a bit more after that to Portland."

"Thanks."

"Pleasure." Arthur slipped the two cups into an insulated paper bag and handed it across the counter. Dane gave the man a nod, then headed back to the sleeping car.

Breakfast in the early morning had been sprinkled

with double entendres, and the hour after that in Dane's
bedroom had led easily to sex. Too easily, even for a
woman on the verge of divorce. The seduction, if that
was what it was, had been managed with practiced
ease, right down to the relevant questions about safe
sex, AIDS, and all the rest. Without being too obvious,
he'd checked those strong hands carefully; no rings,
and no sign that she'd worn them recently. The well-
hung Mr. Falcone was apparently a myth.

The sex had been exquisite, but the fantasy of a
trainboard romance was still just that—a fantasy. Erin
Falcone was not what she appeared to be. And that
meant an almost certain connection to the Hawksworth
situation. He remembered the photographs taken on
board *Terpsichore*. The prostitute had been part-
Chinese, and the message left behind by the killers had
been in Mandarin. Then there was Kim Chee and her
mixed-blood son. He took a deep breath and let it out
slowly, shouldering open the door between cars. What
in God's name had he got himself into? He chewed at
his lip, tasting the musky, lingering tang of Erin Falcone's perfume. It was time to find out.

He stopped in front of roomette 9 and looked both
ways along the narrow corridor. Clear. Transferring the
insulated bag to his left hand, he gently pushed down
on the door handle of Erin's compartment.

It opened, and he let himself in, quickly shutting the
door behind him. The sleeping-car steward had made
up the bed long ago, and it had vanished into its niche
in the wall. The little cell was empty except for the col-
lapsible armchair that folded away when the bed was
down.

The blind was up. On this side of the train there were
no fields of strawberries. Looming hills, dark with ce-
dar. Silence except for the rumbling wheels, errant me-
tallic squeaks, and the hum of the little fan on its ledge
up by the ceiling. There was a faint smell; Erin's perfume in the air, not on his lip.

He put the bag down on the chair and looked around. Two pieces of luggage in the narrow cupboard slot to the left of the door; a soft-sided leather bag and an attaché case. Dane slid out the attaché case, moved the coffee bag onto the floor, and sat down with the case in his lap. Twin combination locks.

Most people had mediocre memories or were too lazy to code their locks with difficult-to-remember sequences. There were too many numbers on this case for a date-of-birth code, which was fortunate since he had no idea what it was. He went through a selection of easy sequences, giving himself a three-minute window before going on to the other bag. He hit the right progression on the third try—zeros right across the locks. He popped open the case.

A file folder, a clip-on telephone pager, and a medium-sized envelope. He took out the file folder, opened it, and glanced at the papers inside. It was a file of personal information relating to one Phillip Dane of Washington, D.C., rarebook dealer, ex-Defense Investigative Services curator. The three-page dossier had a computerized look about it and was not printed on letterhead. He had no idea where it had originated.

He turned to the envelope, emptying its contents into the interior of the case. Half a dozen I.D. wallets dropped out, identifying the bearer as everything from an FBI special agent to a homicide detective with the Vancouver, British Columbia, Police Force. All of the I.D. cards and badges looked totally authentic, and all of them bore a photograph of Erin Falcone. The names were different on each I.D. card, and all of them were Chinese/American combinations: Elaine Wu, Debra Lum, Janet Chung, Cynthia Qwong.

Dane put the I.D. wallets back into the envelope and picked up the pocket pager. A code number had been taped onto the side of the little device, but it told him nothing. He frowned. Cop, spook, or divorcée, why

bother to carry a telephone pager with you when you're
hundreds of miles out of its normal range?

He hefted the little device. Heavy. Too heavy. Examining it closely, he found a narrow plastic hinge on the
underside and a fingernail-sized depression above the
supposed speaker grill. He dug into his pocket, pulled
out a dime, and fitted it into the barely visible notch.
He twisted the dime, and the case popped open.

Inside, firmly held down by a Velcro strap, was a
.25-caliber "mousegun"—a Baby Browning replica
made by Fabrique Nationale in Belgium, with two
spare rounds in a built-in holder. Dane undid the Velcro
hold-down and popped the clip of the tiny automatic.
Six in the clip. He pulled back the slide—another in the
chamber.

It was a brilliantly simple bit of deception. Except
for X-ray machines for international flights the pager
could go through a metal detector without exciting any
interest, and the pager could be worn out in the open.

With a little bit of practice you could probably get
the weapon out at near-holster speed. He slipped the
clip back into the butt of the gun and curled his finger
around the trigger. Tiny but solid: it was no Saturday
Night Special.

The door to the roomette opened suddenly, and Dane
jerked back in his seat, the attaché case dropping to the
floor and knocking over the bag with the two cups of
coffee. He expected to see Erin Falcone, but instead he
found himself staring into the face of an Oriental male
in his late twenties wearing a dark green windbreaker
and blue jeans.

Dane came up out of the chair as the train lurched
over a junction point, spilling the intruder into the
roomette and almost into Dane's lap. The man's right
leg came up in a snap kick, but there was no room to
maneuver in the minuscule cabin.

Dane drove the hand holding the weapon into the
other man's face and heard bone crunch. Blood spurted

from his antagonist's nose, and the Oriental reeled back against the door, slamming it closed.

The man cursed wetly, and Dane had a brief image of his hand sweeping back the windbreaker before he reacted. His adversary was reaching for a weapon. Dane lifted the mousegun and squeezed the trigger almost without thinking.

There was a snapping noise like the sound of a small fire-cracker exploding, and a nailhead-sized hole magically appeared just below the attacker's right eye and black-powder freckles blossomed across his cheek. He dropped like a bundle of dirty laundry, his back propped up against the door.

Sweating, his breath coming in jerking gasps, Dane slumped down into the folding chair, staring at the dead man sharing the roomette with him.

"Jesus!" he whispered. The little room reeked with the rich smell of the coffee seeping into the carpet. There was another smell too; the man's sphincters had loosened as he died.

A woman with a dozen different names and a gun, and now this. Taking deep breaths, Dane put the pistol into his pocket, digging deeper to find his cigarettes and lighter. He found them and lit up, drawing in a huge breath of smoke. He exhaled with a shudder, trying to keep down the shock-shiver in his arms and legs.

This was no time to lose control. He continued to stare at the dead man on the floor. He'd seen plenty of dead bodies in Vietnam, enough to last him a lifetime, but he'd never even come close to killing anybody.

On the other hand, no one had ever tried to kill him. He climbed out of the chair and crouched down beside the corpse, forcing himself to go through the man's pockets, almost losing it when he had to roll the body over to get at the hip pocket of the jeans. Swallowing bile, he stumbled back to the chair, sat down, and examined what he'd found.

Wallet, keys, loose change, a book of matches, and

another handgun—this time a 9-mm Glock 19 in a belt
holster the man had tucked into the waistband of his
jeans at the small of his back. The wallet had a British
Columbia driver's license in a plastic folder identifying
the man as Ngo Tong Cai, age twenty-two, with an address in Vancouver. There was a government of Canada
citizenship registration card, plastic-laminated, showing
Ngo's birthplace as Hong Kong. Born into the hellhole
nightmare of the Dockyard Transit Center. No credit
cards, but a thousand dollars in worn American twenties. The keys had a Corvette tag and a set of miniature
license plates. The book of matches advertised the Timberline Restaurant in Richmond, British Columbia.

There was a double knock on the door, and Dane almost fainted, his heart suddenly pounding against his
ribs.

"Salem!" a muffled voice announced. "The next stop
is Salem, Oregon!" Dane heard footsteps, and then the
announcement was repeated, the words indistinct as the
conductor moved along the corridor.

Working as fast as he could, Dane yanked the attaché
case off the floor, haphazardly replacing its contents.
He also threw in the wallet, keys, matches, and the
Glock pistol, keeping Erin's mousegun in his pocket.
He snapped the case closed, stood, and put it on the
chair.

Using both hands, he wrestled the body of the dead
man into the farthest corner of the roomette and did
some quick calculations. If Erin was actually booked
through to Seattle, it was unlikely that anyone would
enter the roomette until then. Since the name she'd used
to reserved the compartment had almost certainly been
phony, they wouldn't be able to trace her, and except
for a nod and a wink from Arthur in the bar car, there
was nothing to connect Phillip Dane with the dead body
in roomette 9.

In this case discretion was undoubtedly the better
part of valor; if he got off the train in Portland, he'd

have more than an hour before the body was discovered, and perhaps more. He looked at the crumpled body in the corner. A corpse here and a naked woman in his bedroom. He took a last look around the roomette, then pulled down the blind. Ngo Tong Cai had come a long way from Hong Kong, but it hadn't got him far at all. Nowhere, in fact. Taking one last deep breath to calm himself, Dane left the roomette, closing the door softly behind him. Two minutes later he was back in his bedroom.

He closed the door behind him, pushed the locking bolt across, and opened the blind. On the bed Erin Falcone lifted her head off the pillow, confused by the sudden light. Then she noticed the attaché case in Dane's hand.

"No coffee?" she said, sitting up. She kept the sheet up around her breasts, holding it there with one splayed hand.

"No coffee," Dane answered coldly. He dropped the attaché case onto the end of the bed. "It spilled."

"In my roomette?" she asked. Her eyes moved from his face to the attaché case and back again. No fear, no nerves. Waiting.

"Just before I shot the guy with your cute little popgun," he said. Still no fear in her eyes, but sudden surprise.

"I beg your pardon?"

"Vietnamese," Dane said. "I'd guess that from his name anyway. Twenty-two years old. He was going to kill me; I killed him first." He barely paused. "So who the fuck are you?"

"I told you that. My name is Erin Falcone."

"You've got a bunch of other names too ... according to the goodies in your attaché case."

"You opened it?"

"Just before the coffee spilled. Eight zeroes in a row."

"Very James Bond of you," she said.

"Answer the question."

"My name is Erin Falcone."

"Who do you work for?"

"The Royal Hong Kong Police. The Triad Task Force."

"Bullshit. You're American."

"I'm on detached duty to the FBI. I've got dual citizenship."

"I don't believe you."

"So what?" She shrugged. The sheet slipped, and he saw the rounded shape of her breast, the nipple hard. "If you don't believe me, there's nothing I can say that will change your mind."

The train slowed even more and then came to a complete stop, dogging back and forth a few times. It started up again, moving at a snail's pace. Out the window Dane could see a white low-rise building, topped with a truncated tower and a gilded statue of a human figure. He looked back at Erin. She was sitting now, cross-legged, her knees jutting out sharply under the sheet.

"Why do you have a file on me?"

"You're curating Hawksworth," she answered flatly. Dane was surprised.

"You know what a curator does?" he asked.

"What Nixon couldn't. You cover up."

"Why are you interest in me?"

"We're not. We're interested in Hawksworth."

"Who's 'we'?"

"The FBI."

"Crap."

"The Hong Kong Police, the CIA, DIA, NSA ... take your pick." Her voice was cold and hot at the same time. Her eyes were angry now. "You won't believe anything I say, so it doesn't matter."

"That still doesn't explain why you played Mata Hari with me. Hawksworth's dead."

"I didn't sleep with you because I had to, Phillip; I

did it because I wanted to. And the fact that Hawksworth is dead is immaterial. The people he worked for are still very much alive."

"He worked for the Pentagon."

"Among others."

"Who?"

"It's too long a story to tell, especially if there's a dead Vietnamese in my roomette." She looked at him carefully. "Was that true?"

"Yes."

"Then we have to get off the train." Without waiting for his approval, she dropped the sheet and swung her legs off the bed. She began to dress, wriggling into her jeans.

"What's this 'we' shit?" asked Dane. Erin slipped on her dark blue silk blouse, flipping her hair back over the collar.

"You want to try and make it on your own?" she asked, buttoning the blouse. "You think the guy you killed was the only one on the train?"

"The guy was in your room, not mine," said Dane. "And that's where the body's going to be found. You're the one who should be worried . . . whatever your name is."

"You really think that guy was after me?" said Erin, eyes wide with disbelief. She laughed—a single, humorless bark. "From the way your file read, I'd have thought you were smarter than that."

"You're saying _I_ was the one he wanted?" Dane asked. It had never occurred to him.

"Of course, you stupid schmuck!" she said, laughing again. "Odds are that the guy you killed was one of David Long's people. Like it or not, Mr. Dane, you've brought the Holy Ghost down on our necks."

CHAPTER 25

THE ISLAND OF Naloa lies nine miles off Makapuu Beach on the Windward Coast of Oahu, almost directly in line with the Oceanic Institute for Research and Sea Life Park. The closest residential area is the suburban town of Kailua, several miles up the coast.

Naloa itself is five miles long and one mile wide. It is tear-drop-shaped, the broad end facing the open ocean, the point directed toward Oahu. The broad end of the island is volcanic highland, its stony beaches accessible only by sea. The highlands sweep down to the low end of the island, two thirds of which was once used as pastureland by the original owners.

The ranch buildings are all clustered around a small sand beach bay at the point of the island. The only electricity on the island is provided by a bank of diesel generators, and water is collected in a system of concrete cisterns scattered around the island, rainwater from the highlands being piped down to the bay.

The island had been purchased by Limehouse Trading in the late thirties, but the war blocked its development. James Chang's father had intended to make Naloa the centerpiece of his empire, but his capture and eventual death after the fall of Hong Kong prevented the realization of his dream.

Chang himself had taken over Naloa in the late sixties, shutting down the subsistence-ranching operation, paying off the hands, and selling the livestock. The small pineapple plantation on the island had been left to lie fallow, and within a few years the entire island was well advanced on a return to its jungle origins.

The original barns and sheds of the ranch were left in place, but the main house, built in the late 1800s and poorly maintained since well before the war, was demolished. Chang hired an architect from San Francisco, brought in contract workers from Honolulu, and a new house was built—a large one-and-a-half-story villa based on a Ming dynasty estate in the ancient Chinese city of Suzhou.

Half a million roof tiles were ordered from the newly opened imperial kilns in China, as well as several hundred thousand paving bricks. Dark gray Italian granite was used for the floors and arches, and *"Nan"* wood beams, arches, columns, and window frames were all hand-tooled in Hong Kong, numbered, and imported into Hawaii, where they were pegged together.

The gardens, hidden behind a high, skirting wall surrounding the house, were an exact replica of the original in China, complete with stone pools and waterfalls. A year and a half later the house was ready to be occupied at a cost of a little more than a million dollars.

In homage to the house on which it was based, Chang named the estate "Garden of the Master of the Fishing Nets." Although the main house had enough room to accommodate the entire Chang clan, five guest cottages, each with four bedrooms, were erected. Two of the old barns were renovated and transformed into dormitories, one for women and one for men, which were used to accommodate Naloa's regular staff of twenty.

Two or three times a year after the creation of Chang's compound, regular U-2 and SR-71 flights out of Bellows Air Force Base had overflown the island and taken surveillance photographs at the request of various state and federal authorities. At that point there was no evidence, direct or otherwise, that James Change or the Limehouse Trading Corporation were involved in anything illegal, but the fact that any access to the island had been strictly denied by Chang was enough to arouse suspicions.

So was the four-thousand-foot airstrip that had been built two hundred yards behind the house, and so was the thirty-nine-foot twin-hull Blue Thunder speedboat at the dock—an exact match for the go-fasts used by U.S. Customs in Hawaii.

The photographs, taken in every mode throughout the spectrum, showed absolutely nothing. Chang was neither bringing in covert shipments in the dead of night nor growing hidden patches of Kona Gold. Eventually it was assumed that James Chang simply wanted to be left alone, much like Hawaii's other famous hermits, the Robinsons of Niihau. The flights were discontinued except for once-a-year practice jaunts.

More specific surveillance by interested U.S. Customs—Dutch Kapono in particular—proved that the speedboat was used to bring supplies in from Oahu, and the airstrip was used to ferry arriving members of the Chang family from Honolulu International to Naloa. Lifestyles of the Rich and Famous "A-holes."

For James Chang Naloa, especially the house and its gardens, was both the future and the past. The classic rooms, furnished simply but with exquisite taste, represented everything his father and grandfather had worked for, and everything they had lost. In that way it was a memorial. For the future, it was where he would retire. His children and his grandchildren would visit him here, and through them he would watch the world for the last of his days.

With midday light splashing on the lily ponds outside, James Chang sat at the large conference table in the Garden Room, looking out through the carved lattice doors. The sun shone in Hawaii like nowhere else in the world, creating a richness of color that was dreamlike. In front of him on the huge expanse of polished rosewood was a tea set and an ashtray. The tea was Black Turtle green, his favorite. Beside the ashtray was the small green buckram-bound notebook that had once belonged to Vernon Wendell Cates.

Chang sipped the mild, piping-hot liquid and took occasional puffs on his cigarette as he watched the play of sunlight on the ponds outside. He smiled softly; the ponds, silently and gracefully, defined the difference between East and West.

For the Eastern mind and soul it was the liquidity of the ever-changing scene that mattered, a demonstration of fleeting time and man's small place in the universe.

To the Eastern mind, like that of the French Impressionist Monet, the light on the pond was something to be captured and kept. An impossibility, of course—you could not keep the sun or own an instant of time, no matter how infinitesimal the moment.

"Nothing stays the same, and nothing changes," he said aloud. He took another sip of tea and noticed it was cooling. The Confucian conundrum applied as much to the Black Dragon as it did to the ponds outside. The empire he'd spun out of nothing into a global web worth billions would remain in one form or another after he was gone, but its shape and spirit would change with time—that was something he had to face. Black Dragon of the son would not be the Black Dragon of the father.

Which was fair enough. His own father, building on the work of the first Blue-Eyed Chang, had seen two worlds separate. To him, Black Dragon was the physical manifestation of the lineage and was created to work within the realm of his own kind. The classic way of the tongs; prey on your own and the *gwei-lo* will leave you be. Curry favor with the Westerners, but tell them nothing of what you do or what you think. They were, literally, to be treated as ghosts: there, but not there, with no impact on real life.

The concept had worked for both men, at least to a degree, but neither had fully understood, or admitted to themselves, that because of what they were—*ya ou ho chung jen*—half-castes, they stood astride both worlds. His father had believed that the *Hui* would survive despite anything done by the *gwei-lo* as long as he stayed out of their affairs. The Second World War had proved him fatally wrong, and ironically, it was a *gwei-lo,* in the form of William Hawksworth, who had provided the phoenix-fire that gave the *Hui* its new beginning.

Finally returning to England in late 1945 James Chang found the remains of his father's empire in ashes. "Friends" of Limehouse Trading had stripped the company of most of its assets, and except for a small group of loyal men, the *Hui* itself was an empty shell.

The ceremony investing Chang as *Shan Chu* of Black Dragon took place in a basement flat located in a bombed-out section of the East End of London and was overseen by Abbot Fong's uncle, the previous White Paper Fan of the Triad.

To Chang the investiture was an embarrassment. With the exception of a few docklands warehouses and a small trust fund established by his father, Black Dragon and Limehouse had no assets. Its small fleet of tea freighters had either been sunk during the war or seized for debt.

Virtually all the overseas Chinese communities except for New York and San Francisco were impoverished, and Black Dragon's criminal interests had long since been taken over by other groups. Chang knew that it would take a great deal of time and even greater amounts of money to regain the position of honor his father had once occupied, and he had neither. What he did have was William Hawksworth.

Without explaining why, James Chang asked Abbot's uncle to find out anything he could about the war hero. Several weeks later the elder Fong reported that Hawksworth was now deputy head of Air Transport Group in the Pacific, operating out of Tokyo and Wake

Island but headquartered in Honolulu. There also seemed to be a connection between Hawksworth and Conrad Lang of Lang Aviation and Manufacturing.

The aging White Paper Fan had put together files on both Hawksworth and Lang, which he gave to Chang. There was also a rumor that Hawksworth, although married, had a mistress living in Honolulu, a Chinese named Kim Chee Leung who had once been a house servant to the Soong-Chiang *Hui* in Chungking.

Chang took the information and spent several days digesting it, arranging the small string of facts like pearls on a string, realizing intuitively that intelligence like this could often be more valuable than gold.

Hawksworth had been born into a moderately privileged family in New Hampshire. In other times he might have become a doctor or a lawyer at best. But the war had changed more fortunes than Chang's. Hawksworth's adventure with Doolittle's boys had made him a hero, and as a hero he'd married a woman of influence in Washington.

He'd also managed to ally himself with a major industrialist, as well as give himself a mistress with indirect but distinct associations to a family of incredible wealth and power. Madame Chiang was a force in her own right; she had brothers who were international bankers and one who was the Chinese ambassador to the United States. Pearls on a string indeed, and he had the clasp that brought them together.

Against the advice of the elder Fong, Chang dipped deeply into the remaining capital in his trust fund and booked passage to Hawaii, arriving at the Aloha Terminal in Honolulu in early April of 1946.

Under an assumed name he rented a tiny room in a boardinghouse on Hotel Street. It took him four days to discover that Kim Chee Leung was working as a clerk for the Pacific Air Transport Corporation of America and another two days to find out where she lived.

Immediately following the war Honolulu was in a

lively, bureaucratic chaos of rebuilding and expansion, and Chang had no difficulty joining the hordes of illegal immigrants working in Honolulu. He found himself a job as a laborer, spending his days removing the barbed-wire barricades on Waikiki Beach and his evenings standing watch over Kim Chee Leung's apartment. He knew that eventually William Hawksworth would show up.

His patience was rewarded after a fortnight's surveillance. One evening in the third week of May a taxi pulled up in front of the woman's wood-frame building in the tumbledown Iwilei District. A tall man in civilian clothes stepped out, paid off the driver, and entered the building. Chang had memorized the photographs of Hawksworth he'd clipped out of *Life* magazine and knew there was no mistake. His quarry had appeared.

Satisfied, he returned to his rooming house and composed a letter that he mailed to Hawksworth, addressed to the Air Transport Group headquarters at Hickam Field. The letter was brief and to the point:

Dear Colonel Hawksworth:
I believe it would be to your advantage to meet with me in the Banyan Court Room of the Moana Hotel at noon on Wednesday to discuss matters relating to the death of Vernon Wendell Cates, a man with whom you were once acquainted.
A reservation has been made in your name.

Chang left the note unsigned. On Tuesday afternoon he quit his job as a laborer and purchased a plain but well-cut suit. On Wednesday morning he checked out of his room on Hotel Street and took his few possessions to the Aloha Terminal where he had a third-class passage on the *Matsonia,* making her first postwar voyage to San Francisco that evening. He had no intention of leaving anything to chance; if Hawksworth intended him any harm, there would be very little time for him to act.

Escape route arranged, James Chang arrived in front of the Moana at twelve-thirty. The hotel, Hawaii's oldest, was a huge, ornate five-story Victorian pile, its columned main entrance surrounded by towering palms. Located on Kalakaua Avenue, its sprawling rear lanai looked out onto Waikiki Beach.

Crossing the lobby and ignoring the slightly suspicious looks of the hotel staff, Chang entered the ballroom-sized expanse of the Banyan Court and spotted Hawksworth, seated at a small table close to one of the room's high, arched windows. He made his way between the tables and sat down across from Hawksworth. The air-force colonel, dressed again in civilian clothes, looked startled for a moment, then regained his composure. Chang examined him silently.

Tall, clean-shaven, square-jawed, and handsome, the wings of gray hair at his temples that would become his trademark only just beginning to appear. Aquiline nose with deep caliper lines arching down to thin lips. Eyes gray-blue, complexion slightly reddened by too much long exposure to the sun.

"Colonel Hawksworth," Chang said finally, keeping a polite smile on his face. Around them Chang was only dimly aware of the crowded room and the chatter of the other lunchtime guests.

"I'm afraid you have me at a disadvantage," Hawksworth answered. His voice was brittle and his features rigid. He kept his hands clasped in front of him on the bright white linen of the tablecloth.

"Yes." Chang nodded, his voice low. "I suppose I do. But knowing my name wouldn't change the situation, I'm afraid."

"Have we met before?" asked Hawksworth. A waiter shimmered out of nowhere. Hawksworth waved him away with a hand, his eyes hard on the man seated across from him.

"I've seen you from a distance," Chang answered. "In Chungking. At the airfield. You looked much different then."

"We all looked different then." Hawksworth paused. "You're from Chungking?"

"No."

"You speak English well. You have an accent that seems . . ." He let it hang. Chang smiled at the condescending comment.

"Eton," he answered briefly. "And then the Asquith School in Rangoon." He let the smile cool. "With an education like that, even a Chinaman learns to speak the language properly."

"I'm sorry. . . ." Hawksworth's complexion darkened. "I didn't mean to . . . you were in Burma?"

"Yes."

"How did you come to be in Chungking?"

"I was fleeing the Japanese, just like everyone else," Chang answered. There was a long pause.

"How did you know Vern Cates?" Hawksworth asked finally.

"We only met once," Chang said. "I borrowed his jacket."

"Pardon?" Hawksworth looked confused.

"I don't think he minded me taking it," Chang said, smiling again. "He was dead at the time."

"I don't get it," said Hawksworth. He was very nervous now, the fingers of his clasped hands moving like small snakes on the tablecloth. The waiter slid by again, and this time Chang ordered drinks, a gin-and-tonic for himself and a martini for Hawksworth.

"I was a refugee," Chang explained. "I had valid British papers, but I was Chinese, so getting out was very difficult. It was shortly after the Doolittle Raid. You'd arrived and were being wined and dined by Madame Chiang and her family. I was looking for scraps of food and a dry place to sleep." He paused. "It rained hard, do you remember?"

"Yes. I remember," Hawksworth answered stiffly. "It was a swamp."

"A good description." Chang nodded. The drinks arrived, and the waiter vanished. Chang took a sip of his, but Hawksworth ignored the glass in front of him. The olive stared at Chang like a bulbous green eye. At the far end of the room a string quartet began a mooning Island version of "It's a Long Way to Tipperary." "At any rate," Chang continued, "I happened to crawl into a transport, looking for a place to dry off ... maybe a chocolate bar left behind by one of the air crew. I found your friend Vernon Wendell Cates. There were some others with him, all dead."

"But ..." Hawksworth began.

"But that particular aircraft was destroyed, wasn't it?" Chang interrupted. "Burned that night. All the evidence destroyed. You thought you were safe."

Hawksworth snapped, no longer able to contain himself. "Get to the fucking point, you ..."

"Chink?" offered Chang. "Is that what you were going to say?" He leaned forward, pushing his drink aside. "All right, Colonel, I'll do just that." He took a deep breath, trying to keep calm, knowing that the next few moments would define his future.

"You were the seventeenth B-25 in the flight, the last plane off the carrier. There were six of you on board, and that was important, wasn't it? Usually there were only five men in a B-25 crew. You were the pilot, Travsky was the navigator, and Stroud was the copilot. Those were the officers. There were two others—Sergeant Blaine, the engineer-gunner, and Corporal Zabrisky, the bombardier. And then there was the sixth man—Vernon Wendell Cates. He was one of your 'dodo's,' a wingless bird. A writer for *Stars and Stripes*. Doolittle thought it might be a good idea to have a bit of public-relations presence. But just in case, no one put his name down on the flight list. There was no record that he ever climbed into *Holy Ghost*—that was the name you gave your plane, wasn't it? You even had it painted on the nose—a black-shrouded banshee with a sickle in its hand, remember? They ran an old picture of it when they did the *Life* magazine story about you. Congressional Medal of Honor winner William Sloane Hawksworth and his crew. The other four were there but no Vernon Cates."

"How do you know all this?" Hawksworth whispered, his voice raw.

"Because Cates was a writer, Colonel Hawksworth. He wrote it all down, from the days on board the *Hornet* right through to meeting up with you in Heng-yang He kept notes, Colonei.

"That was his job, writing. He was going to go up in *Holy Ghost* while you bombed the hell out of Tokyo, and he was going to win the Pulitzer. But it didn't work out that way, did it? If Vernon Cates had told the real story, you never would have had that medal pinned on your chest by the president of the United States. You would have been court-martialed, Colonel. You would have been disgraced. And you would have been tried. For murder."

"Who are you?" said Hawksworth. "What in God's name do you want from me?"

"I'm a businessman, Colonel Hawksworth. And I want your cooperation."

It had been easy after that. Hawksworth's position as deputy head of ATG had provided an invaluable source of information concerning goods being transshipped through Honolulu and postwar shortages created a thriving black market that Chang tapped into immediately. Using his influence with Lang, Hawksworth had Chang hired on as a "consultant" to Pacific Air Transport, and with San Francisco as his base of operations the young *Shan Chu* of Black Dragon moved back and forth across the Pacific, reestablishing old ties and acting as a middle-man between the dozens of criminal organizations that had been lying dormant through the war years.

Fueled by his share of the proceeds from the Royal Bank of Thailand shipment, Chang began to reconstruct his father's empire, investing heavily in legitimate businesses, Pacific Air Transport included. Conrad Lang, who knew only that Chang was a "business associate" of Hawksworth's, initially balked at partnership with the young Chinese man, but Chang's knowledge of the language and the ways of the Orient quickly proved their worth as PATCOA's interests and Black Dragon's presence spread across the Pacific and into Asia, aided by information provided by Hawksworth.

Within four years, with Chang's help, PATCOA had swallowed up a dozen small air-transport companies, including Oriental Northern, Saigon Air Services, Aero Philippina, Bharat Air Transport, Iran Aero Services, Djibouti Airways, Golden Gulf Airways, and Turkish Air Transit. The complex grid of routes made PATCOA the premier air-cargo carrier from Taiwan to Istanbul.

Not surprisingly it also gave James Chang access to every major produce and processor of opium in the Orient, as well as the means to ship it. At the same time he used the various airlines to move large quantities of gold through the illegal bullion market much more quickly than his competition, often trebling his investments within a few days. By 1950 Chang had regained virtually everything lost by his father during the war, and Limehouse Trading was once again a growing concern in London.

In 1952 Chang severed any direct connection between himself and PATCOA, except for a minority-share position held through several blind corporations in Taiwan. Lang and his company had too high a profile, and its use as a carrier of illicit goods was becoming more and more dangerous. Chang began to develop new methods of transporting his opium. On the other hand, PATCOA was a profitable enough business legitimately, and several years later Limehouse Trading purchased the corporation from Lang and changed its name to Pacific American Transport Corporation, fleshing out its air fleet with half a dozen surplus Liberty freighters and four cargo liners once owned by the Osaka Shosen Line. An enormous number of tea crates could be carried in the belly of a ten-thousand-ton freighter, and those crates provided an almost infinite number of places to secrete large amounts of equally aromatic substances.

Throughout those years Chang maintained his connection with Hawksworth, using information from him to further his successes, each act of treachery further binding the war hero to the fortunes of Black Dragon. Eventually the relationship became almost civil, and the two men occasionally even shared a meal. But never did James Chang ever tell his "business associate" the whereabouts of Vernon Wendell Cates's wartime journal.

Silently a white-jacketed member of the Naloa staff entered the Garden Room carrying a large black-lacquer tray. He replaced the cold pot of tea with a fresh one, emptied Chang's ashtray, and put a clean one in its place. Then the man withdrew as quietly as he had come.

Chang reached into the breast pocket of his open-necked Hawaiian shirt and took out a pair of lightly tinted, horn-rim glasses. He put them on, annoyed by the constricting feel of them, then lit a fresh cigarette. With one hand he reached out and touched the rough, faded cover of Cates's little notebook, seeing the man's face and the small, star-shaped wound in his neck as though it were yesterday.

Peering over the edge of his glasses, he looked out into the gardens again, assuring himself of the present. He sighed; he spent more and more of his time now thinking of the past and avoiding the future. Another sign of age, like the glasses he wore for reading. He turned his attention back to the book and opened it.

A ragged story, nothing more than notes for an article never written, epitaph to a life never lived.

High winds and wild seas ... two men almost drowned today when *Cimarron* was refueling us ... sick as a dog. Not the crew of *Holy Ghost* though, God damn them. I think Zabrisky cheats.

Weather just goes on getting worse. Somehow they keep on launching the patrols from *Enterprise* though. Everyone on the *Hornet*'s getting edgy now. Getting close to the land of the Nips, I guess.

Halsey must have crapped his drawers today. There was a radio report on Jap Radio that mentioned three bombers over Tokio.

April 17. Gale force winds. I'm still sick. Rather be in *Holy Ghost* going for the Japs than down here. Doolittle's rolling the B-25s out. Could be any time now.

The writing in the notebook became jerky, almost unreadable.

Up. Jesus! Doolittle was first in line. We watched him go. Christ! No one thought he was going to make it off the deck. Hawksworth: "I'm fucked if I'm going to follow that crazy buzzard into the soup!" Zabrisky is playing solitaire.

Hawksworth says trouble with #2 engine. Arguing with Blaine and Stroud. H. says it's his decision. What are they talking about?

Should be half hour Tokio. Something wrong. Out of position. Shit—are we aborting mission?

And then a single word.

Coward.

The next few entries were smeared by rain and dirt. Chang let his fingers touch the pages. Chinese rain, Chinese soil. Enough was legible to tell the next part of the tale.

Hawksworth had shifted south well before reaching the target, warned off by flak and a flight of Zeros. They had ditched their bomb load somewhere over the sea between Japan and the mainland, staying at treetop level. According to the notes, there was nothing visibly wrong with any of the engines until they started to run out of fuel.

As it turned out, Hawksworth's cowardice was wasted; heading toward one of their designated bases in a Nationalist-held sector, they ran into another flight of Zeros. Travsky the navigator was killed in the first attack, Zabrisky and Blaine in the second.

Stroud, the copilot, was wounded, but Cates managed to get him into a chute. At that point Hawksworth appeared from the cockpit, sidearm drawn and in his hand. He fired once, the bullet striking Cates in the chest but deflecting off the buckle of his parachute. With the bomb doors open, Cates took the only means of escape and jumped, even though they were still well inside Japanese territory.

According to the journal, Cates spent the next three days dodging Japanese patrols as he desperately tried to make his way into friendly territory. Eventually he made it and was taken to a field hospital near Chuhsien. It was here that he first heard of Hawksworth's "heroism."

Apparently Hawksworth had bailed out with the wounded Stroud, then carried him for two days, searching for a doctor, almost dying in the process. Cates noted in his journal that it was more likely Hawksworth didn't want to leave the copilot's fate in anyone's hands but his own.

Cates managed to track down the doctor in Chuhsien who'd treated Hawksworth for exposure. According to the Chinese medical man, Stroud had been dead when Hawksworth reached safety, killed by several bullet wounds inflicted by Zeros during the Tokyo raid.

Cates took that information with more than a grain of salt, knowing that *Holy Ghost* had never reached Tokyo, and knowing that Stroud's wound had been caused by a piece of razor-sharp Lexan from the B-25's shattered side window, blown out during the attack by the Zeros. Serious perhaps, but not fatal. Cates reached the obvious conclusion: Hawksworth had murdered his fellow officer to prevent him from saying anything about his cowardly action in the face of the enemy.

The doctor told Cates that Hawksworth had been sent on to Heng-yang, where transport would be provided to Chungking. Cates's last journal entry said that it was his intention to follow Hawksworth to Heng-yang and confront him.

The final pages in the book were blank except for one. It was a pencil sketch of the nose of a Mitchell B-25 showing a cowled, faceless figure, skeletal hands holding an upraised scythe. Underneath in flowing script was the name:

HOLY GHOST

Chang closed the book gently. He looked up, suddenly aware of the sound of an aircraft engine. He glanced at his watch: too early for the regular mail and supply flight.

Jeremy Ting appeared in the doorway of the Garden Room, dressed in his usual black suit and green bow tie. Ting was in overall charge of the Naloa staff and managed the island's affairs. Chang had hired him years before as a summer tutor for his son, and the fact that Ting was still there, and in charge of things, infuriated Jimmy.

"What it is, Jeremy?" Chang asked. The hollow-cheeked man approached the far end of the table.

"Your son, sir, returning from Honolulu. Your daughter Victoria is with him, and so is Mr. Kee. It would seem that our guests are beginning to arrive."

"Take a Jeep out to the airstrip," Chang instructed. "Make them welcome and inform my son and Mr. Kee that I will see them after they have settled in."

"Of course, sir." Ting withdrew.

Chang stood up wearily and slipped the little notebook into the pocket of his jacket. He looked out at the changing light that played across the ponds. The end was about to begin.

CHAPTER 26

GENERAL ALEXANDER CORDASCO, dressed in civilian clothes, arrived at Tampa International Airport on a scheduled American Airlines flight from Washington, D.C. He took the complimentary shuttle bus from Terminal A to the Airport Holiday Inn, checking in to his room as "Mr. Allan Blake."

Once in his room he quickly changed into the uniform of an air-force colonel, slipped on a pair of blue-tinted aviator sunglasses, and returned to the lobby. He was met there by a driver from MacDill Air Base who took him to a waiting car.

Taking Shore Boulevard south to Boundary Road and then across to Bayshore Drive, it took less than twenty minutes to reach the base headquarters building, which they proceeded to bypass after Cordasco showed his entirely false identification at the main gate.

From there they followed the MacDill extension of Bayshore Drive even further south along the peninsula, leaving the concentration of buildings around the airfield far behind. Just beyond Catfish Point, with the bright blue of Hillsborough Bay on their right, they reached another checkpoint manned by two heavily armed men in combat fatigues that carried no rank or unit insignia. A small blue sign on the high barbed-wire fence announced that they were entering a "Security Operations Training Facility."

Cordasco switched from his car to a waiting Jeep, which took him to the farthest tip of the peninsula at

Gadsden Point. The Jeep was driven by a black man in his twenties wearing the same unmarked combat fatigues as the gate guards. There wasn't even a name bar over his breast pocket.

It was midafternoon, and even the breeze blowing in off the Gulf couldn't ward off the punishing heat. By the time the Jeep reached the small cluster of cinderblock buildings that marked his destination, he was soaked in sweat.

The unit was completely anonymous. Half a dozen flatroofed administrative buildings, a long, low barracks building, a fenced motor pool, and three extremely large hangar structures, all unmarked. There was tall razor-wire fence running around the tip of the point, and Cordasco could see at least a dozen pylons carrying the spinning pods of perimeter-radar modules. Around the largest of the administrative buildings there was a forest of telecommunications antennae and two microwave dishes.

"This way, Colonel," instructed the Jeep driver. He led the way to a bungalow-sized building tucked in behind the antenna array. The entrance to the building was without signage. Reaching it, the Jeep driver opened the door and stood aside. Cordasco went inside, and the driver closed the door behind him.

The inside of the building was cool, and Cordasco could hear the hum of a hidden air conditioner. He was in a reception room of some kind. Desk, chair, filing cabinets—all fitted with combination locks. A large-scale map of MacDill on the wall.

A door at the far end of the room opened, and yet another figure in combat fatigues appeared. He was in his fifties, dark hair buzzed down to the scalp, craggy face pitted by time, events, and—in the distant past—adolescent acne.

"General Clark?" asked Cordasco, extending a hand. The man stepped forward and took it, gripping briefly. "You must be General Cordasco. We meet at last."

He turned, waving for Cordasco to follow. "Come on into my office, and I'll crack you a beer."

The inner office was more inviting than the reception room, but not by much. Except for the humming air conditioner in the window and a small bar fridge balanced on a filing cabinet, General Clark didn't seem too interested in the privileges of rank. Metal desk, freestanding closet in one corner, and a series of huge map files against the far wall. Directly behind the desk was a large, framed reproduction of "The Last Supper." A neatly cut out photograph of Stormin' Norman Schwarzkopf had been glued over the face of Christ.

"Birthday present from the guys," said Clark, noting Cordasco's interest. He took two Coronas out of the fridge and brought one across the room. He gestured toward the wooden armchair on the other side of his desk and sat down. Cordasco took the beer and followed suit.

"The audit boys at the Pentagon would be impressed," he said, looking around the room. "You're obviously not spending their money on office equipment."

"We're not spending their money at all." Clark grinned. He took a long swallow of beer. "And you know it."

Cordasco sipped his own beer and nodded. Special Operations Command, of which Clark was a divisional commander, had an above-board budget of slightly more than $3 billion a year to administer a forty-five-thousand man organization spread out over a dozen different bases and including navy SEAL, air-force commandos, Green Berets, and Delta Force. Money for specific operations was supposed to be approved on an individual basis by the Pentagon, but SOC had long ago learned how to bypass the normal chain of command, and each of its divisions had created "black" channels for financing that never appeared on the Pentagon's books or anyone else's.

"I guess Desert Storm had its public-relations benefits," said Cordasco blandly.

"Bet your ass," said Clark, taking another slug of beer. "As far as the brass is concerned, we're still the 'crazies in the basement,' but now we're crazies that can bite. A proven commodity, you might say." He put his beer bottle down on the desk. "The paper-chasers are pretty much turning a blind eye these days."

"Speaking of paper . . ." said Cordasco, letting it dangle.

"Clean as a whistle," Clark answered. "All run through an ISA proprietary in Miami." The Special Operations general stood up and came around the desk. He went to one of the map files, pulled out a large-scale sheet, and brought it back to Cordasco. He spread the map out across the desk, pinning down one end with his beer bottle. Cordasco stood up and examined the map. It was a large-scale chart of the Caribbean.

"Can you do it in one jump?" asked Cordasco. Clark shook his head.

"Not quite." He poked one thick finger down on the map. "We ferry down to Homestead first. We've got a legit Op set with the Thirty-first Tactical Wing as cover. They fly into the Everglades; we go the other direction."

"How long?" asked Cordasco.

"We go nap-of-the-earth most of the way. It's two-hundred-twenty-six miles to the target. We figure sixty-eight minutes to contact, four minutes on site, and an hour back. Hundred and thirty-six minutes door to door. Pretty good window—target's a hundred miles inside our operating range."

"You think four minutes over the site will be enough?" Cordasco asked, frowning. Clark let his finger drift across the map, drawing a line from Homestead Air Force Base at the top of the Keys out into the open ocean just below Nassau.

"Four minutes and I'll squash Howard's Cay like a

bug," said Clark. He put his thumb down on the small
dot that marked the island and twisted. "Like a fucking
bug." Clark stood away from the map and glanced at
his companion. "And I'll show you how," he said.
"Come on with me."

Clark took Cordasco out into the baking heat again
and led the way to one of the large hangar buildings.
Fishing a key out of the pocket of his fatigues, he unlocked a small door in one enormous wall and ushered
Cordasco into the hanger's cavernous interior.

The building was a third the size of a football field,
its lattice grid of steel roof beams almost fifty feet overhead. The hanger was lit by dozens of high-intensity
pans dangling from the ceiling, creating pools of light
and pockets of shadow across the concrete floor. There
were a dozen vacant work areas scattered around the
perimeter of the building, but Cordasco's eyes were
drawn to the five Mantalike machines drawn-up in line
abreast directly in front of him.

"Brand-new LHs," said Clark, motioning Cordasco
forward. "On loan from the Army Aviation Center at
Fort Rucker. We're supposed to be doing operational
testing."

The helicopters were each a little more than forty
feet long, snake-headed with a broadening fuselage that
thinned to a chunky tail section, the rear rotor enclosed
in a metal shroud. There was a twin-barreled proboscis
jutting out from below the nose, and stubby wings grew
out of each side. Drooping over everything was a five-
bladed rotor. The gunships were painted a dull, neutral
gray and had no military markings of any kind.

"I've been hearing about these." Cordasco nodded.
"Central beam that everything hangs on. No structural
role for the skin at all."

"That's it," said Clark. "The skin's composite, like
the rotors. Stealthy as shit . . . real voodoo stuff. Not
quite as fast as an Apache, but who cares if they can't
see you coming?"

"Doesn't seem to have a whole lot of weaponry," Cordasco commented. Clark shrugged.

"Twelve Hellfire missiles on the pylons, and the Gatling out front pumps fifteen-hundred rounds a minute of twenty-millimeter cannon fire. Figure it out for yourself."

Cordasco did a rough calculation in his head. The Hellfires carried a forty-pound high-explosive or incendiary payload. The five gunships could place more than a ton of explosive with deadly accuracy and follow up with thirty thousand rounds of cannon fire. All in four minutes.

"I guess they'll do," he said, smiling at Clark. The general grinned fiercely and patted one of the machines on its bulbous nose-end sensor turret.

"Damn right," he said happily. He thumbed thin air. "I told you . . . like a bug."

"A lot of people will sleep easier once it's done," Cordasco said quietly. "And not just in the Pentagon."

"Just so the deal is fair," said Clark. "We get whatever's in the accounts, right?"

"The papers are already cut. Your man from Intelligence Support Activity goes in with a Seized Asset authorization signed off by DEA, and you can siphon the money anywhere you want. The banks won't be a problem; they'll be too embarrassed."

"Just so long as there's no paper trail," Clark grunted. "Brownie points from the Gulf War aside, we can't afford another screw-up like the Yellow Fruit thing." The man shook his head. "Hell of a way to finance a drug war, don't you think, General?"

"It's a hell of a world." Cordasco shrugged. "Sometimes you fuck the enemy, sometimes the enemy fucks you."

"I suppose," Clark answered. "At least on this one we're the fucker and not the fuckee."

The dark green Mercedes drove slowly down Lion's Head Road in Kowloon's Sanpokong District, headlights charting a course through the looming canyon of timeworn factories and warehouses. Every few minutes the night sky overhead blazed with flashing lights and the ground beneath the automobile's tires shook as yet another jumbo jet thundered in for a landing at Kai Tak, giant wheels almost scraping the rooftops as the aircraft made their hair-raising approach to the airport's single runway less than a mile to the east.

The landings were so nerve-racking for pilots that the local government had long since banned flashing neon lights on buildings within a five-mile perimeter of the airport to prevent confusion, but everyone knew that it was only a matter of time before a Cathay Pacific 747 or a Northwest Orient DC-10 turned Sanpokong into an inferno of blast-furnace aviation fuel, melting Samsonite and caramelized human flesh.

The Mercedes turned off Lion's Head into the crowded, filthy jumble of streets and alleys bordering Choi Hung and pulled in behind a row of dark blue overflowing garbage dumpsters. To the right of the automobile there was the blank-walled concrete block facade of a warehouse almost as large as the helicopter hangar at MacDill Air Force Base.

There were two men in the car, one young, one old. The younger man, dark-haired and wearing a plain gray suit, sat behind the wheel smoking a Red Lotus–brand cigarette. His companion, in his sixties, was thin-faced and partially bald, salt-and-pepper hair trimmed short over the age-spotted parchment skin that covered his skull.

The younger man, a Hong Kong agent-in-place for the Communist Chinese Secret Service, spoke Mandarin. The older man beside him, a businessman from Taiwan, spoke Fukienese. When they talked, it was in the only language they shared—English.

For Chinese they were the strangest of bedfellows; Sheng Yu Ti, the younger of the two, was thirty-six years old, a career intelligence officer and a staunch Communist. Huang Man Chun, at sixty-nine, owned three silicone factories, a shipping line, and a company that manufactured expensive tennis rackets. He was also a deeply committed capitalist. But they had one thing in common beyond a knowledge of English: Both men hated the Kuomintang legacy of Chiang Kai-shek.

On the Mainland Chiang and the KMT represented everything the Revolution had been fought for, and contrary to the long-held Western fantasy that Chiang represented the wishes of the Chinese masses, Sheng Yu Ti knew that historically Chiang had never been anything more than a self-aggrandizing minor warlord who was more interested in lining his own pockets than creating a united China.

Huang's hatred was much more specific. The KMT and the 2 million Mainland Chinese Chiang had brought with him in 1949 had ruled more than 17 million native Taiwanese with an iron fist for more than forty years, and more than half of the Taiwanese National Assembly was still made up of Kuomintang members who had installed themselves in their positions for life. By their standards they were "fathers" to their Taiwanese children.

Part of their paternal discipline had resulted in the terrible 2–28 massacre in 1947, a popular uprising that the KMT aborted by killing ten thousand Taiwanese and imprisoning thousands more in the infamous Green Island penal colony just off the eastern coast.

Huang's mother and father had been among the ten thousand killed, and Huang himself, a university lecturer, was sent to Green Island for eleven years. On his release in 1958 he discovered that all his family's land and business interests had been expropriated by the KMT. Everything he had now had been built from nothing.

Seated behind the wheel of the Mercedes, Sheng flipped the butt of his cigarette out the open window and looked at his watch. It was just after three in the morning. Lowering his head, he checked through the windshield. Nothing moved. Another jet pounded through the air less than two hundred feet over their heads, and Sheng felt the sudden pressure wave of its passage push against his eardrums.

"Kang men lou," he muttered under his breath. He tried not to breathe too deeply; the air in the narrow roadway stank like an open sewer.

"I beg your pardon?" said Huang.

"I'm sorry, Uncle," Sheng apologized, using the polite honorific for his companion. "I was thinking out loud."

"And what was your thought?" Huang asked.

"I was observing that if Hong Kong is the asshole of China, then this part of Hong Kong must be one of its hemorrhoids."

"I wouldn't argue the point," Huang agreed. "I have been in this so-called 'Fragrant Harbor' for the better part of a week, and the only conclusion I can come to is that here the color green is synonymous with money. What they call 'parkland,' we would call a 'back garden.' "

"This place is a curse," Sheng grumbled.

"Not looking forward to Turnover?" asked Huang.

"Perhaps once Hong Kong would have provided a much-needed window to the West," the younger man said. "But we have made our own in the meantime. We have troubles enough without inheriting the problems here."

"One of which we must try and solve together . . . now," said Huang. He peered through the windshield again. There was movement at the small door leading into the warehouse. "I think we are ready, Nephew," he said, pointing with his chin. Sheng looked. The door had opened, and a man in the uniform of the Royal Hong Kong Police was standing in a faint spill of light.

"Hao!" Sheng grunted. "It's about time."

The two men left the Mercedes and picked their way through the littered garbage in the alley, eventually reaching the door. A small sign in Cantonese over the entrance announced that this was the Sanpokong Closed Compound. The policeman, a cotton mouth mask covering the lower half of his face, stepped aside and ushered Sheng and Huang inside.

The smell was overwhelming, and Huang gagged, reaching into the pocket of his jacket for a handkerchief. It was the smell of Green Island again—urine, feces, the rot of sweat and death. Fear.

The warehouse was two hundred feet long and fifty feet wide, flat roof supported by dozens of wooden columns that broke the concrete expanse of floor into broad aisles that stretched into the distance. Scores of small cooking fires burned everywhere, smoke clouding the air, slowly rising up between crisscross lines of hanging, tattered rags to the metal roof beams high above. Even at this late hour there was a steady hum of voices, cries in the night from old men and children. The yap and snarl of dogs.

Three thousand people were jammed into the building's interior, each allowed no more than the extent of a five-by-two woven pallet for a living space. They were dressed in rags, small bundles of possessions gathered jealously close to pitifully thin bodies, last of the more than three hundred thousand refugees who had passed through Hong Kong in the years after the end of the Vietnam War. These were the friendless ones, those too poor or too unconnected to have found sanctuary in the United States or Canada. In places like Sanpokong and five or six other hidden compounds in Kowloon and the New Territories, they waited for the skeins of their fate to unravel.

"My God!" Sheng whispered, horrified.

"No gods here," Huang answered. "Even the devils of the world would avoid a place like this."

"Follow me," said the Hong Kong policeman, his

words muffled by the mask. The two men, one young, one old, followed their guide down one of the endless, smoky pathways between the dense patterns of human detritus. An ancient woman, gray hair loose around the narrow shoulders of her filthy apron-dress, stood against one of the wooden beams, a long trickle of urine running along the concrete at her shoeless feet. A man, sunken-cheeked, head shaved against lice and wearing nothing but a torn singlet, defecated into an already overflowing chipped enamel bowl.

For years the secret societies of Hong Kong and their brother organizations around the world had used places like the Sanpokong Compound as recruiting centers. A man, a boy, a child, from a place like this would give utter loyalty to anyone who freed him from its horrors, and fear of being returned would bind the recruit to the *Hui* more fiercely than any family tie.

Finally the policeman stopped and pointed toward a man in his late twenties, standing close to the side wall of the warehouse, smoking a hand-rolled cigarette. He was wearing shorts obviously cut from long trousers and a sweat-stained undershirt several sizes too large for him. But there was meat on his bones, and he bore no signs of the abuse of life in a place like this. Most telling of all was the richly colored dragon tattoo that wrapped itself around the bicep of his right arm. The half-alive occupants of Sanpokong had no money for such decorations. He was in the compound, but he was not of it. Sheng and Huang approached him.

"You are Yang Bo?" asked Sheng, in English. The tattooed man nodded, sucking on the twig-thin cigarette. For the first time Huang noted the odd positioning of the man's sandaled feet. The left heel was tucked against the right instep at right angles.

"Yes, I am Yang Bo."

"You understand the arrangements?"

"Yes."

"How many have you?" asked Sheng.

"Thirty," Yang answered. "Another twenty-five at the Mongkok Compound. Ten in hiding elsewhere."

"No problems?"

"None. They were brought across in two's and three's over the past ten days."

"Good." Sheng nodded. Yang continued to smoke, watching Huang's face.

"We'll need them on board by tomorrow night," said the old man.

"Easily enough done," said Yang. "Your ship has arrived?"

"Tonight." Huang nodded. "She docks in the Cargo Handling Basin at Kellett Island, Hong Kong side. The *Taiwan Commander.*"

"Make sure she's moored in Hung Hom Bay by midnight. I'll ferry the men over from the Typhoon Shelter. Three lights. Two green over white."

"I'll give the order," Huang agreed.

"See that you do," Yang answered, his voice cool. He dropped the tiny end of his cigarette into a small puddle at his feet. To his right a young boy eyed the few flecks of tobacco in their wrapper, watching the paper dissolve in the brown water. Yang gave the two men a brief, searching look, then turned away quickly. The Hong Kong policeman, standing discreetly out of earshot, led the way out of the compound.

Even the fetid air of the street was a relief after the atmosphere inside the warehouse, and both men paused for a moment, taking long breaths as the policeman closed and locked the door behind them. They walked back to the Mercedes and got in.

"You're sure of him?" asked Huang. "I'm putting a great deal at risk."

"He's one of ours," said Sheng.

"I noticed the way he was standing. A code?"

"Perhaps." Sheng smiled. He turned on the automobile's ignition. "He'll do his job."

Huang stared at his younger companion. Very different, but in the end, very much the same.

"We're all Chinese," he said softly. "We're all alike, even you and I."

"You sound like my father," Sheng answered. He put the car in gear, and they began to move off. "I used to argue with him about politics, and he'd say that there were two things I needed to remember in life: In the world there are only two states of being—to be Chinese and to not be Chinese."

"And the other thing?" asked Huang as they turned onto Lion's Head Road again.

"He told me that there was no such thing as politics," Sheng answered. "He said that Time was a dictatorship which held the only vote worth casting."

"So much for Karl Marx," Huang said.

"Malcolm Forbes as well," Sheng replied, and both men laughed as they drove toward the bright lights of the city.

CHAPTER 27

"WAKE UP," SAID Erin Falcone. Phillip Dane opened his eyes. The woman was standing over his bed with a cup of coffee in her hands. She was dressed in jeans, sneakers, and a T-shirt that said SOUVENIR OF VANCOUVER across the chest in pink puffy letters. Her dark hair was pulled back into a ponytail and secured with a rubber band. Rather than go back to her roomette on the train, she'd left her luggage behind except for the attaché case. The new clothes had been purchased in downtown Vancouver the previous afternoon.

Dane sat up in bed and accepted the coffee. His own luggage was piled on the dresser on the far side of the hotel room. He glanced out the window on his left. Rain was spattering against the glass, and he could hear traffic.

"What time is it?" he asked. He sipped the coffee, then put the cup down on the bedside table. He swung his legs out onto the floor. The headache he'd been nursing as he fell asleep was gone.

"Ten," replied Erin. Dane nodded sleepily. Thirty-six hours had passed since the killing of the man on the Amtrak train. He groped for his underwear on the floor, slipped it on, and grabbed his shirt from the back of the chair tucked into the kneehole of the bedside table.

They had booked into the Château Granville, a small, clean, and relatively new hotel on the corner of Helmcken and Granville streets, three blocks north of the Granville Bridge on the outer edge of Vancouver's business district. From the bridge to the corner of Smithe, another couple of blocks north, Granville Street looked like a miniature version of Times Square in New York, complete with transvestite boutiques, peekaboo strip joints, and porn theaters with a sprinkling of S&M leather salons thrown in for good measure. Since the introduction of limited gambling licenses in the city a few years before, a number of casinos had also opened up in the area. There were hookers everywhere.

Dane had specifically asked for a room with twin beds. Since their episode on the train he and the Falcone woman hadn't touched each other. The night before, they'd eaten separately as well, Falcone in the hotel restaurant, Dane in a crowded McDonald's up the street.

Picking up his coffee again, Dane went to the window and looked out. They were on the fifth floor, looking out over the strip. Below him was the curved drive around the front entrance to the hotel. Even at this hour there were hookers on the corner—five of them, walking back and forth as though they were waiting for a bus.

They were dressed in everything from skintight bicycle pants and tank tops to frilled blouses and leather miniskirts. Each of them was holding up a large, conservative black umbrella. The sight was almost charming until you thought about the potential for lingering death that lurked within each one of them. Dane turned away from the window.

"So tell me what you know about David Long," he said bluntly. Erin Falcone sat down at a small round table a few feet away and toyed with her coffee cup. Dane found his pants and put them on.

"We went through all that yesterday," she answered.

"Go through it again," said Dane, sitting down on the edge of the bed and putting on his socks and shoes.

"As David Leung he had a 1-A draft classification.

He drifted into the Haight-Ashbury scene, and when his notification went through, he came up here."

"To Vancouver."

"Not specifically. From what we can tell, he hung around at one of the communes up the coast. There was a big grass bust he just managed to avoid. He had papers in the name of David Long by then . . . went back to San Francisco."

"And got picked up."

"Yes. That's when our file opened up."

"By 'our,' you mean the FBI."

"Yes. I wasn't with them then, of course."

"No," said Dane. "Did he try and get in touch with his father?"

"Not officially. According to his papers, he was a Canadian. The beef was local, so we didn't get word for a long time after, but the bail was high, and he made it with no problem. I think we can assume that the money came from Hawksworth."

"So he skipped bail and came back here?"

"As far as we can tell."

"And then?"

"He got a job on one of the Alaska cruise lines. A steward. He was clean, at least on the surface."

"But you don't think so."

"No. We think that's where he started to get really connected. All the below-deck staff, or a lot of them, anyway, are Chinese, contract labor from Hong Kong. Laundrymen, dishwashers, that kind of thing. It looks like he got things organized, started moving weight up to Alaska. Not a lot at first, but the prices were very high. He was also smuggling booze and cigarettes. Made his nut, established himself."

"Doesn't sound very big time," said Dane.

"It wasn't. But he was smart. Kept his head down, making his connection. Didn't step on anyone's toes, did some favors."

"No connection with the Vancouver groups?"

"None," said Falcone, shaking her head. "The Five Dragons were running things then." The Five Dragons were a group of former Hong Kong policemen who had "retired" from the force with millions in drug money and established themselves in Taiwan and Canada. "He didn't need them, anyway; he had his own scam going."

"The Elmendorf thing?"

"Right," said Falcone. "Up until then he'd been buying his goods in Vancouver at premium prices, then ferrying it north. He saw a way to bring it in himself through the air base. Elmendorf was a Military Air Transport operation, part of it, anyway. Planes coming in from all over the Pacific, up from Taiwan, Tokyo, the Philippines. He started up his own operation, using airforce personnel."

"A weak gateway," said Dane.

"Exactly," said Falcone. "Who the hell thinks about drugs coming in from Alaska? And it was so simple. The junk would come in by air, and he'd get it off the planes, no problem. From Anchorage he'd get it across the Canadian border at a little know-nothing place called Nabesna. From there it would be flown down to Prince Rupert on the coast and loaded onto the cruise ship. The boats were Canadian, so there was no customs at Vancouver. Very neat."

"How much was he bringing in?"

"Five, ten kilos a month, and only during the cruise season."

"Still pretty small time," said Dane.

"He got big. Quick. About three years ago," said Falcone. Dane found his cigarettes on the bedside table and lit one.

"Holy Ghost."

"Holy Ghost," she agreed. "Within a six-month period he was moving three, four hundred kilos, and no one knew where he was getting it. He wasn't part of the loop. He was flying in and out of Hong Kong once or twice a month, but he never tripped over our people, not once. And he wasn't part of the Vancouver scene at all. He stayed right out of Chinatown, away from the bikers and the Teamsters on the docks. All his people were Vietnamese. We picked up a couple here and there, mostly on minor charges—theft, gang-related violence. That's when we first heard the name, and when I got involved."

"Because of his pipeline," said Dane.

"Yes," said Falcone. "And there wasn't a damn thing we could do about it. The stuff was coming in with the regular diplomatic mail to the Chinese Consular Office in Vancouver. Right across the bridge from here. The RCMP wouldn't touch it with a barge pole—said there wasn't enough evidence, and we don't have jurisdiction, so all we could do was sit back and watch. Then Hawksworth was murdered, and everything fell into place."

"This Black Dragon group and Long?"

"That's right. Long, or Leung, or whatever you want to call him, is linked directly to the Communist Chinese. He's also linked with Hawksworth and Defense Intelligence. And now it looks as though they're going to come together with a bang. We can't let that happen. U.S. relations with China are fragile enough without something like this."

"A lot of heads would roll," said Dane. "And not just in China. This all goes back a long way."

"The government of China actively involved in the drug trade, and a Medal of Honor U.S. Air Force general connected to one of the largest organized-crime operations in the world."

"So I sanitize Hawksworth, and you put the clamps on his son," breathed Dane. "We're talking about the status quo here."

"That's right," said Falcone. "We've got to turn off the fan before the shit hits."

"Such an elegant turn of phrase," said Dane. He

stubbed out his cigarette and stood up. He went to the window again and looked out. A blue-and-white police car was parked by the curb. A uniformed cop was sipping coffee from a cardboard cup and chatting with the hookers out the car window. The rain had let up, and the umbrellas were furled. Dane turned back to Falcone. "Maybe it's to late," he said slowly. "If that Viet kid on the train was on to you, then Long knows you're after him, and I'm not getting any response from Washington."

"You think you've been cut loose?" asked Falcone.

"I'd bet on it," said Dane. "Long might have ordered his father killed, but he didn't blow his mother to kingdom come." He shook his head. "I wasn't sent out to curate Hawksworth, I was supposed to bird-dog any weak spots. She was one of them. Now this."

"What do you mean—'now this'?" asked Falcone.

"I tag the woman, she gets hit. She leads me to Long. . . ."

"And they sweep up afterward?" she asked.

"Something like that." Dane nodded. "Which brings us back to your involvement." He stared at her coldly. "Who's to say you're not part of the same scenario?"

"I told you who I was," she answered. "And who I work for."

"Why should I believe you?" he asked.

"Because you don't have any choice," she answered. "If you've been cut loose, you don't have much in the way of options. You either believe me or you run."

"Or I talk," he said.

"To who?" asked Falcone, her voice weary. "You're going to play Robert Redford in *Three Days of the Condor* . . . walk into *The New York Times* or *The Washington Post?* No one would believe you, and you don't have any evidence. And they wouldn't let you get that far anyway."

"Who's 'they'?" Dane asked.

Falcone shrugged. "Take your pick," she answered.

"Mine, yours, theirs. You're a negative asset for anyone involved in this."

"Thanks for the vote of confidence," said Dane. "You make me feel so wanted." But he knew she was right.

"The question is, where do we go from here?" Falcone said thoughtfully.

"The Timberline Restaurant," said Dane.

In a halfhearted attempt to cover their tracks Erin Falcone had traded in the Hertz they'd rented in Portland for a battered Toyota from a place called Rent-A-Wreck in Vancouver, putting down a cash deposit instead of using a credit card.

With Dane beside her as navigator she drove the half-mufflered two-door across the Granville Bridge above False Creek, then headed up the hill to Sixteenth Avenue. The clouds had broken, and bright sunlight was brushing the rain-wet leaves of the cherry trees lining both sides of the broad four-laned thoroughfare.

Just past the lights at Sixteenth Dane noticed a small crowd gathered around the high-fenced entrance to a walled estate on their left. The signs carried by the small assembly of picketers said something about "Free Tibet."

"That's the Chinese Consulate," supplied Falcone. "I've seen the surveillance pictures." She shook her head. "They call this neighborhood Shaughnessy. Timber millionaires, a creep who got out of Iraq with some of Saddam's loot, and our Chinese friends. Nothing but Audis and Mercedes. Mao must be spinning in his grave."

Dane ignored her comments, concentrating on the map book in his lap. A quick check in the telephone book before they left the hotel had revealed that the restaurant was located in an industrial park close to the airport. Not much to go on.

They continued driving south along Granville, slipping from lane to lane through the lunchtime traffic.

After ten or fifteen blocks the larger houses on both sides faded into more modest dwellings, interspersed with car dealerships and gas stations. By Sixty-fifth Street both sides of the street were solidly commercial—video stores, pharmacies, and Chinese restaurants. In the distance Dane could see the arcing shape of a bridge on-ramp.

"Keep to the middle lane," he instructed. "There should be signs for the airport."

Granville Street curved sharply to the left as they neared the North Arm of the Fraser River, and Erin Falcone did as he'd asked, guiding the car onto the Arthur Laing Bridge. To the right Dane could see a stream of tugs hauling heavily loaded barges up and down the wide silt-brown waterway. Directly in front of them an Air Canada jumbo hurled itself toward the main runway of Vancouver International.

They swung through the cloverleaf, following the signs to the main terminal, straightening out behind an airport bus as they headed along Grant McConachie Way, a boulevarded eight-lane strip leading to and from the terminal.

"Now where?" asked Falcone, hands tight on the wheel. The Toyota was sputtering intermittently, sounding like a spin dryer full of sneakers.

"Left at the first set of lights," said Dane, glancing down at the map book. To the right was the huge, windowless blockhouse of the main Canadian Airlines hangar. To the left, beyond another service road, he could see a complex of small and medium-sized industrial buildings. In the midst of the low commercial structures and set off by itself by a grassed playing field was something that looked like an old hockey arena, one wall garishly done up with some kind of illegible graffiti.

Erin turned at the lights, then turned again. A plastic sign on the wall of one of the buildings said TIMBERLINE RESTAURANT. It was directly across the street from the hockey arena. Pulling into the restaurant parking lot, Dane was able to read the twenty-foot-high graffiti on the arena behind them: THUNDERZONE. Purple, scarlet, and lime green sprayed onto the corrugated wall.

"Now what?" asked Erin, pulling into a parking spot in the almost empty lot and turning off the engine. The Toyota bucked, heaved, clattered, and then fell silent.

"Now we sniff around," said Dane.

"All this for a book of matches?" said Erin.

"It's all we've got," Dane answered, climbing out of the car. Erin Falcone followed him out into the sunlight. They walked toward the front door of the restaurant.

The interior of the Timberline was done in sixties-style vinyl variations in shades of brown. The illumination was at the forty-watt level, what light there was shrouded in amber-colored imitation oil-lamp chimneys.

"How could you tell what you were eating?" Erin whispered as they stepped into the gloom.

"I think that's the idea," Dane answered. From what he could see, the management of the Timberline was counting on the fact that it had a captive clientele. The next-closest restaurant was probably at the airport itself.

There was a middle-aged man in a short-sleeved shirt standing at the cash register, flipping through the pages of a newspaper. The man was Chinese, and so was the paper. There were half a dozen people eating at booths. Three in Federal Express uniforms, two in Japan Airlines coveralls, and one man eating alone, still wearing his hard hat. A silent television high on the wall at the rear of the restaurant was tuned in to Much-Music, the Canadian version of MTV. Madonna was having group sex and singing simultaneously.

"Twilight Zone," said Erin.

"Could be worse," Dane commented, approaching the man behind the register. "They could have had the volume turned on."

The Chinese man looked up as they approached, switching on a quick smile.

"Lunch?" he asked.

"Not just now," said Dane. "I'm looking for someone."

"No lunch?" The man glanced at Erin and spoke to her in rapidfire dialect. She ignored him.

"What did he say?" Dane asked.

"How the hell would I know?" Erin answered. "He's speaking Mandarin. I speak Cantonese."

Dane dug into the pocket of his jacket and pulled out the key chain he'd taken from the Vietnamese man on the train. He separated out the Corvette tag and pointed to it.

"Repo," he said. "You know this car?"

"Lunch only," said the man. The quick smile was setting like concrete.

"He hasn't made his last five payments," Dane went on. "I'm here to take back the car."

"No cars," said the man. "Lunch only. Busy time. Lunch only."

"This isn't getting us anywhere," said Erin. "We're just going to piss him off."

The man spit out another stream of dialect, ending it with a braying laugh. Erin shot back something on her own, and the man's face darkened.

"What was that?" Dane asked.

"I know enough Mandarin to figure out when someone's calling me a name," she answered. She plucked at the sleeve of his jacket. "Let's go." She turned on her heel and walked out of the restaurant. Dane followed her.

"A waste of time," said Erin, blinking in the sunlight. A Fed Ex jet roared in three hundred yards away, dropping out of sight behind the arena.

"Maybe not," Dane answered, looking over her shoulder. He pointed. "Check it out."

Across the street, half hidden by a line of trees screening the hockey arena parking lot, Dane could see the gleaming form of an old, split-window Corvette, painted deep blue. It was sandwiched in between a green Ford Econoline and a Browning-Ferris Dumpster.

"You think so?" asked Erin. Dane shrugged.

"Worth a look," he said.

They crossed the street, hopped over a narrow gulley, and stepped out onto the parking lot. As they neared the car, Dane pulled out the key chain again and checked the miniature license-plate tags.

"They match?" asked Erin.

"They match," said Dane.

The Corvette was locked up tight, and Dane went through the keys until he found the right one. He opened the driver's side door and ducked inside. The interior was warm, the air stale. It had been locked up for a while, and it was vacuum-clean. Not even a butt in the ashtray.

"Nothing," he said, stepping back.

"A dead end," said Erin. "Shit."

"Why would he park it here?" Dane asked aloud, glancing around the parking lot. "If he flew out of Vancouver to get on the train, you think he'd have put it into a park-and-fly, or a long-term lot. Not just leave it here." He inspected the Corvette again, letting his finger slide over the sharp-edged fairing over the wheel hump. "This thing is cherry . . . the split windows are worth a lot of money."

"Maybe he works at the restaurant," said Erin. "That would explain the matches."

"If he worked in the restaurant, he'd park in their lot," said Dane, shaking his head. He stared at the arena building. "I wonder what the hell Thunderzone is?"

"Looks like an old recreation center or something," suggested Erin. The building was a hundred feet on a side and windowless except for a narrow strip of glass high under the gently curved roof. Concrete steps led up to a covered entranceway.

Leaving the Corvette behind, they went across the parking lot to the entrance. Two men in their twenties, both dressed in Air Canada coveralls, were playing catch with a softball.

"Know anything about this place?" asked Dane, speaking to the young man closest to the entrance.

"Used to be an air-force recreation center. They call it the Forum," the man answered.

"Thunderzone?" said Erin. The man laughed. He went through a blinding windup and whipped the softball to his companion thirty feet away. It hit the other man's withered old catcher's mitt like a pistol going off. The other man lobbed it back.

"It's the name of a movie they were making out here. Right up until a few days ago," the pitcher said. "Some kind of teen kung fu picture I think."

"What makes you say that?" Dane asked.

"They were all Chinese," said the pitcher, giving Erin a quick look. "I think. Maybe Japanese, who knows?" He cranked out another pitch.

"How long were they here?" said Dane.

"Three weeks, a month."

"And they're gone now?"

"Yup." The pitcher nodded. He caught the softball and looked at the building. "Left a few days ago. One day they were here with all their trucks and stuff, and then poof, they were gone."

"You think anyone would mind if we had a look?" Dane asked. The pitcher laughed.

"I couldn't give a shit, mister, it's not my building." He turned away and went back to his game. Dane and Erin Falcone went up the steps to the main door.

"Making a movie," the woman said. "A perfect cover."

"Cover for what?" asked Dane, looking at her sharply.

"For whatever they were doing," she answered blandly. Dane tested the door. It opened, and they stepped inside.

They found themselves in a low-ceilinged lobby,

walls painted a utilitarian pale yellow, floors worn dark green linoleum. There were bulletin boards pinned with faded photocopies announcing dances and activities. The Bluebirds were taking the Yellowjackets three games to none at Slow Pitch. Howie Grimalkin had won the Hotshot Trophy on the shooting range. A trestle table piled with wooden folding chairs. It looked as though 1968 had simply packed up its bags and gone home one night.

Beyond the lobby there was a narrow dark corridor off-sided by a series of closed doors, all locked. There was a hand-inked cardboard sign on one that said COACH. The corridor ended, and they stepped out into a huge gymnasium. The endless floor was hardwood, the varnish almost worn off, laid out with inlaid strips outlining a basketball court. Dane could almost hear the echo of squeaking high-top runners. Boy sweat. Cheerleaders with their pleated skirts flipping up to show tight adolescent buttocks sheathed in satin. It was eerie. And dark—the only light came from the grimy clerestory windows fifty feet up. Empty bleachers rose skeletally beneath them.

"Strange," whispered Erin.

"No kidding," Dane answered, looking around. "A blast from the past."

"No . . . the floor."

Dane looked, following the pointing finger. For the first time he noticed that more than just a basketball court had been laid out on the hardwood. Strips of black grip tape criss-crossed back and forth in some kind of pattern. They walked out onto the floor together. Broader strips of masking tape were tacked down here and there, scrawled with Chinese characters in Magic Marker.

"Can you read any of it?" Dane asked.

"Some." She nodded. She bent down. *"L'i t'ou t'i."*

"Which means?"

"Barber shop."

"What the hell?" said Dane. He raked a hand through his hair.

"Here's another," said Erin. She stood up, frowning. "Water closet, first class. A toilet?"

"I've got an idea," Dane muttered. He turned on his heel and walked back to the bleachers. Erin Falcone followed. Dane climbed up through the seats until he reached the wall. He turned and looked back down onto the floor.

From his vantage point the lines of tape resolved themselves into a long outer rectangle broken into dozens of smaller squares. Two "corridors" of tape ran almost the full length of the rectangle grouping the smaller squares into three sections. Most of the squares were the same size, but at various points within the rectangle there were larger, odd-shaped forms. Dane nodded to himself.

"I don't get it," said Erin, joining him and looking down.

"I think I do," said Dane. "First-class toilet and a barber shop. The small squares are staterooms, the long rectangles between them are passageways. Jesus! It's the deck of a ship!"

There was a loud barking sound from the shadowed entrance to the gymnasium. A single word. Three men stepped out into the dim light. They were short, dark-haired with sunglasses. Each man was wearing an identical deep blue windbreaker. All three carried machine pistols. The man in the lead called out again, waving his weapon in their direction.

"What's he saying?" asked Dane.

"Does it matter?" asked Erin Falcone.

"No, I suppose not," said Dane. They raised their hands above their heads and began climbing down out of the bleachers.

CHAPTER 28

"I WONDER HOW you say 'fly on the wall' in Chinese?" said Dutch Kapono, eyes glued to the high-powered binoculars in his hands. He was standing on the open bridge of *Island Lady,* the U.S. Customs sparkling new fifty-eight-foot interdiction catamaran. In service for less than a year the high-powered vessel had a top speed of thirty-eight knots and a range of over five hundred miles. Even the newspapers were using her nickname, "Weed Whacker," instead of the formal name on her transom.

For the last three hours the ship had been standing off the entrance to the small harbor at the western end of Naloa. From his perch on the fly bridge Dutch Kapono had a clear view of the harbor itself and the walled compound beyond. Beside him Frank Stanner, his surveillance photographer, was banging off dozens of exposures with a motor-drive Nikon fitted with a massive, 1,000-mm low-light lens.

Kapono lowered the binoculars for a moment and wiped the sweat away from his eyes. It was hot, the sun beating down hard, and he was getting frustrated. He picked up a can of Pepsi from the console in front of him and took a sip of the warm, sweet liquid. Beside him the short, bald photographer continued shooting.

"What the hell are you taking pictures of?" Kapono asked, grumbling. "There's nothing going on."

Stanner lowered the camera briefly and shrugged.

"Comparisons," he answered. "Funny what you don't see on the spot that you pick up in the darkroom."

"I don't give a sweet shit for the nuances of stakeout pictures," said Kapono. "I want to know what the fuck is going on in there."

"Lunch probably," said Stanner, lifting the camera again. Kapono snorted.

"Funny man." He raised the binoculars.

At last count there were now twenty-three major organized-crime heavyweights roaming around Hawaii as though it were their private turf. Everyone was here, from Hiroshi Sato of the Inagawa-kai to Joey "Pizza Man" Priziola from Kansas City, the one they called the Double-Cheese Don. The night before Chan Muk Wen, *Shan Chu* of United Bamboo, had come in from Taiwan, and this morning it had been Yellow Shu from the On Leongs in L.A. and Micky Ma from the Green Gang in Hong Kong.

Each of the twenty-three high-rollers was traveling with an entourage, and the total count of triad Dragon Heads, yakuza *kobuns,* Mafia capos, and their assorted bodyguards, was climbing past the two hundred mark.

So far everything was peaceful, but Kapono knew that a swarm of that many hoods was a bomb waiting to go off. None of them had been stupid enough to bring any kind of ordnance onto the Islands, but getting a gun in Hawaii was as easy as buying a package of cigarettes.

Almost as bad was the sudden interest by just about any crime-buster outfit in the free world. Since Kapono had sent out the first tentative word on the wire, everyone from the DEA to the Hong Kong police was trying to put his oar in. The beaches along Waikiki were littered with undercover cops all trying to look like tourists.

And they all had their own secret agendas. Kapono had a horrible vision of two hundred hoods and twice that many cops trying to blow each other away through the open windows of unmarked cars zooming up and down Ala Moana Boulevard. It was the kind of thing that gave the chamber of commerce nightmares, and it wasn't all that farfetched; Mike Yee over at HPD had told Kapono that he'd filled out more than sixty temporary carry permits for off-Island cops in the past few days.

"A-holes," he said hotly.

"Pardon?" said Stanner.

"Nothing," snapped Kapono. "Just do your fucking job." Kapono put down the binoculars again and looked around for Styrofoam cups to shred. There weren't any.

"Shit," he muttered. This time Stanner didn't say anything.

Kapono frowned, then took another slug of Pepsi. His stomach was beginning to act up after rolling around on the mild swell for too long. He thought about packing it in but fended off the temptation. Even if there was nothing going on, simply keeping up the surveillance was worthwhile. At least the bastards would know they were being watched.

Not that it would do much good. There were no laws being broken . . . at least not yet, and there was nothing in the rules that said crooks couldn't take a holiday. Of the twenty-three big-timers not one had an outstanding warrant, and none of the soldiers accompanying them had done so much as a day behind bars. They'd obviously been handpicked for their clean records.

"Shit, fuck, piss, and corruption!" Kapono spit out angrily. What was the use having all the intelligence and surveillance information in the world when you couldn't act on it? He turned to Stanner. "I'm going below for a while. Let me know if anything starts to go down."

"Sure thing," the photographer answered easily. Kapono's face twisted into a grimace, and he climbed down off the fly bridge. Maybe there'd be a foam cup for him in the galley.

James Chang, Samson Kee, and Abbot Fong sat at the umbrella-shaded round table in the walled garden, relaxing after the noon meal. The kitchen staff had prepared a dozen courses of dim sum for the entire family, but the men had eaten in the garden, away from the women and children. There were still a few plates and woven bamboo steamers on the table with a large, delicately patterned finger bowl of lemon water as a centerpiece. A small cup and a ceramic flagon stood at each of the four place settings.

Jimmy Chang, only son of the *Shan Chu,* appeared in the doorway of the Garden Room and crossed the tiled expanse of the lanai. He sat down at his place, poured himself a small portion of rice liquor from his flagon, and drank it down. His father, Kee, and Abbot Fong were dressed in jackets and ties; Jimmy Chang wore white tennis shorts and a brilliantly patterned Hawaiian shirt.

"Still there," said Jimmy, in rapidfire Cantonese. "Bobbing up and down like a turd in the water." He put down his cup.

"Do you know who it is?" Abbot Fong asked quietly.

"It's the 'Weed Whacker'," the younger Chang replied. "Customs boat. That means Dutch Kapono. Son of a bitch has been on our ass for years."

"Presumably we have done nothing to cause him concern," said Jimmy Chang's father.

"He's playing dick games," Jimmy answered. "Peekaboo, I'll-show-you-mine-even-if-you-won't-show-me-yours shit. It doesn't mean anything, Father, believe me."

"It means something," said James Chang. "It means he is becoming nervous. We can assume he has been alerted by the sudden influx of his enemies."

"He's not the only one who's feeling nervous," said Samson Kee, speaking for the first time. "I prefer to keep our business private."

"Don't be such a bookkeeper," scoffed Jimmy Chang. "Kapono doesn't have anything on us, and neither does anyone else. Relax, I've got it covered."

"There is a case to be made for caution," murmured Abbot Fong. Jimmy Chang's arrogance and self-confidence were dangerous; it wasn't a long step from there to overconfidence and bluster, and at this point such a stance could be fatal for all of them. Virtually the entire upper tier of Black Dragon was present in Hawaii, and the men Dutch Kapono worried about were as much the *Hui*'s enemies as they were the enemies of the customs man.

"This Kapono represents no real threat," said James Chang. He paused and glanced at Fong. "But we must maintain our vigilance. The United States Customs is the least of our enemies. And we have other concerns at the moment," he added.

Fong smiled. The *Shan Chu* had read his mind.

"Things are going according to schedule," said Fong, taking his cue and turning things back to the business at hand. *"Orient Star* left Anchorage two days ago. Our people at Halpro arranged it just the way we wanted. It was a one-way cruise, with all the passengers flying back to Vancouver, so the ship is deadheading. Gives the crew plenty of time to get things ready." He glanced down at the open laptop computer on the empty chair beside him. "She'll be here in three days."

"Good." Chang nodded. He stared across the table at Samson Kee. "The special crates I asked for . . . did they arrive?"

"Yes, as you requested, *Shan Chu.* I sent them . . ."

"There is no need to discuss the matter further," Chang interrupted. His son frowned, then glowered at his brother-in-law.

"What crates are these, Father?" he asked. Abbot Fong fought to keep his features expressionless. The *Shan Chu* was teaching his son a lesson in humility.

"They do not concern you," said Chang coldly. "It is between myself and your *mei-fu.* "

"That is the point, Father," Jimmy Chang responded. "He is *mei-fu,* my sister's husband, not truly family. If something is going on within the *Hui,* then I should know about it. I *am* the *Fu Chan Shu* . . . aren't I?" As the *Hui*'s second in command and son of the *Shan Chu,* he felt the exclusion by his father as a slap in the face; but it was no more so than his own insult to Samson Kee. Abbot Fong waited tensely. It was the first time Jimmy had made such an obvious move.

"You are my son," Chang said finally. "And Samson is my *hsiao hsu* . . . my son-in-law. Both of you have important positions within the *Hui.*"

"Mine by right, his by marriage," Jimmy Chang interrupted.

"Indeed." Chang nodded. His expression turned to stone. "But *I* am the Dragon Head, and until that changes, both of you will follow my orders without question, is that clear?"

Jimmy Chang held his father's stare for a long moment, and then his head slowly inclined.

"Yes, *Shan Chu,*" he said, his voice almost a whisper. Fong let out his breath slowly. At least Jimmy had been smart enough not to press the point. The plump man could feel prickles of sweat at his temples. Jimmy had acquiesced for the moment, at least to his father's power, but the confrontation would divide the younger man from Samson Kee even more decisively than before.

It did not bode well for either man or for himself. Jimmy Chang might have taken his lesson in humility to heart, but Abbot Fong had read the message too: The *Shan Chu* had seen fit to exclude him as well—he'd been told nothing about the "special crates."

"Where is Han Chao?" Fong asked, gently trying to ease the tension around the table. "I thought he was supposed to be at this meeting." The manager of the *Hui*'s New York branch had arrived the night before but had left the island earlier that morning.

"He *was* supposed to be here," said Jimmy Chang.

"I spoke to him at breakfast," offered Samson Kee. "He said he had business to attend to in Honolulu." Kee hesitated for a moment and then continued weakly, "Perhaps he's been delayed."

"I wonder what sort of business he's doing," said

Jimmy Chang, his tone acidic. There was a long pause. Everyone knew, the *Shan Chu* included, that his daughter was a rampant alcoholic, and that Han Chao regularly took his pleasure elsewhere. Fong was also aware that this was a delicate subject, especially since Jimmy was married to Han's younger sister, Mu-Chen. It wasn't so much the infidelity that posed a problem— monogamy, at least for men, was not essential to a proper Chinese marriage, but rather Han's lack of discretion.

"I'm sure my daughter's husband has good reason for his absence," Chang said finally. Fong winced, noting the formal description of Han's position used by the *Shan Chu*. He had put as much distance between himself and his son-in-law as possible. Another crack in the wall of the *Hui*'s defenses.

"Perhaps I should . . ." said Fong, leaving the rest unsaid. If necessary he could send someone out to bring Han back to Naloa. James Chang shook his head.

"Thank you, Abbot, but that won't be necessary." He smiled blandly. "Kom is watching over him."

"Ah," said Fong. He cast up a silent prayer, warding off ghosts and ill omens. Kom Tong-Ho, Black Dragon's gray-haired demon, the Red Pole.

"Now then!" said Chang, clapping his hands together. "Let us get back to business."

Kom Tong-Ho sat alone at a table near the window of Elsie's Bar on Hotel Street, peeling an orange and keeping one eye on the entrance to the Commodore Hotel across the street. Han Chao had disappeared inside with his slut a few moments before, but from all the reports he'd heard, Han wouldn't be very long.

It was too early for much trade in places like Elsie's, and Kom was alone with the sleepy-eyed bartender. He liked it that way. He was odd even for Hotel Street, and he didn't like being stared at, even when people who did stare inevitably turned away almost instantly. Kom knew he looked fearsome, even cultivated that impression with his longer-than-shoulder-length hair and his undertaker's apparel. But that was something for those he pursued, not strangers. The power was wasted on them.

He'd seen it in their eyes, though; a split second recognizing his power, fearing it, then denying they had seen what they had seen—the turnaway. He smiled to himself, then dug his long, slim fingers into the peeled orange, splitting it into a dozen sections. He laid the sections out neatly in a row on the table in front of him, then sat back in his chair and examined them.

He reached into the pocket of his black suit jacket and took out a package of cigarettes. He lit one and glanced out the smoke-clouded window. The entrance to the Commodore was dark and empty. Kom turned his attention back to the table, examining the row of orange sections. He chose one, placed half of it in his mouth, and bit down quickly with his small, sharp teeth, cutting into the meat of it, juice spilling out onto his tongue.

More than any other food in the world, he loved oranges. When he was a child, they had been magic things, unattainable for someone like him. Even now, with the fruit available to him whenever he desired, he treated them as treasures to be savored, allowing himself only one each day.

Kom was fifty-six years old and knew that he was Shanghainese, but any memory of his first years was hidden behind a shadowed curtain of fear. He had been born under the threat of a savage Japanese occupation and raised in a concentration camp, orphaned by the time he was six. At ten, in the chaos and horrors that followed the war, he had killed for the first time. By twenty it was his profession. At forty, after almost twenty years of service to his *Shan Chu*, he had officially been made Red Pole of the *Hui*.

He found no pleasure in what he did; he took cold

satisfaction from doing the job quickly, cleanly, and without disturbance. And this was the source of his power; he was not motivated by strange lusts or mad passions—lusts and passions that could be used as weaknesses by his enemies. He had lost his heart and soul so long ago in the shrouded past that he never regretted losing them. People knew instinctively that Kom Tong-Ho was not just a killer; he was Death itself.

His work for Black Dragon these days rarely involved actual killing, however; there simply wasn't any need. If a Soho gambling den in London was late in paying its "dues," a single appearance of Kom at the mah-jongg tables was usually enough to put the owners of the den in line. If a major drug transaction was being made, and money was about to change hands between people who had never done business before, Kom's presence generally assured that there would be no problems. Often, the knowledge that Kom *might* appear was enough to keep any tempted member of Black Dragon's flock from straying.

But Kom was no mindless symbol of the *Hui*'s power. Contrary to the tales told about him behind his back, he thought, analyzed, and had doubts just like everyone else. And he had his doubts now. He was Red Pole, not a lowly *Sze Kau* foot soldier, so why had he been asked by the *Shan Chu* to keep a close eye on Han Chao?

Kom allowed himself another section of orange. Was the *Shan Chu* trying to tell him something? Had he somehow offended, or not done any task set before him? Or did the surveillance say something about Han Chao? If Han was prey and he was predator—his proper role as the *Hui*'s Red Pole—then Han was in serious trouble.

That was clearly a more likely scenario. The Black Dragon Triad had almost seven thousand active members around the world, and there was not one of them, from the Dragon Head himself down to the lowest 49 in a Hong Kong Lotto booth, who took Han Chao seriously. Without his marriage to Lily Chang he would have been nothing within the *Hui,* and as it was, the way the *Shan Chu* and Abbot Fong had arranged things, New York and Toronto were really run by trusted *Hui* members several rungs down the official ladder. Han's power was hollow.

Which brought Kom back to his first thought. The plump, weasely little man was not a real factor within the *Hui,* except for his relationship with the *Shan Chu*'s eldest child. Kom, with no family tie to the *Hui,* had an equal rank number—438, so why had he been given the job of watching Han?

Kom blanked the thoughts from his mind and bit into another section of orange. The *Shan Chu* had a reason for asking him to keep a watch over the man, and until he was told otherwise, that was exactly what he'd do. He sucked on the orange section, draining it of pulp and juice, leaving nothing but the pale, veined membrane. He looked across at the dark mouth of the Commodore and wondered if Han was enjoying himself. Kom let a small smile creep across his thin, pocked face. Take your pleasure now, Han Chao, he thought to himself, life is short and can easily be made even shorter.

The meeting had been arranged in New York, and the pickup had gone flawlessly. Thankfully Lily hadn't shown the slightest interest in going to Naloa with him, so at least he didn't have to deal with her drunken hysterics, or the flat-eyed, reproachful stare of his daughter, Alice. He loathed both women and blamed them both for all his failures. He had assumed he was marrying wealth and power when he joined the *Hui,* but instead he had found only humiliation, alcoholism, and stupidity. It wasn't fair.

He flew out of Naloa just after breakfast, arrived at the Honolulu domestic terminal, and took a taxi to Hotel Street and Nuuanu, telling the driver to drop him off at the HPD downtown substation. As he looked back into the downtown area, Hotel Street was a mixed bag of pagoda-roofed chop-suey houses, vegetable markets, and souvenir stores; as he walked toward River Street, it was an Oriental version of Place Pigalle with the police station acting as the dividing line between the two worlds.

Han moved slowly along the strip, passing the Hubba Hubba Club with its billboard ads promising to astound him with the antics of the Vegetable Twins and Wanda's Disappearing Coins. A littler farther on, the Zig Zag was already open for morning trade, and the chippies were yawning on every corner.

Ignoring them all, he continued down Hotel Street past a row of one-story gin joints, tattoo parlors, and flophouses, his shoulders tensing, waiting for the contact.

She came at him out of an alley between Smith and Maunakea. Taller than he was by six inches, the difference made even greater by her spike heels, dressed in a pair of skintight denim shorts and a spandex top in electric blue. She wore a short, silver-tipped blond wig in a shag cut and dark glasses. From her cheekbones and her coloring, Han guessed that she was either Taiwanese or Korean.

The woman linked her arm in his and leaned down to whisper in his ear.

"Talk. Walk," she said in English. "Make it look good," Han swallowed and did as he was told. The woman smelled of some exotic spice, and he began to feel aroused, despite the currents of fear that coursed through his body.

She took him down Hotel Street for another few blocks, eventually turning in at the Commodore. The hotel was a five-story frame building with a kiosk-sized lobby manned by a hugely fat Hawaiian attendant. He ignored Han and the woman as they entered.

The woman led the way up three flights of narrow stairs into a corridor that smelled strongly of urine and beer. Faintly Han could hear the sound of music playing on a radio and muffled laughter.

Walking along the corridor behind the woman's swaying hips, he noticed that the scuffed green-painted doors on either side had their room numbers painted on. The woman stopped in front of room 326, plucked a key out of some secret niche behind her belt, and unlocked the door. She opened it and stood back. Han stepped inside, and the woman followed him, closing the door behind her.

The room was small, not much larger than a jail cell. The walls were papered in a faded blue pattern, and the floor was linoleum in gray. A narrow window looked out onto an alley, feeding in the sound of distant traffic and the smell of rotting fish and vegetables from the market directly behind the hotel. There was an iron bed in the room, a small table, a chest of drawers with a large mirror above it, and two wooden kitchen chairs. The chairs were covered in a dozen dripping coats of ancient yellow enamel.

There were two other men in the room as well as the woman. One of the men was standing by the window; the second was sitting on the bed. The man standing was Chinese, taller than Han and slim, wearing sunglasses, a well-cut dark blue suit, and expensive, tasseled brogues. He was in his forties, black hair slicked back close to his delicate-looking skull. He had hands like a woman, and he was smoking.

The second man was white, in his mid-fifties, with thinning, light brown hair and a long, thick-lipped horsey face. He wore an open-necked Hawaiian shirt bloused over loose sweatpants, and everything about him said "cop."

"I see Melinda managed to find you," said the Chinese man. He looked over Han's shoulder and nodded at the girl. She nodded back and opened the door, stepping outside again. The door closed, and the three men were alone.

"My name is Howlitt," said the man on the bed. He had the cracked voice of a longtime smoker. "HPD. Narcotics." Han looked startled for a moment, but the Chinese man put up a soothing hand.

"Don't be alarmed, Mr. Han. Sergeant Howlitt and I have been associated for some time." The Chinese man gestured toward one of the wooden chairs that stood in front of the chest of drawers. "Why don't you sit down, Mr. Han?" He did so. The Chinese man made no move away from the window. He turned slightly, flicking ash from his cigarette into a tinfoil ashtray on the sill.

"I didn't think there would be anyone else here," said Han, his eyes fixed on Howlitt. The police sergeant didn't seem concerned at the attention.

"I merely wanted to demonstrate our relative positions," said the Chinese man. "You have indicated that you wish to join us. Mr. Howlitt is proof that our reach is at least equal to that of your father-in-law, the *Shan Chu.*"

"Chang is getting old," said Han, making no effort to conceal his contempt. "He is weak, and his weakness is destroying Black Dragon."

"Brittle bones rarely bend." The Chinese man smiled. "Instead they break. Chang Chin-Kang is not one given to change."

"He gives me no respect," said Han. "I've worked for him loyally for years, but there is nothing. Except for Abbot Fong I am eldest in the *Hui* after him, but he gives me no honor. I will have even less when Jimmy becomes *Shan Chu.*"

"Is such an event imminent?" asked the Chinese man.

Han shrugged. "Perhaps. The results of this so-called 'convention' called by the *Shan Chu* may hold the answer to that."

"And what does he know of Holy Ghost?" asked the Chinese man.

"No more than any of us," said Han. "A rogue triad with no connections. They claim responsibility for the loss of our shipment from Vancouver, and for the death of Hawksworth. That is Abbot Fong's assessment, and he is adviser to the *Shan Chu.*"

"Is that all?"

"It is all that I know."

"But they may not tell you everything," said the Chinese man.

Han reddened. "If there was anything more, I would know it," he said hotly. "I have my ways. I have my sources."

"Ah, good." The Chinese man nodded. "I'm glad." There was a long silence, broken finally by Howlitt. He belched loudly, then pressed both palms down on the bed, ready to stand.

"I don't like to press or nothing, but I've got to get back to work eventually."

"Of course," said the Chinese man. He looked at Han. "You have the information we requested?"

"Yes." Han reached into the inside pocket of his jacket and withdrew a sealed business envelope, thick with paper. He handed it over. The Chinese man slit the envelope and withdrew the stapled document, quickly flipping through the pages.

"These are the correct numbers?" he asked. Han nodded.

"Yes."

"This shows all the leaders on the sundeck, with the exception of the *Shan Chu.*"

"Yes." Han nodded again. "He will be in the owner's suit, on the boat deck, directly behind the main bridge."

"Will there be anyone with him?" asked the Chinese man. Han shook his head.

"Not directly. Abbot Fong will occupy the inside owner's cabin. They connect."

"I see." The Chinese man nodded. He squashed the remains of his cigarette into the ashtray. "You have done well for us, Mr. Han, we appreciate it."

"You will remember your promises?" said Han.

"And honor them, Mr. Han, you have my word." He stepped forward and extended his hand. Han rose from his chair and shook it.

"You should leave first, Mr. Han," said Howlitt. "Just in case someone's watching. Melinda will take you back to Nuuanu Street if you want."

"She's very pretty," said Han. "Is she really a . . . ?"

"She's not a cop, if that's what you mean." Howlitt laughed. "Why? You want to give her a shot?"

"I . . ."

"Perhaps it would be wise to indulge yourself some other time," suggested the Chinese man. Han nodded. He bowed his head briefly, then turned and left the room.

"Is he really that stupid?" asked Howlitt from the bed.

"I'm afraid so, Sergeant," sighed the Chinese man.

"I don't trust stupid people," said Howlitt. "They have this tendency to fuck up . . . large."

"It never occurred to me that I should trust Mr. Han," replied the Chinese man. "That would be very foolish." Howlitt nodded, then stood up, grunting with the effort. He crossed the small room, leaned over the chest of drawers, and tapped lightly on the large mirror above it.

"You get all that?" he called out. A few seconds later there was a muffled, affirmative reply from the next room.

"Well done," murmured the Chinese man approvingly.

"It's all tied up." Howlitt grinned.

"Not yet," cautioned the Chinese man. "Not quite yet."

CHAPTER 29

T. J. GOLLINGER stood on the front steps of his house on Howard's Cay, shading his eyes with one hand in the dusky light as the twin-engined Fairchild did a final turn over the island and began its approach. There was still plenty of light to come in visually, but he'd had the boys light the firepot lights along the runway as a welcoming gesture. His squinting smile hardened; he'd be needing the lights himself in a little while.

As the wheels of the Floridair charter thudded down, Gollinger turned and went back into the house. He went to the living room and gave it the quick once-over. A fresh pot of coffee waited on the warming plate, and there was a pitcher of iced tea on the table in front of the couch. No liquor. Cigarettes in a small, carved box on the smaller end table beside his favorite chair. Nothing looked out of place. No sign that this would be his last night on the island. He went to the chair and sat down, taking a cigarette from the box and lighting it.

He'd grown fond of the room; for a while at least it had represented some kind of permanency in his life. It was a facade, of course, but he liked the flavor of it. Amateur watercolors framed on the thick plaster walls, dried flowers in a vase on the buffet, cricket bat leaning against the floor-to-ceiling bookcase behind the couch.

Years before he'd visited Ian Fleming at Goldeneye in Jamaica, and the famous writer's living room had looked a lot like this. Except Bond's creator had a gold-plated Remington on a writing table in the corner instead of a roomful of computer equipment.

Gollinger smiled sadly to himself. He'd managed to accumulate great wealth and power over the years, beyond anything Fleming had ever wished on his heroes or his villains, but he'd never achieved fame. When he died, he'd die alone, with no one to stand over his coffin extolling his virtues—or describing his sins, for that matter. Silence for a eulogy; fitting enough, considering how he'd lived his life.

He made a small grunting sound, dragging on the cigarette, watching the splinters of fading light fan across the Persian carpet, broken into broad gold bars by the slats of the jalousies. Outside he heard the sound of an approaching Jeep. His guests had arrived. He put out the cigarette and waited.

A few moments later, Morris, black, shaven-headed, and silent, ushered Conrad Lang and Tucker Barnes into the room. Both men were dressed in lightweight tropical suits, but even so they looked absurdly overdressed.

"Conrad, Tucker." Gollinger waved the two men toward the couch. They sat down. Their white-haired host nodded to Morris, and the muscular servant slipped out of the room.

"Very nice," said Senator Lang, looking around the room. "You've done well for yourself."

"It suits." Gollinger shrugged. He poked his chin at the warming coffeepot and the iced tea on the table. "Get you anything, fellows?"

"No, thank you," said Lang.

"Right to business?" Gollinger smiled. He stood up and poured himself a tall glass of iced tea. He took it back to his chair and sat down again.

"We don't have a lot of time," said Lang. "I have to be back in Miami tonight."

Gollinger took a small sip from his glass, then set it

down carefully on the table beside his chair. He smiled at Lang's companion.

"You've lost more hair since the last time I saw you, Tuck," he said. Barnes lifted his shoulders.

"Other things I could've lost," the old pilot answered philosophically.

"True enough." Gollinger grinned. "None of us spends a lot of time impressing the ladies anymore." There was a long silence. Gollinger waited patiently, listening to the faint sounds of waves breaking in the distance.

"I suppose you know why we've come," said Lang finally.

"Hawksworth?" said Gollinger.

"That . . . and other things," the senator replied.

"You want to know if your ass is covered," stated Gollinger. "You want to know if his murder is the first ripple in the pond."

"I want to know if we've been compromised," said Lang.

"We?" asked Gollinger.

"You're involved, T. J., you have been almost from the start." The senator was working hard to keep his voice calm and even. Gollinger smiled. The man was frightened.

"Hawksworth was high profile," Gollinger said slowly. "Even more than you. The president wanted him as the new drug czar, a frontline soldier in the battle against the foreign scourge of narcotics. You supported him."

"I had no choice," said Lang.

"The president needed a hero," said Gollinger. "You gave him one. And that's what got Hawksworth killed. You must have known he was too vulnerable, Conrad." He smiled. "When the old buzzard went down, I figured you for the one to finger him. I bet I wasn't the only one."

"Don't be absurd," said Lang. "He was my friend."

"That's never stopped you in the past," said Gollinger. "You've burned your buddies before when it suited your purposes."

"I've never condoned murder."

"Even when it was expedient?" said Gollinger.

"Things like that . . ."

"Are best left to other people?" Gollinger interjected smoothly. "Quite so."

"A man named Cordasco has put a curator onto the Hawksworth situation," said Lang. "He's very good, very thorough. He knows too much already. I'd like your assessment."

"You're talking about Phillip Dane," said Gollinger, nodding. Lang looked surprised. "Oh, sure, I know all about him." The white-haired man smiled. "Not much gets by me, even out here. And you're right. Dane is good. Give him enough time and he'll tumble to the whole thing."

"So what do we do about it?" Lang said.

"Nothing," said Gollinger. "Time is something Dane doesn't have." He took another sip from his glass. "As the British say, the entire thing is a wank."

"I'm not sure I understand." Lang frowned.

"Put the pieces together, Senator," said Gollinger. "It comes out pretty as the picture on the boxtop for a jigsaw puzzle."

"Explain," the senator demanded, his voice tight. Tucker Barnes sat silently beside his boss like an aging schoolboy, hands clasped in his lap.

"Sure," said Gollinger. "If it'll make you feel any better." He sighed. "Okay . . . anybody with a brain in his head can tell you that the Senate and the House are full of people like you; so is the judiciary, right down to a county level. Not to mention the cops. The Colombians have banned extradition, Noriega's in a country-club prison, and the Mafia's still got a lock on the unions. The triads own banks on Wall Street, and the yakuza in Japan make Jimmy Hoffa look like a pansy. What does that tell you?"

"Hawksworth was enlisted to put a stop to it," Lang answered. "That was his mandate . . . the president had no idea of the man's involvement."

"Bullshit," said Gollinger succinctly. "Hawksworth was never a factor in any of this. He was a figurehead. And every president going back to Truman and Eisenhower has been aware of the government's complicity in the drug trade. The pickings have just gotten richer over the years. Chiang greased the KMT with opium dollars, and Truman knew it. Kennedy's Bay of Pigs boys were funded by dope, and so were the Contras. Bush was head of the CIA—you don't think he knew what Noriega was up to?"

"What are you saying?" asked Lang.

"I'm saying that there is an underground economy in place that keeps the wheels turning. Within the next five years it will have infiltrated every sector of life in the United States. It's already halfway there. It works, it's efficient. You're a perfect example of it."

"Don't be absurd!" said Lang.

"Balzac said it a long time ago," said Gollinger. " 'Behind every great fortune there is a crime.' You're no exception, Connie." He shook his head. "And here you are, trying to cover your ass, trying to bury the crime that took you to where you are."

"Get to the point," the senator barked.

"Simple," Gollinger answered. He glanced at Tucker Barnes. "Remember, Tuck? Back in the war? We had the Jap codes cracked, and we heard that Yamamoto was flying out on an inspection run. There was a big flap in intelligence. What the hell were we supposed to do? And what *did* we do, Tuck?"

"We shot him down," said the old flyer. "Blew him away."

"Precisely," said Gollinger.

"What are you saying?" asked Lang.

"I'm saying that the government of the United States has been backed into a corner. It's not a drug war, Connie, it's a money war, and we're losing. Too much dirty laundry, too much complicity, too much public awareness. They've got a dragon with a hundred heads, breathing fire. Hire as many drug czars as you want, mount as many Just Say No campaigns as you want, bust a thousand crack dealers, and it won't do a Goddamned bit of good. Tom Clancy can write any amount of back-patting hooey he wants about high-tech interdiction, but it's all just fiction, Sesame Street for grown-ups. It's not reality. There's only one *real* option left. Only one way to slay the dragon and keep all that dirty laundry buried."

"Cut off the hundred heads," Lang whispered, suddenly understanding what Gollinger was talking about. "My God!"

"That's it," said the white-haired man. "Kill them all. It's the only way. Hawksworth was the first. He won't be the last. Who knows? Maybe we're on the list too."

"Jesus!" groaned Tucker Barnes.

"It's insane," the senator whispered. Gollinger lifted his broad shoulders.

"Sometimes madness is the appropriate state of mind," he answered. "At the very least it can often be the best defense."

Behind Lang and Tucker Barnes, Morris, Gollinger's servant, had silently reentered the room. He picked up the cricket bat from its place against the bookcase and took two steps forward, placing himself directly behind the couch. He lifted the bat to his shoulder and brought it down in a sweeping arc, putting all his strength into the swing. Years before Morris had been champion batsman for the Bahamas National Team, and he had lost none of his prowess.

The twenty-ounce, cane-handled ashwood club struck Lang at the base of his skull, crushing bone and rupturing his spinal cord. Caught completely by surprise,

Tucker Barnes barely had time to acknowledge the wet splash of brain tissue on his cheek before the bat fell again, catching him edge-on, cracking with incredible force across the bridge of his nose as he turned on the couch. The entire procedure had taken less than thirty seconds.

"Well done," said Gollinger. He swallowed the last of his iced tea and stood up.

"Nah problem," Morris answered. He returned the soiled bat to its position against the bookcase. Blood and brains dripped down to the floor in a small puddle. Gollinger checked his watch.

"Get your people into the boat," he instructed. "It should take you about three hours to get to Nassau. I'll meet you at the airport at eleven-thirty, and we'll proceed from there. All right?"

"Nah problem," Morris repeated.

"Good," said Gollinger. "Tell Johnathan I'll be at the airplane in about twenty minutes. I've still got a few things to do here." He smiled briefly. "Our friends shouldn't be appearing out of the wild blue yonder for another few hours."

"Nah problem." Morris turned on his heel and left the room, ignoring the results of his batsmanship as the draining bodies of Lang and Barnes began sagging forward on the couch.

Gollinger went to his study and loaded the last of his floppy disks into his briefcase. There were more than two hundred of them, containing the entire library of his dossiers. Enough material for a book. Call it *Perfidy,* he thought idly.

He checked to make sure that all his banking documents were safely put away in the briefcase's file sleeve, then closed it up, snapping the locks. He went back into the living room and looked around.

His late companions had slipped down onto the couch, shoulders touching like tentative lovers at a drive-in. Both men had voided bowels and bladders as

they died. The room smelled like shit. Gollinger wrinkled his nose, crossed to the far side of the room, and
plucked one of the framed watercolors off the wall. He
breathed in through his mouth, trying to ignore the
stench.

Twenty pounds of plastic explosive in the bilges of
the boat would take care of Morris and the other members of the staff an hour after the engines fired.
Johnathan, his pilot, would be dealt with later. Everything was in order.

With his briefcase in hand and the painting under his
arm, T. J. Gollinger left the room. Half an hour later the
Floridair Fairchild lifted off the runway of his abandoned home and headed north toward Nassau, into the
fall of the night.

The five LH helicopters from the special-operations
base at MacDill reached Howard's Cay two hours after
sunset, flying directly from Homestead Air Base with a
brief stop at an uninhabited island some twenty miles
from their objective. The landing allowed them to re-
group and wait out the twelve-minute schedule change
from an unexpected tailwind and also gave them time
to peel away the covering from the roughly painted Cu-
ban Air Force markings that had been applied to each
of the helicopters.

Flying at more than two hundred miles per hour, it
was unlikely that anyone would be able to make out the
bogus designations and even more unlikely that anyone
would believe that the Cubans owned anything as sophisticated as the LHs, but on the off-chance that they
were spotted, the markings would serve to confuse the
issue of who had attacked Howard's Cay. As far as
General Clark was concerned, the Cubans were perfectly acceptable patsies.

The five helicopters, weapons armed, flew the last
few miles to Howard's Cay at less than fifty feet above
the moonless waves, arriving off the southern end of

the tiny island in line-abreast formation. Targets were
acquired, laser sights locked on, and the one-sided battle began, witnessed only by the corpses of Lang and
Tucker Barnes as well as several families of gulls who
had made the unfortunate choice of nesting at the end
of the island's runway.

Shells for the 20-mm cannon were listed in the General Electric Aircraft Armament Catalog at a discounted
price of three dollars net per unit on orders for one million shells or more, while the Rockwell International/
Martin-Marietta Hellfires went for a stiff twenty-five
thousand bucks apiece, considered to be a bargain after
their exceptional 83 percent rating during Desert Storm.

Over a seven-minute period $1,590,000 worth of ord-
nance was dumped on Howard's Cay, pulverizing every
building into powder, cindering the two bodies in
Gollinger's house, and cremating seventeen sea gulls.
Factoring in crew flight time and aviation fuel, the operation bottom-lined at slightly less than $1.7 million
and was deemed to be a complete success. Cutting
through the roiling pall of smoke billowing up into the
darkness over the island, the five helicopters swung
away over the water, departing the island less than ten
minutes after they arrived. Below them and behind
them there was nothing left alive.

At midnight T. J. Gollinger boarded a British Airways direct flight to London, his hair cut short and
dyed a nondescript light brown. Seven-and-a-half hours
later, briefcase still in hand, he left Heathrow Airport
on a Swissair flight to Geneva. He was never seen or
heard from again.

CHAPTER 30

PHILLIP DANE WOKE with a raging headache and a mouth that tasted like the bottom of a bird cage. Eyes still closed, he lifted a weak hand and brushed it across his gummy lips. He opened his eyes and blinked in the sudden glare. He found himself staring directly up at a circular light fixture in the ceiling.

But where exactly was the ceiling? He sat up, groaning, aware that he was lying on a narrow bed. There was a single pillow behind him, covered in striped ticking. The mattress beneath him was thin and without a sheet. His back hurt; it felt as though he had been lying there for a long time.

He swung his legs over the edge of the bed and almost threw up at the sudden surge of vertigo. He gripped the mattress with both hands and waited for it to pass. If he closed his eyes, the vertigo returned; if he opened them, the room heaved like a ship at sea, making him equally nauseous.

"Shit," he groaned. His senses began to return in fragments. The smell of mold, the bad taste in his mouth, the crackling of the fluorescent over his head. The room.

It was small, and it had no windows. The walls were white plaster, cracked with age, the ceiling covered in pinhole acoustic tile. The brown linoleum floor was cold against his bare feet. There was a door, closed, a few feet away. Plain wood with a crystal knob. No lock.

Why were his feet bare, and why was he wearing green cotton pajamas? No, not pajamas. More like surgical greens. Or something else. What? It took him a moment. The kind of clothes he'd seen the men wearing in North Vietnamese POW camps.

Dully he noticed that there was a pair of plastic sandals on the floor beside the bed. He slipped his feet into them and waited, trying to remember.

He'd been with the woman. He reached for her name, fighting the fog that seemed to be drifting back and forth across his consciousness. Something stupid. Green, like his clothes. No, not green—Irish. Erin the Italian. Erin Falcone.

The Chinese men had taken them to a van outside the movie-set auditorium. No windows in the truck either, but two other men. Hoods had been put over their heads, and then they'd been driven off. Not far, no more than four or five minutes, the sounds of aircraft landing and taking off getting louder and louder. He'd felt the prick of a needle in his arm just after they stopped. There'd been echoing sounds of slamming doors before he faded out, as though they'd driven into some kind of large building or underground garage. And that was all.

Drugged. He let out a jaw-cracking yawn and turned his head slowly, wincing as a bolt of pain rocketed between his eyes, the pain buried deep inside his head. They'd drugged him. He watched his right hand come up and push back the sleeve of his pajama top. It felt as if his arm belonged to someone else. He glanced blearily at a bruised spot in the crook of his elbow. Little red dots. Half a dozen of them. More than one needle. Multiple doses. They'd kept him out for a while.

He felt his heart jerk in his chest. They'd kept him out, but now the effects of the drug were fading. No more shots. Something was changing. He groaned again and pushed himself up onto weak legs, feeling the floor begin to turn and slide again, fighting off the nausea.

Time to get his shit together, face whatever was coming.

And where was the woman?

Put it together, Phillip, there's no time to waste. Make for the door. He tried, stumbled, and almost fell. He gritted his teeth, forcing one foot in front of the other, feeling like an invalid: *Make for the door, make for the door, make for the door, hang on to the knob, for Christsake, or you'll fall.*

He waited, letting the wave of dizziness pass, then dragged open the door. Another room, larger than the first, decorated in motel-room modern. Cheap-paneled walls, furniture in a Scotch-tape tartan, thin fake Persian carpet on the floor. Television and VCR in a sleazy "Media center" on wheels in one corner.

The far side of the room was outfitted as a kitchenette—refrigerator, stove, counters, and cupboards. It all looked as though it came from the fifties. A window in front of the couch was shuttered. There was another door, more substantial.

He shuffled over to the door and tried it: locked. Next was the window. The shutters were locked as well, a small padlock hanging from the hasp. He peered through the narrow slats—plywood beyond the shutters. Mind games. He was sealed up like someone in a *Twilight Zone* episode.

He yawned again, feeling his tongue scrape on the roof of his mouth. Awful. He made his way to the kitchen counter and ducked his head under the faucet, turning on the water. He took a long drink. The water was soft and sweet-tasting, but it told him nothing.

The slaking of his thirst and the passage of time were easing the last effects of the drug. He realized that he was feeling a lot better. Turning away from the sink, he checked the cupboards and then the refrigerator, looking for some clue. Still nothing. The soup was Campbell's, the ketchup was Heinz, and the package of hot dogs he found, rock-hard in the freezer, was Oscar

Meyer with a stale date two weeks away. The pots and pans below the sink said nothing. An efficiency house-keeping unit in Limbo.

Crossing the room again, he squatted down in front of the television and flipped it on. Running through the channels, all he could find was snow. The tape in the VCR was a collection of Rocky and Bullwinkle cartoons. A fly walked across the glowing screen, huge, wings folded back, blotting out the stalwart features of Dudley, the square-jawed Mountie, in his scarlet uniform.

Dane sat back on his heels, trying to think. Christ! He didn't even know if it was day or night. He watched the fly, something scratching at the back door of his memory. What?

A book. In his grandfather's store. And where was that? Ten thousand miles away or two blocks away? Where the hell was he? Dane concentrated, furiously throwing off the trailing tendrils of the drug. What book? Black and red, textbook bound, Elsevier's old-fashioned woodcut imprint. Dane struggled, keeping his eyes on the fly; he could almost see the "card" for the book in the computer file. Then he had it.

Geberth's *Practical Homicide Investigation,* chock-full of ghastly color photographs of decomposing bodies, floaters, and rape victims. There'd been an anecdote about the value of forensic entomology, something about maggot eggs establishing place and time of death.

Dane remembered the story. Half a dozen packages had begun to stink in the "no such address" bin at an L.A. United Parcel Service depot. When the packages were opened, they were found to contain the butchered pieces of a woman.

No one knew where the body parts had come from or who the woman was. A forensics expert at UCLA went to work, examining the crawling swarms of maggots infesting the putrid remains, and came up with the answer. The egg castings proved that she'd been murdered two weeks before, and the maggots themselves blossomed into *Drosophila simulans,* a huge variant of the common "garbage can" fruit fly. The flies established the murder site beyond any doubt, since they lived in only one place.

Dane stared at the giant fly crawling across the television screen. It was identical to the example he'd seen in the book, like an ordinary fruit fly under a magnifying glass. Definitely *Drosophila simulans.*

"Son of a bitch," Dane whispered. "I'm in Hawaii."

The pink stucco sprawl of the Royal Hawaiian Hotel on Waikiki Beach had been a Honolulu Landmark since its construction in 1927. Along with the Moana, a few hundred yards farther along the beach, it was a favorite choice of passengers arriving from San Francisco on the Matson liners. During its early years its guest list included the likes of Mary Pickford, Douglas Fairbanks, and Al Jolson, and even with the massive development of Waikiki over the next half-century, it still maintained a certain cachet among luxury-class travelers.

It also had at least a dozen points of entry, both from the beach itself and the street, labyrinthine corridors and a complex system of elevators and stairways that made it an ideal place for a covert meeting.

The "Pink Lady," now dwarfed by the thirty-one-story tower of the Sheraton, still hosted nightly soirees in the giant Monarch Ballroom, and the high-ceilinged lobby was always crowded with people intent on an evening of dancing to the mellow tones of an endless succession of Big Bands.

Chang had chosen the Royal for reasons other than logistical convenience. During his time as a laborer on Waikiki after the war, he had asked to use the hotel's toilet facilities and had been refused. Now, a world of time away from those days, it pleased him to occupy the Royal Hawaiian's most expensive suite. In a subtle way it was also politically expedient; the Royal Hawaiian was owned by Kenji Osano.

Osano, the billionaire Japanese industrialist who had been involved in the Lockheed/Tristar bribery scandal in the 1970's was a close friend of Susumu Ishii, second in command of the powerful Yamaguchi-inagawa combine. To place the meeting at the Royal Hawaiian was a deferential acknowledgment of the yakuza's presence in Hawaii, yet involved no loss of face for Chang since there was no clear connection between Osano's business interest and the Yamaguchi-inagawa.

In addition to James Chang and Abbot Fong there were four other people seated in the drawing room of the Royal Hawaiian's presidential suite: Hiroshi Sato, *kobun* leader of the Yamaguchi-inagawa, Chan Muk Wen, *Shan Chu* of the United Bamboo Triad Society of Taiwan, Yui Keong Ma of the Sun Yee On in Hong Kong, and Tommy Denano, capo of the Mafia combine that ruled the Pacific Coast from Mexico to the Canadian border. With the exception of Chang and Abbot Fong, the men in the room were all in their mid-to-late forties.

"I'm feeling a little outnumbered," said Denano, seated in a fan-backed bamboo armchair. Denano, slim, stoop-shouldered, and wearing glasses, looked more like an accountant that a major crime figure. Chang knew that his looks were deceiving. Denano had single-handedly taken over the motion-picture union scams in Los Angeles and then bludgeoned his way into the Heroin trade, leaving a trail of unmarked graves behind him in the Nevada desert.

Denano shook his head, smiling lightly, then took a sip from the glass in his hand. "But I guess there's always been more of you than us when you get right down to it." He paused. "No disrespect, gentlemen," he added.

"None taken," said Chang. "What you say is a simple truth."

"I'm still not sure why we are here," said Hiroshi Sato. The Yamaguchi-inagawa leader frowned. He was short, had his hair in a crew cut, and wore a three-piece dark suit. The missing joint of the baby finger on his right hand was fitted with a pink plastic prosthesis held on by a large diamond ring. "I was told that our discussion would take place on board your vessel the *Orient Star.*"

"One place is as good as another," Chang answered. "I trust you have no objections?" He waited for an answer. Sato scowled and said something under his breath in Japanese.

"I am a little confused, Uncle," said Yui, *Shan Chu* of the Hong Kong Sun Yee On Society. Although he and Chang were of equal rank, the age of the Black Dragon *Shan Chu* required the honorific. Chang was pleased by the younger man's adherence to tradition. "I was under the impression that there would be many more people in attendance," Yui continued. "I see no representative of the Fourteen K, and Yellow Shu from the On Leongs is also absent."

"Circumstances have changed," Chang said quietly.

"Apparently," said Chan Muk Wen dryly, speaking from an upholstered chair close to the balcony. The United Bamboo leader was closest in age to Chang, hugely fat, his close-cropped hair graying and the skin of his jowled face loose with the effects of too much liquor and nicotine over too many years.

"I dunno." Tommy Denano shrugged. "I can do without those other guys. I saw Nick Rugetti on the beach today. Shit! He's got a belly on him like a truck driver and a babe on each arm. No style at all." Realizing his faux pas, he glanced at Chan, but the United Bamboo man didn't appear to have noticed the insult.

"The meeting on board *Orient Star* has been compromised," said Abbot Fong, speaking for the first time. "We have received word that it was to be sabotaged."

"By who?" asked Denano, sitting forward. "The feds?"

"No," Fong replied. "A group known as Holy Ghost."

"Your people?" asked Sato roughly.

"By my people I assume you mean Chinese?" Chang asked. Sato nodded.

"Yes," he said. Chang turned to Abbot Fong again.

"Holy Ghost is Chinese," said Fong. "Although they seem to employ a great many Vietnamese as well."

"We all do," said Chan, the Taiwanese.

"Your version of niggers." Denano grinned.

"A vulgar term," said Chang blandly. "But true enough."

"So what about these people?" asked Denano. "Tough guys making a move or what?"

"According to our information, Shen Ling—Holy Ghost—is directly associated and funded by the Chinese Black House in Hong Kong. *Guojia Anquanbu,*" said Abbot Fong, using the Chinese term. Yui, the Hong Kong triad leader, almost leapt from his chair.

He swore. "The fucking Secret Service?"

"It would seem so," said Fong. "It has also come to our attention that they are working in concert with several federal agencies in the United States."

"What kind of crap is this?" asked Denano. "The chinks . . . sorry, the Communist Chinese working with the feds? Give me a fucking break."

"It is a question of common cause," said Chang, smoothly breaking in. "It is our feeling that Holy Ghost was created to do what the Red Chinese and the Americans could not."

"Which is?" asked Chan, the United Bamboo leader.

"Break the back of organized crime once and for all," said Chang bluntly. "Wholesale assassination on a global scale."

"That's nuts!" said Denano. "A bunch of fucking

ninja Elliot Nesses running around offing the bad guys?"

"How good is your information?" asked Chan, ignoring the Sicilian.

"Excellent," Chang answered. "We have, as they say, a highly placed informant. The meeting on *Orient Star* was to be their first, and perhaps last, major operation."

"I still think it's crazy," said Denano.

"Not so crazy when you think about it," said Sato. He stood up, went to the bar, and poured himself a glass of mineral water. He sipped, standing with his back to the wall. "A variation on the theme of 'set a thief to catch a thief.' "

"Precisely." Chang nodded. "For the Black House to operate on its own would be suicidal politically, yet they know that to secure Hong Kong for the future, they must deal with people like Mr. Yui and myself. The same holds true for the Americans. Twenty years of escalating problems with the Colombians has proven their present methods are useless. Our own inroads have proven that as well."

"So they get together and make up this Holy Ghost bunch?" said Denano. "I'm not convinced."

"Look to your own history." Chang shrugged. "Internecine gang wars in New York and Chicago did more harm to your organization than Mr. Ness and his socalled Untouchables."

"And it favors a certain racist bent," said Sato from the bar, nodding to himself.

"You mean, who cares what a bunch of slants and gooks do to each other as long as it's not us?" said Denano.

"Your eloquence is astounding," Sato said, his smile tight. "But, yes, that is the essence of what I am saying."

"I still don't see how this connects to all of us, and why the others are not here," said Yui.

"Whatever you believe about Holy Ghost, it is clear

that there is a fundamental change going on," Chang answered. "This meeting is an anticipation of that change."

"Forgive me, Uncle," said Yui, "but I'm not sure I understand what you are saying."

"In a few years the Mainland will absorb Hong Kong. Mr. Chan's organization in Taiwan could fall to the growing democratic movement within a decade as the Old Guard KMT die off, and Mr. Denano's colleagues, both in the United States and abroad, have become weak over time. Neither is Mr. Sato safe from the sweeping broom of reform. His gangster boys are no longer quite so acceptable to the common Japanese."

"Your organization has somehow managed to escape this scourge?" asked Sato. Chang ignored the sneering tone.

"By no means," he answered, shaking his head. "Black Dragon is the oldest single organization represented in this room. We have been in existence as a family business for more than one hundred and thirty years. It is inevitable that there should be a certain amount of ... deterioration."

"In other words, you got some weak links in the chain," said Denano.

"True." Chang nodded. "Which means that new links must be forged."

"This meeting," said Yui.

"Yes," said Chang. "When Mr. Fong here began setting up the arrangements for us to gather some months ago, I had a single focus to my thought. A network of organizations around the world, fully independent, but able to call on each other's resources and special skills.

"Japanese technology and transportation, Taiwanese intrusion into the manufacturing industries, Hong Kong's banking experience, and the exceptional political, judicial, and trade-union connections of Mr. Denano's people. All of this tied together by a mutually owned and operated 'switchboard' located here in Hawaii, or somewhere else that was agreeable to the parties concerned."

"Quite a speech," grunted Sato, frowning. "But you still haven't answered Mr. Yui's question about the others. My colleague Mr. Kimura of the Ichiwa-kai will not be pleased if he finds out that he has been excluded."

"Mr. Kimura's organization is small and riddled with corruption," said Abbot Fong. "Our information concerning him is quite clear—within six months he will either fall to his own people or become a witness for the National Tax Agency, which is preparing to indict him."

"Ah," said Sato quietly. It was relatively easy to corrupt the various police forces in Japan, but the NTA was another matter altogether.

"What about me?" asked Denano. "I've got Priziolla in New York, Riccabono and Zacotti in Chicago . . . even Rugetti and his Cubans. You saying that we get together and try to cut these guys out? Some balls, Mr. Chang!"

"There is a difference between cutting someone out and simply not including them," said Chang. He stood up and went to the glass doors leading out onto the balcony, feeling the eyes of the other people in the room upon him. Outside he could see lights on the water— booze cruises setting out from the Aloha Terminal. He turned and faced the room.

"You are the best, the strongest, the most shrewd, and above all you are the youngest," he said softly. "More than half of those invited to meet aboard *Orient Star* are old men like me. They wish only to protect what they have—their vision has gone."

"You put yourself with them?" asked Denano.

"In some ways, yes," Chang answered. "I'm old . . . like Don Corleone in *The Godfather.*" He smiled at the younger man. "I wish nothing more than to play with my grandchildren and perhaps raise tomatoes in the garden."

"I'm afraid your reputation suggests otherwise, Uncle," said Yui, choosing his words carefully. "How are we to believe all this simply on the strength of your word?"

"You don't have to," said Chang, impressed by Chan's boldness. A strong ally or a dangerous adversary. "Mr. Fong will provide you with documentation." He looked at the other men in the room. "There is one more thing, another reason I wanted to speak with you. A warning that you may choose to interpret as you wish." He glanced at Fong and nodded.

"Holy Ghost will realize their plans have failed within the next twenty-four hours," said the Black Dragon's White Paper Fan. "We have taken a number of steps to see that this occurs. When they find out, they may well act precipitously. Mr. Chang thinks that it might be wise for you to leave Hawaii as soon as possible. I concur."

"By precipitous you mean violent?" said Yui.

"It is a definite possibility." Fong nodded.

"So we cut and run?" said Denano, standing up. "Maybe you've got us pegged, Mr. Chang. Maybe you do see us as the up-and-comers, and you don't want *us* around for the big meeting."

"I've been accused of many things, Mr. Denano," Chang said, smiling, "but not of being that circuitous in my thinking."

"I think," said Yui, who now also stood, "that Mr. Denano would like some concrete evidence of your intentions."

"I agree," said Chan, remaining in his seat. "You are asking us to accept a great deal on good faith. So far there has been nothing but talk."

"This is the strength behind the power of our friends in Taiwan," said Chang, verbally stroking the United

Bamboo *Shan Chu.* "Its leader thinks only of the business at hand."

He nodded to Abbot Fong. The White Paper Fan rose and left the living area, disappearing briefly into the adjoining bedroom. He returned a moment later carrying four large manila envelopes. He went around the room, handing one to each of the other men.

"Good faith requires a gesture," Chang began. "And a gesture is meaningless unless it has value. Inside these envelopes you will find the documentation I promised you regarding Holy Ghost. You will also find some information we have gathered which will be of personal interest to each of you concerning the activities of our absent friends. Finally you will discover that there are registration certificates in each of your envelopes for twenty million escrow shares of the Signal Group.

"Ostensibly the Signal Group is a film production company with extensive real estate holdings in British Columbia; in fact it is a shell company listed on the Vancouver Stock Exchange which we can use for a variety of purposes in the future. It has already helped to solve some delicate immigration problems for several of our friends in Hong Kong and in Thailand. The share certificates have a current book value of two dollars each. You may sell them, trade them, or keep them; the choice is yours." Chang waited, his glance turning to each of the four men in turn. Finally Chan, the heavyset Taiwanese, rose to his feet.

"Elder Brother has given us much to consider," he said ponderously. Standing beside Chang, Abbot Fong could almost see the wheels turning inside the man's close-cropped bullet head. If Chang was right, a discreet withdrawal would be a prudent move with a $40 million gift as an incentive. "I suggest we leave now and think about our options."

Fong smiled to himself. Roughly translated, that meant he wanted to read the material inside the envelope and do a quick check with his broker about the value of the Signal Group shares.

"I'll go along with that," said Denano, nodding. "It's getting late."

"We shall be in touch," said Sato, stepping forward. He bowed stiffly in Chang's direction, then turned and let himself out of the suite. The others followed a few moments later, leaving Chang and Abbot Fong alone together.

"Well, Abbot, what do you think?" asked Chang, easing himself down into a chair.

"About those four?" Fong asked rhetorically. "As you said, they are the strongest, that much I'm sure of. They represent the future, not the past."

"Yui is interesting," said Chang. "I'd heard a number of things about him. A great deal of maturity in one so young."

Fong nodded without speaking. He knew what was going through the *Shan Chu*'s mind. The leader of the Sun Yee On in Hong Kong was roughly the same age as Jimmy, his son. There was no comparison between them, though—Yui was by far the stronger. "I wouldn't wish him as an enemy," he said finally.

"No," Chang murmured. He rose to his feet and went to the balcony doors. Opening them, he stepped out into the cool evening air. Floating up from the patio bar four floors below, he could hear the sound of Hawaiian music. He clasped the balcony railing, drifting on an eddying current of memories. He was vaguely aware of Abbot Fong joining him.

"Only a few elements left, *Shan Chu*," Fong said quietly. "And then we can all relax."

"Yes, only a few," Chang said, nodding absently. "Cordasco first, and then the rest until it's done."

General Alexander Cordasco lived in a large red brick colonial house in Kenwood, one of the more prestigious neighborhoods in Chevy Chase, Maryland. The

house was set back thirty yards from the street, surrounded by old-growth oak and elm, the grounds land-
scaped with flowering bushes and topiary hedges. The
one-and-a-half-acre "estate" was enclosed by a waist-
high dry stone wall. The house had seven bedrooms,
five bathrooms, an attached solarium, and a three-car
garage. Cordasco, widowed for the past nine years, his
children long since gone away, lived there alone.

It was almost one o'clock in the morning when the
general, out of uniform, returned from his evening in
Washington. A boring dinner for a retiring colleague at
the Foreign Studies Institute had led to drinks at the
Hotel Washington's rooftop bar with a woman friend of
long standing, and eventually to her bed at the Water-
gate.

Pulling into his driveway, Cordasco paused, keyed
the garage-door opener, then drove the late-model
Mercedes forward. As he reached the midpoint of the
driveway, the security system automatically turned on
the spots hidden in the bushes, bathing the house in
light.

The man frowned. Every time that happened, it reminded him that all of this had been his wife's, none of
it his. Even a general didn't make the kind of money
you needed to live in Chevy Chase, and he'd been only
a bird colonel when they married.

She was rich, and he was handsome, that was the arrangement right from the beginning. He drove the car
into the garage and listened as the door slid shut behind
him. He wasn't handsome anymore, but by the same to-
ken, she was dead, so what the hell.

He climbed out of the car, feeling the liquor finally,
or maybe it was old age creeping into his bones. It
didn't matter, what he wanted was one stiff shot of
Remy and then bed—his own bed. He slammed the
door of the Mercedes, yawned, then crossed the garage
to the door leading into the house. He unlocked the
door, fumbling with his key, and let himself into the

mudroom and then the kitchen, switching on lights as he went.

A professional drinker, Cordasco had bottles for all occasions, one of them being the kitchen Remy. He kept the bottle on a nice cool shelf beside the window, cuddled up to the Chinese cooking wine and the Worcestershire sauce he used for Bloody Marys.

He took a glass down from another shelf, poured a double of brandy, then carried glass and bottle through the kitchen and dining room into the solarium. It was a regular ritual, sitting in the dark, drinking, looking out over the lawn, confessing his sins to the night. He slumped down into one of the ghastly white-painted wrought-iron chairs his wife had loved so much. Confess his sins? By God, he had enough of them to last until dawn broke!

"General?" The voice was soft, barely audible. Cordasco turned blearily in his seat and peered into the darkness. There wasn't supposed to be anyone here.

"Who the hell is that?" he grunted. Absurdly there seemed to be a young Chinese man sitting in the shadows holding something that looked remarkably like an old-fashioned peashooter in his hands.

"My name is Nelson Fong," the young man said with a smile. He lifted the peashooter to his lips and blew hard. Cordasco felt something sting his cheek. A mosquito. He lifted his hand to brush it away, felt a skewering bolt of pain shoot through his chest, and died, eyes bulging grotesquely as though pressed out by some hidden fist within his skull.

Fong stood up, slipped the peashooter into the inside pocket of his suit jacket, and examined Cordasco's corpse. The needles with its cotton-batten wadding still dangled from the raspberry flesh of his cheek. The young man left the needle in place. It would save the coroner time.

The needle had been dipped in a mucoid secretion given off by the cooked flesh of the tiny South American dart frog. A single frog gave off enough toxin to kill a dozen adult men. The creature was native to Colombia, and the poison was used by jungle hunters. It was also a method of assassination favored by major drug dealers in Bogotá.

Fong smiled, pleased with his work; the *Shan Chu* would certainly be convinced of his value to the *Hui* now, and the poison would confuse the issue of motive for a while. He would thank the Red Pole personally for his advice. Fong glanced at the luminous dial of his watch and clucked his tongue. He'd have to hurry if he wanted to catch the San Francisco red-eye. There was still a great deal to be done.

CHAPTER 31

"GOD DAMN!" SNARLED Dutch Kapono, ripping apart a Styrofoam cup as he watched the tape slow-motion through the monitor once again. "It's the dance of the Sugar Plum A-holes!"

"Picture's worth a thousand words," said the young man at the Security Office console.

"Cute," snapped Kapono. "There, stop the damn tape right there!"

The customs man at the video controls suppressed a grin and did as he was told. A figure on the screen stopped in midstride, halfway through the X-ray bull-pen for domestic departures. Kapono checked the mug-shot photograph in his hand, just to be sure. There was no doubt. The man going through the checkpoint was Thomas Denano. The digital readout at the lower right-hand edge of the screen filed it at 8:35 that morning.

"He got on the plane?" said Kapono, frowning at the image on the screen.

"Eight fifty-five Cathay Pacific to Los Angeles," said the man at the console, checking his notes. "He went first class; four of his boys went tourist."

"And the others?" asked Kapono angrily.

"Chan went out on a China Air Lines flight to Taipei an hour later ... alone. Sato went JAL to Kobe at eleven-ten, and the other one, Yui, he left about twenty minutes ago ... picked up a seat on a Wardair charter from Vancouver heading for Kai Tak." The customs officer paused and looked over his shoulder at Kapono. "You want to see the tapes for them again too?"

"No! Goddamnit! I don't want to see the fucking tapes again!" Kapono was furious. It was all unraveling in front of his face. First they came, then they went.

He pitched the ragged remains of the Styrofoam cup at a wastebasket in the corner. He missed. "Shit!" he breathed. He hitched his rump off the edge of the tape-storage unit he'd been leaning on and grabbed at a package of Winstons on the console beside the video operator. Furiously he pulled a cigarette out of the pack and jammed it into his mouth. Using the man's lighter, he fired it up and dragged in a harsh lungful of smoke.

"I thought you quit . . . sir," said the video operator. Smoke flared out of Kapono's nostrils.

"Oh shut up!" Kapono snorted. He took another drag on the cigarette. "I've got to think about this." He stared at the screen in the dark room. Some of the rats were leaving the ship, and he didn't have the faintest idea why.

The video operator waited, trying not to breathe too loudly. At least they wouldn't have to put up with foam chips being scattered all over the airport anymore.

On Naloa a light rain was falling from an almost cloudless sky. James Chang watched, standing at the open doors leading out of the Garden Room. Just enough to dimple the water in the lily ponds and stain the stone tiles on the lanai a darker red. It would pass. He turned and went back to the men gathered around the conference table.

"Perhaps the weather will be better on Oahu," suggested Han Chao Shun, trying to inject a bright tone into his voice.

On the *Shan Chu*'s orders a family outing had been arranged for the afternoon by Abbot Fong. All of them, women and children included, were to meet at the Ala Moana Yacht Harbor for a picnic cruise on board the

Kokuryu, a hundred-and-two-foot Blanchard built in the twenties and operated as a private charter vessel by one of Limehouse Trading's subsidiaries in Honolulu.

Chang had repurchased the wooden-hulled ship, owned by his father during the thirties, from the Coast Guard, which had used it as a coastal auxiliary during the war. Returning the yacht to its previous brass-and-teakwood elegance, Chang occasionally used it when he was in Hawaii. The name was his private joke; in Japanese *Kokuryu* meant Black Dragon.

Han was so worried his belly was roiling with anxiety. As far as he knew, the only person not invited on the trip was Kom Tong-Ho, the *Hui*'s ominous, gray-haired Red Pole. Which was strange; if the Red Pole wasn't joining them for the picnic, why was he with them in the Garden Room now?

Han glanced down the table. Kom sat silently, eyes focused on some unseen spot in the air. Han, like the five other men in the room, was dressed casually; the Red Pole was wearing his usual plain black suit.

James Chang took his place at the head of the table, glancing at each of the others in turn. Abbot Fong, looking slightly ridiculous in shorts and an open-necked mauve-and-pink shirt, sat on his right, his son Jimmy on the left. Han sat directly across from Samson Kee, while Kom waited, meditating, at the far end of the table.

"I still think this picnic thing is a waste of time," said Jimmy Chang. "*Orient Star* will be here tomorrow, and we've got a lot left to do before she docks."

"The situation has changed," said James Chang quietly, his eyes on the Red Pole. "*Orient Star* will not be docking in Honolulu."

"What?" said Chang's son, gaping at his father. "For Christ's sake! . . ."

"Hold your tongue," said Chang coldly. "As I said, *Orient Star* will not be docking. She has been rerouted to San Francisco."

"But . . ." his son began. Chang lifted one hand, silencing him.

"The meeting with our colleagues has been canceled," said Abbot Fong. "On the *San Chu*'s orders."

"Is there some problem?" asked Han Chao Shun. He felt his chest tighten as Chang looked down the table in his direction.

"No," the *Shan Chu* answered. "Everything is going exactly as I had planned."

"You knew you were going to cancel?" asked his son.

"The meeting was never to take place," Chang replied. He frowned, searching for the right word; even after a lifetime of thinking in two languages, both sometimes failed him. "It was a . . ."

"A ruse," supplied Fong.

"Thank you, Abbot." Chang nodded. "A ruse." He smiled thinly, looking directly at Han. "It was also bait for a trap," he added. "A way of flushing out those whose honor is questionable."

"I don't understand, *Shan Chu.*" Samson Kee frowned. "It all seems . . ."

"The bait was not for you," said Chang. He looked around the table again. "Neither was it for Abbot, nor my son, nor my old friend Tong-Ho."

"Han?" said Jimmy Chang, staring down the table at his brother-in-law. The man's features had frozen into a rigid stare. His eyes began to blink like shutters.

"He is brother to your wife and husband to my daughter," said Chang. "He was given everything that could be offered. He was taken into the *Hui* as one of our own."

Chang clasped his hands loosely together and leaned forward slightly, his cold blue glance raking across Han's terrified features. "He was the other meaning of his name . . . a traitor."

"*Shan Chu,* please . . ." whispered Han. The words were a rasping squeak. "I can explain . . . please."

"Greed is excusable," said Chang, speaking quietly. "Vice less so, but still acceptable within limits. Betrayal cannot be condoned."

Kom Tong-Ho rose from his seat at the end of the table and took three steps to stand behind Han's chair. He drew a snub-nosed .357 magnum revolver from the pocket of his jacket, pressed the barrel against the thick flesh at the base of Han's neck, aiming slightly upward, and pulled the trigger.

There was a sharp sound, like the slapping of a palm against wood, and Han's brains, teeth, and face exploded across the table, spattering onto Samson Kee's flower-patterned shirt. What was left of Han's skull smacked down on the surface of the table with a dull, wet thud.

Kom put the revolver back into his pocket and returned to his seat. A smell like burned sugar hung in the air for a moment, then dissolved in the breeze blowing in from the garden. James Chang stood up, pushing his chair away from the table.

"No one shall betray this family again," he said calmly. "No one shall steal from it. No one shall lie to any of its members. No one shall defy its Dragon Head, its *Shan Chu*. No one."

Chang placed his hand on Abbot Fong's shoulder, squeezing with a strong, affectionate pressure. "As of this moment I am no longer *Shan Chu* of Black Dragon, nor is Abbot Fong its White Paper Fan. Mr. Kom will remain as Red Pole until the new *Shan Chu* is invested." Chang smiled, ignoring the pool of offal spreading across the table in front of him. "Mr. Kom will ensure the smooth transition of power," he said. He lifted his hand from Fong's shoulder.

"Who . . ." began Chang's son. He made no attempt to hide the eagerness in his voice.

"Not you," said Chang coldly. "Not any one of you here." He paused, glancing at Han's remains. "Abbot will explain the changes which I have decided upon."

He moved away from the table, crossing to the doors leading out into the garden. The rain had stopped. He turned. "There will be no excursion today aboard *Kokuryu,* I'm afraid." He walked out onto the tiled lanai, alone, and disappeared from view.

Sixteen hundred eighty miles due west of Naloa, the fourteen-thousand-ton tramp steamer *Taiwan Commander* had just crossed the international date line and was in the process of making a minor course change. She carried a standard mix of cargo for a ship of her type, including bulk fertilizer, some machine-tool equipment, and a large stock of knock-off computer clones destined for the gray markets of Honolulu and Los Angeles.

She also carried several containers of small arms and other weaponry for the 212 Taiwanese and Hong Kong Chinese mercenaries billeted in cramped quarters below decks.

Neither the captain of the vessel, her crew, nor the men below decks were aware that the fifteen medium-sized crates that had been added to the cargo manifest just before they sailed from Tainan Harbor did not contain the powdered deer horn and freeze-dried bear gallbladder specified on the shipment's forged customs-clearance papers.

Instead the "special" crates held a dozen home-made variants of the Durandel airborne penetration bomb, each one capable of blowing a ten-foot hole through a yard-thick concrete wall. The other three crates each contained 136 kilograms of weapons-grade phosphorus. All the material for the bombs, including the specialized, long-duration timing fuse, came from Kadena Air Base in Okinawa. Most of it bore the stenciled markings of the United States Air Force 400th Munitions Maintenance Squadron.

Eighteen minutes after crossing the international date line the first of the fifteen crates exploded. The remainder followed within the space of less than three-and-a-half seconds.

The concussion wave created by the enormous explosion killed the entire 212-man mercenary complement and eleven members of the crew. Those who survived the initial blast were either burned to death by the white-hot phosphorus fire that blowtorched through the *Taiwan Commander* over the next few minutes or drowned when the fuming hulk sank into the abysmal depths of the Central Pacific Basin shortly thereafter. No distress message was sent; *Taiwan Commander* simply vanished.

The ship's owner, Huang Man Chun, would have been greatly distressed to know that his ship had been blown off the face of the earth, but he was unaware of the sinking since he had experienced a smaller-scale version of the event when his chauffeured Mercedes became a funeral pyre several hours previously.

Four hundred miles southwest of Taiwan, on the far side of Formosa Strait, two bodies were delivered to the Hong Kong Morgue, a low, dank building discreetly tucked in behind the Railway Terminus and the Hung-Hom Ferry Pier, Kowloon side.

Given the enormous number of corpses in varying states of deterioration that come through the morgue on any given day, it wasn't surprising that no connection was made between the two dead men.

One, nameless and without any identification other than an expensive dragon tattoo around one arm, was found floating belly-up under the Jordan Road Ferry Pier with his throat slit, while the second, apparently a minor clerk at the Bank of China named Sheng, was discovered just outside the Walled City.

It was hard to tell the cause of death in his case, since the rats had clearly had quite some time to feed. On further examination it was discovered that the back of Sheng's head had been penetrated by a six-inch electric-drill bit, a favorite triad method of relatively slow execution.

In San Francisco Charlie Ong was last seen entering the Burlingame premises of T.K. Manufacturing Ltd. He was not seen leaving the building, at least not in one piece.

Also in San Francisco, Norma Chung, overseer of the Black Dragon brothels in the area, was the victim of a drive-by shooting at a restaurant on Stockton Street. It was assumed by police that Ms. Chung was an innocent bystander and that the real targets had been Big-Eared Son of the Suey Sings and his Red Pole, Screwdriver Kong, also killed in the shooting. Witnesses on the street said the killers appeared to have been Vietnamese.

Tobias Woo, chairman of the First Pacific Orient Bank and the secret CEO of Kwikchek International, was killed in a hit-and-run accident involving a black-visored motorcyclist. The motorcycle was later found abandoned on a back street in Oakland. It had been stolen the night before.

Marvin Lok, *Fu Chan Chu* of the Vancouver division of Black Dragon, was discovered in a parking lot on Hamilton Street, directly across from the headquarters of the Canadian Broadcasting Corporation.

An autopsy would later show that he had died as the result of a massive overdose of 96 percent pharmaceutically pure Heroin. Analysis proved that the Heroin was Two Rabbit brand, usually marketed by the Suey Sings and the On Leongs.

At 6:30 P.M., eastern daylight saving time, a Federal Express flight from Los Angeles containing a transshipment of parcels from the Far East arrived at Dulles Airport. A package addressed to the President's Office on Drug Abuse, the White House, Washington, D.C., was put through the standard sniff-'n'-peek routine, and a curious X-ray machine operator alerted the FBI. The parcel was taken to the Bomb Disposal Facility at Quantico, where it was then opened.

The package contained the severed, fast-frozen tongueless and earless head of a Thailand Provincial Police major named Chakri. Identification was simplified by the fact that Chakri's wallet was included with his head. His eyes had been stapled shut, and an adult penis had been inserted into his empty mouth, replacing the tongue. The skin color of the sexual organ and the head did not appear to match. Also included in the package was a small recipe card, wrapped in plastic, like the wallet. There were two words on the card, in English, printed with a wide-nib black felt pen:

HOLY GHOST

At 2:30 P.M., Hawaiian time, James Chang flew out of Naloa with a large picnic basket on his lap. He was dressed in lightweight cotton trousers, a gray silk open-neck shirt, and Topsiders. Thirty-five minutes later he landed at the Honolulu Domestic Terminal, then took a short limousine ride to the Ala Moana Yacht Harbor.

CHAPTER 32

THE OLD YACHT moved at an easy twelve knots through the calm seas a mile and a half off Koko Head, the sound of her twin Cummins diesel engines no more than a deep-throated rumble on the open lounge deck at the stern. *Kokuryu* had been heading south for more than an hour and was now turning steadily east into the Kaiwi Channel. The scattering of rain clouds had long since cleared, and the sky was an infinite amphitheater of brilliant blue.

A white-jacketed steward came up the galley companionway and stepped out onto the lounge deck carrying a tray with tall glasses, a pitcher of iced tea, and a bowl of ice cubes. He placed the tray down on the table between the two men, bowed, then turned and went back the way he'd come.

James Chang set out the glasses and poured a drink for himself and Phillip Dane. The curator, dressed in his own clothes, freshly washed and pressed, took a sip of the iced tea, then put the glass back down on the table. He reached out, plucked a cigarette from the open box in front of him, and lit it, looking out over the low deck railing at the distant coastline. The beaches and bluffs fringing the ancient volcanic crater were nothing more than a green blur on the horizon, marked by white featherlines of breaking surf. They were alone on the empty sea.

"A long and complicated story, Mr. Chang," said

Dane finally, turning back to his host. "I'm not entirely sure that I believe it."

"What part of it do you find so difficult to comprehend?" Chang smiled. He took a brief swallow of his own drink and sat back in his chair.

"No one thing in particular," Dane answered. "It's just so incredibly Machiavellian. Ten thousand puzzle pieces all fitting together as though the design was preordained."

"Not so unlikely," said Chang. "Nothing more than history—supposedly your forte, from what I understand about your background." He smiled again. "In retrospect events form patterns never seen when they occurred."

"And all of this hinges on Hawksworth."

"I suppose you could say that. He was a pivotal element certainly. His cowardice was compounded by the weakness of others, the temper of the times. I simply took advantage of the situation."

"You were very young," said Dane.

"But not a fool," Chang answered. "Hawksworth piloted *Holy Ghost* over Japan and failed in his mission. Cates documented his failure and died for his efforts."

"In other words, he gave you an edge," said Dane.

"I beg your pardon?" Chang said, frowning.

"Jackie Gleason and Paul Newman in *The Hustler,*" Dane explained. "The edge . . . the leverage you have to make you a winner."

"Ah." Chang nodded. "Yes . . . Cates and his little book became my edge. The more important Hawksworth became, the more useful the edge became."

"Until now," said Dane quietly. "All these years later."

"Indeed," said Chang. "All these years."

"And Hawksworth, and the Doolittle Raid, and all of that, is meaningless," said Dane. "Dusty stuff for the history books."

"Just because the roots of an oak aren't seen doesn't mean they aren't important to the tree," said Chang. "If you'll pardon my inscrutability."

"You enjoy that, don't you?" said Dane, a certain coolness creeping into his voice. "All this Confucian sage business, playing on race."

"A mirror only reflects what is there," Chang answered. "I have spent a lifetime living in your white world, Mr. Dane. Like my father and his father before him, I have been spit upon for my differences, reviled and shunned for what I am rather than who. An old Chinaman is supposed to quote Confucius. I simply do what is expected of me. Ten million overseas Chinese all over the world do exactly the same thing, Mr. Dane. They have a face for the white world and a face for their own. For almost two centuries it has been the only way to survive. We wouldn't have stood a Chinaman's chance otherwise." Chang paused. "Do you know the origins of that phrase, Mr. Dane?"

"No."

"It's American slang," Chang explained. "Dating back to the time of the gold rush. Up to the early 1900s it was perfectly legal to shoot a Chinese person in the United States. To murder with impunity, Mr. Dane, because the Chinese were not considered to be human beings. After the San Francisco earthquake in 1906 the National Guard was called in and given orders to shoot looters on sight . . . except in Chinatown. In Chinatown looting was acceptable."

"So you . . . this Black Dragon is some kind of revenge? Retribution visited upon the round-eye?"

"Black Dragon is the *Hui,*" said Chang quietly. "The family and all its members. What is done is done to ensure the continuity and prosperity of the *Hui.*"

"With you as some kind of Oriental Godfather?" said Dane.

"The Sicilians didn't invent organized crime, Mr. Dane," said Chang, laughing. "We did." He shook his head. "There were Chinese secret societies in existence when the people Mr. Puzo wrote about so eloquently were scrabbling in the dirt for grubs and fornicating with goats. Their Cosa Nostra—Our Thing—is a pale imitation of what we are."

"But they believe in 'family' the way you do."

"Their notion of family has very limited boundaries," said Chang. "It is what they can see, what they can gather around themselves. For us the family is all of the past and all of the future.

"There are a million families who carry the name Chang, but each member of each family can trace his ancestry back a thousand years simply through his name, and no one will be common with the other.

"*That* is the power of the *Hui*, Mr. Dane, not the angry sentiment of Don Corleone's imaginary world. What we were in the past and what we can be in the future defines who we are in the present."

"More Confucius," said Dane skeptically.

"A better role model than Al Capone," Chang replied dryly. "And it is a philosophy which applies to all Chinese, not just members of a triad group."

"You people just twist it into a rationale for killing, is that the difference?"

"The modern triads were conceived as a way of battling an oppressive rule in China during the mid-1600s," said Chang. "The common man in Manchu China was confronted by a system riddled with corruption, and the triads were a way of fighting back. The oppressor has changed since then, but the oppressed are still the same, and if anything, the systems of the world have become even more corrupt."

"This is all very nice," said Dane. "But by your own admission you're part of a multibillion-dollar operation—I'd hardly call that oppression."

"It's simply business." Chang shrugged. "Your government understands that . . . more than they would ever admit in public."

"You call selling Heroin simply business?"

"Of course," said Chang. "It was simply business for the British when they exchanged Patna opium for silver. The American government has been involved in the drug trade, officially and otherwise, for two hundred years. Opium is not native to China, Mr. Dane; it was imported by your people and the British."

"So now you're turning the tables?" said Dane. "Getting your own back after all these years?"

"The Chinese are well known for their patience," Chang answered. "But no, it isn't revenge or retribution. It is money, pure and simple. Heroin is a commodity, like pork bellies or pineapple juice. We exchange one commodity for another, we invest, we expand."

"And take over the world." Dane snorted. "You and Adolf Hitler or Saddam Hussein or Qaddafi." He stubbed out his cigarette and lit another. "It's an old story, Chang, and it doesn't really make it."

"I don't want to take over the world," Chang answered calmly. "I merely wish the opportunity to take my place in it. An opportunity which has been denied to me and others of my race. If it requires enterprises which you deem to be criminal, then so be it.

"Hawksworth was a traitor and a coward—a criminal. So were Senator Lang and a hundred others like him. You have elected presidents with family fortunes built on crime and supported criminal regimes like those of Batista and Noriega. Standard Oil, American Airlines, and IT&T supported the Nazis until it became economically expedient to change horses in midstream.

"In Canada they once charged a head tax before a Chinese was allowed to enter the country. It used to be fifty dollars, now it's a five-hundred-thousand-dollar investment in a Canadian business. Instead of a head tax, they now call it 'immigration financing.' "

"Nice speech," said Dane. "But it was your Heroin that created a couple of hundred thousand new smackhead addicts in Vietnam. I know, I was there."

"Quite so." Chang nodded. "And the Heroin was flown into Saigon on aircraft owned and operated by the Central Intelligence Agency. Business."

"And I'm supposed to go along with all of this?" asked Dane. "Let's cut the crap, Mr. Chang. You're a thug. A hood. You've got a nice boat here, and you spin a good story, but it doesn't change the facts of who and what you are. A kidnapper, for one thing." He turned slightly and looked over his shoulder.

"Hawaii might be a long way from the Mainland, but it's still the United States. Kidnapping is a capital offense."

"Please, Mr. Dane, spare me the melodrama. You're hardly in a position to depend on federal statutes." Chang slipped two fingers into his glass, pulled out a slice of lemon, and took a small, sour bite of pulp. He tossed the rind over his shoulder and into the sea. "The water here is around two hundred fathoms—twelve hundred feet."

"Now who's being melodramatic?" said Dane.

"Hardly that." Chang shrugged. "A fact. Business."

"All right," said Dane. "I've listened to you, now how about if I ask a few relevant questions before we go on?"

"Certainly," said Chang.

"Holy Ghost. How do they fit into this?"

"It is an organization designed by the Chinese Black House—their Secret Service—in conjunction with certain vested political interests in the United States and the United Kingdom."

"Intelligence and business interests."

"Correct."

"And their purpose was to remove the upper management of the triads and the yakuza? Assassinate them?"

"Quite so." Chang nodded. "As well as several higher-echelon Cosa Nostra. Such a plan would be 'inappropriate' for any government body, so Holy Ghost was created as a rival enterprise. The deaths would appear to be a result of internecine warfare between opposing groups. Much like the gangster wars of the twenties and thirties in Chicago and New York."

"You said Cordasco was part of this? DIA."

"He was the comptroller." Chang nodded. "Which is how you came to be involved. Among other things you were supposed to identify weak security elements in the event of a future investigation."

"And Cordasco's dead?" Dane asked bluntly. "Killed by Holy Ghost?"

"I'm afraid so, yes," said Chang. "A number of other people as well, including Senator Lang."

"It doesn't make any sense," said Dane, shaking his head. He was beginning to feel slightly dizzy, either from the lazy motion of the yacht or the increasingly complex web of events he was struggling to comprehend. "Why would Holy Ghost kill its own people?"

"What Holy Ghost was is not necessarily what it became," said Chang obscurely.

"You told me it was being run by this David Long, Hawksworth's illegitimate kid."

"Kim Chee Leung's son," agreed Chang.

"That's too much to swallow," said Dane. "He has his father tortured and then hideously murdered in Washington, and a few days later he kills his mother as well. What kind of psychopath are we talking about?"

"He had nothing to do with the death of Kim Chee," answered Chang, his features hardening. "We are reasonably sure she was murdered by Cordasco's own people. You were discovering too much too soon."

"How do you know that?"

"The man you killed on the train," Chang answered. "He had been infiltrated into Holy Ghost by the general. Apparently he didn't trust the Black House any more than they trusted him. He had been shadowing you in San Francisco and noticed Miss Falcone's interest in you as well. What Kim Chee knew was too sensitive, and so she died. You would have been next."

"What about Erin, if that really is her name?" asked Dane. "Who the hell is she?"

"Exactly who she said," Chang answered. "A special agent for the FBI who had been seconded to the Royal Hong Kong Police to liaise with their Triad Squad." He smiled thinly. "Her father was a distant cousin to me. Her family has been involved with Black Dragon for three generations."

"I'll be damned!" Dane whispered. He stood up and walked toward the stern, coming out from under the deck cabin overhang and into the full punishment of the brilliant sun.

He stood on the fantail, staring down into the *Kokuryu*'s creaming wake for a moment. He lifted a shading hand to his forehead, letting his eyes follow the long V of spume that marked their course. He squinted; far in the distance he thought he could see another, smaller boat coming after them. He turned and went back to the table.

"Do you have any other questions?" asked Chang as Dane took his seat again.

"I should be dead," he said flatly. "I have no place in this, no reason for being here. If everything you say is true, then I'm a speck of fly shit on the wall. I'm a loose end, an annoyance you shouldn't even be bothering with." He stared across the table into the hard blue of Chang's eyes. "So what am I doing having iced tea and history lessons with the Chinese Boss of Bosses on his yacht?"

"Learning," said Chang. "Receiving necessary information."

"Necessary to what?" asked Dane.

"Your continued existence," Chang answered blandly.

"Why do I get the feeling you're about to be inscrutable again?" Dane asked. Chang laughed.

"I'm impressed," he said smiling. "To retain your sense of humor under such circumstances is admirable. You bear out Miss Falcone's impressions." Chang paused. "At any rate . . ."

"You were about to be inscrutable," said Dane.

"I was about to tell you a story," Chang replied.

"Another one?"

"An ancient one," said Chang. "A legend, really, told to Chinese children by their mothers." He paused again and turned to look back toward the stern. Dane followed the look. He'd been right; there was another boat behind them, getting closer by the minute. Chang didn't seem concerned. Dane noticed a small change in the engine vibration beneath his feet. They were slowing down. Chang went on with his story.

"Many thousands of years ago the Chinese neither tilled the soil nor fished the sea. They hunted only, and during the months of winter hundreds died.

"The empress at that time, an unmarried girl, prayed so that the gods would save her people from this recurring tragedy, and one day the god of earth and heaven appeared to her and said that he would grant her wish. Nine months later she gave birth to a son.

"The people of her court thought the child was an evil omen, since she was unmarried, and powerful members of the council of elders decided that the only way to get rid of the evil was to get rid of the child.

"This they tried to do, stealing the boy from the empress and carrying him off to the woods. But he did not die. Seven times they tried to kill him, and seven times they failed, taking him farther and farther away from the imperial palace each time. Finally he was rescued by a woodcutter who knew nothing of the evil omen associated with the boy, and the man raised him as his own.

"In the distant valley where he grew up the boy discovered the secrets of plants and poisons, and which seeds if planted would raise crops. Over the years he turned rank wilderness into fruitful, well-tended land.

"Eventually his knowledge spread across the land, and finally reached the empress's court. She was reunited with her son, and the hunters ruled no more, nor did the people die each winter for lack of food."

"Very nice," said Dane. "What's the connection?"

"The story is called 'The Legend of the Child No One Wanted,' " said Chang. Dane could hear the powerful engine of the new boat as it approached. He turned and glanced back over the stern. She was big—a huge, flush-decked cigarette boat like the ones the coke runners in Florida used. He looked back at Chang. Light dawned.

"The child no one wanted? David Long? Kim Chee Leung's son?"

"Yes."

Dane began to laugh, the sound tinged with something close to hysteria. The man seated across from him was immensely rich, incredibly powerful, and a homicidal megalomaniac. He had somehow become a character in this madman's nightmare fantasy.

"Jesus!" Dane cried, still laughing. "What's the analogy I'm supposed to draw? You're trying to tell me a freak who has his father's tongue hacked away and his eyes gouged out is some sort of New Age Johnny Appleseed, spreading civilization to us peasants? Better living through assassination and Heroin addiction?!"

"Wait," Chang murmured, ignoring Dane's outburst. *Kokuryu* had slowed almost to a dead stop, a gentle cross chop making the yacht sway from side to side in a mild corkscrew. The cigarette boat, engines thundering, turned across their wake, the raked bow of her lime-green hull slicing through the waves as she moved up on the yacht's port side. The cigarette slowed, matching the yacht, and pulled in even closer. Dane heard raised voices, speaking Chinese, then felt a gentle bump as the big speedboat nudged against the foam bumpers protecting *Kokuryu*'s hull. A few moments later the cigarette pulled away, the sound of her engines increasing to a pounding roar as she raced off, back toward Koko Head.

A man appeared at the top of the lounge-deck companionway and stepped out into the sunlight. He was tall, dark-haired, wearing sunglasses, a crisp seersucker suit over a pale blue shirt, and expensive tasseled loafers. He was carrying a heavy dark brown leather attaché case in his right hand. He crossed the deck and sat down with James Chang and Phillip Dane, placing the attaché case on the table in front of him. He smiled at Dane. It was the boy in the coonskin cap. The mug shot from the police file. Hawksworth's son. Holy Ghost.

"We meet finally," said the man. "I've heard a great deal about you." The voice was pleasant and unaccented. "My name is David Long."

He reached up and took off the sunglasses. Eyes a slightly darker shade of blue than the sky overhead stared at Dane curiously. The man turned to Chang.

"Hello, Father," he said.

"*Shan Chu,*" Chang answered formally. He glanced at Dane, a stern look of pride on his face. "This is my firstborn son, fourth of the Chang Chin-Kang, the new *Shan Chu* of Black Dragon."

CHAPTER 33

PHILLIP DANE OPENED the door of Blind Justice and took a deep breath of the musty, familiar air. He put down the heavy attaché case he'd carried as his only luggage from Hawaii, then closed the door and locked it, twisting the dead bolt and resetting the alarm. In front of him the rows of floor-to-ceiling bookcases stood like shadowed sentinels. He sighed, feeling knots of tension in his muscles begin to ease. Home again, even if its comfortable security was only an illusion.

He was exhausted, but he knew that if he didn't begin now, be might never make the attempt. Leaving the lights off, he looked down the length of the store. All the books, all the knowledge they contained. And knowledge was power, wasn't it? Someone had said that; he couldn't remember who. He glanced down at the attaché case. Whoever it was didn't know the half of it. He picked up the case, feeling its weight through the handle, the weight he'd carried on his lap for the past twelve hours. The weight he'd be carrying for the rest of his life.

He walked over to his desk and set the attaché case down beside the keyboard for his computer. He sat down, switched on the machine, and waited for the stuttering lines of text as the boot program went through its cycle. Lighting another in a long gray line of cigarettes consumed between Honolulu and Washington, he set the combination David Long had given him and opened the case. Stacks of carefully sleeved floppy disks sat in neat piles.

A universe of information compiled by the man Chang and his son had told him about—Gollinger. During Dane's days with Intelligence Gollinger had been only a rumor referred to as "Mr. Wizard," or sometimes "the Bank of Information." Now here he was, the myth made manifest and just as quickly turned to myth again, the disks his passport to a new life, and his legacy.

Dane closed his eyes for a few seconds, then forced himself awake again. A drink, sleep, oblivion—Christ!, how he wanted that. But not yet, not with those last hours in the company of Chang and his son so vivid in his mind.

Chang's son, not Hawksworth's. The unbelievable irony of it. Kim Chee had been Chang's thrall from the beginning, perhaps as far back as Chungking; the aging man had never made that clear.

The blue-eyed child had been Chang's, accepted by Hawksworth and used as a blackmailing buttress to Vern Cates's damning notebook, all the while watched from a distance by his real father. Biding his time.

Cordasco hadn't known, nor had his colleagues. To them, Kim Chee's bastard was the perfect figurehead for their plan; even the name, Holy Ghost, was the perfect slight. An angry abandoned son using the same name as the aircraft his father had flown to fame.

Then the aging *Shan Chu* of Black Dragon had revealed himself, acknowledged his son, offered him his rightful place in the *Hui,* explained *his* plan.

Holy Ghost had been co-opted almost from the beginning, Chang and his child by Kim Chee manipulating both East and West. And the result was hegemony for Black Dragon; it stood unopposed among the rest, with Gollinger's vast library as its perfect breastplate. Gollinger, the man who'd first gone to Chang almost half a century before with his information about the

Thai bullion shipment, another strand in the web that bound Hawksworth to Black Dragon.

Gollinger, supported, aided, financed by Chang in return for his information and analyses. Black Dragon's private spy, its *gwei-lo* eyes in the East, its burrowing mole.

Chang and his son had sent clear signals to Cordasco's people and the Black House that Holy Ghost and Black Dragon were now one. Any attempt, from the East, West, or otherwise, to interfere with their activities would result in Gollinger's files being made public as well as revealing the truth about Hawksworth's life and the circumstances of his death. The same thing would happen if any member of the *Hui* came to harm.

And Dane was to be made keeper of the keys—those were the words Chang had used aboard the yacht. Black Dragon had a set of the disks, and presumably so did Gollinger, wherever he was, but Dane would be the stand-alone arbiter should anything untoward happen to Chang, his son, or any other member of his family. A human deterrent.

According to Chang's bland estimation, the task would be simple enough. Read through the files, copy them onto his own computer, and ensure that the disks themselves were hidden safely away for his lifetime. To refuse the job would mean his immediate death, since there was no other reason for Black Dragon to keep him alive. Refusing to act, when and if it was requested, would have the same result.

If any of Cordasco's people or those who would almost certainly follow threatened Dane, they would be dealt with; he had that assurance. The perfect stalemate while Chang, his family, his myriad companies, and those of others like him slowly but surely spread their influence throughout the world.

Phillip Dane picked a disk at random from the attaché case, loaded it into his hard drive, and began the

simple process of copying the files. He put out his cigarette, sitting in the darkened bookstore, watching the
glowing screen, and he felt a chilling tremor run the
length of his spine and raise the hairs on the back of his
neck. There were no choices, no alternatives, no options, no place to turn, and for the first time since his
childhood he wanted to weep. He had a brief, terrible
vision of Chang, sitting across from him aboard the
yacht, the strong sun harsh on his age-lined face. He
felt the chill course through his body a second time and
shivered with its force.

During his lifetime Phillip Dane had never been particularly religious, had never believed in any God. But
sitting there, weary in the night, he realized he knew
the Devil's name, and the color of his eyes.

AFTERWORD

THE MAN REFERRED to in *Black Dragon* as the first Chang Chin-Kang, or "Brilliant" Chang, as he was known to Scotland Yard, really existed, and established a wide-spread criminal empire out of London's Limehouse District during the mid-1870s. Fugitive from a Hong Kong murder charge, Brilliant Chang spent fifteen years in London, then suddenly vanished. There is some evidence that he fled to New York and then San Francisco.

The Royal Hong Kong Police Triad Squad estimates that there are presently fifty major triad organizations actively operating out of Hong Kong, Taiwan, Europe, the United Kingdom, Canada, and the United States. It estimates that in Hong Kong alone there are three-hundred thousand triad members. This compares to two thousand active members of the Mafia, or Cosa Nostra, in the United States.

Information contained within *Black Dragon* concerning the complicity of various government agencies in the trafficking of narcotics, particularly Heroin, is accurate.

Information relating to the drug-trafficking activities of specific individuals, such as Chiang Kai-shek, is also accurate.

Following the Doolittle Raid on Tokyo, a number of those fliers involved, including Doolittle himself, were entertained by Madame Chiang (neé Soong) at her residence in Chungking; however, according to official records, there were only sixteen Mitchell B-25s involved in the raid. *Holy Ghost,* the aircraft flown by General William Sloane Hawksworth, was the seventeenth and last B-25 to leave the deck of the U.S.S. *Hornet* on April 18, 1942.

For those of you with a bent for historical accuracy, the tail designation for General Hawksworth's aircraft was 130177-A.

Although rarely acknowledged by its owner, Heroin is a registered trade name of the Bayer Pharmaceutical Corporation, the inventors of Aspirin, and the name has therefore been capitalized throughout.

—Christopher Hyde

Tough, Suspenseful Novels by
Edgar Award-winning Author

LAWRENCE BLOCK

FEATURING MATTHEW SCUDDER

A DANCE AT THE SLAUGHTERHOUSE
71374-8/$4.99 US/$5.99 Can

A TICKET TO THE BONEYARD
70994-5/$4.99 US/$5.99 Can

OUT ON THE CUTTING EDGE
70993-7/$4.95 US/$5.95 Can

THE SINS OF THE FATHERS
76363-X/$4.50 US/$5.50 Can

TIME TO MURDER AND CREATE
76365-6/$4.50 US/$5.50 Can

A STAB IN THE DARK
71574-0/$4.50 US/$5.50 Can

IN THE MIDST OF DEATH
76362-1/$4.50 US/$5.50 Can

EIGHT MILLION WAYS TO DIE
71573-2/$4.50 US/$5.50 Can

Coming Soon

A WALK AMONG THE TOMBSTONES
71375-6/$4.99 US/$5.99 Can

GRITTY, SUSPENSEFUL NOVELS
BY MASTER STORYTELLERS
FROM AVON BOOKS

FORCE OF NATURE
by Stephen Solomita
70949-X/$4.95 US/$5.95 Can

"Powerful and relentlessly engaging...Tension at a riveting peak" *Publishers Weekly*

A MORNING FOR FLAMINGOS
by James Lee Burke
71360-8/$4.95 US/$5.95 Can

"No one writes better detective novels...truly astonishing"
Washington Post Book World

A TWIST OF THE KNIFE
by Stephen Solomita
70997-X/$4.95 US/$5.95 Can

"A sizzler...Wambaugh and Caunitz had better look out"
Associated Press

BLACK CHERRY BLUES
by James Lee Burke
71204-0/$4.95 US/$5.95 Can

"Remarkable...A terrific story...The plot crackles with events and suspense...Not to be missed!"
Los Angeles Times Book Review

JAMES ELLROY